RIPLEY UNDER WATER

PATRICIA HIGHSMITH was born in Fort Worth, Texas, in 1921. Her parents moved to New York when she was six, and she attended Julia Richmond High School and Barnard College. In her senior year she edited the college magazine, having decided at the age of sixteen to become a writer. Her first novel, *Strangers on a Train*, was made into a film by Alfred Hitchcock in 1951. *The Talented Mr Ripley*, published in 1955, was awarded the Edgar Allan Poe Scroll by the Mystery Writers of America and introduced the fascinating anti-hero Tom Ripley, who was to appear in many of her later crime novels. Patricia Highsmith died in Locarno, Switzerland, in February 1995. Her last novel, *Small g: A Summer Idyll*, was published posthumously just over a month later.

BY THE SAME AUTHOR

The Blunderer

Deep Water

A Game For The Living

This Sweet Sickness

The Cry of The Owl

The Two Faces of January

The Glass Cell

A Suspension of Mercy

Those Who Walk Away

The Talented Mr Ripley

The Tremor of Forgery

Eleven

Ripley Under Ground

A Dog's Ransom

Ripley's Game

The Animal-Lover's Book of Beastly Murder

Little Tales of Misogyny

Edith's Diary

Slowly, Slowly In The Wind

The Boy Who Followed Ripley

The Black House

Mermaids on the Golf Course

Found In The Street

Carol

Tales of Natural and Unnatural Catastrophes

People Who Knock on the Door

Small g: A Summer Idyll

RIPLEY UNDER WATER

Patricia Highsmith

BLOOMSBURY

LONDON · BERLIN · NEW YORK

First published in Great Britain 1991
This paperback edition published 2010

Copyright © 1991 by Patricia Highsmith

The moral right of the author has been asserted

A CIP catalogue record for this book
is available from the British Library

Bloomsbury Publishing Plc, 36 Soho Square, London W1D 3QY

Bloomsbury Publishing, London, Berlin and New York

ISBN 978 1 4088 1317 1

10 9 8 7 6 5 4 3 2 1

FSC
Mixed Sources
Product group from well-managed
forests and other controlled sources
Cert no. SGS-COC-2061
www.fsc.org
© 1996 Forest Stewardship Council

Printed in Great Britain by Clays Ltd, St Ives plc

www.bloomsbury.com/patriciahighsmith

To the dead and the dying among the Intefada and the Kurds, to those who fight oppression in whatever land, and stand up not only to be counted but to be shot.

1

Tom stood in Georges and Marie's bar-tabac with a nearly full cup of café express in his hand. He had paid, and Héloïse's two packs of Marlboros bulged his jacket pocket. Tom was watching a slot-machine game that someone else was playing.

The screen showed a cartoon motorcyclist hurtling into the background, the illusion of speed given by a forward-moving picket fence on either side of the road. The player manipulated a half-wheel, making the cyclist swerve to pass a slower car, or leap like a horse to hurdle a fence that had suddenly appeared across the road. If the motorcyclist (game-player) didn't hurdle in time, there was a silent impact, a black and gold star appeared to indicate a crash, the motorcyclist was finished and so was the game.

Tom had watched the game many a time (it was the most popular he had ever known Georges and Marie to acquire), but he had never played it. He somehow didn't want to.

'Non-*non*!' From behind the bar Marie's voice sang out over the usual din as she contested some customer's opinion, probably political. She and her husband were left-wing no matter what. 'Ecoutez, *Mitterand* . . . '

It crossed Tom's mind that Georges and Marie didn't like the influx of people from North Africa, however.

'Eh, *Marie*! Deux *pastis*!' That was fat Georges with a somewhat soiled white apron over shirt and trousers, serving the few tables, where people drank and occasionally ate pommes chips and hard-boiled eggs.

The juke-box played an old cha-cha-cha.

A silent black and gold star! Spectators groaned sympathetically. Dead. All was over. The screen flashed its silent, obsessed message, 'INSERT COINS INSERT COINS INSERT COINS', and the workman in blue jeans groped obediently in a pocket, inserted more

1

coins, and the game began again, motorcyclist in tiptop shape, zooming into the background, ready for anything, neatly dodging a barrel that appeared in his lane, smoothly jumping the first barrier. The man at the controls was intent, determined to make his man come through.

Tom was thinking now about Héloïse, about her trip to Morocco. She wanted to see Tangier, Casablanca, maybe Marrakesh. And Tom had agreed to go with her. After all, it wasn't one of her adventure cruises requiring hospital visits for vaccines before departure, and it behoved him as her husband to accompany her on some of her jaunts. Héloïse had two or three inspirations a year, not all of which she acted on. Tom wasn't in the mood for a holiday now. It was early August, Morocco would be at its hottest, and Tom loved his own peonies and dahlias at this time of year, loved cutting a fresh two or three for the living-room almost daily. Tom was fond of his garden, and he rather liked Henri, the handyman who helped him with big jobs, a giant when it came to strength, though not the man for some tasks.

Then there was the Odd Pair, as Tom had begun calling them to himself. He wasn't sure they were married, and of course that didn't matter. He felt they were lurking in the area and had their eye on him. Maybe they were harmless, but who knew? Tom had first noticed them a month or so ago in Fontainebleau, when he and Héloïse had been shopping one afternoon: a man and woman who looked American and in their mid-thirties, walking towards them, eyeing them with that look Tom knew well, as if they knew who he was, perhaps knew his name, Tom Ripley. Tom had seen the same look a few times at airports, though rarely, and not lately. It could come after one's picture had been in the newspapers, he supposed, but Tom's hadn't been in any newspapers for years, he was sure of that. Not since the Murchison business, and that had been about five years ago – Murchison, whose blood still stained Tom's cellar floor, and which Tom said was a wine stain, if anyone remarked on it.

In truth, it was a mixture of wine and blood, Tom reminded himself, because Murchison had been hit over the head with a wine bottle. A bottle of Margaux wielded by Tom.

Well, the Odd Pair. *Crash* went the motorcyclist. Tom made himself turn away and took his empty cup over to the bar counter.

The male of the Odd Pair had dark straight hair, round-rimmed glasses, and the woman light brown hair, a slender face and grey or

2

hazel eyes. It was the man who stared, with a vague and empty smile. Tom felt that he might have seen the man before, at Heathrow or Roissy airport, giving him that I-know-your-face look. Nothing hostile, but Tom didn't like it.

And then Tom had seen them once cruising slowly in their car down the main street of Villeperce at midday when he was coming out of the bakery with a *flute* (must have been Mme Annette's day off or she'd been busy with a lunch), and again Tom had seen them looking at him. Villeperce was a tiny town, several kilometres from Fontainebleau. Why should the Odd Pair have come here?

Both Marie with her big red smile and balding Georges happened to be behind the bar just as Tom pushed his saucer and cup away. 'Merci et bonne nuit, Marie – Georges!' Tom called and gave a smile.

'Bon soir, M'sieur Reepley!' cried Georges, one hand waving, the other pouring Calvados.

'Merci, m'sieur, à bientôt!' Marie threw at him.

Tom was almost at the door when the male of the Odd Pair walked in, round glasses and all, and seemingly alone.

'Mr Ripley?' His pinkish lips again wore a smile. 'Good evening.'

'Evening,' said Tom, still on his way out.

'We've – my wife and I – may I invite you for a drink?'

'Thanks, I'm just leaving.'

'Another time, maybe. We've rented a house in Villeperce. This direction.' He gestured vaguely north, and his smile widened to reveal squarish teeth. 'Looks like we'll be neighbours.'

Tom was confronted by two people entering, and had to step back into the bar.

'My name's Pritchard. David. I'm taking courses at the Fontaine-bleau educational combine – INSEAD. I'm sure you know of it. Anyway, my house here is a two-storey white one with garden and a little pool. We fell in love with it *because* of the pool, reflections on the ceiling – the water.' He chuckled.

'I see,' Tom said, trying to sound reasonably pleasant. He was now out of the door.

'I'll telephone you. My wife's name is Janice.'

Tom managed a nod and forced a smile. 'Yes – fine. Do that. Good night.'

'Not too many Americans around here!' the determined David Pritchard called after him.

Mr Pritchard would have a hard time finding his number, Tom

3

was thinking, because he and Héloïse had managed to keep it out of the telephone book. The outwardly dull David Pritchard – nearly as tall as Tom and a bit heavier – looked like trouble, Tom was thinking as he walked homeward. A police officer of some kind? Digging up old records? Private detective for – for whom, really? Tom couldn't think of any active enemies. 'Phoney' was the word Tom thought of in regard to David Pritchard: phoney smile, phoney goodwill, maybe phoney story about studying at INSEAD. That educational institution at Fontainebleau could be a cover, in fact such an obvious one that Tom thought it might be true that Pritchard was studying something there. Or maybe they weren't man and wife but a CIA pair. What would the USA be after him for, Tom wondered. Not income tax, that was in order. Murchison? No, that was settled. Or case abandoned. Murchison and his corpse had disappeared. Dickie Greenleaf? Hardly. Even Christopher Greenleaf, Dickie's cousin, wrote Tom a friendly postcard now and then, from Alice Springs last year, for instance. Christopher was now a civil engineer, married, working in Rochester, New York, as Tom recalled. Tom was even on good terms with Dickie's father Herbert. At least, they exchanged Christmas cards.

As Tom approached the big tree opposite Belle Ombre, a tree whose branches leaned a little over the road, his spirits rose. What was there to worry about? Tom pushed open one big gate just enough to slip through, then closed it with as gentle a clang as he could manage and slid the padlock home, then the long bolt.

Reeves Minot. Tom stopped short and his shoes slid on the gravel of the forecourt. Another fence job for Reeves was in the offing. Reeves had telephoned a few days ago. Tom often vowed he would not do another, then found himself accepting. Was it because he enjoyed meeting new people? Tom gave a laugh, short and barely audible, then continued walking towards his front door with his usual light tread that hardly disturbed the gravel.

The light was on in the living-room, and the front door was unlocked, as Tom had left it forty-five minutes ago. Tom went in, then locked the front door behind him. Héloïse sat on the sofa, poring over a magazine – probably an article on North Africa, Tom thought.

''Ello, chéri – *Reeves* telephoned,' Héloïse said, looking up, tossing her blonde hair back with a swing of her head. 'Tome, did you –'

'Yes. Catch!' Smiling, Tom tossed the first red and white packet to her, then the second. She caught the first, the second hit her blue shirt-front. 'Anything pressing concerning Reeves? *Répassant* – ironing – *buegelnd* – ?'

'Oh, Tome, stop it!' said Héloïse, and used her lighter. She inwardly enjoyed his puns, Tom thought, though she would never say so, would hardly permit herself to smile. 'He will telephone back but maybe not tonight.'

'Somebody – well – ' Tom stopped, because Reeves didn't go into detail with Héloïse, ever, and Héloïse professed to be uninterested, even bored, with Tom's and Reeves's doings. It was safer: the less she knew, the better, Tom supposed Héloïse thought. And who could say that wasn't true?

'Tome, tomorrow we go and buy the tickets – to Maroc. All right?' She had tucked her bare feet up on the yellow silk sofa like a comfortable kitten, and now she looked at him calmly with her pale lavender eyes.

'Y-yes. All right.' He had promised, he reminded himself. 'We fly first to Tangier.'

'Oui, chéri, and then we go on from there. Casablanca – of course.'

'Of course,' Tom echoed. 'Right, dear, we'll buy the tickets tomorrow – Fontainebleau.' They always went to the same travel agency there, where they knew the staff. Tom hesitated, then decided to say it now. 'Darling, do you remember the pair – the American-looking couple we saw in Fontainebleau one day – on the pavement? Walking towards us, and I said later I thought he was staring at us? Dark-haired man with glasses?'

'I think – yes. Why?'

Tom could tell that she did remember. 'Because he just spoke to me in the bar-tabac.' Tom unbuttoned his jacket and shoved his hands in his trouser pockets. He had not sat down. 'I don't care for him.'

'I remember the woman with him, with lighter hair. Americans, no?'

'He is, anyway. Well – they've rented a house here in Villeperce. Remember the house where the – '

'*Vraiment*? Villeperce?'

'Oui, ma chère! The house where the pond water is reflected on the ceiling – in the living-room?' He and Héloïse had marvelled at the oval moving like water itself on the white ceiling.

5

'Yes. I remember the house. Two-storey white, not such a pretty fireplace. Not very far from the Grais', is it not? Someone with us thought about buying it.'

'Yes. Right.' An American acquaintance of an acquaintance, looking for a country house not too far from Paris, had asked Tom and Héloïse to accompany him while he inspected a couple of houses in the vicinity. He had bought nothing, at least nothing near Villeperce. That had been more than a year ago. 'Well – to the point, the dark-haired man with glasses intends to be neighbourly with me or us, and I'm not having it. Just because we speak English or American, ho-*ho*! Seems he's connected with INSEAD – that big school near Fontainebleau.' Tom added, 'How does he know my name in the first place, and why is he interested?' Lest he seem too concerned, he calmly sat down. Now he faced Héloïse from his straight chair with the coffee table between them. 'David and Janice Pritchard, they're called. If they manage to telephone, we're – polite, but we're busy. All right, dear?'

'Of course, Tome.'

'And if they have the nerve to ring the bell, they're not to be let in. I'll warn Madame Annette, you can be sure.'

Héloïse's usually clear blonde brow became thoughtful. 'What is the matter with them?'

The simplicity of the question made Tom smile. 'I have a feeling – ' Tom hesitated. He did not usually talk to Héloïse about his intuitions, but in this case he might be protecting her if he did. 'They don't look normal to me.' Tom glanced down at the carpet. What was normal? Tom couldn't have answered that question. 'I have the feeling they're not married.'

'And – so what?'

Tom laughed, and reached for the blue pack of Gitanes on the coffee table, lit one with Héloïse's Dunhill lighter. 'True, my dear. But why are they eyeing me? Didn't I tell you, I think I recall the same man, and maybe the pair, staring at me at some airport not long ago?'

'No, you didn't,' said Héloïse, sounding sure of herself.

'I'm not saying it's important – but I suggest we be polite – and distant – if they make any approaches. All right?'

'Yes, Tome.'

He smiled. 'There've been people before this we didn't like. No great problem.' Tom got up, walked around the coffee table, and pulled Héloïse up by the hand that she extended. He embraced her,

6

closed his eyes, and enjoyed the fragrance of her hair, her skin. 'I love you. I want to keep you safe.'

She laughed. They loosened their embrace. 'Belle Ombre looks *very* safe.'

'They won't set foot here.'

2

The next day, Tom and Héloïse went to Fontainebleau to buy their Royal Air Maroc tickets, as it turned out, though they had asked for Air France.

'They are closely connected,' said the young woman in the travel agency, a new employee to Tom. 'The Hotel Minzah, double room, three nights?'

'Hotel Minzah, that's correct,' Tom said in French. They could stay a day or so longer, if they were enjoying themselves, Tom was sure. The Minzah was said to be the best in Tangier at present.

Héloïse had gone to a nearby shop to buy shampoo. Tom found himself glancing at the door during the long time it took for the girl to write out the tickets, and realized that he was vaguely thinking of David Pritchard. But he didn't really expect Pritchard to walk in. Weren't Pritchard and mate busy getting settled in their rented house?

'Have you been to Maroc before, M'sieur Ripley?' asked the girl, looking up at him with smiling face as she stuffed a ticket into its big envelope.

Did she care, Tom wondered. He smiled back politely. 'No. I'm looking forward.'

'Open end. So if you fall in love with the country, you can stay on a while.' She handed him the envelope with the second ticket.

Tom had already signed a cheque. 'Right. Thank you, mademoiselle!'

'Bon voyage!'

'Merci!' Tom walked towards the door, which was flanked by two walls of colourful posters – Tahiti, blue ocean, one small sailing boat, and there – yes! – the poster that always made Tom smile, at least inwardly: Phuket, an island off Thailand, as Tom recalled, and he had troubled to look it up. This poster also showed a blue sea, yellow beach, a palm tree leaning towards the water, bent by years of wind. Not a soul in sight. 'Had a bad day – or year? *Phuket!*' might be a good come-on, Tom thought, enticing any number of holiday-makers.

Héloïse had said she would wait for him in the shop, so Tom turned to his left on the pavement. The shop lay on the other side of the St Pierre church.

And there – Tom could have cursed, but he bit the tip of his tongue instead – before him, walking towards him, was David Pritchard and his – concubine? Tom saw them first, through the thickening flow of pedestrians (it was midday, lunchtime), but within seconds the Odd Pair had focused on him. Tom looked somewhere else, straight ahead, and was sorry that his airline ticket envelope was still in his left hand, visible on their side. Would the Pritchards notice it? Would they cruise the road past Belle Ombre, explore the lane to one side of it, once they ascertained that he was absent for a while? Or was he worrying too much, absurdly? Tom trotted the last metres towards the gold-tinted windows of Mon Luxe. Before going through the open door, he stopped and looked back to see if the pair was still staring at him, even drifting into the travel agency. Nothing would surprise him, Tom told himself. He saw Pritchard's broad shoulders in his blue blazer just above the crowd, saw the back of his head. The Odd Pair were, apparently, passing the travel agency by.

Tom entered the perfumed air of Mon Luxe, where Héloïse was talking with an acquaintance whose name Tom had forgotten.

''Ello, Tome! Françoise – tu te rappelles? Friend of the Berthelins.'

Tom didn't, but pretended to. It didn't matter.

Héloïse had made her purchase. They went out, after an *au revoir* to Françoise, who Héloïse said was studying in Paris and also knew the Grais. Antoine and Agnès Grais were old friends and neighbours, who lived on the north side of Villeperce.

'You look worried, mon cher,' said Héloïse. 'The tickets are all right?'

'I think so. Hotel confirmed,' said Tom, slapping his left jacket pocket, from which the tickets protruded. 'Lunch at L'Aigle Noir?'

'Ah – oui!' said Héloïse, pleased. 'Sure.'

That was what they had planned. Tom loved to hear her say 'sure' with her accent, so he had stopped reminding her that 'surely' was correct.

They lunched on the terrace in the sunlight. The waiters and the head waiter knew them, knew that Héloïse liked Blanc de Blanc, fillet of sole, sunlight, salad probably of endive. They talked of pleasant things: summer, Moroccan leather handbags. Maybe a brass or copper pitcher? Why not? A camel ride? Tom's head swam. He'd once done it, he thought, or had that been an elephant in a zoo? Suddenly to be swayed upwards yards above the ground (where he'd surely land if he lost his balance) was not to his taste. Women loved it. Were women masochists? Did that make sense? Child-birth, a stoic tolerance of pain? Did all that hang together? Tom bit his lower lip.

'You are nervous, Tome.' She pronounced it 'nervuse'.

'No,' he said, emphatically.

And he made himself look calm for the rest of the meal, and on the drive home.

They were to leave for Tangier in about two weeks. A young man called Pascal, a friend of Henri the handyman, would come with them in their car to the airport and drive the car back to Villeperce. Pascal had done it before.

Tom took a spade to the garden and did some weeding by hand as well. He had changed into Levis and the waterproof leather shoes which he liked. He chucked the weeds into a plastic sack destined for the compost, then began deadheading, and was at this when Mme Annette called to him from the french windows on the back terrace.

'M'sieur Tome? Téléphone, s'il vous plaît!'

'Merci!' He snapped the clippers as he walked, left them on the terrace, and picked up the telephone in the downstairs hall. 'Hello?'

'Hello, I'm – is this Tom?' asked a voice which sounded like that of a young man.

'Yes.'

'I'm phoning from Washington, D C.' Here there was an *ooey-ooey* interfering sound as if from under water. 'I'm . . . '

'*Who* is phoning?' Tom asked, unable to hear anything. 'Hang on, would you? I'll take it on another telephone.'

Mme Annette was using the vacuum cleaner in the dining area of the living-room, sufficiently distant for a normal telephone conversation, but not for this one.

Tom took the call upstairs in his room. 'Hello, back again.'

'This is Dickie Greenleaf,' said the young man's voice. 'Remember me?' A chuckle.

10

Tom had an impulse to hang up, but the impulse did not last long. 'Of course. And where are you?'

'Washington, DC, as I said.' Now the voice was a bit falsetto.

The faker was overdoing it, Tom thought. Was it a woman? 'Interesting. Sight-seeing?'

'Well – after my experience under water, as you remember – maybe – I'm not in good shape physically for *sight-seeing*.' A falsely merry laugh. 'I was – was – '

There was some confusion here, almost a cut-off, a clicking, but the voice resumed.

'. . . was found and resuscitated. As you see. Ha-ha. Old times are not forgotten, eh, Tom?'

'Oh, no, indeed,' Tom replied.

'Now I'm in a wheelchair,' the voice said. 'Irreparable – '

Here came more noise on the line, a clatter as if of a pair of scissors or something larger falling.

'Wheelchair collapsed?' asked Tom.

'Ha-ha!' A pause. 'No. I was saying,' the adolescent voice continued calmly, 'irreparable damage to the autonomic nervous system.'

'I see,' said Tom politely. 'It's been nice to hear from you again.'

'I know where you *live*,' said the youthful voice, hitting a high note on the last word.

'I suppose so – since you've telephoned,' said Tom. 'I do wish you the best of health – recovery.'

'You should! Goodbye, Tom.' The speaker hung up, hastily, perhaps to cut short an irrepressible giggle.

Well, well, Tom thought, realizing that his heart was beating faster than usual. Due to anger? Surprise? Not fear, Tom told himself. What had sprung to his mind was that the voice might be that of the female companion of David Pritchard. Who else was it likely to be? No one that he could think of, at the moment.

What a lousy, gruesome – prank. *Mentally sick*, Tom thought, the old cliché. But who? And why? Had that been an overseas call or a pretence at one? Tom wasn't sure. Dickie Greenleaf. The beginnings of his troubles, Tom thought. The first man he had killed, and the only one he regretted killing, really, the only crime he was sorry about. Dickie Greenleaf, a well-to-do (for those times) American, living in Mongibello on the Italian west coast, had befriended him, shown him hospitality, and Tom had respected and admired him, in fact, perhaps too much. Dickie had turned against him, and Tom had resented that, and without planning too much Tom had picked up an oar and killed Dickie one afternoon when they had been alone in a small boat. Dead? Of course Dickie had been dead these many years! Tom had weighted Dickie's body with a rock and pushed it out of that boat, and it had sunk, and – well, in all these years Dickie hadn't surfaced, and why should he now?

Frowning, Tom walked slowly about his room, staring at the carpet. He was aware that he felt a bit nauseous, and took a deep breath. No, Dickie Greenleaf was dead (that voice hadn't been like Dickie's anyway), and Tom had stepped into Dickie's shoes and clothing, had used Dickie's passport for a while, but even that had soon come to a stop. Dickie's informal will, written by Tom, had passed inspection. Therefore, who was showing the audacity to bring the matter up again? Who knew or cared enough to look up his past association with Dickie Greenleaf?

Tom had to yield to his nausea. Once Tom thought he might be going to be sick, he couldn't repress it. It had happened before. Tom bent over the raised seat of the toilet. Fortunately only a little liquid came up, but his stomach ached for a few seconds. He flushed the toilet, then brushed his teeth at the basin.

Damn the bastards, whoever they are, Tom thought. He had the feeling that two people had been on the line just now, not both talking, but another listening, hence the mirth.

Tom went downstairs and encountered Mme Annette in the living-room, carrying a vase of dahlias, whose water she had probably changed. She wiped the bottom of the vase with a dishcloth before she set it back on the sideboard. 'I am going out for half an hour, madame,' Tom said in French to her, 'in case anyone rings.'

'Oui, M'sieur Tome,' she replied, then went on with her activities.

Mme Annette had been with Tom and Héloïse for several years. Her bedroom and bath were on the left side of the house as one approached Belle Ombre, and she had her own television set and radio. The kitchen was also her domain, approached from her quarters via a small hall. She was of Normandy stock, with pale blue eyes and lids that drew down at their outer corners. Tom and Héloïse loved her, because she loved them, or seemed to. She had two great friends in the town, Mmes Geneviève and Marie-Louise, also housekeepers, and the three seemed to rotate their TV evenings at the house of one or another on their days off.

Tom got his clippers from the terrace, and put them into a

wooden box that lurked in a corner for such items. The box was more convenient than walking all the way to the greenhouse at the back right corner of the garden. He took a cotton jacket from the front closet, and made sure he had his wallet with his driving licence in it, even for this short journey. The French were fond of spot-checking, using non-local and therefore merciless policemen. Where was Héloïse? Maybe up in her room, choosing clothes for the trip? What a good thing Héloïse hadn't picked up the telephone when the creeps had rung! She surely hadn't, or she'd have come immediately into his room, puzzled, asking questions. But then, Héloïse had never been an eavesdropper, and Tom's business affairs didn't interest her. If she realized that a telephone call was for Tom, she hung up right away, not hastily, but as if without thinking about it.

Héloïse knew the Dickie Greenleaf story, had even heard that Tom was suspected (or had been), Tom was sure. But she made no comment, asked no questions. Certainly she and Tom had had to minimize Tom's questionable activities, his frequent trips for inexplicable causes, in order to placate Jacques Plissot, Héloïse's father. He was a manufacturer of pharmaceuticals, and the Ripley household partly depended upon his generous allowance to Héloïse, who was his only offspring. Héloïse's mother Arlène was even quieter than Héloïse re Tom's activities. A slender and elegant woman, she seemed to make an effort to be tolerant of the young, and was fond of giving Héloïse, or anybody, household tips about furniture care, and, of all things, economy, thrift.

These details ran through Tom's head as he drove the brown Renault at moderate speed towards the centre of town. It was nearly 5 p.m. This being Friday, Antoine Grais might be home, Tom thought, though maybe not quite, if Antoine had put in a full day in Paris. He was an architect, and he and his wife now had two children in their early teens. The house that David Pritchard said he had rented was beyond the Grais' house, which was why Tom turned right at a certain road in Villeperce: he could tell himself he was going by the Grais to say hello or some such. Tom had driven through the comforting main street of the town, with its post office, one butcher's shop, one bakery, and bar-tabac, which was about all Villeperce consisted of.

There was the Grais' house, just visible behind a handsome stand of chestnuts. It was a round house, shaped like a military turret, now prettily overgrown, almost, by climbing pink rose-vines. The Grais had a garage, and Tom could see that its door was closed, meaning that Antoine hadn't arrived as yet for the weekend, and that Agnès and maybe the two children were out shopping.

Now the white house – not the first in view but the second, Tom saw through some trees, on the left side of the road. Tom shifted to second gear. The macadam road, on which two cars could just comfortably pass, was now deserted. There were few houses on this northern side of Villeperce, and the land was more meadow than farm field.

If the Pritchards had rung him fifteen minutes ago, they were probably home, thought Tom. He might at least see if they were lounging in the sunshine in deckchairs by the pond, which Tom thought was visible from the road. A green lawn in need of cutting lay between the road and the white house, a flagstone path went from the driveway to a few steps which led up to the porch. There were also some steps on the road-side of the porch, on which side the pond lay. Much of the property lay behind the house, as Tom recalled.

Tom heard laughter, certainly a woman's laugh, maybe mingled with a man's. And yes, it had come from the pond area between Tom and the house, an area nearly hidden by a hedge and a couple of trees. Then Tom glimpsed the pond, saw twinkles of sunlight on it, and had an impression of two figures lying on the grass there, but he wasn't sure. A male figure stood up, tall, in red shorts.

Tom accelerated. Yes, that had been David himself; Tom was 90 per cent sure.

Did the Pritchards know his car, the brown Renault?

'Mr *Ripley*?' The voice had come faintly but clearly.

Tom drove on at the same speed, as if he'd heard nothing.

Damned annoying, Tom thought. He took the next turning left, which brought him into another small road with three or four houses along it, farm fields on one side. This was the way back into the centre of town, but Tom turned left in order to take a road at right-angles to the Grais' road and to approach the Grais' turret house again. He kept the same easy rate of speed.

Now Tom saw the Grais' white station wagon in the driveway. He disliked dropping in without telephoning first, but perhaps with the news of new neighbours he could risk a breach of etiquette. Agnès Grais was carrying two great shopping bags from the car when Tom drove up.

'Hello, Agnès. Give you a hand?'

'That would be nice! Hello, Tom!'

Tom took both bags, while Agnès lifted something else out of their estate car.

Antoine had carried a case of mineral water into the kitchen, and the two teenagers had opened a large Coca-Cola bottle.

'Greetings, Antoine!' said Tom. 'I happened to be passing by. Nice weather, is it not?'

'That it is,' said Antoine in his baritone voice which sometimes made his French suggest Russian to Tom. Now he was in shorts, socks, tennis shoes and a T-shirt of a green Tom especially disliked. Antoine had dark and slightly wavy hair and was always a few kilos overweight. 'What is new?'

'Not much,' said Tom, setting the bags down.

The Grais' daughter Sylvie had begun unloading in an experienced way.

Tom declined a glass of Coke or wine. Soon Antoine's lawnmower, which ran on benzine and not electricity, would start buzzing, Tom supposed. Antoine was nothing if not diligent in his Paris office and here in Villeperce. 'How are your Cannes tenants working out this summer?' They were still standing in the big kitchen.

The Grais had a villa in or near Cannes which Tom had never seen, and which they rented during July and August, the months when they could get the best rent for it.

'They paid in advance – plus deposit for the telephone,' Antoine replied, then shrugged. 'I would think – all is okay.'

'You've got some new neighbours here, did you know?' Tom asked, gesturing in the direction of the white house. 'A couple of Americans, I think – or maybe you know about them? I don't know how long they've been here.'

'No-on-n,' said Antoine thoughtfully. 'Not the *next* house.'

'No, the one beyond. The big one.'

'Ah, the one that is for sale!'

'Or rent. I think they rented it. His name is David Pritchard. With his wife. Or – '

'American,' said Agnès musingly. She had heard the last part. Hardly pausing, she put a head of lettuce into the bottom compartment of the fridge. 'You met them?'

'No. He – ' Tom decided to go ahead. 'The man spoke to me in the bar-tabac. Maybe someone told him I was American. I thought I'd let you know.'

'Children?' asked Antoine, with black brows coming down. Antoine liked quiet.

'Not that I know of. I'd say not.'

'And they speak French?' asked Agnès.

Tom smiled. 'Not sure.' If they didn't, Tom thought, the Grais would not wish to meet them and would look down on them. Antoine Grais wanted France for the French, even if the outsiders were temporary and merely rented a house.

They talked of other things, Antoine's new compost box that he was going to set up this weekend. It had come in a kit that was now in the car. Antoine's architectural work was going well in Paris, and he had acquired an apprentice who would start in September. Of course Antoine was not taking August off, even if he went to an empty office in Paris. Tom thought of telling the Grais that he and Héloïse were going to Morocco, and decided not to just now. Why? Tom asked himself. Had he unconsciously decided not to go? Anyway, there was time to ring up the Grais and inform them, in a neighbourly way, that he and Héloïse would be absent for perhaps two or three weeks.

When Tom said goodbye, after invitations on both sides to come in for a glass or a café, Tom had the feeling that he had told the Grais about the Pritchards mainly for his own protection. Hadn't the telephone call purporting to be from Dickie Greenleaf been a menace of sorts? Definitely.

The Grais children, Sylvie and Edouard, were kicking a black and white football back and forth on the front lawn as Tom drove away. The boy waved to him.

3

Tom arrived back at Belle Ombre to find Héloïse standing in the living-room. She had a restless air.

'Chéri – a telephone call,' she said.

'From whom?' asked Tom, and felt an unpleasant start of fear.

'From a man – he said he was Deekie Graneleaf – in Washington – '

'*Washington?*' Tom was concerned about Héloïse's unease. 'Greenleaf – it's absurd, my sweet. A rotten joke.'

She frowned. 'But why – this choke?' Héloïse's accent had come back in force. 'Do you know?'

Tom stood taller. He was the defender of his wife, and also of Belle Ombre. 'No. But a joke from – somebody. I can't imagine who. What did he say?'

'First – he wanted to speak with you. Then he said – something – about sitting in a fauteuil roulant – wheelchair?'

'Yes, dear.'

'Because of an accident with you. The water – '

Tom shook his head. 'It's a sadistic joke, my darling. Somebody pretending to be Dickie when Dickie was a suicide – years ago. Somewhere. Maybe in water. No one ever found his body.'

'I know. So you told me.'

'Not only I,' Tom said calmly. 'Everyone. The police. The body was never found. And he'd written a will. Just a few weeks before he was missed, as I recall.' Tom believed it utterly as he said it, even though he had written the will himself. 'He wasn't with me, anyway. This was in Italy, years ago – when he went missing.'

'I know, Tome. But why does this – person annoy us now?'

Tom pushed his hands into his trouser pockets. 'A bad joke. Some people want some kind of – kick, a thrill, you know? I'm sorry he has our telephone number. What kind of voice?'

'He sounded young.' Héloïse seemed to choose her words carefully. 'Not so deep voice. American. The line was not so clear – the connection.'

'Really from America?' Tom said, not believing that it was.

'Mais oui,' said Héloïse, matter-of-factly.

Tom managed a smile. 'I think we should forget it. If it happens again, if I'm here, just pass the telephone to me, my sweet. If I'm not here, you must sound calm – and as if you don't believe a word he's saying. And hang up. You understand?'

'Oh, yes,' said Héloïse, as if she did understand.

'Such people *want* to disturb other people. That's how they get their pleasure.'

Héloïse sat down at her favourite end of the sofa, the end towards the french windows. 'Where were you just now?'

'Driving around. A tour of the town.' Tom made such a tour perhaps twice a week in one of their three cars, the brown Renault or the red Mercedes usually, doing something useful on the way, such as filling the tank at a supermarket near Moret, or checking the air in the tyres. 'I noticed Antoine had arrived for the weekend, so I stopped and said hello. They were just unloading groceries. Told them about their new neighbours – the Pritchards.'

'Neighbours?'

'They're fairly close. Half a kilometre, no?' Tom laughed. 'Agnès asked if they spoke French. If not, they're off Antoine's list, you know? I told her I didn't know.'

'And what did Antoine think of our Afrique du Nord trip?' Héloïse asked, smiling. 'Ex-tra-va-*gant*?' She laughed. The way she said the word made it sound very expensive.

'Matter of fact I didn't tell them about it. If Antoine makes a remark about expense, I'll remind him that things are pretty cheap there, the hotels, for instance.' Tom walked towards the french windows. He wanted to stroll around his land, look at the herbs, at the triumphant and waving parsley, the sturdy and delicious rucola. Maybe he'd cut a bit of the latter to go into the salad tonight.

'Tome – you are not going to do anything about that telephone call?' Héloïse had the slightly pouting but determined air of a child asking a question.

Tom didn't mind, because there was not a child's brain behind her words, and the childlike air could be due to the long straight blonde hair falling over half her forehead now. 'Nothing – I think,'

Tom said. 'Tell the police? Absurd.' He knew Héloïse was aware of how difficult it was to put the police on to any 'annoying' or porno (they'd never had any) telephone calls. One had to fill out forms and submit to a monitoring device, which would of course monitor everything else. Tom had never gone through it, nor would he. 'They're ringing from America. They'll get tired of it.'

He looked at the half-open french windows, and chose to walk past them and go on to Mme Annette's realm, the kitchen in the front left corner of the house. A smell of complex vegetable soup greeted his nostrils.

Mme Annette, in polka-dot blue and white dress and dark blue apron, was stirring something at the stove.

'Good evening, madame!'

'M'sieur Tome! Bon soir.'

'And what is the main dish this evening?'

'Noisettes de veau – but not big ones, because it is a warm evening,' madame said.

'True. It smells divine. Warm or not, I have an appetite. Madame Annette, I want to be sure you feel happy and free to invite your friends when my wife and I are gone. Did Madame Héloïse say anything to you?'

'Ah, oui! About your trip to Maroc! Of course. All will be as usual, M'sieur Tome.'

'But – good. You must invite Madame Geneviève and – the other friend?'

'Marie-Louise,' said Mme Annette.

'Yes. An evening with television, even dinner. Some wine from the cellar.'

'Ah, m'sieur! Dinner!' said Mme Annette as if that were too much. 'We are very happy with tea.'

'Tea and cake then. You will be mistress of the house for a while. Unless of course you might want to spend a week with your sister in Lyon, Marie-Odile. Madame Clusot – we could arrange for her to water the indoor plants.' Mme Clusot was younger than Mme Annette, and did what Tom called the serious cleaning in the house once a week, the baths and the floors.

'Oh – ' Mme Annette pretended to consider, but Tom felt that she preferred to stay at Belle Ombre in August, when householders often went on holiday, leaving the servants free, unless they were taken along. 'I think non, M'sieur Tome, merci quand même. I think I prefer to stay here.'

19

'As you wish.' Tom gave her a smile, and walked out through the servants' door on to the side lawn.

In front of him was the lane, barely visible through some pear and apple trees and low bushes that grew wild. Down this unpaved way he had once wheeled Murchison in a barrow in order to bury him – temporarily. Also through this lane an occasional farmer still drove a small tractor towards the main streets of Villeperce, or appeared out of nowhere with a barrow full of horse manure or tied-up kindling. The lane belonged to no one.

Tom went on to his well-tended plot of herbs near the greenhouse. He had taken a long pair of scissors from the greenhouse, and now he snipped some rucola, and one parsley frond.

Belle Ombre looked as handsome from its back garden as from the front: two rounded corners with bay windows on the ground floor and the second floor, or first floor as the Europeans said. Its pinkish tan stone looked as impregnable as the walls of a castle, though Belle Ombre was softened by a Virginia creeper's reddish leaves, flowering bushes, and a few large pots of plants near its walls. It occurred to Tom that he must get in touch with Henri the Giant before they left. Henri had no telephone, but Georges and Marie could give him messages. He lived with his mother in a house in a court behind the main street in Villeperce. Henri was not bright or quick, but was possessed of unusual strength.

Well, Henri had the height, too, six feet four at least, one metre ninety-three, as Tom figured. Tom realized that he had been thinking of Henri fending off a real assault on Belle Ombre. Ridiculous! What kind of assault, anyway? And from whom?

What did David Pritchard do all day, Tom wondered as he walked back towards the three french windows. Did Pritchard really drive to Fontainebleau every morning? And return when? And what did the rather dainty, pixie-like Janice or Janis do all day to amuse herself? Did she paint? Write?

Should he drop in on them (unless of course he could get their telephone number), bringing a handful of dahlias and peonies, by way of being neighbourly? At once the thought lost its appeal. They'd be boring. He himself would be a snoop for trying it.

No, he'd stay put, Tom decided. He'd read more about Morocco or Maroc, Tangier, and wherever else Héloïse wanted to go, get his cameras in order, prepare Belle Ombre for at least two weeks without a master and mistress.

So Tom did just that, bought a pair of dark blue Bermuda shorts in Fontainebleau and a couple of drip-dry white shirts with long sleeves, as neither Tom nor Héloïse liked shirts with short sleeves. Héloïse sometimes had lunch with her parents up in Chantilly, drove up alone as she always did in the Mercedes, and used part of the morning and afternoon for shopping, Tom supposed, as she returned with at least six plastic bags with shops' names on them. Tom almost never went to the once-a-week lunch at the Plissots, as lunches bored him, and Tom knew that Jacques, Héloïse's father, merely tolerated him, and was aware that some of Tom's affairs were shady. Well, whose weren't, Tom often thought. Wasn't Plissot himself covering up in the income-tax department? Héloïse had let it drop (not that she cared) one time that her father had a numbered account in Luxembourg. So had Tom, and the money in it was derived from the Derwatt Art Supply Inc., and even from Derwatt sales and resales of paintings and drawings in London – less and less activity here, of course, as Bernard Tufts, the forger of Derwatts for at least five years, had died years ago, a suicide.

At any rate, who was quite clean?

Did Jacques Plissot mistrust him because he didn't know *all* about him, Tom wondered. One thing nice about Plissot, he didn't seem to be nudging Héloïse, nor did Héloïse's mother, Arlène, to produce a child so that they could be grandparents. Tom had of course brought up this delicate subject with Héloïse and in private: Héloïse wasn't keen on having a child. She wasn't firmly set against it, it seemed, just didn't crave one. And now years had gone by. Tom did not mind. He had no parents to make ecstatic by the announcement of the blessed event: his parents had drowned in Boston Harbor, Massachusetts, when Tom had been a small boy, and then he had been adopted by Aunt Dottie, the old skinflint also of Boston. Anyway, Tom felt that Héloïse was happy with him, at least content, or she'd have lodged complaints before now – or, indeed, departed. Héloïse was wilful. And old bald-headed Jacques must surely realize that his daughter was happy, that they maintained a highly respectable house in Villeperce. Maybe once a year the Plissots came for dinner. Arlène Plissot's visits by herself were slightly more frequent and definitely more pleasant.

Tom had not thought of the Odd Pair, except fleetingly, for several days, when in the 9.30 a.m. post one Saturday came a square envelope addressed in a hand he didn't know and at once disliked: puffy capitals, a circle instead of a dot over an i. Conceited and stupid, Tom thought. Since it was addressed to Mme et M., Tom opened the envelope, and opened it before anything else. Héloïse was at that moment upstairs having her bath.

Dear Mr and Mrs Ripley,
We would be most pleased if you would come and have a drink with us Saturday (tomorrow). Can you come around 6? I realize this is short notice, and if not convenient for both of you, we can propose another date.
So looking forward to making acquaintance with you both!
Janice and David Pritchard
Other side: map to show where we are.   Tel: 424-6434

Tom turned the paper over and glanced at the simply drawn plan of Villeperce's main street and the street at a right-angle to it, on which the Pritchards' house and the Grais' house were indicated, plus the smaller vacant house in between.

Tum-tee-tum, Tom thought, and flipped the letter against his fingers. The invitation was for today. He was curious enough to go, that was certain – the more one knew about a possible enemy, the better – but he didn't want to take Héloïse along. He would have to invent something to tell Héloïse. Meanwhile, he should confirm, but not at 9.40 a.m., Tom thought.

He opened the rest of the post, except for one envelope addressed to Héloïse in what Tom thought was Noëlle Hassler's hand. She was a good friend of Héloïse's who lived in Paris. There was nothing interesting, a bank statement from Manny Hanny in New York, where Tom kept a current account, junk mail from Fortune 500, which for some reason thought him sufficiently moneyed to be interested in a magazine about investments and stocks. Tom left that task (where to invest) to his tax accountant Pierre Solway, who was also employed by Jacques Plissot, through whom Tom had made his acquaintance. Sometimes Solway had good ideas. This kind of work, if it could be called that, bored Tom, but it did not bore Héloïse (perhaps handling money or at least being interested in it was bred in her bones), and she was always willing to check something out with her father before she and Tom made a move.

Henri the Giant was due at 11 that morning, and vague though he was about the difference between Thursday and Saturday, sometimes, Henri did turn up at two minutes past 11. Henri as usual wore his faded blue overalls with their old-fashioned shoulder straps, and his broad-brimmed straw hat which could be described as tattered.

He also had a reddish brown beard, which he apparently whacked now and then with scissors, an easy way out of shaving. Van Gogh would have loved him as a sitter, Tom often thought. Curious to think that a pastel portrait of him by Van Gogh could and would sell today for something like thirty million dollars. Of which Van Gogh would get not a penny, of course.

Tom pulled himself together and began to explain to Henri what he would need during his two or three weeks' absence. The compost. Could Henri please turn it? Tom had a circular wire compost bin now, high as his own chest, a bit less than a metre in diameter, with a door that could open if one extracted a metal pin.

But as Tom went on, following Henri towards the greenhouse and talking about the new rose spray (was Henri listening?), Henri took a fork from just inside the greenhouse and began to attack the compost. He was so tall, so strong, Tom was loath to stop him. Henri did know how to handle compost, because he understood what it was for.

'Oui, m'sieur,' Henri murmured now and then, in a gentle voice.

'And – well – I mentioned the roses. No spots at the moment. Now – just to make things look nice – the laurel row – with the clippers.' Henri did not need the ladder as Tom did, just, if he tackled the sides near the top. Tom let the top grow any old way, straight up, as to flatten it by trimming would give the look of a formal hedge.

With envy, Tom watched Henri push the wire basket with his left hand, and with his right use the fork to rake out excellent-looking dark compost from the bottom. 'Oh, great! *Très* bien!' When Tom tried to push that wire basket, it seemed to have taken root.

'C'est vraiment bon,' Henri confirmed.

Then the seedlings in the greenhouse, and some geraniums there. They would need watering. Henri clumped about on the wooden slatted floor, nodding his understanding. Henri knew where the key to the greenhouse was, under a round rock behind the greenhouse. Tom locked it only when he and Héloïse were not in residence in the main house. Even Henri's scuffed brown brogues looked of Van Gogh's time, with soles nearly an inch thick and uppers that came above the ankle. Heirlooms? Tom wondered. Henri was a walking anachronism.

'We'll be gone at least two weeks,' Tom said. 'But Madame Annette will be here the whole time.'

A few more details, and Tom considered Henri sufficiently

briefed. A little money would not be amiss, so Tom pulled his wallet from a back pocket and gave Henri two 100-franc bills.

'Here's to start with, Henri. And you keep track,' he added. Tom was ready to return to the house, but Henri showed no sign of departing. Henri was always that way, drifting around the edges, picking up a fallen twig or tossing a stone to one side before he finally sloped off without a word. 'Au revoir, Henri!' Tom turned and walked towards his house. When he looked back, Henri was apparently going to give the compost another whack of some kind with the fork.

Tom went upstairs, washed his hands in his bathroom, and relaxed in his armchair with a couple of brochures on Morocco. The ten or twelve photographs showed a blue mosaic interior of a mosque, five cannons lined up at a cliff's edge, a market with brightly coloured striped blankets hanging, a blonde tourist in scantiest of bikinis spreading a pink towel on yellow sand. The map of Tangier on the other side of the brochure was schematic and clear in blue and dark blue, the beach in yellow and the port a pair of curves extending protectively into the Mediterranean or the Strait. Tom looked for the rue de la Liberté, where the Hotel El Minzah was, and it seemed to be within walking distance of the Grand Socco, or big market.

The telephone rang. Tom had a phone by his bed. 'I'll get it!' Tom shouted down the stairs to Héloïse, who had been practising her Schubert on the harpsichord. 'Hello?'

'Hi, Tom. Reeves here,' said Reeves Minot on a clear connection.

'You in Hamburg?'

'Sure am. I think – well, Héloïse probably told you I called before.'

'Yes, she did. Is everything all right?'

'Oh, yes,' said Reeves in a calm and reassuring voice. 'Just that – I'd like to mail something to you, small as a cassette. In fact – '

It is a cassette, Tom was thinking.

'And it's not explosive,' Reeves went on. 'If you could hold it for about five days, and then mail it to an address which will be enclosed in the envelope it's coming in – '

Tom hesitated, a bit annoyed, yet knowing he would oblige, because Reeves did him favours when he needed favours – a new passport for someone, shelter for the night in Reeves's big apartment. Reeves did favours quickly and for no charge. 'I'd say yes, old pal, but Héloïse and I are going to Tangier in a few days and travelling on from there.'

'Tangier! Fine! There's time, if I express it. It'll come to your house maybe tomorrow. No problem. I'll get it off today. Then you send it on – from wherever you're going to be in four or five days from now.'

They'd still be in Tangier, Tom supposed. 'Okay, Reeves. In principle.' Tom had unconsciously lowered his voice, as if someone might be trying to eavesdrop, but Héloïse was still at the keyboard. 'It'll be Tangier. Do you trust the post from there? I've been warned – about slowness.'

Reeves gave his dry laugh, which Tom knew well. 'There's nothing like *The Satanic Verses* on this one – *in* this one. Please, Tom.'

'All right – what *is* it, exactly?'

'Not saying. Not now. Weighs hardly an ounce.'

They hung up within seconds after that. Tom wondered if the addressee was to post it to another intermediary. Reeves had always cherished the theory, maybe self-created, that the more hands something passed through, the safer it was. Reeves was a fence, essentially, and loved his work. Fencing – what a word. Rather, to *act* as a fence had a make-believe charm for Reeves, as hide-and-seek games had for children. Tom had to admit that Reeves Minot up to now had been successful. He worked alone – at least, he was always alone in his Altona apartment, and had survived a bombing there, aimed at his apartment, too, and survived whatever it was that had given him a five-inch-long scar down his right cheek.

Back to the brochures, and Casablanca next. There were some ten folders on his bed. Tom thought of the express arriving. He was sure he would not have to sign for it; Reeves was shy about registering anything, so anyone at the house could receive it.

Then, this evening, drinks with the Pritchards at 6 p.m. Past 11 a.m. now, and he ought to confirm. What to say to Héloïse? He didn't want her to know he was going to visit the Pritchards, first because he didn't want to take her there, and to complicate things didn't want to state, plainly, to Héloïse that he felt protective of her and didn't want her near those oddballs.

Tom went downstairs, intending to take a turn around the lawn, and perhaps beg a coffee of Mme Annette, if she were in the kitchen.

Héloïse stood up from the beige harpsichord and stretched.

'Chéri, Noëlle telephoned while you were talking with Henri. She would like to come for dinner tonight, maybe stay the night. Is that all right?'

'But of course, my sweet. Certainly.' It had happened before, Tom thought, Noëlle Hassler ringing up and inviting herself. She was pleasant, and Tom had nothing against her. 'I hope you said yes.'

'I did. La pauvre – ' Héloïse started to laugh. 'A certain man – Noëlle should never have thought he was *serious*! He was not nice to her.'

Walked out, Tom supposed. 'So she's depressed?'

'Oh, not much, not for long. She is not driving, so I pick her up at Fontainebleau. The station.'

'What time?'

'Around seven. I shall check with the horaire.'

Tom was relieved, or slightly relieved. He decided to come out with the truth. 'This morning, believe it or not, an invitation from the Pritchards – you know, the American pair. For us to come for a drink around six tonight. Do you mind if I go – alone – just to learn a little more about them?'

'No-o,' said Héloïse, sounding and looking like a teenager instead of someone in her late 20s. 'Why should I? And you are back for dinner?'

Tom smiled. 'You can be sure of that.'

4

Tom decided after all to cut three dahlias and take them to the Pritchards. He had confirmed his acceptance of their invitation at noon, and Janice Pritchard had sounded pleased. Tom had said he would come alone, as his wife had to fetch a friend from the station around 6.

So at a few minutes past 6, Tom rolled up the Pritchard driveway in the brown Renault. The sun had not set and it was still warm. Tom wore a summer jacket and trousers, a shirt with no tie.

'Oh, Mr Ripley, welcome!' said Janice Pritchard, who was standing on her porch.

'Evening,' said Tom, smiling. He went up the steps and presented her with the red dahlias. 'Just cut. From my place.'

'Oh, how lovely! I'll get a vase. Please come in. David!'

Tom went into a short foyer that led to a square white living-room which he remembered. The almost ugly fireplace was unchanged, its wood painted white with an unfortunate dubonnet trim. Tom had an impression of false rusticity in all the furniture except for the sofa and armchair, and then David Pritchard came in, wiping his hands on a dishcloth. He was in shirtsleeves.

'Good evening, Mr Ripley! Welcome. I am slaving over canapés.'

Janice laughed dutifully. She was thinner than Tom had thought, and wore pale blue cotton slacks and a black and red blouse with long sleeves and ruffles at her neck and wrists. Her light brown hair was rather a pleasant apricot colour, cut short and combed so that it fluffed around her head.

'Now – what would you like to drink?' asked David, peering politely at Tom through the black-rimmed glasses.

'There's everything – probably,' said Janice.

'Um-m – gin and tonic?' asked Tom.

27

'No sooner said than done. Maybe you'd like to show Mr Ripley around the house, hon,' David said.

'Of course. If he'd like.' Janice tilted her narrow head in a pixie-like way that Tom had noticed before. It gave her eyes a skewed look that was vaguely disturbing.

They looked into the dining-room behind the living-room (kitchen to the left), where Tom's impression of horrid made-yesterday antique was confirmed by the heavy dining-table and the high-backed chairs around it, with seats that looked as uncomfortable as church pews. The stairs up were on one side of the gaudy fireplace, and he climbed them with Janice, who was talking all the while.

Two bedrooms, a bathroom in between, and that was it. Wall-paper of a modest floral pattern everywhere. One picture in the hall, also floral, of the kind one saw in hotel rooms.

'You're renting,' Tom said as they went down the stairs.

'Oh, yes. Not sure we want to live here. Or in *this* house – but just look at the reflection *now*! We left the side shutters wide open so you could see.'

'Yes – Isn't that pretty!' From the stairs, just below eye-level with the ceiling, Tom could see rippling grey and white designs created on the Pritchards' ceiling by the pond on the lawn.

'Of course, when the wind blows it's even more – *lively*!' Janice said with a shrill giggle.

'And you bought this furniture yourself?'

'Ye-es. But some of it's lent – by the people we're renting from. The dining-room suite, for example. A little heavy, I think.'

Tom made no comment.

David Pritchard had the drinks ready on the sturdy made-yesterday antique coffee table. The canapés were melted cheese bits stuck with a toothpick. There were also stuffed olives.

Tom took the armchair; both the Pritchards sat on the sofa, which was covered, like the armchair, in a chintz-like flowered material, the least offensive items in the house.

'Cheers!' said David, apronless now, lifting his glass. 'To our new neighbours!'

'Cheers,' said Tom, and sipped.

'We're sorry your wife couldn't come,' said David.

'So is she. Another time. How are you liking – just what is it you do at INSEAD?' Tom asked.

'I'm taking courses in marketing. All aspects. Marketing and how

28

to keep track of results in same.' David Pritchard had a clear and direct way of speaking.

'All *aspects*!' said Janice, and giggled again, nervously. She was drinking a pinkish something, which Tom supposed was kir, a mild concoction with wine.

'The courses are in French?' asked Tom.

'French and English. My French isn't bad. Wouldn't hurt me to try harder though.' He spoke with hard r's. 'With marketing training a variety of jobs open up.'

'Where are you from in the States?' Tom asked.

'Bedford, Indiana. Then I worked for a while in Chicago. Always in the sales end of things.'

Tom only half believed him.

Janice Pritchard fidgeted. She had slender hands, nails painted a pale pink and well cared-for. She wore one ring with a small diamond that looked more like an engagement ring than a wedding ring.

'And you, Mrs Pritchard,' Tom began pleasantly. 'You're from the mid-west too?'

'No, Washington, D C, originally. But I've lived in Kansas and Ohio and – ' She hesitated, like a small girl who had forgotten her lines, and looked down at her gently writhing hands in her lap.

'And *lived* and *suffered* and *lived* – ' David Pritchard's tone was only partly humorous, and he stared at Janice in a rather cold way.

Tom was surprised. Had they been quarrelling?

'*I* didn't bring it up,' Janice said. 'Mr Ripley asked me where I'd – '

'You didn't *have* to go into detail.' Pritchard's broad shoulders turned slightly towards Janice. 'Did you?'

Janice looked cowed, speechless, though she tried to smile, and gave Tom a glance, a quick glance that seemed to say: Think nothing of this, sorry.

'But you like to do that, don't you,' Pritchard went on.

'Go into detail? I fail to see – '

'What on earth's the *matter*?' Tom interrupted, smiling. 'I asked Janice where she's *from*.'

'Oh, thanks for calling me Janice, Mr Ripley!'

Now Tom had to laugh. He hoped his laugh relieved the atmosphere.

'You see, David?' said Janice.

David stared at Janice in silence, but he had leaned back against the sofa cushions, at least.

Tom sipped his drink, which was good, and pulled cigarettes from a jacket pocket. 'Are you people going anywhere this month?'

Janice looked at David.

'No,' said David Pritchard. 'No, we still have cartons of books to unpack. Cartons are in the garage just now.'

Tom had seen two bookcases, one up and one downstairs, empty except for a few paperbacks.

'Not *all* our books are here,' Janice said. 'There are – '

'I'm sure Mr Ripley doesn't want to hear where our books are – or extra winter blankets, Janice,' said David.

Tom did, but he kept silent.

'And you, Mr Ripley,' David went on. 'A trip this summer – with your lovely wife? I saw her – once, and only from a distance.'

'No,' Tom replied somewhat thoughtfully, as if he and Héloïse could still change their minds. 'We don't mind staying put this year.'

'Our – most of our books are in London.' Janice sat up straighter, looking at Tom. 'We have a modest apartment there – direction of Brixton.'

David Pritchard looked sourly at his wife. Then he took a breath and said to Tom, 'Yes. And I think we might have some acquaintances in common. Cynthia Gradnor?'

Tom at once knew the name, the girlfriend and fiancée of the now dead Bernard Tufts. She had loved Bernard but parted from him because she couldn't bear his forging of Derwatts. 'Cynthia . . . ' said Tom, as if searching his memory.

'She knows the Buckmaster Gallery people,' David went on. 'So she said.'

Tom could not have passed a lie-detector test at that moment, he thought, because his heart was beating palpably faster. 'Ah, yes. A blondish – well, fair-haired woman, I think.' How much had Cynthia told the Pritchards, Tom wondered, and why should she have told these bores *anything*? Cynthia wasn't the talkative type, and the Pritchards were a few cuts below her social level. If Cynthia had wanted to hurt him, ruin him, Tom thought, she could have done that years ago. Cynthia could have exposed the Derwatt forgeries too, of course, and never had.

'You maybe know the Buckmaster Gallery people in London better,' said David.

'Better?'

'Better than you know Cynthia.'

'I don't really know any of them. I've been to the gallery a few times. I like Derwatts. Who doesn't?' Tom smiled. 'That gallery specializes in Derwatts.'

'You've bought some from there?'

'Some?' Tom laughed. 'At Derwatt's prices? I have two – bought when they weren't so costly. Old ones. Well-insured now.'

Several seconds of silence. Pritchard might have been planning his next move. It occurred to Tom that Janice might have impersonated Dickie Greenleaf on the telephone. Her voice had a wide range, from shrill to a quite deep tone when she spoke softly. Was his suspicion correct, that the Pritchards had briefed themselves on Tom Ripley's past as far as they could – via newspaper archives, talks with people like Cynthia Gradnor – just to have fun with him, pique him and perhaps make him admit something? What the Pritchards believed would be interesting to know? Tom did not think Pritchard was a police agent. But one never knew. There were sub-employees of the C I A, and F B I too. Lee Harvey Oswald had been one for the C I A, Tom thought, and the fall guy in that story. Was extortion, money, on the Pritchards' minds? Horrid thought.

'How's your drink, Mr Ripley?' asked David Pritchard.

'Thanks. Maybe a half one.'

Pritchard went into the kitchen to make it, taking his own glass too, ignoring Janice. The kitchen door leading off the dining-room was open – it wouldn't be much of a problem to hear what was said in the living-room, Tom supposed, from the kitchen. But he was going to wait for Janice to begin. Or was he?

Tom said, 'And do you work too, Mrs – Janice? Or did you?'

'Oh. I was a secretary in Kansas. Then I studied singing – voice-training – first in Washington. So many schools there, you wouldn't believe it. But then I – '

'She met me, tough luck,' said David, coming in with the two drinks, again on the little round tray.

'If *you* say so,' said Janice with deliberate primness. She added in her quieter and deeper tone, 'You should know.'

David, who had not yet sat down, took a mock swat at Janice with fingers crumpled against his palm, narrowly missing her face and right shoulder. 'I'll fix you.' He did not smile.

Janice had not flinched. 'But sometimes it's *my* turn,' she replied.

They played little games, Tom saw. And made it up in bed? Unpleasant to contemplate. Tom was curious about the Cynthia

31

connection. That was a can of worms, if the Pritchards or anybody else – especially Cynthia Gradnor, who knew as well as the Buckmaster Gallery people that the last sixty-odd 'Derwatts' were forgeries – ever opened it, and told the truth. No use trying to put the lid back on, because all those very expensive paintings would become next to worthless, except for eccentric collectors who were amused by good forgeries; like Tom, in fact, but how many people in the world were like him, with a cynical attitude towards justice and veracity?

'How *is* Cynthia – Gradnor, is it?' Tom began. 'It's been ages since I've seen her. Very quiet, as I remember.' Tom also remembered that Cynthia detested him, because Tom had thought up the idea of Bernard Tufts's forging Derwatts, after Derwatt's suicide. Bernard had done the forgeries brilliantly and successfully, working slowly and steadily in his little London garret-cum-studio, but he had ruined his life in the process, because he had adored and respected Derwatt and his work, and had finally felt that he had betrayed Derwatt unforgivably. Bernard had committed suicide, a nervous wreck.

David Pritchard was taking his own sweet time answering, and Tom saw (or thought he saw) that Pritchard was thinking that Tom was worried about Cynthia, that Tom wanted to pump Pritchard about her.

'Quiet? No,' said Pritchard finally.

'No,' said Janice with a flash of a smile. She was smoking a filter cigarette, and her hands were calmer, though still clasped, even when they held the cigarette. She looked constantly from her husband to Tom and back.

And what did that mean – that Cynthia had blabbed the whole story out to Janice and David Pritchard? Tom simply could not believe that. If so, let the Pritchards say it right out: the Buckmaster Gallery people are phoney as to the last sixty-odd Derwatts.

'Is she married now?' Tom asked.

'I think *so*, isn't she, David?' asked Janice, and rubbed her right arm above the elbow with the palm of her hand for a few seconds.

'I forget,' David said. 'She was alone the – the couple of times we saw her, anyway.'

Saw her where, Tom wondered. And who had introduced Cynthia to them? But Tom was shy about probing further. Were Janice's arms bruised, Tom wondered. Was that the reason for the rather quaint long-sleeved cotton blouse on this hot August day? To hide bruises inflicted by her aggressive husband? 'You go often to art exhibitions?' Tom asked.

'Art – ha-ha!' David, after a glance at his wife, had given a genuine laugh.

Cigaretteless, Janice was again twiddling her fingers, and her knees were pressed together. 'Can't we talk about something more pleasant?'

'What's more pleasant than art?' Tom asked, smiling. 'The pleasure of looking at a Cézanne landscape! Chestnut trees, a country road – those warm orange colours in the house roofs.' Tom gave a laugh, and it was good-natured. Time he was leaving, but he tried to think what to say in order to learn more. He accepted a second cheese canapé when Janice extended the plate. Tom was *not* going to say anything about Jeff Constant, a photographer, and Ed Banbury, a freelance journalist, who years ago had bought the Buckmaster Gallery on the strength of Bernard Tufts's forgeries and the profit they would derive from them. Tom also was deriving a percentage from Derwatt sales, a sum merely steady in recent years, but that was normal, considering no more forgeries were coming since Bernard Tufts's death.

Tom's sincere remark on Cézanne might have fallen on deaf ears. He took a glance at his wristwatch. 'Thinking of my wife,' Tom said. 'I must be getting home.'

'And suppose we kept you for a while?' said David.

'Kept me?' Tom was on his feet now.

'Didn't let you out.'

'Oh, David! *Games* with Mr Ripley?' Janice writhed with apparent embarrassment, but she was grinning with her head tipped sideways. 'Mr Ripley doesn't like *games*!' Her voice had gone shrill again.

'Mr Ripley's very fond of games,' said David Pritchard. Now he was sitting upright on the sofa, his sturdy thighs in evidence, big hands on his hips. 'You couldn't leave now, if we didn't want you to leave. And I know judo too.'

'Really.' The front door, or the door Tom had come in by, was some six metres behind him, he thought. He didn't relish a fight with Pritchard, but was ready to defend himself if it came to that. He'd grab the heavy ashtray between them now, for instance. An ashtray in the forehead had done for Freddie Miles in Rome good and proper. One blow. Dead was Freddie. Tom gazed at Pritchard. A bore, an overweight, everyday, mediocre bore. 'I'll be off. Many thanks, Janice. And Mr Pritchard.' Tom smiled and turned.

Tom heard nothing behind him, and turned again in the doorway that led to the hall. Mr Pritchard was merely strolling towards him, as if his game was forgotten. Janice fluttered near. 'Are you people finding everything you need in the neighbourhood?' Tom asked. 'Supermarket? Hardware shop? Moret's still the best bet for everything. Nearest, anyway.'

Affirmative replies.

'Ever hear from the Greenleaf family?' asked David Pritchard, throwing his head back as if to increase his height.

'Now and then. Yes.' Tom still wore his bland expression. 'Do you know Mr Greenleaf?'

'Which one?' asked David, jokingly and a bit roughly.

'Then you don't,' said Tom. He looked up at the circle of quivering water reflected on the ceiling in the living-room. The sun had nearly disappeared behind the trees.

'Big enough to drown in when it rains!' said Janice, noticing Tom's glance.

'How deep is that pond?'

'Oh – five feet or so,' replied Pritchard. 'Soggy bottom, I think. Not for wading.' He grinned; the square teeth showed.

The grin might have seemed pleasant and naïve, but Tom knew him better now. Tom descended the steps to the grass. 'Thank you both. We'll see each other soon, I hope.'

'No doubt! Thanks for coming,' David said.

Weirdos, Tom thought as he drove homeward. Or was he 100 per cent out of touch with America by now? Was there a couple like the Pritchards in every small town in the United States? With funny hang-ups? Just as there were young men and women – seventeen, nineteen years old – who ate until they were two metres and more in girth? These were to be found mostly in Florida and California, Tom had read somewhere. These extremists went on draconian diets after food binges, and once they had become skeletons started the cycle again. A form of self-obsession, Tom supposed.

Tom's gates were open, and he rolled on to the soothing crunch of Belle Ombre's grey gravel forecourt, then into the garage at the left, parallel with the red Mercedes.

Noëlle Hassler and Héloïse sat in the living-room on the yellow sofa, and Noëlle's laugh rang out as merrily as ever. This evening Noëlle's dark hair was her own, longish and straight. She was fond of wigs – disguises, almost. Tom never knew what to expect.

'The ladies!' he said. 'Good evening, mesdames. How are you, Noëlle?'

'Bien, merci,' said Noëlle, 'et toi?'

'We discuss life,' Héloïse added in English.

'Ah, the supreme subject,' Tom went on in French. 'I hope I did not delay the dinner?'

'Mais non, chéri!' said Héloïse.

Tom loved looking at her slender form on the sofa now, left foot bare and propped on her right knee. Héloïse was such a contrast to the taut, writhing Janice Pritchard! 'Because I'd like to make one telephone call before dinner, if I may.'

'And why not?' said Héloïse.

'Excuse me.' Tom turned and went up the stairs to his own room, washed his hands quickly in his bathroom as was his wont after a disagreeable episode such as the one he'd just been through. His bathroom would be shared by Héloïse tonight, he realized, as she gave hers to any guest they might have. Tom ascertained that the second door to the bathroom, giving on to Héloïse's bedroom, was unlocked. Damned unpleasant, that moment when the beefy Pritchard had said, 'And suppose we kept you for a while?' and Janice had stared on, fixated. Would Janice have aided her husband? Tom thought she would have. Maybe like an automaton. *Why?*

Tom flipped the hand towel back on to its rod, and went to his telephone. His brown leather address book was there, and he needed it, as he didn't know Jeff Constant's or Ed Banbury's telephone numbers by heart.

Jeff first. He was still living in NW8, where he had his photographic studio, as far as Tom knew. Tom's watch said 7.22. He dialled.

An answering machine came on after the third ring, and Tom seized a ballpoint, and wrote down another number: ' . . . until 9 p.m.,' Jeff's voice said.

That meant 10, Tom's time. He dialled the number he'd been given. A male voice answered, and the background noise sounded as if a party were in progress.

'Jeff *Constant*,' Tom repeated. 'Is he there? He's a photographer.'

'Oh, the photographer! Just a moment, please. And your name?'

Tom hated it. 'Just say Tom, would you?'

A fairly long wait before Jeff came on, sounding a bit out of breath. The party racket continued. 'Oh, *Tom*! I was thinking of another Tom . . . Oh, it's a wedding – after-the-ceremony reception. What's new?'

Tom was glad of the background noise now. Jeff had to shout and strain to hear. 'Do you know of somebody called David Pritchard? American about thirty-five? Dark hair. Wife called Janice, blondish?'

'No-o.'

'Could you ask Ed Banbury the same thing? Ed's reachable?'

'Yes, but he moved not long ago. I'll ask him. I don't know his address by heart.'

'Well, look – these Americans have rented a house in my village, and they claim to have met Cynthia Gradnor recently – in London. They're making very snide remarks, the Pritchards. Nothing about – Bernard, however.' Tom gulped at the name. He could hear Jeff's brain ticking, almost. 'How could he have met Cynthia? Does she ever come to the gallery?' Tom meant the Buckmaster Gallery in Old Bond Street.

'No.' Jeff was firm on that.

'I'm not even sure he *has* met Cynthia. But even that he's heard of her – '

'In connection with the Derwatts?'

'I don't know. You don't suppose Cynthia would play the bitch, do you, drop – ' Tom stopped, horribly aware that Pritchard or the Pritchards had been boning up on *him*, and as far back as Dickie Greenleaf.

'Cynthia's not a bitch,' Jeff said, deep and earnest, as the maniacal din in the background continued. 'Look, I'll sound out Ed and – '

'Tonight, if you can. Ring me back, doesn't matter – well, up to midnight your time. Then I'm home tomorrow, too.'

'What's this Pritchard up to, do you think?'

'Good question. It's some kind of malice, don't ask me just what kind. Can't tell yet.'

'You mean he might know more than he's saying?'

'Yes. And – I don't have to tell you Cynthia hates *me*.' Tom spoke as softly as he could and still be heard.

'She doesn't like any of us! You'll hear from me or Ed, Tom.'

They hung up.

Then dinner, served by Mme Annette, a most delicious clear soup which tasted as if it had fifty ingredients, followed by écrevisses with mayonnaise and lemon, accompanied by a cool white wine.

The evening was still warm, and a pair of french windows stood open. The women talked of North Africa, as Noëlle Hassler had been there at least once, it seemed.

'. . . no meters on the taxis, you just have to pay what the driver says . . . And a lovely climate!' Noëlle lifted her hands in near ecstasy, then picked up her white napkin and wiped her fingertips. 'The breeze! It is not hot, because of the wonderful steady breeze all day . . . Oh, yes! French! Who can speak Arabic?' She laughed. 'You will do fine with French – everywhere.'

Then some tips. Drink the mineral water, the kind called Sidi something, in plastic bottles. And in case of intestinal difficulties, pills called Imodium.

'Buy some antibiotics to take home. No prescription,' said Noëlle cheerfully. 'Rubitracine, for example. Cheap! And it has a shelflife of five *years*! I know, because . . .'

Héloïse was drinking it all in. She did love new places. Amazing that her family had never taken her to the former French protector-ate, Tom thought, but the Plissots had always preferred Europe, it seemed, for holidays.

'And the Prickerts, Tom! How were they?' Héloïse asked.

'The Pritchards, dear. David and – Janice. Well – ' Tom glanced at Noëlle, who was listening with only polite interest. 'Very American,' Tom went on. 'He is studying marketing at the Fontainebleau INSEAD. I don't know what she does to pass the time. Awful furniture.'

Noëlle laughed. 'How so?'

'*Style rustique*. From the supermarket. Truly heavy.' Tom winced. 'And I don't much care for the Pritchards either,' he finished gently, and smiled.

'Any children?' asked Héloïse.

'No. Not the kind of people we like, I think, my dear Héloïse. So I'm glad I went and you didn't have to endure it.' Now Tom laughed, and reached for the wine bottle to add a bit of cheer to their glasses.

After dinner, they played Scrabble in French. It was just what Tom needed to relax. He was becoming obsessed with the mediocre David Pritchard, with wondering what he was up to, as Jeff had put it.

By midnight, Tom was upstairs in his room, ready to go to bed with *Le Monde* and the *Trib* whose edition today combined Saturday and Sunday.

Some time later, Tom's telephone rang in the darkness and woke him up. Tom at once recalled that he'd asked Héloïse to disconnect the telephone in her room, in case he had a late call, and he was glad of that. Héloïse and Noëlle had sat up late enough talking.

'Hello?' Tom said.

'Hi, Tom! Ed Banbury. Sorry to ring so late, but I had a message from Jeff when I got in a couple of minutes ago, and I gather it's rather important.' Ed's light and precise diction sounded more precise than ever. 'Someone called Pritchard?'

'Yes. And wife. They – they've rented a house in my village. And they claim to have met Cynthia Gradnor. Do you know anything about that?'

'N-no,' said Ed, 'but I heard about this guy. Nick – Nick Hall is our new manager at the gallery, and he mentioned an American coming in, asking about – about Murchison.'

'Murchison!' Tom echoed, softly.

'Yes, it *was* a surprise. Nick – he's been with us barely a year, and didn't know anything about a Murchison who disappeared.'

Ed Banbury said it as if Murchison had done just that, disappeared, whereas Tom had killed him. 'If I may ask, Ed, did Pritchard say or ask anything about me?'

'Not that I know of. I questioned Nick, not wanting to rouse his suspicions by doing so, of course!' Here Ed gave a whoop of laughter that sounded like his old self.

'Did Nick say anything about Cynthia – Pritchard talking to her, for instance?'

'No. Jeff told me about that. Nick wouldn't know Cynthia.'

Ed had been fairly well acquainted with Cynthia, Tom knew. 'I'm trying to figure how Pritchard met Cynthia – or if he really did.'

'But what's this Pritchard *on* about?' asked Ed.

'He's delving into my past, damn his eyes,' Tom replied. 'I hope he drowns in murk – in *anything*.'

A short laugh from Ed. 'Did he mention Bernard?'

'No, thank God. And he didn't mention Murchison – to *me*. I've had a drink with Pritchard, that's all. Pritchard's a tease. He's a prick.'

They both enjoyed a brief laugh.

'Hey,' Tom said. 'May I ask, does this Nick know anything about Bernard et cetera?'

'I don't think so. He might, but if so he chooses to keep his suspicions to himself.'

'Suspicions? We're open to blackmail, Ed. Either Nick Hall

38

doesn't suspect – or he's with us. Got to be.'

Ed sighed. 'I have no reason to think he suspects, Tom – we have friends in common. Nick's a failed composer, still trying. He needs a job and he has one with us. Doesn't know or care much about paintings, that's certain, just keeps some basic facts about prices on hand in the gallery, so he can ring up Jeff or me in case of a serious interest in anything.'

'How old is Nick?'

'About thirty. He's from Brighton. Family's there.'

'I don't want you to ask Nick anything about – Cynthia,' Tom said, as if thinking aloud. 'But it worries me, what she might have said. She knows everything, Ed,' Tom said very softly. 'One word from her, a couple of words – '

'She's not the type. I swear, I think she'd feel she was hurting Bernard somehow if she spilled the beans. She has a respect for his memory – a certain respect.'

'You see her sometimes?'

'Nah. She never comes to the gallery.'

'You don't know if she's married now, for instance?'

'No,' said Ed. 'I could take a look in the phone book, see if she's still listed under Gradnor.'

'Um-m, yes, why not? I seem to remember she had a Bayswater number. I never had her address. And if it occurs to you how Pritchard might have met her, *if* he did, tell me, Ed. Might be important.'

Ed Banbury promised he would.

'Oh, and what's your number, Ed?' Tom wrote it down, plus Ed's new address which was in the Covent Garden area.

They wished each other well, and signed off.

Tom went back to bed, after listening for a moment in the hall, looking for a streak of light under a door (he saw none) to see if the telephone call had disturbed anyone.

Murchison, good God! Murchison had last been heard of when staying overnight at Tom's in Villeperce. His luggage had been found at Orly, and that was that. Presumably – no, definitely – Murchison had not boarded the aeroplane that he was supposed to. Murchison, what was left of him was sunk in a river called the Loing, or a canal off it, not far from Villeperce. The Buckmaster Gallery boys, Ed and Jeff, had asked the minimum of questions. Murchison, who suspected forgeries of Derwatts, had been erased from the scene. They were all saved, therefore. Of course Tom's name had been in the newspapers, but briefly, as he had told a convincing story of driving Murchison to Orly airport.

That had been another murder he had regretfully, reluctantly, done or perpetrated, not like the couple of Mafia garrotte jobs, which had been a pleasure and a satisfaction to Tom. Bernard Tufts had helped him dig Murchison's corpse out of the shallow grave behind Belle Ombre, where Tom by himself had tried to bury him several days earlier. The grave hadn't been deep or safe enough. He and Bernard in the dead of night had taken the corpse, in a tarpaulin or canvas of some kind, Tom remembered, in the station wagon to a certain bridge over the Loing waters, where it had not been too difficult for the two of them to heave Murchison – weighted with stones – over the parapet. Bernard had obeyed Tom's orders like a soldier at that time, being then on some solitary plane of his own where different standards of honour prevailed, concerning different matters: Bernard's conscience had not been able to bear the weight of his guilt in creating sixty or seventy paintings and countless drawings over the years, deliberately in the style of Bernard's idol Derwatt.

Had the London or American (Murchison had been American) newspapers ever mentioned Cynthia Gradnor during the days of enquiry about Murchison? Tom didn't think so. Bernard Tufts's name had definitely not been mentioned in relation to Murchison's disappearance. Murchison had had an appointment with a man at the Tate to discuss his forgery theory, Tom remembered. He had first gone to the Buckmaster Gallery, to speak with its owners, Ed Banbury and Jeff Constant, who had very soon alerted Tom. Tom had gone over to London to try to save the day, and had succeeded, disguising himself as Derwatt and verifying a few paintings. Then Murchison had visited Tom at Belle Ombre, in order to see Tom's two Derwatts. Tom had been the last person Murchison was known to have seen, according to Murchison's wife in America, with whom Murchison must have spoken by telephone in London before coming to Paris and then Villeperce to see Tom.

Tom thought he might be visited that night by unpleasant dreams of Murchison slumping to the cellar floor in a cloud of blood and wine, or of Bernard Tufts trudging in his worn-out desert boots to the edge of a cliff near Salzburg, and disappearing. But no. Such was the whimsicality, the illogic of dreams and the subconscious, that Tom's sleep was untroubled, and he awoke the next morning feeling particularly refreshed and cheerful.

5

Tom took a shower, shaved and dressed, and went downstairs just after 8.30. The morning was sunny, not yet warm, and a lovely breeze made the birch leaves flicker. Mme Annette was of course up and in the kitchen, with her little portable radio, which lived by the breadbox, on for the news and the chatter-and-pop programmes in which the French radio abounded.

'Bon jour, Madame Annette!' Tom said. 'I am thinking – since Madame Hassler probably departs this morning, we might have a substantial breakfast. Coddled eggs?' He said the last two words in English. Coddle was in his dictionary, but not in regard to eggs. 'Oeufs dorlotés? Remember the trouble I had translating? In the little porcelain cups. I know where they are.' Tom fetched them from a cupboard. There was a set of six.

'Ah, oui, M'sieur Tome! Je me souviens. Quatre minutes.'

'At least. But first I shall ask if the ladies want them. Yes, my coffee. Most welcome!' Tom waited the few seconds while Mme Annette poured from her ever-ready kettle of hot water into his filter coffee-maker. Then he carried it on a tray into the living-room.

Tom liked to stand and drink a cup while gazing out across the back lawn. His thoughts wandered, and he could also think about what the garden needed.

A few minutes later, Tom was out in his herb section, cutting some parsley, in case the coddled eggs idea met with approval. One dropped some cut parsley, plus butter and salt and pepper, into the cups with the raw egg in each, before screwing the lids on and immersing the jars in hot water.

''Allo, Tome! Working already? Good morning!' It was Noëlle, dressed in black cotton slacks, sandals, and a purple shirt. Her English was not bad, Tom knew, but she nearly always spoke French to him.

41

'Morning. Very hard work.' Tom extended his parsley bouquet. 'Would you like a taste?'

Noëlle took a sprig and began nibbling. She had already applied her pale blue eyeshadow and her pale lipstick. 'Ah, délicieux! You know,' she continued in French, 'Héloïse and I were talking last evening after dinner. I may join you in Tangier, if I can arrange a couple of matters in Paris. You two go next Friday. Maybe I can take off by Saturday. That is, if it doesn't bother you. Maybe for five days –.'

'But what a nice surprise!' Tom replied. 'And you know the country. I think it's a splendid idea.' Tom meant it.

The ladies did opt for coddled eggs, one egg each, and the cheerful breakfast required more toast and tea and coffee. They were just finished when Mme Annette came in from the direction of the kitchen with an announcement.

'M'sieur Tome, I believe I should tell you, there is a man across the road taking pictures of *Belle Ombre*.' She pronounced Belle Ombre with a certain reverence.

Tom was on his feet. 'Excuse me,' he said to Héloïse and Noëlle. Tom had a suspicion who it was. 'Thank you, Madame Annette.'

He went to the kitchen window to have a look. Yes, the sturdy David Pritchard was at work, stepping out of the shadow of the great leaning tree which Tom loved, opposite the house, into the sunlight, camera lifted to his eye.

'Perhaps he thinks it a pretty house,' Tom said to Mme Annette in a tone calmer than he felt. He could have shot David Pritchard gladly, if he'd had a rifle in the house, and of course if he could have got away with it. Tom gave a shrug. 'If you notice him on our grass,' Tom added with a smile, 'that's a different matter, and tell me.'

'M'sieur Tome – he may be a tourist but I believe he lives in Villeperce. I think he is the American who rented a house down there with his wife.' Mme Annette gestured, and in the right direction.

How news travelled in a small town, Tom thought, and most of the *femmes de ménage* had no cars of their own, only windows and telephones. 'Really,' said Tom, and felt at once guilty, as Mme Annette might know, or soon know, that he had been in this same American's house yesterday evening at the aperitif hour. 'Probably not important,' Tom said as he moved towards the living-room.

He found Héloïse and their guest looking out of a living-room front window, Noëlle holding a long curtain back a little, smiling as

42

she said something to Héloïse. Tom was now sufficiently far from the kitchen not to be overheard by Mme Annette, but he still glanced behind him before he spoke. 'That's the American, by the way,' he said in French in a soft voice. 'David Pritchard.'

'Where you *were*, chéri?' Héloïse had whirled around to face him. 'Why is he photographing *us*?'

Indeed, Pritchard hadn't stopped, had moved across the road to where the famous lane began, no-man's land. There were trees and bushes near. Pritchard would not be able to get a clear picture of the house from the lane.

'I don't know, dear, but he's the type who loves to irritate others. He'd love for me to go out and show some annoyance, which is why I prefer to say nothing.' He gave Noëlle an amused glance, and walked back to the dining area where his cigarettes lay on the table.

'I think he saw us – looking out,' said Héloïse in English.

'Good,' Tom replied, relishing his first cigarette of the day. 'Really, he'd like nothing better than for me to go out and ask him why he's taking photographs!'

'What a strange man!' Noëlle said.

'Indeed,' Tom replied.

'He didn't say last evening he wanted to take pictures of your house?' Noëlle went on.

Tom shook his head. 'No. Let's forget him. I asked Madame Annette to tell me if he sets foot on – on our land.'

They did talk of other things – traveller's cheques versus Visa cards for North African countries. Tom said he preferred a little of both.

'A little of both?' asked Noëlle.

'You find hotels that won't take Visa, only American Express, for instance,' Tom said. 'But – a traveller's cheque can always do it.' He was near the french windows at the terrace, and he took the opportunity to scan the lawn from the left, where the lane was, to the right corner where the greenhouse squatted in tranquillity. No sign of a human figure or of movement. Tom saw that Héloïse had noticed his concern. Where had Pritchard left his car, Tom wondered. Or had Janice dropped him and was she going to swoop by and pick him up?

The ladies consulted a timetable for the trains to Paris. Héloïse wanted to drive Noëlle to Moret, where there was a train direct to the Gare de Lyon. Tom offered to do it, but it seemed that Héloïse really wanted to drive her friend. Noëlle had the smallest of overnight cases, and was already packed, and she was downstairs in a trice with it.

'Thank you, Tome!' said Noëlle. 'So it seems we shall see one another sooner than usual – in just six more days!' She laughed.

'Let us hope. That'll be fun.' Tom wanted to carry her case, but Noëlle wouldn't let him.

Tom walked out with them, and watched the red Mercedes turn left and head towards the village. Then he saw a white car approaching from the left, slowing, and a figure stepped out from the bushes into the road – Pritchard in rumpled tan summer jacket and dark trousers. He got into the white car. Now Tom stepped behind a conveniently tall hedge at one side of the gates of Belle Ombre, a hedge taller than a Potsdamer guard, and waited.

The self-assured Pritchards cruised by, David grinning at the excitable Janice, who was looking at him rather than at the road. Pritchard glanced at the open gates of Belle Ombre, and Tom almost wished he had dared to order Janice to stop, back up and drive in – Tom felt like taking them both on with his fists – but apparently Pritchard did not give such an order, because the car rolled slowly away. The white Peugeot had a Paris licence, Tom noticed.

What was left of Murchison by now, Tom wondered. The flow of the river over the years, slow and steady, would have done as much or more than predatory fish to diminish Murchison. Tom was not sure there were types of fish in the Loing there that would be interested in flesh, unless of course there were eels. Tom had heard – he checked his sickening thoughts. He did not want to imagine it. Two rings, Tom recalled, which he had decided to leave on the dead man's fingers. The stones just might have held the corpse in the same spot. Would the head have come loose from the neck bones, and rolled away on its own somewhere, dispelling dental identification? The tarpaulin or canvas would certainly have rotted.

Stop it! Tom told himself, and lifted his head. Mere seconds had passed since he had seen the creepy Pritchards, and he was only now at his own unlocked door.

Mme Annette had by now cleared the breakfast table and was probably doing the most minor of chores in the kitchen, such as checking the black and white pepper supplies. Or she might even be in her own room, sewing for herself or a friend (she had an electric sewing machine), or writing a letter to her sister Marie-Odile in

Lyon. Sunday was Sunday, and exerted its influence, Tom had noticed, also on him: one simply didn't try to work as hard on Sunday. Monday was Mme Annette's official day off.

Tom stared at the beige harpsichord with its black and beige keys. Their music teacher, Roger Lepetit, was coming Tuesday afternoon to give a lesson to them both. Tom was practising some old English songs now, ballads, which he didn't love as much as he loved Scarlatti, but the ballads were more personal, warmer, and of course a change. He liked to listen to, or overhear (Héloïse did not like attention paid), Héloïse's efforts with Schubert. Her naïveté, her goodwill, seemed to Tom to bring out a new dimension in the familiar tunes of the master. Tom was further amused by her Schubert playing, for the reason that M. Lepetit rather resembled the young Schubert – of course Schubert had always been young, Tom realized. M. Lepetit was under forty, somewhat soft and rotund, and wore rimless glasses, as had Schubert. Unmarried, he lived with his mother, as did the giant Henri, the gardener. What a difference in the men!

Stop dreaming, Tom told himself. What was he logically to expect from Pritchard's photographic efforts this morning? Would the photographs or negatives be sent to the CIA, that organization which, as Tom recalled, J.F.K. had once said he would like to see hanged, drawn and quartered? Or would David and Janice pore over the photos, some of them, perhaps, enlarged, giggle and chatter about invading the Ripley stronghold, which was apparently unguarded by dog or man? Would the Pritchards' chatter be dreams or real plans?

What did they have against him, and why? What did they have to do with Murchison, or Murchison with them? Were they related? Tom couldn't believe it. Murchison had been reasonably well educated, a cut above the Pritchards. Tom had also met his wife; she had come to Belle Ombre to meet Tom after her husband's disappearance, and she and Tom had talked for an hour or so. A civilized woman, Tom remembered.

Creepy collectors, of sorts? The Pritchards had not asked for his autograph. Would they try to do some harm to Belle Ombre in his absence? Tom debated saying something to the police, that he'd seen a man who might be a prowler, and because the Ripleys were going to be away for a while –

Tom was still debating when Héloïse returned.

Héloïse was in good humour. 'Chéri, why didn't you ask this

man – photographing – to come in? Prickard – '

'Pritchard, dear.'

'Pritchard. You were at his house. What's the trouble?'

'He is not really friendly, Héloïse.' Tom, who had been standing at the french windows that gave on to the back lawn, had taken a stance with feet slightly apart. He deliberately relaxed. 'A boring little snoop,' Tom went on more calmly. '*Fouineur* – that's what he is.'

'Why is he snooping?'

'I dunno, darling. I know – we must keep a distance – and ignore him. And his wife.'

The next morning, Monday, Tom chose a moment when Héloïse was in her bath and telephoned the institute at Fontainebleau, where Pritchard had said he was taking courses in marketing. Tom took some time over this, saying first that he wished to speak with someone in the department of marketing studies. Tom was prepared to speak in French, but the woman who answered spoke English, and without an accent.

When Tom got the right person he asked if David Pritchard, an American, was in the building now, or could he leave a message. 'In marketing, I think,' Tom said. Tom said he had found a house Mr Pritchard might be interested in renting, and it was important that he leave a message for Mr Pritchard. Tom could tell that the man in INSEAD took his words seriously, as people there were always looking for housing. He came back to the telephone and told Tom that there was no David Pritchard on their register, in marketing or any other department.

'Then I've made a mistake somewhere,' Tom said. 'I thank you for your trouble.'

Tom took a turn around the garden. He might have known, of course, that David Pritchard – if that was his real name – made a game of telling lies.

Now Cynthia. Cynthia Gradnor. That mystery. Tom bent quickly and plucked a buttercup, shiny and delicate, from his lawn. How had Pritchard got her name?

Tom took a breath, and turned towards the house again. He had decided that the only thing to do was to ask either Ed or Jeff to ring up Cynthia and ask her straight if she knew Pritchard. Tom could have done it, but he strongly suspected that Cynthia would hang up on him, or be deliberately unhelpful, no matter what he wanted. She hated him more than she did the others.

Just as Tom entered the living-room, the front doorbell sounded, a buzz, twice. Tom drew himself up, clenched and unclenched his fists. The door had a spy-hole, and Tom took a look through it. He saw a stranger in a blue cap.

'Who's there?'

'Express, m'sieur. Pour M'sieur Reepley?'

Tom opened the door. 'Yes, thank you.'

The messenger handed Tom a small sturdy manila envelope, gave a vague salute and departed. He must have come from Fontainebleau or Moret, Tom thought, and enquired the position of Tom's house perhaps from the bar-tabac. This was the mystery object from Reeves Minot of Hamburg, whose name and address was on the upper left corner. Tom found inside a small white box, and in this something that looked like a miniature typewriter ribbon in a transparent plastic case. There was also a white envelope on which Reeves had written 'Tom'. Tom opened it.

Hello, Tom,

Here it is. Please post it about five days from now to George Sardi, 307 Temple St, Peekskill, NY 10569, but not registered, and please label it tape or typewriter ribbon. Airmail, please.

All the best, as always,

R.M.

And what was on this, Tom wondered, as he put the transparent case back into the white box. International secrets of some kind? Financial transactions? A record of drug-money movements? Or some revolting private and personal blackmail material, a pair of voices taped when the owners of the voices thought they were alone? Tom was glad to know nothing about the tape. He was not paid nor did he wish to be paid for work such as this, and he wouldn't have accepted pay, or even danger money, if Reeves had offered it.

Tom decided to try Jeff Constant first and ask him, insist even, that he find out how David Pritchard might have learned Cynthia Gradnor's name. And what was Cynthia doing these days – married, working in London? Easy for Ed and Jeff to take a rather unanxious attitude, Tom thought. He, Tom Ripley, had eliminated Thomas Murchison for them all, and now Tom had a vulture cruising over him and his household in the form of Pritchard.

Héloïse was out of her bath, Tom was sure, and in her own room upstairs, but still Tom preferred to venture this call from his room with the door closed. He nipped up the stairs two at a time. Tom looked up the St John's Wood number and dialled, expecting an answering service.

A strange voice, male, answered, saying that Mr Constant was busy just now, and could he take a message? Mr Constant was photographing someone at an appointed sitting.

'Can you tell Mr Constant that Tom is on the line and wants to speak just a moment?'

In less than half a minute, Jeff was on the line. Tom said, 'Jeff. Sorry, but this is a bit urgent. Can you *and* Ed make another effort to find out how this David Pritchard got hold of Cynthia's name? It's very important. And – did Cynthia ever meet him? Pritchard's a sick liar, if I ever saw one. I spoke with Ed the night before last. Did he ring you?'

'Yes, this morning before nine.'

'Good. My news – Pritchard was standing on the road outside, photographing my house yesterday morning. How do you like that?'

'Photographing! Is he a cop?'

'I'm trying to find out. I've got to find out. I'm leaving in a few days for a holiday with my wife. I hope you'll understand why I'm thinking about the safety of my house. It might be a good idea to invite Cynthia for a drink or lunch, or whatever – to get the information we want.'

'That won't – '

'I know it won't be easy,' Tom said, 'but it's worth a try. It's worth as much as a good bit of your income, Jeff, and Ed's too.' Tom didn't want to add, on the telephone, that it might also prevent a charge of fraud against Jeff and Ed, and a charge of first-degree murder against himself.

'I'll try,' said Jeff.

'And Pritchard again: American about thirty-five, dark straight hair, about six feet, sturdy build, wears black-rimmed glasses, has a receding hairline that's going to leave him with a widow's peak.'

'I'll remember.'

'If for some reason Ed might be better at the job – ' But between the two, Tom couldn't have told which might be better. 'I know Cynthia's difficult,' Tom went on, more gently, 'but Pritchard's on to Murchison – or at least mentioning his name.'

'I *know*,' said Jeff.

'Okay.' Tom felt exhausted. 'Right, Jeff, you and Ed do your best and keep me posted. I'm here till Friday morning early.'

They hung up.

Tom seized a half-hour to practise with unusual concentration, he thought, at the harpsichord. He did better with definite short periods of time in view, twenty minutes, one half-hour, made more progress, if he dared use the word. Tom was not aiming at perfection, or even adequacy. Ha! What was that? He didn't, wouldn't, ever play for other people, so what did his mediocre level matter to anyone but himself? To Tom his practice, and the weekly visits and sessions with the Schubertly Roger Lepetit, were a form of discipline which he had come to love.

The half-hour in Tom's mind and on his wristwatch was two minutes short of being up, when the telephone rang. Tom went to take it in the hall.

'Hello, Mr Ripley, please – '

Tom at once recognized Janice Pritchard's voice. Héloïse had picked up her telephone, and Tom said, 'It's all right, my dear, I think it's for me.' He heard Héloïse hang up.

'This is Janice Pritchard,' the voice went on, tense and nervous. 'I want to apologize for yesterday morning. My husband has such absurd, sometimes *rude* ideas – such as photographing your house! I'm sure you saw him or your wife did.'

As she spoke, Tom recalled her face, apparently smiling approval as she gazed at her husband in the car. 'I think my wife did,' said Tom. 'No serious matter, Janice. But why does he want pictures of my house?'

'He *doesn't*,' she said on a high note. 'He just wants to annoy you – and everybody else.'

Tom gave a laugh, a puzzled laugh, and repressed a statement that he longed to make. 'Finds it fun, does he?'

'*Yes*. I can't understand him. I've told him – '

Tom interrupted the phoney-sounding defence of husband with, 'May I ask you, Janice, where you got my telephone number, or your husband did?'

'Oh, that was easy. David asked our plumber. He's the local plumber and he gave it to us right away. The plumber was here because we had a small problem.'

Victor Jarot, of course, the indefatigable voider of rebellious cisterns, the rammer of clogged pipes. Could such a man have any

49

idea of privacy? 'I see,' said Tom, at once livid, but at a loss what to do about Jarot, except to tell him please not to give his number out to anyone, under any circumstances. The same thing could happen with the *mazout* – the heating-fuel – people, he supposed. Such people thought the world turned around their *métiers*, and nothing else. 'What does your husband really do?' Tom asked, taking a wild chance. 'That is – I can hardly believe he's studying marketing. He probably knows everything about marketing! So I felt he was kidding.' Tom wasn't going to tell Janice he'd checked at INSEAD.

'Oh – one minute – yes, I *thought* I heard the car. David's back. Got to sign off, Mr Ripley. Bye!' She hung up.

Well! Had to ring him on the sly! Tom smiled. And her objective? To apologize! Was apologizing further humiliation for Janice Pritchard? Had David really been coming in the door?

Tom laughed aloud. Games, games! Secret games and open games. Open-looking games that were really sly and secret. But of course beginning-and-end secret games went on behind closed doors, as a rule. And the people concerned merely players, playing out something not in their control. Oh, sure.

He turned and stared at the harpsichord, which he was not going back to now, then went out and trotted to his nearest circle of dahlias. He cut with his pocketknife just one of the type he called frizzy orange, his favourite, because its petals reminded him of Van Gogh sketches, of fields near Arles, of leaves and petals depicted with loving, wriggling care, be it with crayon or brush.

Tom walked back to the house. He was thinking of the Scarlatti Opus 38, or Sonate en Ré Mineur, as M. Lepetit called it, which Tom was working on and had hopes of improving. He loved the (to him) main theme which sounded like a striving, an attack upon a difficulty – and yet was beautiful. But he did not want to practise it so much that it became stale.

He was also thinking of the telephone call to come from Jeff or Ed re Cynthia Gradnor. Depressing to know that it probably wouldn't come for twenty-four hours, even if Jeff was successful in having some kind of conversation with Cynthia.

When the telephone rang around 5 that afternoon, Tom had a small hope, very small, that it might be Jeff, but it was not. Agnès Grais' pleasant voice announced itself, and asked Tom if he and Héloïse could come for an aperitif that evening around 7. 'Antoine had a prolonged weekend, and he wants to leave so early tomorrow morning, and you both so soon go away.'

'Thank you, Agnès. Can you wait a moment while I speak with Héloïse?'

Héloïse agreed, and Tom came back and so informed Agnès.

Tom and Héloïse left Belle Ombre almost at 7. The newly rented Pritchard house lay on the same road and beyond, Tom was thinking as he drove. What had the Grais noticed about the 'renters'? Maybe nothing. The inevitable wild trees – Tom liked them – grew in the fields between houses in this area, sometimes blocking the points of distant house lights, even cutting down noise when leaves were on the trees, as now.

As was usual, Tom found himself standing and talking with Antoine, though he had vowed in a mild way not to be so entrapped this time. He had little to talk about to Antoine, the hardworking right-wing architect, whereas Héloïse and Agnès had that feminine talent for bursting into conversation on sight, and keeping it up – with pleasant expressions on their faces too – for a whole evening, if need be.

This time, however, Antoine talked about Morocco instead of the influx of non-French in Paris demanding housing. 'Ah oui, my father took me there when I was about six. I never forgot it. Of course I went a few times since then. It has a charm, a magic. To think that once the French had a protectorate over it, the days when the *postal service* was functioning, the *telephone service*, the streets . . .'

Tom listened. Antoine waxed almost poetic as he described his father's love of Tangier and Casablanca.

'It *is* the people, of course it is,' said Antoine, 'who make the country. They rightly possess their country – and yet they make such a mess from a French point of view.'

Ah, yes. What to say about that? Only sigh. Tom ventured: 'To change the subject' – he swirled his tall gin and tonic and the ice rattled – 'are your neighbours here quiet?' He nodded towards the Pritchard estate.

'Quiet?' Antoine's lower lip came out. 'Since you ask,' he said with a chuckle, 'they were twice playing loud music. Late, around midnight. After! Pop music.' He said pop music as if it was amazing that anyone over twelve would play pop music. 'But not for long. One half-hour.'

Suspicious length of time, Tom thought, and Antoine Grais was just the man to time such a phenomenon by his watch. 'You can hear it here, you mean?'

'Oh, yes. And we're nearly half a kilometre away! They had it really loud!'

Tom smiled. 'Other complaints? They are not borrowing your lawn-mower yet?'

'Non-n,' Antoine growled, and drank his Campari.

Tom was not going to say a word about Pritchard photographing Belle Ombre. Antoine's vague suspicion of Tom would congeal a bit, the last thing Tom wanted. The whole village had finally known that the police, both French and English, had come to speak with Tom at Belle Ombre just after Murchison's disappearance. The police had not made a noise about it, no cars with sirens, but in a small town everyone knew everything, and Tom could not afford more. He had warned Héloïse before coming to the Grais that she was not to mention seeing Pritchard taking pictures.

The boy and girl came in, back from swimming somewhere, smiling, damp-haired and barefoot, but still not obstreperous: the Grais wouldn't have permitted that. Edouard and his sister said their 'Bon soir' and departed for the kitchen, Agnès following.

'A friend in Moret has a pool,' Antoine explained to Tom. 'Very nice for us. He has kids too. And he brings ours back. I take them.' Antoine gave another rare smile that creased his well-fed face.

'When are you back?' asked Agnès, pushing her fingers through her hair. The question was for Héloïse and Tom. Antoine had gone off somewhere.

Héloïse said, 'Perhaps in three weeks? It is not fixed.'

'Back again,' said Antoine, coming down the curving staircase with something in each hand. 'Agnès chérie, some small glasses? Here is a fine map, Tom. Old but – you *know*!' His tone implied that old was best.

It was a much used roadmap of Morocco, Tom saw, folded many a time and repaired with transparent tape.

'I'll be most careful with it,' Tom said.

'You should rent a car. No doubt about it. Get around to the little places.' Then Antoine attended to his speciality, Holland gin from a cold crock bottle.

Tom recalled that Antoine had a small fridge up in his atelier here.

Antoine poured and then passed the tray of four small glasses first to the ladies.

'Oooh!' Héloïse exclaimed politely, though she was not fond of gin.

52

'Santé!' said Antoine as they all raised their glasses. 'A happy trip and safe return!'

Bottoms up.

The Holland gin was particularly smooth, Tom had to admit, but Antoine acted as if he had made the stuff, and Tom had never known him to offer a second nip. Tom realized that the Pritchards had not yet tried to scrape acquaintance with the Grais, perhaps because Pritchard didn't know that the Ripleys were old friends of the Grais. And that house between the Grais and the Pritchards? Empty for years, as far as Tom knew, maybe for sale; of no matter, no importance, Tom thought.

Tom and Héloïse took their leave, promising a postcard, which prompted Antoine to warn that the post in Maroc was *abominable*. Tom thought of Reeves's tape.

They had just got home when the telephone rang.

'I'm expecting a call, dear, so – ' Tom picked up the telephone on the hall table, prepared to have to go up to his own room, in case it was Jeff and the conversation became complex.

'Chéri, I want some yaourt, I don't like that gin,' Héloïse said, and went off in the direction of the kitchen.

'Tom, this is Ed,' said Ed Banbury's voice. 'I got through to Cynthia. Jeff and I were sharing – efforts. I couldn't make a date, but I learned a few things.'

'Yes?'

'It seems Cynthia was at a party some time ago for journalists, a big stand-up thing where nearly anybody could get in and – it seems this Pritchard was there.'

'One minute, Ed, I think I'll take this on another phone. Hang on.' Tom leapt up the stairs to his room, took the telephone off the hook, and ran down again to hang up the hall telephone. Héloïse, paying no attention, was turning on the TV in the living-room. But Tom did not want to say the name Cynthia within her hearing, lest she remember that Cynthia had been the fiancée of Bernard Tufts, *le fou*, as Héloïse called him. Bernard had frightened Héloïse when she had met him here at Belle Ombre. 'Back again,' said Tom. 'You talked with Cynthia.'

'By telephone. This afternoon. A man at the party whom Cynthia knew came over and told her there was an American there, asking if he knew Tom Ripley. Just out of the blue, it seems. So this man – '

'American also?'

'I don't know. Anyway, Cynthia told her friend – this man – to tell the American to look into Ripley's connection with Murchison. That's how it all came about, Tom.'

Tom found it extremely fuzzy. 'You don't know the go-between's name? Cynthia's friend who spoke with Pritchard?'

'Cynthia didn't drop it and I didn't want to – to press it too much. What was my excuse for ringing her in the first place? That a rather gauche type of American knows her name? I didn't say that *you'd* told me that. Talk about out of the blue! I had to play it that way. I think we learned at least something, Tom.'

True, Tom thought. 'But Cynthia never met Pritchard? That night?'

'I gather not.'

'The go-between must've said to Pritchard, "Let me ask my friend Cynthia Gradnor about Ripley." Pritchard had her name right and it's not an everyday name.' Maybe Cynthia had taken the trouble, via her go-between, Tom thought, to give her name like a calling card, thinking it might strike the fear of God into Tom Ripley, if it ever got to him.

'You still there, Tom?'

'Yep. Cynthia means us no good, my friend. And neither does Pritchard. But he's simply cracked.'

'Cracked?'

'Some kind of mental case, don't ask me what.' Tom took a deep breath. 'Ed, I thank you for your trouble. Tell Jeff thanks too.'

When they had hung up, Tom suffered a shaky few moments. Cynthia had her suspicions with regard to Thomas Murchison's disappearance, that was certain. And she had the courage to stick her neck out about it. She must know that if anyone were a candidate for elimination on Tom's agenda, it would be herself, because she knew all about the forgeries, down to the first picture Bernard Tufts ever forged (which not even Tom was sure of) and its date, very likely.

Tom was thinking that Pritchard would have come across the name Murchison while reading up on Tom Ripley in newspaper archives, probably. Tom's name had been mentioned only one day that Tom knew of in the American newspapers. Mme Annette had seen Tom carrying Murchison's suitcase out to his (Tom's) car at the right time to reach Orly for Murchison's flight, and had mistakenly but innocently told the police that she had seen M. Ripley and M. Murchison going out to M. Ripley's car with the luggage. Such was the power of suggestion, of acting, Tom thought.

At that moment Murchison had been clumsily wrapped in an old canvas in Tom's cellar, and Tom had been terrified that Mme Annette might go down for wine before he could do something about the corpse.

Cynthia's bringing Murchison's name up might well have given the Pritchards new enthusiasm. Tom had no doubt that Cynthia knew Murchison had 'disappeared' just after visiting Tom. That had been in the newspapers in England, as Tom recalled, even if the items had been small. Murchison had had a conviction that all the late Derwatts were forgeries. As if Murchison's belief wasn't strong enough, Bernard Tufts had further strengthened it by telling Murchison to his face in London, at Murchison's hotel, 'Don't buy any more Derwatts.' Murchison had told Tom of this curious meeting with a stranger in the bar of the hotel. Bernard had not told Murchison his name, Murchison had said to Tom. Tom, himself spying on Murchison just then, had seen him and Bernard tête-à-tête, viewing it with a horror Tom could still feel: Tom had known what Bernard must be saying.

Tom had often wondered if Bernard Tufts had then gone to Cynthia and tried to win her back, on the grounds that he had sworn to himself not to paint any more forgeries. But if Bernard had, Cynthia hadn't taken him back.

6

Tom had thought that Janice Pritchard might make another effort to 'contact' him, as she would put it, and so she did, on Tuesday afternoon. The telephone rang at Belle Ombre around 2.30 p.m. Tom heard it faintly. He was then weeding in one of the rose-beds near the house. Héloïse answered, and after a few seconds called, 'Tome! Telephone!' She had come to the open french window.

'Thank you, my sweet.' He dropped the hoe. 'And who is it?'

'The wife of Prickard.'

'Aha! Pritchard, dear.' Annoyed but curious, Tom took it in the hall. The time he would not be able to go upstairs to talk without explaining that move to Héloïse. 'Hello?'

'Hello, Mr Ripley! I'm so glad you're home. I was wondering – you may think this presumptuous of me – I would so much like to say a few words to you face to face.'

'Oh?'

'I have the car. I'm free until nearly five. Can – '

Tom did not want her at his house, nor did he want to go to the house of the shimmering ceiling. They agreed to meet near the obélisque in Fontainebleau (Tom's idea) at a working-class bar-café called Le Sport or some such on the north-east corner at a quarter past 3. Tom and Héloïse had M. Lepetit coming at 4.30, for their music lesson, but Tom did not mention that.

Héloïse looked at him with an interest in her eyes that his telephone calls seldom evoked.

'Yes, of all people.' Tom hated saying it, but went ahead. 'She wants to see me. I might learn something. So I agreed. This afternoon.'

'Learn something?'

'I don't like her husband. I don't like either of them, my dear,

56

but – if I learn something, it helps.'

'They are asking funny questions?'

Tom smiled a little, grateful for Héloïse's understanding of their mutual problems, mainly his problems. 'Not too many. Don't worry. They tease. *Ils taquinent.* Both of them.' Tom added on a more cheerful note, 'I'll give you a full report when I return – which will be in time for M'sieur Lepetit.'

Tom left the house a few minutes later, and found a parking place near the obélisque, dubious as to parking ticket, but he didn't care.

Janice Pritchard was already there, standing uneasily at the bar. 'Mr Ripley.' She gave Tom a warm smile.

Tom nodded, but ignored the hand she extended. 'Good afternoon. Can't we find a booth?'

They did. Tom ordered tea for the lady, and an express for himself.

'What's your husband doing today?' Tom asked with a pleasant smile, expecting Janice to say he was at the Fontainebleau INSEAD, in which case Tom was going to ask her to be more specific about her husband's studies.

'His massage afternoon,' replied Janice Pritchard with a weaving motion of her head. 'In Fontainebleau. I'm supposed to pick him up at four-thirty.'

'Massage? He has a bad back?' The word massage was disagreeable to Tom; he associated it with sex parlours, although he knew respectable massage parlours existed.

'No.' Janice's face looked tortured. She stared as much at the table top as at Tom. 'He just likes it. Anywhere, everywhere, twice a week, anyway.'

Tom swallowed, hating the conversation. The loud cries for '*Un Ricard*!' and the roars of triumph from the games-machine players were more pleasant than Janice talking about her oddball husband.

'I mean – even if we're in Paris, he can find a masseuse parlour right away.'

'Curious,' Tom murmured. 'And what's he got against me?'

'Against *you*?' Janice said, as if surprised. 'Why, nothing. He has a respect for you.' She looked Tom in the eyes.

Tom knew that. 'Why does he say he's at INSEAD, when he isn't?'

'Oh – you know that?' Now Janice's eyes were steadier, amused, and mischievous.

'No,' Tom said. 'I'm not at all sure. I just don't believe all of what your husband says.'

Janice laughed, giggling with a curious glee.

Tom didn't smile back, because he didn't feel like it. He watched Janice rub her right wrist with her thumb, as if performing some kind of unconscious massage. She wore a crisply clean white shirt above her same blue slacks, with a turquoise (not real, but pretty) necklace under the shirt collar. And now Tom saw definite bruise marks as her massaging pushed her cuff back. Tom realized that a bluish spot on the left side of her neck was a bruise also. Did she want him to see her bruises? 'Well,' Tom said finally, 'if he doesn't attend INSEAD – '

'He likes to tell unusual stories,' said Janice, looking down at the glass ashtray, in which three stubs from preceding customers lay, one a filter.

Tom smiled indulgently, doing his best to make it look genuine. 'But of course you love him all the same.' He saw Janice hesitate, frown. She was putting on the damsel-in-distress act, Tom felt, or something close to it, loving his drawing her out.

'He needs me. *I'm* not sure he – I mean, that I love *him*.' She glanced up at Tom.

Oh, Christ, as if it mattered, Tom thought. 'To ask a very American question, what does he do for a living? Where does his money come from?'

Janice's brow suddenly unfurrowed. 'Oh, that's no problem. His family had a lumber business in Washington State. It was sold when the father died, and David got half along with his brother. It's all invested – somehow – so income comes from that.'

The way she said 'somehow' told Tom that she didn't know a thing about stocks and bonds. 'Switzerland?'

'No-o. Some bank in New York, they handle it all. It's enough for us – but David always wants more.' Janice smiled almost sweetly, as if talking about a child's penchant for another helping of cake. 'I think his father got impatient with him, threw him out of the house when he was about twenty-two, because he wasn't working. Even then, David had a good allowance, but he wanted more.'

Tom could imagine. Easy money nourished the fantasy element in his existence, guaranteed the continued unreality, and at the same time food in the fridge and on the table.

Tom took a sip of his coffee. 'Why did you want to see me?'

'Oh – ' His question might have awakened her from a dream.

58

She shook her head a little, and regarded Tom. 'To tell you he's playing a game with you. He wants to *hurt* you. He wants to hurt me too. But you – interest him now.'

'How can he hurt me?' Tom pulled out his Gitanes.

'Oh, he suspects you – of everything. So he just wants to make you feel aw-w-ful.' She drawled the word out, as if this kind of hurt was unpleasant, but just a game.

'He hasn't succeeded yet.' Tom extended the packet. She shook her head and took one of her own. 'Suspects me of what, for instance?'

'Oh, I'm not saying. He'd beat me, if I ever told.'

'Beat you?'

'Oh, yes. He loses his temper sometimes.'

Tom feigned mild shock. 'But you must know what he's got against me. It's surely not personal, because I never met him till a couple of weeks ago.' Then he ventured, 'He knows nothing about me.'

Her eyes narrowed, and her weak smile could hardly be called a smile now. 'No, he just pretends.'

Tom disliked her as much as he disliked her husband, but tried not to let it show in his face. 'He makes a habit of going around annoying people?' Tom asked it as if he were amused by the idea.

Again the juvenile giggle from Janice, though the little wrinkles around her eyes would indicate that she was at least thirty-five, the age her husband looked also. 'You could say that.' She glanced at Tom and away.

'Who was it before me?'

Silence, as Janice looked into the sordid ashtray as if it were a fortune-teller's crystal ball, as if she glimpsed fragments of old stories there. Her brows even lifted – was she acting some part now, for her own pleasure? – and Tom saw for the first time a scar of crescent shape on the right side of her forehead. Result of a flying saucer one evening?

'What does he hope to gain by annoying people?' Tom asked gently, as if posing a question at a seance.

'Oh, his idea of fun.' Now Janice gave a real smile. 'There was a singer in America – *two* singers!' she added with a laugh. 'One a pop singer and the other – much more important, a female soprano in the opera. I forgot her name, maybe that's for the best, ha-ha! Norwegian, I think. David – ' Janice gazed at the ashtray again.

'A pop singer?' Tom prompted.

59

'Yes. David just wrote insulting notes, you see. "You're slipping," or "Two assassins are waiting," something like that. David wanted to throw him *off*, make him give a shaky performance. *I'm* not even sure the letters ever reached this one, they get so many letters, and he was pretty big among the kids. First name was Tony, I remember that. But I think drugs happened to him and not – ' Janice paused again, then came out with, 'David just likes to see people *wilt* – if he can. If he can make them wilt.'

Tom listened. 'And he collects dossiers on these people? Newspaper items?'

'Not so much,' Janice said casually with a glance at Tom, and she drank some of her tea. 'For one thing, he doesn't want them in the house, in case he's – well, successful. I don't think he was successful with the Norwegian opera singer, for example, but he kept the TV on, watching her, I remember, and saying she's becoming shaky – failing. Why, *nonsense*, I thought.' Janice looked into Tom's eyes.

A phoney frankness, Tom thought. If she felt so strongly, what was she doing living under the same roof as David Pritchard? Tom took a deep breath. One didn't ask a logical question of each and every married woman. 'And what's he planning for me? Just heckling?'

'Oh – probably.' Janice squirmed again. 'He thinks you're too sure of yourself. Conceited.'

Tom repressed a laugh. 'Heckle me,' Tom mused. 'And what comes next?'

Janice's thin lips rose at one corner in a sly, amused line that he'd never seen before, and her eyes avoided his. 'Who knows?' She rubbed her wrist again.

'And how did David happen to alight on me?'

Janice glanced at him, then pondered. 'I seem to remember he saw you at an airport somewhere. Noticed your coat.'

'*Coat?*'

'Leather and fur. Something nice, anyway, and David said, "Isn't that a good-looking coat, I wonder who he is." And somehow he found out. Got behind you in a line, maybe, so he could find out your name.' Janice shrugged.

Tom tried hard to recall anything, and couldn't. He blinked. It was possible, of course, discovering his name at an airport, noticing that he had an American passport. Then checking – what? Embassies? Tom wasn't registered, didn't *think* he was, in Paris, for instance. Then newspaper files? That took perseverance. 'How long have you been married? And how did you meet David?'

'Oh – ' Again mirth in her narrow face, a hand pushed through the apricot-coloured hair. 'Y-yes, I suppose we've been married more than three years. And we met – at a big conference for secretaries, bookkeepers – even bosses.' Another laugh. 'In Cleveland, Ohio. I don't know how David and I got to talking, there were so many people. But David has a certain charm, maybe you can't see it.'

Tom couldn't. Types like Pritchard looked as if they intended to get what they wanted, even if it meant twisting a man's or woman's arm or half-throttling them, and Tom knew this had a charm for certain female types. He pushed his cuff back. 'Excuse me. I have a date in a few minutes, but I'm all right for time now.' He was dying to mention Cynthia, to ask what Pritchard intended to use her for, but Tom did not want to drum the name in. And of course he didn't want to seem worried. 'What does your husband want from me – if I may ask? Why was he taking pictures of my house, for instance?'

'Oh, he wants to make you afraid of him. Wants to see that you're afraid of him.'

Tom smiled tolerantly. 'Sorry, no way.'

'It's simply a show of *power* on David's part,' she said on a shriller note. 'I've said that many a *time* to him.'

'Another blunt question – has he ever gone to a shrink?'

'Ha-ha! *Hee!*' Janice squirmed with mirth. 'Certainly not! He laughs at them, says they're phoneys – if he ever *mentions* them.'

Tom signalled for the waiter. 'But – Janice, don't you think it's unusual that a husband beats his wife?' Tom could hardly control his smile, since Janice surely enjoyed the treatment.

Janice shifted, and frowned. 'Beats – ' She stared at the wall. 'Maybe I shouldn't have said that.'

Tom had heard of the cover-up-for-mate type, and Janice was that, at least for now. He took a note from his wallet. The bill was less, and Tom motioned for the waiter to keep the rest. 'Let's be cheerful. Tell me David's next move,' Tom said pleasantly, as if it were an amusing game.

'Move where?'

'Against me.'

Her gaze clouded as if a multitude of possibilities had filled her brain. She managed a smile. 'I honestly can't say, maybe couldn't put it into words if I – '

'Why not? Try.' Tom waited. 'Tossing a stone through one of my windows?'

She didn't answer, and Tom, disgusted, stood up.

'If you'll pardon me – ' he said.

Silent, maybe affronted, she got up, and Tom let her precede him to the door.

'By the way, I saw you picked David up on Sunday in front of my house,' Tom said. 'And now you pick him up again. You're very attentive.'

Again no answer.

Tom felt suddenly a boiling anger, caused by frustration, he realized. 'Why don't you pull out? Why do you stick around and take it?'

Naturally Janice Pritchard wasn't going to answer that one, that was hitting too close to home. Tom saw a tear brighten her right eye as they walked, presumably towards Janice's car, as she was leading.

'Or are you even married?' Tom pursued.

'Oh, stop it!' Now the tears overflowed. 'I so much wanted to like you.'

'Don't bother, ma'am.' Tom was at that moment recalling her satisfied smile as she drove David Pritchard away from Belle Ombre last Sunday morning. 'Goodbye.'

Tom turned and walked towards his own car, and trotted the last few yards. He felt like hurling his fist against something, a tree-trunk, anything. On the road homeward, he had to be careful not to press too hard on the accelerator.

The front door was locked, Tom was glad to find, and Héloïse opened it for him. She had been at the harpsichord. Her Schubert Lieder book was on its stand.

'Mother of God and God's *teeth*!' Tom said with profound exasperation, and held his head with both hands for an instant.

'What happened, chéri?'

'The woman is cracked! And it's depressing. Awful.'

'What did she say?' Héloïse was calm.

It took a lot to rattle Héloïse, and it did Tom good to look at her composure. 'We had a coffee. I did. She – well, you know, these Americans.' He hesitated. Tom still felt he, he and Héloïse, could simply ignore the Pritchards. Why upset Héloïse with their quirks? 'You know, my sweet, I am often bored by people, some people. Bored enough to explode, sorry.' Before Héloïse could ask another question, Tom said, 'Excuse me,' and went to the lavatory off the front hall, where he washed his face in cold water, his hands with soap and water, and his nails with a brush. With M. Roger Lepetit, he would soon be in another atmosphere entirely. Tom and Héloïse never knew which of them would come first for the half-hour with M. Roger, as he chose suddenly and with a polite smile, saying, 'Alors, m'sieur' or, 'Madame, s'il vous plaît?'

M. Lepetit arrived a few minutes later, and after the usual pleasantries about the good weather, the garden in such fine condition, he gestured to Héloïse with his rosy little smile, lifted a rather pudgy hand and said, 'You, madame? Would you like to begin? Shall we?'

Tom kept in the background, still on his feet. He knew that Héloïse did not mind his presence when she played, a fact which Tom appreciated. He would have detested the role of Harsh Critic. He lit a cigarette, stood behind the long sofa, and gazed at the Derwatt over the fireplace. *Not* a Derwatt, Tom reminded himself, but a Bernard Tufts forgery called 'Man in Chair'. It was reddish-brown with some yellow streaks, and like all Derwatts had multiple outlines, often with darker strokes, which some people said gave them headaches; from a distance the images seemed lifelike, even slightly moving. The man in the chair had a brownish, apelike face, with an expression that could be described as thoughtful, but was by no means defined by clear-cut features. It was the restless (even in a chair), doubting, troubled mood of it which pleased Tom; that and the fact that it was a phoney. It had place of honour in his house.

The other Derwatt in the living-room was 'The Red Chairs', another medium-large canvas, of two small girls about ten years old, sitting on straight chairs in tense attitudes, with wide, frightened eyes. Again the reddish-yellow outlines of chairs and figures were tripled and quadrupled, and after a few seconds (Tom always thought, imagining a first view) the observer realized that the background could be flames, that the chairs might be on fire. What was that picture worth now? A six-figure sum in pounds, a high six-figure. Maybe more. It depended on who was auctioning it. Tom's insurer was always upping his two paintings. Tom had no intention of selling them.

If the vulgar David Pritchard managed to blow all the forgeries, he could never touch 'The Red Chairs', of course, whose provenance was old and from London. Pritchard *couldn't* stick his clumsy nose in and cause devastation, Tom thought. Pritchard had never heard of Bernard Tufts. The lovely measures of Franz Schubert gave Tom strength and heart, even though Héloïse's playing was not of concert standard: the intention, the respect for Schubert, was there, just as in Derwatt's – no, Bernard Tufts's – 'Man in Chair' the respect for Derwatt had been there when Bernard painted it in Derwatt's style.

Tom relaxed his shoulders, flexed his fingers and looked at his nails. All neat and proper. Bernard Tufts had never wanted to share in the profits, in the rising income of the false Derwatts, Tom recalled. Bernard had always accepted just enough to keep himself going in his studio in London.

If a type like Pritchard exposed the forgeries – how? – Bernard Tufts would also be exposed, Tom supposed, dead though he was. Jeff Constant and Ed Banbury would have to answer the question, who had been forging, and of course Cynthia Gradnor knew. The interesting question was, would she have enough respect for her former love Bernard Tufts not to betray him by name? Tom felt a curious and proud desire to do just that, protect the idealistic and childlike Bernard, who had finally died by his own hand (or action, jumping off a cliff in Salzburg) for his sins.

Tom's story had been that Bernard had left his duffelbag with Tom while he, Bernard, went off to look for a hotel room, as he wanted to change his hotel; and Bernard had never come back. In truth, Tom had followed Bernard, who had jumped off a cliff. And Tom had cremated the body the next day as best he could, and claimed that the body had been that of Derwatt. And Tom had been believed.

Funny, if Cynthia nourished a smouldering resentment, asking herself: Where is Bernard's body, after all? And Tom knew that she hated him and the Buckmaster Gallery boys.

7

The plane began its descent with a dramatic dip of its right wing, and Tom was on his feet, as much as his seatbelt would permit. Héloïse had the window seat, Tom had insisted on that, and there it was – the dramatic two prongs, curved inward, of the port of Tangier, reaching out into the Strait as if wanting to capture something.

'Remember the map? There it is!' Tom said.

'Oui, mon chéri.' Héloïse seemed not as excited as he, but she did not take her eyes from the round window either.

Unfortunately the window was dirty, and the view not clear. Tom stooped, trying to see Gibraltar. He couldn't, but he did see the southern tip of Spain, where sat Algeciras. It all looked so small.

The plane straightened, bent the other way and turned left. No view. But again the right wing dipped, and Tom and Héloïse were given a prospect, closer now, of white, jammed-together houses on a rise of land, chalky-white little houses with tiny squares of windows. On the ground, the plane taxied for ten minutes, people unfastened seatbelts, and grew too impatient to keep their seats.

They walked into a passport control room with a high ceiling, where sunlight poured down through high and closed windows. Warm, Tom removed his summer jacket and put it over his arm. The people on the two slowly moving lines seemed to be French tourists, and there were Moroccan natives also, Tom thought, some wearing djellabas.

In the next room, where Tom claimed their luggage from the floor – a most informal arrangement – he changed 1000 French francs into dirhams, then enquired of a dark-haired woman sitting at the Information Desk the best way to get to the centre. Taxi. And the price? About 50 dirhams, she replied in French.

Héloïse had been 'reasonable' and the two of them could manage their few suitcases without a porter. Tom had reminded Héloïse that she could buy things in Morocco, and even another suitcase to carry them in.

'Fifty to the city, all right?' Tom said in French to the taxi driver who opened his car door. 'Hotel Minzah?' Tom knew there were no taxi meters.

'Get in,' was the brusque reply in French.

Tom and the driver did the loading.

Off they went like a rocket, Tom felt, but the sensation was due to the somewhat bumpy road plus the wind through the open windows. Héloïse was holding on to her seat and a strap. Dust came in through the driver's window. But at least the road was straight, and they seemed to be heading for the cluster of white houses that Tom had seen from the aeroplane.

Houses rose on either side, rather crude-looking red-brick dwellings, four and six storeys high. They rolled into a main street of some sort, with sandalled men and women walking on the pavements, a sidewalk café or two, and small children dashing recklessly across the street, causing the driver to brake suddenly. This was undoubtedly the city proper, dusty, greyish, busy with shoppers and strollers. The driver turned left and stopped after a few yards.

Hotel El Minzah. Tom got out and paid, adding another 10 dirhams, and a bellhop in red came out to assist them.

Tom registered in the rather formal and high-ceilinged lobby. At least it looked clean, and had a predominance of red and dark red in its colours, though the walls were creamy white.

A few minutes later, Tom and Héloïse were in their 'suite', a term Tom always found ludicrously elegant. Héloïse washed her hands and face in her quick and efficient way, and set about unpacking, while Tom surveyed the scene from the windows. They were on the fourth floor by European counting. Tom looked down on a busy panorama of greyish and white buildings, none more than six storeys high, a disorder of hanging laundry, some tattered and unidentifiable flags from a few roof poles, television aerials aplenty, and more laundry spread out on the rooftops. Directly below, visible from another window in the room, the moneyed class, of which he was presumably one, sunned itself and sprawled on hotel grounds. The sun had disappeared from the area around the Minzah's swimming pool. Beyond the horizontal forms in bikinis and swimming trunks was a border of white tables and chairs, and beyond these, pleasant and well cared-for palm trees, bushes and bougainvillaeas in bloom.

At the level of Tom's thighs, an air-conditioner blew up cool air, and he held out his hands, letting the coolness go up his sleeves.

'Chéri!' A cry of mild distress. Then a short laugh. 'L'eau est coupée! Tout d'un coup!' She continued, 'Just as Noëlle said. Remember?'

'For four hours a day in toto, didn't she say?' Tom smiled. 'And what about the toilet? And the bath?' Tom went into the bathroom. 'Didn't Noëlle say – yes, look at this! A bucket of clean water! Not that I'd want to drink it, but to wash with – '

Tom did manage to wash his hands and face in cold water, and between them they unpacked nearly everything. Then they went out for a stroll.

Tom jingled strange coins in his right-hand trouser pocket, and wondered what to buy first. A café, postcards? They were at the Place de France, an intersection of five streets, including the Rue de la Liberté, where their hotel was, according to Tom's map.

'This!' said Héloïse, pointing at a tooled leather purse. It hung outside a shop along with scarves and copper bowls of questionable utility. 'Pretty, Tome? Unusual.'

'Um-m – won't there be other shops, my sweet? Let's look around.' It was already nearly 7 p.m. And a couple of shopkeepers were starting to close for the day, Tom observed. He took Héloïse's hand suddenly. 'Isn't it terrific? A new country!'

She smiled back at him. He saw the curious dark lines in her lavender eyes that went from the pupil like spokes from a hub; a heavy image for something as beautiful as Héloïse's eyes.

'I love you,' Tom said.

They walked into the Boulevard Pasteur, a broad street which sloped slightly downward. More shops, and denser everything. Girls and women in long gowns swept by, their bare feet in sandals, while the boys and young men seemed to prefer blue jeans and sneakers and summer shirts.

'Would you like an iced tea, my pet? Or a kir? I bet they know how to make a kir.'

Back towards their hotel then, and at the Place de France, according to Tom's undetailed map in the brochure, found the Café de Paris, which had a long and noisy row of tables and chairs along the pavement. Tom captured what seemed the last little round table, and wangled a second chair from a table nearby.

'Some money, my dear,' Tom said, pulling out his wallet and offering Héloïse half the paper dirhams.

She had a graceful way of opening her handbag – this one was something like a saddle-bag, but smaller – and making the banknotes or whatever disappear instantly, yet in the right place. 'And what is this?'

'About – four hundred French. I'll change more this evening at the hotel. The Minzah has the same rate, I noticed, as at the airport.'

Héloïse showed no sign of interest in his remark, but Tom knew she would remember. He heard no French around him, only Arabic or what he had read was a Berber dialect. Either way, it was unintelligible to Tom. The tables were taken almost entirely by men, several middle-aged and a bit heavy, in short-sleeved shirts. Only one distant table, in fact, was occupied, by a blondish man in shorts and a woman.

And the waiters were scarce.

'Should we make sure, Tome, the room for Noëlle?'

'Yes, no harm in double-checking.' Tom smiled. He had, when registering, asked about the room for Mme Hassler, arriving tomorrow evening. The clerk had said that a room had been reserved. Tom signalled for the third time for a waiter, this one in white jacket and bearing a tray, and with no air of attention to anything. But this time he approached.

Tom was informed that wine and beer were unavailable.

They both ordered coffee. *Deux cafés.*

Tom's mind was on Cynthia Gradnor, of all people to be thinking about in North Africa. Cynthia, the epitome of cool, blond, English aloofness. Hadn't she been cool to Bernard Tufts? Unsympathetic finally? Well, Tom couldn't answer that, as it got into the realm of sexual relations, so different in privacy from what the pair might show the public. How far would she go in the direction of exposing him, Tom Ripley, without exposing herself and also Bernard Tufts? Curious that, though Cynthia and Bernard had never married, Tom considered them as one, spiritually. Surely they had been lovers, and for many a month – but that physical factor did not matter. Cynthia had respected Bernard, loved him profoundly, and Bernard in his tortured way had perhaps finally thought himself 'unworthy' of even making love to Cynthia, because he had felt so guilty about forging Derwatts.

Tom sighed.

'What is the matter, Tome? You are tired?'

'No!' Tom wasn't tired, and he smiled broadly again, with a real sense of freedom, based on the realization of where he was:

hundreds of miles from his 'enemies', if he could call them enemies. He could call them hecklers, he supposed, and that included not only the Pritchards but Cynthia Gradnor.

For the moment – Tom couldn't finish that thought, and his frown was back. He felt it, and rubbed his forehead. 'Tomorrow – what'll we do? The Forbes Museum, the toy soldiers? That's up in the Casbah. Remember?'

'Yes!' said Héloïse, her face alight suddenly. 'Le Casbah! Then the Socco.'

She meant the Grand Socco, or grand market. They would buy things, bargain, argue about prices, which Tom didn't like but knew he had to do or look like a fool, and pay a fool's price.

On their way back to the hotel, Tom did not bother bargaining for some pale green figs and some darker ones, both varieties in a stage of ideal ripeness, plus some beautiful green grapes and a couple of oranges. Tom loaded the two plastic bags the pushcart vendor had given him.

'They'll look pretty in our room,' Tom said. 'And we'll give Noëlle some too.'

The water was back on, Tom discovered to his pleasure. Héloïse took a shower, followed by Tom, then they relaxed in pyjamas on the outsized bed, basking in the air-conditioned coolness.

'And there is television,' said Héloïse.

Tom had seen it. He went and turned it on, or tried to. 'Just for curiosity,' he said to Héloïse.

It didn't come on. He checked the plug, and it seemed to be connected properly, in the same outlet in which the standard lamp worked.

'Tomorrow,' Tom murmured, resigned, not caring. 'I'll ask somebody about it.'

The next morning they visited the Grand Socco before the Casbah, necessitating a meterless taxi ride back to the hotel with Héloïse's purchases: a brown leather handbag and a pair of red leather sandals, which neither of them wished to carry around all day. Tom had the taxi wait while he left the parcel at the front desk. Then they rode to the post office, where Tom sent off the mysterious item that looked like a typewriter ribbon. He had rewrapped it in France. Airmail but not registered, as Reeves desired. Tom did not write a return address, even an invented one.

Then on in another taxi to the Casbah, an upward drive through

69

some narrow streets. York Castle was here – hadn't he read that Samuel Pepys had been employed or stationed here for a while? – overlooking the harbour, its stone walls looking enormously strong and huge because of the smaller white houses on either side of it. Nearby was a mosque with a high green dome. As Tom gazed, a loud chant began. Four times a day, Tom had read, the muezzin's call to prayer sounded forth, all done by recorded voice these days. People too lazy to get out of bed and climb the stairs, Tom thought, but merciless when it came to waking other people up at 4 a.m. He supposed that believers had to get out of bed and face Mecca, recite something, then get back into bed.

Tom enjoyed the Forbes Museum with its lead soldiers more than did Héloïse, he supposed, but he was not sure. Héloïse said little, but seemed fascinated, as was Tom, by the scenes of battle, the camps for the wounded with blood-stained bandages round their heads, the parade of this and that regiment, many on horseback – all displayed on long counters under glass. The soldiers and their officers all looked about four and a half inches high, cannon and wagons in proportion. Amazing! How thrilling it would be to be seven years old again – Tom's thoughts stopped abruptly. His parents had been dead, drowned, by the time he would have been old enough to appreciate lead soldiers. He had been in the care of Aunt Dottie then, and she would never have understood the charm of lead soldiers, and also never have advanced the money to buy any.

'Isn't it great to be so alone here!' Tom said to Héloïse, because oddly not a soul was in any of the big rambling rooms through which they wandered.

There had been no admission charge. The caretaker was a youngish man in white djellaba in the big foyer, and he asked merely if they would be kind enough to sign his visitors' book. Héloïse obliged, and then Tom. It was a thick book with cream-coloured pages.

'Merci et au revoir!' they all said.

'A taxi now?' Tom asked. 'Look! Do you think that might be a taxi?'

They went down the front walk between big green lawns to what might be a taxi rank at the curb, where there was one dusty car at present. They were in luck. It was a taxi.

'Au Café de Paris, s'il vous plaît,' Tom said through the window before they got in.

Now Noëlle was on their minds – Noëlle boarding the plane in a few hours at Roissy. They would put a plate of fresh fruit in her room (which was on the floor above theirs), and take a taxi to the airport to meet her. Tom sipped tomato juice with a lemon slice floating on top, and Héloïse a mint tea, which she had heard about and never tried. It smelt lovely. Tom tried a sip. Héloïse said she was boiling hot, that the tea was supposed to help, but she could not imagine how.

Their hotel was just a few steps away. Tom paid, and was taking his white jacket from the back of his chair when he thought he recognized a familiar head and shoulders on the main boulevard to his left.

David Pritchard? The head in profile had looked like Pritchard. Tom raised himself on his toes, but so many people were walking back and forth that Pritchard, if it had been he, had vanished in the crowd. Not worth dashing to the corner and staring, Tom thought, much less running after him. More than likely he'd been mistaken. That dark-haired head with round-rimmed glasses: didn't one see a type like that a couple of times a day?

'This way, Tome.'

'I know.' Tom espied a flower vendor *en route*. 'Flowers! Let's get some now!'

They bought bougainvillaea fronds, several day lilies, and a shorter bouquet of camellias. These were for Noëlle.

Any messages for the Ripleys? *Non, m'sieur*, Tom was told by the red-liveried clerk behind the desk.

A telephone call to the housekeeper resulted in two vases, one for Noëlle's room, one for Tom's and Héloïse's. There were, after all, enough flowers. Then quick showers before going out to find a place for lunch.

They decided to look for The Pub, recommended by Noëlle, 'just off Boulevard Pasteur, middle of town,' Tom remembered her saying. Tom asked a pavement vendor of ties and belts if he knew where The Pub was. Second street and on the right, he would see it.

'Merci infiniment!' said Tom.

The Pub might or might not have been slightly air-conditioned, but at any rate it was comfortable and amusing. Even Héloïse appreciated it, as she knew what some English pubs looked like. Here, the owner or owners had made an effort: brown rafters, an old pendulum clock fastened to the wall, along with photographs of sports teams, menu on a blackboard, and Heineken bottles in evidence. It was a smallish place and not too crowded. Tom ordered a cheddar sandwich, and Héloïse a cheese plate of some kind, and also a beer, which she drank only under the warmest conditions.

'Should we telephone Madame Annette?' Héloïse asked after their first sips of the beer.

Tom was mildly surprised. 'No, darling. Why? You're worried?'

'No, chéri, you are worried. No?' Héloïse frowned, very slightly, but she so seldom frowned that it was as if she scowled.

'No, my sweet. About what?'

'About this Preekard, no?'

Tom put his hand over his eyes, and felt that he blushed. Or was it the heat? 'Pritchard, dear. No,' Tom said firmly, as his cheese sandwich and cup of relish were set down before him. 'What can he do?' Tom added. 'Merci,' Tom said to the waiter, who was serving Héloïse second, or maybe that was an accident. Tom felt that his 'What can he do?' was a silly, empty question, uttered to soothe Héloïse. Pritchard could do plenty, depending exactly on how much he could prove. 'How's your cheese?' Tom asked, by way of posing another void question.

'Chéri, Prik-shard was not the one who telephoned and pretended to be Graneleaf?' Héloïse delicately spread a little mustard on some cheese.

The way she pronounced Greenleaf, omitting Dickie too, made Dickie and therefore his corpse seem miles away, even unreal. Tom said calmly, 'Most unlikely, my dear. Pritchard's got a deepish voice. Not young-sounding, anyway. You said the voice sounded young.'

'Yes.'

'Telephone calls,' Tom said musingly, as he spooned relish on to the edge of his plate. 'I'm reminded of a silly joke. Want to hear it?'

'Yes,' said Héloïse, with mild but steady interst in her lavender eyes now.

'Loony bin. Maison de fous. A doctor sees a patient writing something and asks what. A letter. A letter to whom, asks the doctor. To myself, says the patient. What's in the letter, asks the doctor. The patient answers, I don't know, I haven't received it yet.'

Héloïse did not greet this with a laugh, but at least she smiled. 'I think it *is* silly.'

Tom took a deep breath. 'My sweet – postcards. We must buy a fistful. Camels galloping, marketplaces, desert views, chickens upside down – '

'Chickens?'

'They're often upside down on postcards. Mexico, for instance. On their way to market.' Tom didn't want to add, to have their necks wrung.

Two more Heinekens to finish the lunch. The bottles were smallish. Back to El Minzah's high-ceilinged elegance, and another shower, this time together. Then they found themselves in the mood for a siesta. There was ample time before leaving for the airport.

Tom at some time after 4 put on blue jeans and a shirt, and went down to buy postcards. He bought a dozen from the hotel desk. He had brought a ballpoint with him, and intended to begin a card that Héloïse could add to, to the faithful Mme Annette. Ah, gone were the days – and had there ever been many? – when he had written a postcard from Europe to Aunt Dottie, Tom admitted to himself, with the purpose of keeping in her good graces in order to inherit something. She had bequeathed him $10,000 but had given her house, which Tom had liked and had had some hopes of acquiring, to another person, whose name Tom had forgotten, perhaps because he wanted to forget.

He sat on a stool at the Hotel Minzah's bar, because the light was rather good. A card to the Cleggs also would be friendly, Tom supposed, good old neighbours who lived near Melun, both English, he a retired lawyer. Tom wrote in French:

Dear Mme Annette,
                    Very hot here. We have seen a pair of goats walking on the pavement without a lead!

That was true, but the sandalled boy with them was doing a good job of control by grabbing their horns when necessary. And where had they been going? He continued:

Please tell Henri the little forsythia near greenhouse needs water *now*. A bientôt,

                                                    Tom

'M'sieur?' said the barman.

'Merci, j'attends quelqu'un,' Tom replied. The red-jacketed barman knew he was staying here, Tom supposed. The Moroccans, like the Italians, had that look of observing and remembering strangers' faces.

Tom hoped that Pritchard was not drifting around Belle Ombre, disturbing Mme Annette, who surely recognized him from a distance as well as Tom did now. The Cleggs' address? Tom was not certain of their street number, but he could start the card anyway. Héloïse was always delighted to be relieved as much as possible of the chore of postcards.

With pen poised again, Tom glanced to his right.

He need not have worried about Pritchard at Belle Ombre, for there he sat at the bar, his dark eyes on Tom, just four stools away. He had his round-rimmed glasses on, a blue short-sleeved shirt, a glass before him, but his eyes were steady on Tom.

'Afternoon,' said Pritchard.

Two or three people from the pool behind Pritchard came in from the door there, and strolled in sandals and bathrobes toward the bar.

'Good afternoon,' Tom replied calmly. His worst, most *outré* suspicions seemed to have come true: the goddam Pritchards had espied him in Fontainebleau with airline tickets still in his hand or his pocket, when he, Tom, had been not far from the travel agency! *Phuket*! Tom thought, recalling the halcyon beach of that island on the travel-agency poster. Tom looked down again at his postcard, which was divided into four images: camel, a mosque, market girls in striped shawls, a blue and yellow beach. *Dear Cleggs.* Tom gripped his pen.

'How long are you here for, Mr Ripley?' Pritchard asked, now venturing to approach Tom, glass in hand.

'Oh – I think we leave tomorrow. You're here with your wife?'

'Yes. But we're not at this hotel.' Pritchard's tone was cold.

'By the way,' Tom said, 'what do you intend to do with the pictures you took of my house? Sunday, remember?' Tom had asked Pritchard's wife the same question, he recalled, and was still trusting, hoping, that Janice Pritchard hadn't told her husband about her teatime rendez-vous with Tom Ripley.

'Sunday. Yes. I saw your wife or somebody looking out of the front window. Well – the photos are just for the record. As I said, I – I have a fair dossier on you.'

Pritchard hadn't exactly said it, Tom thought. 'You work for some kind of investigations bureau? International Prowlers Incorporated?'

'Ha-ha! No, just for my pleasure – and my wife's,' he added with some emphasis. 'And you're a fertile field, Mr Ripley.'

Tom was thinking that the rather dull girl in the travel agency had probably answered David Pritchard's question: 'Where did your last customer buy a ticket for? He's a neighbour, Mr Ripley. We hailed him just now, but he didn't see us. We can't make up our minds, but we'd like to go to some place different.' The girl might have said, 'Mr Ripley just bought a ticket to Tangier for himself and his wife.' She might have been obtuse enough to volunteer the hotel, Tom thought, especially as an agency got a percentage from hotels where the client was booked. Tom said, 'You and your wife came all the way to Tangier just to see me?' His tone might have meant that he was flattered.

'Why not? It is interesting,' said Pritchard, his dark brown eyes steady on Tom.

And annoying. Every time Tom saw Pritchard, he seemed to be a pound or so heavier. Curious. Tom glanced to his left, to see if Héloïse had come into the lobby, because she was due now. 'Some trouble for you, I'd think, considering that we'll stay such a short time. We're leaving tomorrow.'

'Oh? You've got to see Casablanca, no?'

'Oh, definitely,' Tom replied, 'we'll go to Casablanca. What hotel are you and Janice in?'

'The – um – Grand Hotel Villa de France, just' – he waved a hand towards Tom – 'a street or so away.'

Tom didn't completely believe him. 'And how are our mutual friends? We have so many.' Tom smiled. He was on his feet now, left hand clutching cards and pen and resting on the black leather-covered bar stool.

'Which ones?' Pritchard chuckled, sounding rather like an old man.

Tom would have loved to sock him in his bulging solar plexus. 'Mrs Murchison?' Tom ventured.

'Yes, we're in touch, and with Cynthia Gradnor too.'

Once more the name rolled easily from Pritchard's tongue. Tom backed a few inches, indicating his imminent departure via the broad doorway. 'You talk with each other – across the Atlantic?'

'Oh, yes. Why not?' Pritchard showed his square teeth.

'But – ' Tom began in a bemused way. 'What do you talk about?'

'*You*!' Pritchard replied with a smile. 'We pool our facts.' Again his nod for emphasis. 'And we plan.'

'And your objective?'

'Pleasure,' replied Pritchard. 'Maybe revenge.' He gave a full-throated chuckle here. 'For some, of course.'

Tom nodded, and said pleasantly, 'Good luck.' He turned and left.

Tom found Héloïse, spotted her, in one of the easy chairs in the lobby. She was looking at a French newspaper, or at least one printed in French, but Tom saw also a column in Arabic down the front page. 'My *dear* – ' Tom knew she had seen Pritchard.

Héloïse bounced up. 'Again! That so-and-so! Tom, I can't believe that he is *here*!'

'I'm just as annoyed as you,' Tom murmured in French, 'but let's be calm now, because he might be watching us from the bar.' Tom stood up straight and calm. 'He claims to be at the Grand Hotel something near here, with his wife. I don't necessarily believe him. But he's no doubt at a hotel somewhere tonight.'

'And he follows us *here*!'

'My dear, my sweet, we could – ' Tom stopped abruptly, and felt at the edge of a cliff, as to his reasoning. He had been about to say that he and Héloïse could move that afternoon, change their hotel and give Pritchard the slip, and maybe successfully, in Tangier, but it would be less fun for Noëlle Hassler, who had probably told her friends that she was at the Hotel El Minzah for a few days. And why should he and Héloïse inconvenience themselves because of the creep called Pritchard? 'Did you leave the key at the desk?'

Héloïse said she had. 'Preeckard's wife is with him?' she asked as they went out through the front door.

Tom hadn't even looked to see if Pritchard had left the bar. 'He said she was, which probably means that she isn't.' His *wife*! What a relationship, his wife admitting to Tom in the Fontainebleau café that her husband was a tyrant and a brute. Yet they clung together. Sick-making.

'You are tense, chéri.' Héloïse was holding his arm, mainly so that they could stay together in the jostling crowd on the pavement.

'I am thinking. Sorry.'

'About what?'

'About us. About Belle Ombre. Everything.' He took a quick glance at Héloïse's face, just as she brushed her hair back with her left hand. *I want us to be safe*, Tom might have added, but he didn't want to upset Héloïse any further. 'Let's cross the street.'

Once more, they had begun walking down the Boulevard Pasteur, as if the throngs and the shop fronts were a magnet. Tom saw a red and black shingle hanging over a doorway: Rubi Bar and Grill, in English with Arabic letters under it.

'Shall we look in?' Tom asked.

This was a smallish bar and restaurant, with three or four non-tourist types standing or sitting.

Tom and Héloïse stood at the bar, and ordered a café express and a tomato juice. The barman pushed a little saucer of cold beans and another of radishes and black olives towards them, plus forks and paper napkins.

A well-built man on a stool behind Héloïse, reading an Arabic newspaper with an air of serious absorption, seemed to be lunching from the saucers. He wore a yellowish djellaba, which hung down almost to his black business shoes. Tom saw him shove a hand into a slit in order to get at the pocket of his trousers. The edges of the slit looked a bit soiled. The man blew his nose, then shoved the handkerchief back in his pocket, never taking his eyes from the newspaper.

Tom was inspired. He would buy a djellaba, and, with some courage, wear it. He so informed Héloïse, and she laughed.

'And I'll photograph you – in the Casbah? Outside our hotel?' she asked.

'Oh, anywhere.' Tom was thinking how practical the loose garment was, because one could wear shorts or a business suit under it, even a bathing suit.

Tom was in luck: just around the corner from the Rubi Bar and Grill was a shop where djellabas hung amid bright scarves on the shop front.

'Djellaba – s'il vous plaît?' Tom said to the proprietor. 'Not pink, no,' he continued in French, on seeing the shop owner's first offering. 'And long sleeves?' Tom indicated with a forefinger on his wrist.

'Ah! Si! Ici, m'sieur.' His heelless sandals clap-clapped on the old wooden floor. 'Ici – '

A rack of djellabas, partly obscured by a couple of display counters. No room even to sidle to where the shop owner was, but Tom pointed to a pale green number. This had long sleeves and two slits for reaching pockets. Tom held it up against himself to verify the length.

Héloïse doubled over, and for politeness' sake coughed and made her way towards the door.

'Bon, c'est fait,' Tom said, after enquiring the price, which struck him as reasonable. 'And these?'

'Ah, si – ' There followed a eulogy – Tom could not make out every word, though the man spoke in French – on the quality of his knives. For the hunt, for *le bureau*, and for the kitchen.

These were clasp-knives. Tom made his choice quickly: one with a haft of light brown wood with inlaid brass fittings, a blade sharp and pointed, and concave on its non-cutting edge. Thirty dirhams. Folded, his knife was not six inches long, suitable for any pocket.

'A taxi ride?' Tom said to Héloïse. 'A quick tour – any direction, Does that appeal?'

Héloïse took a look at her wristwatch. 'We could. Aren't you going to change into your djellaba?'

'Change? I can do that in the taxi!' Tom waved to the shopkeeper, who was watching them. 'Merci, m'sieur!'

The shopkeeper said something Tom did not understand, and Tom hoped it was 'God be with you' no matter what God.

The taxi driver asked, 'Yacht Club?'

'That's for lunch some day,' Héloïse said to Tom. 'Noëlle wants to take us.'

A drop of sweat slid down Tom's cheek. 'Some place cool? With a breeze?' he said in French to the driver.

'La Haffa? Brize – ocean. V'near. Thé!'

Tom was lost. Still, they got in and gave the driver his head. Tom made a statement: 'We must be at Hotel Minzah in one hour,' and made sure the driver understood it.

Checking of watches. They were to pick up Noëlle at 7.

Again high speed, and faulty springs in the taxi. The driver was clearly aiming for somewhere. They headed west, Tom thought, and the city began to fade away.

'Your dress,' said Héloïse, slyly.

Tom pulled the folded garment from its plastic bag, got it into position, ducked and hauled the flimsy pale green gown over his head. Then a shimmy or two and it was over his white trousers, and he made sure he could sit down without splitting it before he did sit down. 'There!' he said triumphantly to Héloïse.

She surveyed him with a sparkle in her eyes, approvingly.

Tom checked his trouser pockets: accessible. The knife was in his left pocket.

'La Haffa,' said the driver, pulling up at a cement wall with a couple of doors in it, one open. The blue Atlantic Strait lay beyond, visible through a break in the wall.

'What is it? A museum?' asked Tom.

'Thé-café,' said the driver. 'J'attends? Demi-heure?'

Wisest to say yes, Tom thought, and replied, 'Okay, demi-heure.'

Héloïse had already got out, and with head lifted was gazing out at the blue water. The breeze blew her hair steadily out to one side.

A figure in black trousers and limp white shirt slowly beckoned to them from a stone doorway, like some evil spirit, Tom thought, leading them into hell or at least corruption. A skinny mongrel, black and much underfed, started to sniff at them, apparently lost the energy, and went limping away on three legs. Whatever the problem with his fourth leg was, he seemed to have had it for a long time.

Tom almost reluctantly followed Héloïse through the primitive stone doorway on to a stone path that led in the direction of the sea. Tom saw a kitchen of sorts to their left, with a stove capable of heating water. Broad, railless stone steps descended towards the ocean. Tom glanced into cubicles on either side, rooms with no walls on the sea side, and with straw mats on poles for a roof, mats on the floor, and no furnishings otherwise. No customers just now either.

'Curious,' Tom said to Héloïse. 'Would you like some mint tea?'

Héloïse shook her head. 'Not now. I don't like this.'

Neither did Tom. The waiter was not hovering. Tom could imagine the place being fascinating at night, or at sunset, with friends, with a little liveliness, an oil lamp on the floor. One would have to sit cross-legged on those mats, or recline like the ancient Greeks. Then Tom heard laughter from one cubicle, where three men sat smoking something, legs folded on the mat-covered floor. Tom had an impression of tea cups, a white plate in the shade there, where the sunlight fell like tiny flecks of gold.

Their taxi was waiting, the driver talking and laughing with the skinny fellow in the white shirt.

Back to El Minzah, where Tom paid the driver off, and he and Héloïse entered the lobby. Tom did not see Pritchard anywhere, from where he stood. And his djellaba excited not the least notice, he was glad to see.

'Darling, there's something I want to do just now – for an hour, maybe. Can you – would you mind going alone to the airport to pick up Noëlle?'

'Non-n,' said Héloïse thoughtfully. 'We will come back here at once, of course. What are you going to do?'

Tom smiled, hesitated. 'Nothing important. Just – be on my own for a while. See you then around – eight? Or soon after? My greetings to Noëlle. See you both soon!'

8

Tom walked out into the sun again, hiked up his djellaba and pulled his schematic map from a back pocket. The Grand Hotel Villa de France that Pritchard had mentioned was indeed two steps away, apparently, approachable by the Rue de Hollande. Tom started walking, wiped sweat from his forehead with the upper part of the pale green djellaba, then hoisted it up at the sides, and pulled it over his head as he walked. Pity he had no plastic bag, but the garment folded into a rather small square.

No one looked at him, and Tom did not stare at the passers-by either. Most of the people, male and female, carried shopping bags of some kind, and were not out for a walk.

Tom entered the lobby of the Grand Hotel Villa de France and looked around. Not so plush as the Minzah; four people occupying chairs in the lobby, none Pritchard or wife. Tom went to the desk and asked if he could speak with M. David Pritchard.

'Ou Madame Pritchard,' Tom added.

'Who shall I say?' asked the young man behind the desk.

'Just say Thomas.'

'M'sieur Thomas?'

'Oui.'

M. Pritchard was not in, it seemed, though the young man looked behind him and remarked that his key was absent.

'May I speak with his wife?'

Hanging up the telephone, the young man remarked that M. Pritchard was alone.

'Thank you very much. Please say that M'sieur Thomas called, would you? No, thank you, M'sieur Pritchard knows where to reach me.'

Tom turned towards the door, and at that moment saw Pritchard emerging from a lift, with camera on a strap over one shoulder. Tom strolled towards him. 'Afternoon, Mr Pritchard!'

'Well – hello! Nice surprise.'

'Yes. Thought I'd come and say hello. Have you got a few minutes? Or have you an appointment?'

Pritchard's deep pinkish lips parted in surprise, or was it pleasure? 'Y-um – yes, why not?'

Favourite phrase of Pritchard's, it seemed, why not. Tom put on an affable manner, and moved towards the door, but had to wait while Pritchard deposited his key.

'Nice camera,' Tom remarked, when Pritchard came back. 'I was just at a great place on the coast near here. Well, it's all on the coast, isn't it.' He gave an easy laugh.

Out of the air-conditioning into the hot sunlight again. It was close to 6.30, Tom saw.

'How well do you know Tangier?' Tom asked, ready to play the knowledgeable. 'La Haffa? That's the spectacular-view place. Or – a café?' He made a circular gesture with a finger to indicate the immediate neighbourhood.

'Let's try the first place you mentioned. The view place.'

'Perhaps Janice would like to come?' Tom stopped on the pavement.

'She's taking a nap just now,' said Pritchard.

They got a taxi after a few minutes' effort on the boulevard. Tom asked the driver please to go to La Haffa.

'Isn't the breeze lovely,' said Tom, letting the air rush through an inch of open window. 'Do you know any Arabic? Or the Berber dialect?'

'Very little,' said Pritchard.

Tom was prepared to fake that a bit too. Pritchard wore white shoes with a basket-weave structure that let the air in, the kind of shoes Tom couldn't abide. Funny how everything about Pritchard irked him, even the wristwatch, the stretchable gold-bracelet variety, expensive and flashy, with gold surround for the watch, gold-coloured face even, suitable for a pimp, Tom thought. Tom preferred infinitely his conservative Patek Philippe on a brown leather strap, which looked like an antique.

'Look! I think we're already here.' As usual, the second time to the destination seemed to be shorter than the first. Tom paid over Pritchard's protest, 20 dirhams, and dismissed the driver. 'It's a tea place,' Tom said. 'Mint tea. Maybe other things.' Tom gave a chuckle. Kif, cannabis, might be obtainable on request, he supposed.

They entered via the stone doorway and descended the path, remarked by one of the white-shirted waiters, Tom noticed.

'Now look at that view!' Tom said.

The sun still floated above the blue Strait. Looking out to sea, one might think no dust particle existed, yet underfoot and to right and left the dust and sand lay thinly, bits of man-made straw mats were visible on the stone path, plants looked thirsty in the dry soil. One cubicle, or whatever the partitioned spaces were called, was rather full, with six men sitting and reclining, talking animatedly.

'Here?' Tom asked, pointing. 'Just so we can order, if the waiter comes. Mint tea?'

Pritchard shrugged, and turned some dials on his camera.

'Why not?' Tom said, beating Pritchard to it, he thought, but Pritchard said it at the same time.

Stony-faced, Pritchard lifted his camera to his eyes and aimed it at the water.

The waiter came, with empty tray hanging in one hand. This waiter was barefoot.

'Two mint teas, please?' asked Tom in French.

An affirmative response, and the boy went away.

Pritchard took three more pictures, slowly, his back mostly towards Tom, who stood in the shade of the cubicle's sagging roof. Then Pritchard turned and said with a faint smile, 'One of you?'

'No, thank you,' Tom replied genially.

'Are we supposed to sit here?' asked Pritchard, strolling farther into the sun-speckled cubicle.

Tom gave a short laugh. He was in no mood for sitting. He took the folded djellaba from under his left arm and dropped it gently to the floor. His left hand returned to his trouser pocket, where his thumb moved over his folded knife. There were a couple of cloth-covered pillows on the floor also, Tom noticed, no doubt comforting for the elbow, if one was reclining.

Tom ventured, 'Why'd you say your wife was here with you, when she isn't?'

'Oh – ' Despite his faint smile, Pritchard's brain was busy. 'Just joking, I suppose.'

'Why?'

'Fun.' Pritchard lifted and pointed his camera at Tom, as if to pay Tom back for his insolence.

Tom made a violent gesture towards the camera, as if to swat it to the ground, though he didn't touch it. 'You can stop that right now. I'm camera-shy.'

'Worse'n that, you seem to hate cameras.' But Pritchard had lowered his camera.

What a good place to kill the bastard, Tom thought, since nobody knew they had a date, nobody knew they had a date *here*. Knock him out, wound him enough with the knife so that he'd bleed to death, drag him into another cubicle (or not), and depart.

'Not really,' said Tom. 'I have two or three at home. I also don't like people taking pictures of my house with the look of making a survey – as if for future use.'

David Pritchard held his camera in his hands, at the level of his waist, and smiled benignly. 'You are worried, Mr Ripley.'

'Not at all.'

'Maybe you're worried about Cynthia Gradnor – and the Murchison story.'

'Not at all. You've never met Cynthia Gradnor, for one thing. Why did you imply you had? Just to have fun? What kind of fun?'

'You know what kind.' Pritchard was warming, but ever so cautiously, to the fray. He obviously preferred the cynical, cool-looking front. 'The pleasure of seeing a snob crook like yourself go belly up.'

'Oh. Best of British luck, Mr Pritchard.' Tom was balanced on his feet, both hands in his trouser pockets now and itching to strike. He realized that he was waiting for the tea, and here it came.

The young waiter set the tray smack on the floor, poured out two glasses from a metal pot, and wished the gentlemen pleasure in the imbibing.

The tea did smell lovely, fresh, almost enchanting, everything that Pritchard wasn't. There was also a saucer of mint sprigs. Tom pulled his wallet out and insisted on paying, over Pritchard's protests. Tom added a tip. 'Shall we?' said Tom, and stooped for his glass, taking care to remain facing Pritchard. He wasn't going to hand Pritchard his glass. The glasses were in metal holders. Tom dropped a mint sprig into his tea.

Pritchard bent and picked his glass up. 'Ouch!'

Maybe he'd spilt some drops on himself, Tom didn't know or care. Was Pritchard, in his sick way, enjoying this tea hour with him, Tom wondered, even when nothing happened except that the relationship between them became more hateful on both sides? Did

Pritchard like it the more hateful it became? Probably. Tom thought of Murchison again, but in a different way: oddly, Pritchard was now in Murchison's position, acting like someone who could betray him, and possibly the Derwatt forgeries, and the Derwatt Art Supply business, now owned in name by Jeff Constant and Ed Banbury. Was Pritchard going to stick to his guns, like Murchison? Had Pritchard any guns, or only vague threats?

Tom sipped his tea, standing up. The similarity, Tom realized, was that he had to ask both men whether they preferred to stop their enquiries or be killed. He'd pleaded with Murchison to let the forgeries be, let them alone. He hadn't threatened Murchison. But then when Murchison had been adamant –

'Mr Pritchard, I'd like to ask what is perhaps the impossible for you. Just get out of my life, quit your snooping and why not get out of Villeperce? What're you doing there besides heckling me? You're not even at INSEAD.' Tom laughed in an indifferent way, as if Pritchard's tales about himself were puerile.

'Mr Ripley, I have a right to live where I want to. The same as you.'

'Yes, if you behave like the rest of us. I've a mind to put the police on to you, ask them to keep an eye on you in Villeperce – where I've been living for several years.'

'*You* calling on the police!' Pritchard tried to laugh.

'I could tell them about your photographing my house. I've three witnesses for that, besides myself, of course.' Tom might have mentioned a fourth, Janice Pritchard.

Tom put his tea down on the floor. Pritchard had also set his down after burning himself, and had not picked it up.

The sun dropped ever closer to the blue water on Tom's right, and beyond Pritchard. For the moment Pritchard was trying his cool act. Tom remembered that Pritchard knew judo, or so he'd said. Maybe he'd been lying? Tom suddenly lost his temper, exploded, and swung his right leg to give Pritchard a kick in the abdomen – ju-jitsu style, maybe – but the kick was low and got Pritchard in the crotch.

As Pritchard doubled over, holding himself in pain, Tom delivered a neat right to the jaw with his fist. Pritchard hit the mat over the stone floor with a thud that sounded utterly limp and unconscious, but perhaps wasn't.

Never kick a man when he's down, Tom thought, and gave Pritchard another kick, hard, in the midriff. Tom was furious enough to have pulled out his new knife and got in a few stabs, but the time might be short here. Still, Tom yanked Pritchard by the shirt-front and delivered another right-handed blow under his jaw.

This little fracas he had decidedly won, Tom thought as he pulled the djellaba over his head. No tea spilt. No blood, Tom thought. A waiter coming in might think from Pritchard's recumbent position on his left side, his back to anyone entering the cubicle, that he was snoozing.

Tom departed, took the stone steps upward and climbed, effortlessly it seemed, up to the kitchen level, walked out, and nodded to the young man in limp shirt who stood outside.

'Un taxi? C'est possible?' Tom asked.

'Si – peut-être cinque minutes?' He waggled his head, and looked as if he didn't believe the five minutes.

'Merci. J'attendrai.' Tom didn't see any other means of transportation, such as a bus; no bus stop in sight. Still bursting with energy, he walked with deliberate slowness along the edge of the road – there was no pavement – relishing the breeze that blew against his damp forehead. *Clump, clump, clump.* Tom walked like a pensive philosopher, looked at his watch, 7.27, then turned and idled back towards La Haffa.

Tom was thinking, imagining Pritchard lodging a complaint against him for assault and battery with the Tangier police. Imagine that? Tom couldn't really. Unspeakable difficulties. Pritchard would *never* do it, Tom thought.

And now, if a waiter came dashing out (as a waiter might in England or France) saying, 'M'sieur, your friend is injured!' Tom would profess not to know a thing about the mishap. But the tea hour (when wasn't it the tea hour here?) being so leisurely, and the waiter having been already paid, Tom doubted that any excited figure was going to dash through the stone doorway of La Haffa, in quest of him.

After some ten minutes, a taxi approached from the Tangier direction, stopped and disgorged three men. Tom hastened to secure it, and also had time to hand the boy at the door the loose change that was in one pocket.

'Hotel El Minzah, s'il vous plaît!' said Tom, and settled back to enjoy the ride. He pulled out his rather bent packet of Gitanes and lit one.

He was beginning to like Morocco. The lovely whitish cluster of little houses in the Casbah area came ever nearer, then Tom felt that the taxi was swallowed by the city, became unnoticeable in a long boulevard. A left turn and there was his hotel. Tom pulled out his wallet.

On the pavement in front of the Minzah's entrance, he calmly reached for his hem, pulled the djellaba over his head, and folded it as before. A nick on the second finger of his right hand had caused a couple of spots on the djellaba, Tom had noticed in the taxi, but it was hardly bleeding now. Truly minor compared to what might have happened, a real cut from one of Pritchard's teeth, for example, or from his belt buckle.

Tom went into the high-ceilinged lobby. It was nearly 9. Héloïse was surely back from the airport with Noëlle.

'The key is not here, m'sieur,' said the man at the desk.

No message either. 'And Madame Hassler?' asked Tom.

Her key was also absent, so Tom asked the man to ring Mme Hassler's room, please.

Noëlle answered. ''Allo, Tome! We are talking – and I am dressing.' She laughed. 'Nearly finished. 'Ow do you like Tangier?' For some reason Noëlle was speaking English, and sounded in merry mood.

'Most interesting!' Tom said. 'Fascinating! I think I could almost rave about it!' He realized that he sounded excited, over-enthusiastic, perhaps, but he was thinking of Pritchard lying on that mat, more than likely not discovered yet. Pritchard was not going to feel so well tomorrow. Tom listened to Noëlle explaining that she and Héloïse could be ready to join him in less than half an hour downstairs, if that was agreeable to Tom. Then she passed Héloïse to him.

'Hello, Tome. We are talking.'

'I know. See you downstairs – in twenty minutes or so?'

'I come to our room now. I want to freshen.'

That displeased Tom, but he had no idea how to stop it. And also, Héloïse had the key.

Tom took the lift to their floor, and got to their room door seconds before Héloïse, who had used the stairs.

'Noëlle sounds in top form,' Tom said.

'Yes. Oh, she loves Tangier! She wants to invite us to a restaurant on the sea front tonight.'

Tom was opening the door. Héloïse went in.

'Velly good,' said Tom, putting on his Chinese accent, which sometimes amused Héloïse. He quickly sucked at his nicked finger. 'Possible use bathroom first? Velly shot time. Chop-chop.'

'Oh, yes, Tome, go ahead. But if you shower, I use the basin.' Héloïse made her way to the air-conditioner which was beneath the wide windows.

Tom opened the bathroom door. There were two basins, side by side, as in many hotels aiming to give their guests comfort, Tom supposed, but he inevitably thought of a wedded pair, scrubbing away at their teeth, or the wife plucking eyebrows while the husband scraped at his beard, and the unaesthetic picture depressed him. He got the plastic bag of washing powder which he and Héloïse always travelled with from his own toilet kit. But first, cold water, Tom reminded himself. There was a minimum of blood, but Tom wanted it all out. He rubbed at the couple of spots, which looked paler now, then let the water out. A second wash now with warm water and some soap of the kind that made no suds, but was still effective.

He went into the big bedroom – two king-sized beds, no less, also side by side and pushed together – and to a front closet for a plastic hanger.

'What did you do this afternoon?' Héloïse asked. 'Did you buy anything?'

'No, sweet.' Tom smiled. 'Walked around – and had tea.'

'Tea,' Héloïse repeated. 'Where?'

'Oh – little café – looking like all the others. I just wanted to watch the people go by for a while.' Tom returned to the bathroom and hung up his djellaba behind the shower curtain, so it would drip into the tub. Then he stripped and hung his clothes over a towel rack, and had a quick, cool shower. Héloïse came in and used the basin. In a bathrobe and barefoot, Tom went in quest of fresh underwear.

Héloïse had changed, and now wore white slacks and a green and white striped blouse.

Tom pulled on black cotton trousers. 'Does Noëlle like her room?'

'You washed your djellaba already?' Héloïse called to him from the bathroom, where she was applying make-up.

'Dusty!' Tom replied.

'What are the stains? Grease?'

Had she spotted some that he'd missed? At that moment, Tom heard the wailing, high-pitched voice of the prayer-caller from a nearby tower. It could be taken as an alarm, Tom thought, a warning of worse to come, if he chose to think of it that way, which he didn't. Grease? Could he get away with it?

'This looks like blood, Tome,' she said in French.

He advanced, buttoning his shirt. 'Surely not much, my sweet. Yes, I cut my finger a little. Hit it on something.' That was true. He held out his right hand, palm down. 'Tiny. But I didn't want the stains to stay in.'

'Oh, they are feeble,' she said solemnly. 'But how did you do that?'

Tom had realized in the taxi that he would have to explain a few things to Héloïse, because he was going to suggest that they move by tomorrow noon, before tomorrow noon. He was even a little worried about staying here tonight. 'Well, my dear – ' He sought for words.

'You saw this – '

'Pritchard,' Tom supplied. 'Yes. We had a little scuffle. Dust-up – outside a teashop – a café. He so annoyed me that I hit him. Socked him. But I didn't hurt him badly.' Héloïse was waiting for more, as she so often had in the past. It was seldom that he and she were together like this, when something happened, and he was not used to sharing information with her – not any more than necessary, at any rate.

'Well, Tome – you found him somewhere?'

'He's at a hotel near here. And his wife's not with him, though he told me she was, when I saw him in the bar downstairs. I suppose she's in Villeperce. Makes me wonder what she's up to.' He was thinking of Belle Ombre. A female prowler was creepier than a male one, Tom felt. She'd be less likely to be challenged by other people, for one thing.

'But what is the matter with these Pree-shard?'

'My dear, I told you they're cracked. *Fous*! It needn't spoil your holiday. You've got Noëlle. This creep wants to annoy *me*, not you, I'm sure of that.' Tom wet his lips, and walked to the bed to sit down and put on his socks and shoes. He wanted to get back to Belle Ombre to check on things, then to London. He tied his shoes rapidly.

'Where was the fight? About what?'

He shook his head, wordless.

'Is your finger still bleeding?'

Tom looked at it. 'No.'

Héloïse went into the bathroom, and returned with a Band-aid, stripping it for application.

In a trice the little bandage was in place, and Tom felt better, at least as if he weren't leaving a trail, the faintest pink smudge somewhere.

'What are you thinking?' she asked.

Tom looked at his watch. 'Don't we have to meet Noëlle downstairs?'

'Ye-es,' Héloïse said calmly.

Tom put his wallet into his jacket pocket. 'I came out the better in the fight today. Tom pictured Pritchard 'resting' this evening, when he got back to his hotel, but what he would do tomorrow was anybody's guess. 'But I think Mr Pr – Pritchard is going to want to hit back. Maybe tomorrow. Best if you and Noëlle change hotels. I don't want any unpleasantnesses here for you.'

Héloïse's eyebrows trembled slightly. 'Hit back how? And you want to stay here?'

'That's what I don't know yet. Let's go down, darling.'

They had kept Noëlle waiting five minutes, but she seemed in good humour. She looked as if she had come back to some place she liked, after a long absence. As they approached, she was chatting with the barman.

'Bon soir, Tome!' Noëlle said, and continued in French. 'What may I offer you as aperitif? This evening is mine.' Noëlle tossed her head, and her straight hair stirred like a curtain. She wore large thin gold circles as earrings, an embroidered black jacket and black slacks. 'Are you both warm enough for tonight? Yes,' said Noëlle, checking like a mother hen to see if Héloïse had a sweater in her hand.

Tom and Héloïse had been forewarned: evenings in Tangier were decidedly cooler than the daytime.

Two Bloody Marys, one gin and tonic for the gentleman.

Héloïse brought the matter up. 'Tom thinks he may have to leave the hotel tomorrow – *we* might. You remember the man photographing our house, Noëlle?'

Tom was pleased to realize that Héloïse hadn't mentioned Pritchard when she had been alone with Noëlle. Noëlle did indeed remember.

'He is here?' cried Noëlle, really astonished.

'And still making trouble! Show your hand, Tome!'

Tom gave a laugh. *Show his hand.* 'You will have to take my word for my wound,' Tom said solemnly, showing his Band-aid.

'A fist fight!' said Héloïse.

Noëlle looked at Tom. 'But why is he angry with you?'

'That is the question. He is like a prowler – willing to buy an aeroplane ticket, as most are not,' Tom replied in French, 'to be nearer. Strange.'

Héloïse told Noëlle that Pritchard was here without his wife, at a hotel in the vicinity, and in case Pritchard intended to try some odd attack, it would be better if they all left the Minzah, because Pritchard knew that she and Tom were here.

'There are other hotels,' Tom said unnecessarily, but he was trying to sound more at ease than he felt. He found he was glad that Noëlle and Héloïse knew of his plight, or his present strain, even if Noëlle didn't know the reason for Murchison's mysterious disappearance and the Derwatt business. *Business*. That had two meanings, Tom thought as he sipped his drink: industry, which it was, and phoneyness, which by now half of it was. Tom with difficulty refocused his attention on the ladies. He was standing, as was Héloïse, and only Noëlle was perched on a stool.

They were talking about buying jewellery in the Grand Socco, both talking at the same time, though they no doubt managed, as ever, to make themselves perfectly clear to each other.

A man came in selling red roses, a street peddler judging from his garb. Noëlle waved him away, still rapt in her conversation with Héloïse. The barman escorted the man to the door.

Dinner at the Nautilus Plage. Noëlle had made reservations. It was a terraced restaurant on the sea coast, busy but rather elegant, with plenty of room between the tables and lighted candles to read the menu by. Fish was the speciality. Only gradually did they return to the subject of tomorrow, the next hotel. Noëlle was sure she could extricate them easily from their unwritten obligation to stay five days at the Minzah. She knew the Minzah people: the Minzah was fully booked, and she would just say there was someone coming whom she wished to avoid.

'Which is true, I believe?' she asked, arching her eyebrows at Tom, smiling.

'Quite,' said Tom. Noëlle seemed to have forgotten her recent lover, Tom thought, the one who had depressed her.

9

Tom was up early the next day, and his accidental awakening of
Héloïse before 8 didn't seem to bother her.

'I'm going to have a coffee downstairs, my dear. What time did
Noëlle say she wanted to check out – ten?'

'Tennish,' said Héloïse, eyes still closed. 'I can do the packing,
Tome. Where are you going?'

She knew he was going somewhere. But Tom didn't know exactly
where he was going. 'On patrol,' he said. 'Want me to order a
continental for you? With orange juice?'

'I will – when I feel like it.' She snuggled into the pillow.

There was a nice, relaxed spouse, Tom thought, as he opened the
door and blew a kiss back to her. 'Back in about an hour.'

'Why are you taking your djellaba?'

Tom had it again in one hand, folded. 'I dunno. To buy a hat to
match?'

Downstairs, Tom spoke again with the desk, and reminded them
that he and his wife were leaving that morning. Noëlle had told them
late last night, near midnight, but Tom thought it courteous to say a
word now, as the staff had changed. Then he went to the men's
room, where a middle-aged American was shaving at a basin, or at
least he looked American. Tom shook out his djellaba and put it on.

The American watched him in the mirror. 'Don't you guys trip on
those things?' With battery razor in one hand, the American
chuckled, and looked unsure of whether he'd been understood.

'Oh, sure,' Tom replied. 'Then we make a bad joke, like – enjoy
your trip?'

'Ha-ha!'

Tom waved and departed.

Once more the gentle slope downward of the Boulevard Pasteur,
where shopkeepers had already set up pavement stalls, or were in

the act of doing so. What were the men wearing in the way of headwear? Most wore nothing, Tom saw as he looked around. A couple had white cloths of some kind, resembling a barber's hot towel more than a turban. Tom finally bought a straw hat with a wide brim, yellowish in colour, for 20 dirhams.

Thus attired, Tom walked towards the Villa de France. *En route*, he stopped at the Café de Paris for an express and something like a croissant. Then onward.

He loitered for two or more minutes outside the entrance of the Grand Hotel Villa de France, hoping Pritchard might emerge, in which case Tom would pull his hat-brim down in front and keep gazing. But Pritchard did not.

Tom entered the lobby, looked around, and went to the front desk. He tilted his hat back, like a tourist come in from the sun, and said in French, 'Good morning. May I speak with M'sieur David Pritchard, please?'

'Preechard – ' The clerk referred to a ledger, then dialled a number on a desk to Tom's left.

Tom saw the clerk nodding, frowning. 'Je suis désolé, m'sieur,' he said, returning, 'mais M'sieur Preechard ne veut pas être dérangé.'

'Tell him I am Tom Ripley, please,' Tom said with urgency in his voice. 'I am quite sure – it is *very* important.'

The clerk tried it again. 'It is M'sieur Reepley, m'sieur. Il dit – '

The clerk was interrupted by Pritchard, apparently, and after a moment came and told Tom that M. Preechard did not wish to speak with anyone.

Rounds one and two for Tom, Tom thought, as he thanked the clerk and walked away. Did Pritchard have a broken jaw? A tooth knocked loose? Pity it wasn't a good deal worse.

Back to the Minzah now. He must change more money for Héloïse when they paid and checked out. What a shame not to have seen more of Tangier! But then – Tom's spirits rose and consequently his self-confidence – maybe he could get a late afternoon plane today to Paris. Must ring Mme Annette, he thought. Ring the airport first. Air France, if possible. Tom wanted to lure Pritchard back to Villeperce.

He bought a tightly bound bunch of jasmine from a pavement vendor. It had an interesting and authentic smell.

In their room, Tom found Héloïse dressed and packing their suitcases.

'Your hat! I want to see it on.'

Tom had unconsciously removed his hat on entering the hotel, and now he put it on. 'Don't you think it's too much like Mexico?'

'No-n, chéri, not with your dress,' said Héloïse, surveying him quite seriously.

'What is the news from Noëlle?'

'We go first to the Hotel Rembrandt, and then – Noëlle has an idea of a taxi to Cap Spartel. We must see it, she says. Maybe have lunch there. Un snack. Not a big lunch.'

Tom remembered Cap Spartel on the map, a cape or promontory west of Tangier. 'How long does it take to get there?'

'Noëlle said no more than forty-five minutes. *Camels*, Noëlle said. And marvellous view. Tome – ' Now Héloïse's eyes were suddenly sad.

She sensed that he might be leaving, Tom knew, and today. 'I – well – I must ring the airlines, my sweet. I am thinking of Belle Ombre!' he added, like a knight before departure. 'But – I'll try for a late plane this afternoon. I'd also like to see Cap Spartel.'

'Did – ' Héloïse dropped a folded blouse into her suitcase. 'Did you see Preechaud this morning?'

Tom smiled. Héloïse had infinite variations on that name. He thought of saying that the expletive-deleted had been in but had not wanted to see him, but finally said, 'No. I just walked around, bought the hat, had a coffee.' He liked to keep certain little things back from Héloïse, little things that could only disturb her.

By a quarter to noon, Noëlle, Héloïse and Tom were in a taxi heading westward towards Cap Spartel, across empty and dryish land. Tom had telephoned from the Hotel Rembrandt lobby, and with the aid and clout of the hotel manager got a reservation on an Air France plane leaving Tangier at 5.15 p.m. for Roissy. The manager had assured Tom that the confirmed reservation would be at the Tangier airport on his arrival. Therefore Tom could turn his attention to the scenery, or so he felt. There had been no time to ring Mme Annette, but his unexpected appearance would not terrify her, and he had the house key on his ring.

'Now *zees* was very important – always,' said Noëlle, beginning her speech on Cap Spartel, after Tom with difficulty had paid off the taxi over Noëlle's protestations. 'The Romans were here – everyone was here,' she said in English, opening her arms.

Her leather handbag hung over one shoulder. Now she wore

yellow cotton slacks and a loose jacket over her shirt. The steady breeze blew their clothing and their hair in an unvarying westerly direction, or so it seemed to Tom. It ballooned men's shirts and trousers and at the same time was gentle. Two longish bar-cafés seemed the only structures in the area. The Cap stood high above the Strait, and the view was better than Tom had ever seen it, because the Atlantic spread widely to the west.

Smirking camels regarded them from a few yards away, two or three comfortably installed on the sand, with legs folded under them. A white-gowned attendant in a turban lingered near the camels, but seemed never to look at them. He was eating something like peanuts out of his hand.

'A ride now or after lunch?' asked Noëlle in French. 'Look! You see? I almost forgot!' She pointed to the coast, which curved magnificently on the western side, where Tom could see what looked like tan adobe ruins, the low remains of halls and rooms. 'The Romans made fish oil here and sent it to Rome. The Romans once owned *all* this here.'

At that moment, Tom was looking at a hillside, where a man dismounted from a motorcycle and at once assumed a prayer position, head down, buttocks high, facing Mecca, no doubt.

Both cafés had indoor and outdoor tables, one with a terrace on the ocean side. They chose that one and sat at a white metal table.

'A beautiful sky!' said Tom. It was indeed impressive, something to remember, a great dome of cloudless blue, without even an aeroplane or a bird at the moment, only silence, and a feeling of timelessness. After all, he thought, had the camels changed over the thousands of years when, far back in time, their passengers had no cameras?

They ate titbits for lunch, a favourite kind of meal for Héloïse. Tomato juice, Perrier, olives, radishes, little pieces of fried fish. Under the table, Tom looked at his wristwatch. Nearly 2 p.m.

The ladies were talking about a camel ride. Noëlle's slender face, her narrow nose, had already become suntanned. Or was it protective make-up? And how long would Noëlle and Héloïse be staying in Tangier?

'Maybe three more days?' Noëlle asked, looking at Héloïse. 'I have some friends here. There's the Golf Club, nice for lunch. I reached only one friend this morning.'

'You will be in touch, Tome?' said Héloïse. 'You took the Rembrandt telephone number.'

'Of course, darling.'

'What a shame,' said Noëlle with vehemence, 'that these *barbare* types like Preetchard can spoil one's vacation!'

'Oh – ' Tom gave a shrug. 'He didn't spoil it. And I have some business to take care of at home. And elsewhere.' Tom didn't feel that he was being vague, although he was. Noëlle wasn't in the least interested in the details of his activities, of how he made his living. Noëlle lived on family income, plus something from a former husband, Tom vaguely recalled.

Their snack over, they drifted towards the camels, but first petted 'baby donkey', whose presence was announced in English by its owner, a sandalled man in charge of mother donkey. Baby donkey with fuzzy coat and ears kept very close to the side of mother donkey.

'Picture? Photo?' asked the owner of both. 'Baby donkey.'

Noëlle had a camera in her capacious reticule or satchel. She pulled it out and gave the donkey owner a 10 dirham note. 'Put your hand on baby donkey's head,' Noëlle said to Héloïse. *Click*! Héloïse was grinning. 'You, Tome!'

'No.' Or maybe yes. Tom took a step towards mother and baby donkey and Héloïse, Then shook his head. 'No, I'll take one of you two.'

Tom did. Then he left the women talking in French to the camel driver. He had to get a taxi back to Tangier, to collect his luggage, which he could have brought, but he wanted to return to the Rembrandt to see if Pritchard had snooped them out there. They'd told the Minzah that they were going on to Casablanca.

Tom had to wait for a taxi. Several minutes before, he had asked the café barman if he could telephone somewhere for one, and the barman had done this. Meanwhile, Tom paced the terrace floor, making himself walk slowly.

The taxi or a taxi arrived with people intending to get out here. Tom got into the taxi and said, 'To the Hotel Rembrandt, Boulevard Pasteur, s'il vous plaît.'

They tore off.

Tom had not looked back at the camels, not wanting to see Héloïse perhaps being tossed from side to side as the camel got to his or her feet. Tom didn't want to think about looking down from a camel's back to the distant sand, though Héloïse would probably be smiling broadly and looking in all directions as she rode. And she'd make it to the ground later with no bones broken. Tom closed the window except for a quarter-inch, as the speed of the taxi made the air whip in.

Had he ever been on a camel? Tom wasn't quite sure, even though the discomfort of being lifted up high seemed so real, so within his memory, that he felt it had happened. He would hate it. It would be something like looking down at a swimming pool while standing on a diving board five or six metres above the surface of the water. *Jump*! Why should he? Had anybody ever commanded him to jump? At summer camp? Tom wasn't sure. Sometimes his imagination was as clear as a remembered experience. And some remembered experiences faded, he supposed, such as that of killing Dickie, Murchison, even the couple of well-fed Mafia members around whose throats he had pulled a garrotte. The latter two alleged humans, as Doonesbury would say, had meant nothing to him, except that he particularly detested the Mafia. Had he really killed those two on the train? Was his unconscious mind shielding the conscious by making him feel that he might *not* have killed them? Or not quite? But of course he'd read about the two corpses in the papers. Or had he? Naturally, he wouldn't have cut the item out to keep in the house! There was indeed a screen between fact and memory, Tom realized, though he could not have given it a name. He could, of course, he thought a few seconds later, and it was self-preservation.

Now again the dusty, busy, populated streets and four-storey edifices of Tangier took form all round, and he glimpsed the red-brick tower of the San Francisco, looking somewhat like that of the Piazza San Marco in Venice, despite its Arabic designs in white brick. Tom sat on the edge of his seat. 'It's very near,' he said in French, because the driver was going fast.

At last a left swerve to the other side of Pasteur, and Tom was out, paying the driver off.

He had left his luggage in the care of the concierge downstairs. 'Any messages for Ripley?' he asked at the desk.

There was none.

That pleased Tom. He had only one small suitcase and an attaché case. 'Now I'll need a taxi – please,' Tom said. 'To the airport.'

'Yes, sir.' The man raised a finger and said something to a bellhop.

'No one came in to ask for me? Even someone who didn't leave a message?' asked Tom.

'No, m'sieur. I do not think so,' said the desk man, earnestly.

Tom entered the taxi that had arrived. 'L'aéroport, s'il vous plaît.'

They headed south, and once they had left the city, Tom sat back and lit a cigarette. How long would Héloïse want to stay in Morocco? Would Noëlle persuade her to go on somewhere else? Egypt? Tom couldn't see Egypt, but he could see Noëlle wanting to linger in Morocco. That suited Tom perfectly, because he sensed some danger ahead, maybe violence, and around Belle Ombre. He must try to steer the odious Pritchards away from Villeperce, Tom thought, because as an outsider – worse, an American – he did not want to bring trouble and disturbance upon that quiet little town. He'd brought enough, in truth, but had so far kept it pretty quiet and under cover.

On the Air France plane, the atmosphere was French, and Tom, having a first-class ticket, accepted a glass of champagne (not his favourite wine) as he watched the coastline of Tangier and Africa recede from his vision. If any coastline contour could be called unique, a popular and abused word in travel brochures, it was the two-pronged port of Tangier. Tom wanted to come back one day. He picked up his knife and fork for his dinner, just as the Spanish land mass also faded and yielded to the usual oyster whiteness and boredom-from-the-window which was the fate of aeroplane travellers. There was a new (to Tom) issue of *Le Point* ready for him, and Tom intended to look at it after his meal, then deliberately snooze until landing.

Tom wanted to ring Agnès Grais to ask how things were, so this he did from Roissy, after claiming his suitcase. Agnès was at home.

'I'm at Roissy,' Tom said in answer to her question. 'I decided to come home early . . . Yes, Héloïse is staying on with her friend Noëlle. Is everything all right on the home front?' he went on in French.

Tom was told that it was as far as Agnès knew. 'You are coming home by train? Let me pick you up at Fontainebleau. Doesn't matter how late . . . But of course, Tome!'

Agnès consulted a timetable. She would pick him up just after midnight. It would be a pleasure, fun, she assured Tom.

'One more thing, Agnès. Can you ring Madame Annette now and tell her I'll be coming home by myself tonight? So that I don't frighten her when I use my key?'

Agnès said she would.

Tom felt much better then. He did similar favours for the Grais sometimes, and for their children. It was part of life in the country, part of the satisfaction, helping neighbours. The other part, of course, was the hassle of getting from the country to anywhere, or back, such as now. Tom took a taxi to the Gare de Lyon, then the train, on which he bought the ticket from the conductor, choosing to pay a tiny fine rather than fool with the slot machines at the Gare. He could have taken a taxi all the way home, but he was wary of letting taxi drivers go all the way to Belle Ombre's gates. It was like letting a potential enemy know exactly where you lived. Tom recognized this fear in himself, and asked himself if he was becoming paranoid. But if a taxi driver turned out to be an enemy, it would be too late for academic questions.

At Fontainebleau, there was Agnès, smiling, good-humoured as ever, and Tom answered her questions about Tangier as they drove towards Villeperce. He did not mention the Pritchards, and was hoping Agnès might say something, anything, about Janice Pritchard, who lived a couple of hundred metres away from her, but Agnès did not.

'Madame Annette said she would wait up for you. Really, Tome, Madame Annette – '

Agnès could not find words for Mme Annette's devotion, and just as well. Mme Annette had even opened the big gates.

'You are not sure, then, when Héloïse is back?' asked Agnès as they rolled into Belle Ombre's forecourt.

'No. That's up to her. She needs a little vacation.' Tom got his case from the boot and said goodnight to Agnès, with his thanks.

Mme Annette opened the front door. 'Soyez le bienvenu, M'sieur Tome!'

'Merci, Madame Annette! I am happy to be here.' He was happy to smell again the faint and familiar scent of rose petals and furniture polish, to hear Mme Annette asking if he were hungry. Tom assured her he was not, and that he wanted merely to go to bed. But first the post?

'Ici, M'sieur Tome. Comme toujours.'

It was on the hall table, and not much of a stack, Tom saw.

'Madame Héloïse, she is well?' Mme Annette asked anxiously.

'Oh, yes. With her friend Madame Noëlle, you remember.'

'These tropical countries – ' Mme Annette shook her head slightly. 'A person must be very careful.'

Tom laughed. 'Madame was riding a camel today.'

'Oooh, *la*!'

It was unfortunately rather late to ring Jeff Constant or Ed

Banbury without being rude, but Tom did anyway, Ed first. It would be nearly midnight in London.

Ed answered, somewhat sleepily.

'Ed, my apologies for ringing so late. But it's an important – ' Tom moistened his lips. 'I think I should come over to London.'

'Oh? What's happening?' Ed had come awake.

'Anxieties,' Tom said with a sigh. 'Better if I talk with – some people there, you know? Can you put me up? Or can Jeff? For a night or so?'

'I think very likely either of us could,' said Ed, his tense, clear voice sounding like his own now. 'Jeff's got a spare bed and so have I.'

'The first night at least,' Tom said, 'till I see how things go. Thanks, Ed. Anything from Cynthia?'

'N-no.'

'No hints, no rumours anywhere?'

'No, Tom. You're back in France? I thought you – '

'David Pritchard turned up in Tangier, believe it or not. Followed us there.'

'*What?*' Ed sounded genuinely surprised by this.

'He means us no good, Ed, and he'll do his damnedest. His wife stayed at home – in my town. I'll save the details for London and I'll ring you again tomorrow, when I have my ticket. What's a good time to get you?'

'Before ten-thirty my time,' Ed said. 'Tomorrow morning. Where's Pritchard now?'

'Tangier, as far as I know. At the moment. I'll ring you tomorrow morning, Ed.'

10

Tom slept well, and was up before 8. He went down to have a look at the garden. The forsythia he had worried about had been watered, or at least it looked all right, and Henri had been here, Tom saw from some new deadheads of roses near the compost heap by the greenhouse. In two days, a disaster could hardly have happened, unless a hailstorm had hit.

'M'sieur Tome! – Bonjour!' Mme Annette stood in one of the three french windows that opened on to the terrace.

No doubt his black coffee was ready, and Tom went at a trot back to the house.

'I had not expected you up so early, m'sieur,' said Mme Annette, after she had poured his first cup.

His tray was in the living-room, with the filter pot.

'Nor I.' Tom sat on the sofa. 'Now you must tell me the news. Sit down, madame.'

That was an unusual request. 'M'sieur Tome, I have not yet gone to buy the bread!'

'Buy it from the man who honks his van!' Tom smiled. A bread truck honked from the road, and women in dressing-gowns went out to buy loaves. Tom had seen it.

'But he doesn't stop here, because – '

'You are right, madame. But there will still be bread at the bakery this morning, if you speak with me for two minutes.' She preferred walking to the village for bread, because she met people she knew at the bakery, and they exchanged gossip. 'Has everything been quiet?' He knew such a question would make Mme Annette rack her brain for something unusual.

'M'sieur Henri was here once. Not for long, not an hour.'

'No more people photographing Belle Ombre?' Tom asked with a smile.

Mme Annette shook her head. Her hands were clasped just below her waistline. 'No, m'sieur. But – my friend Yvonne told me that Madame – Pichard? The wife – '

'Pichard, something like that.'

'She is weeping – when she goes shopping. Tears! Can you imagine?'

'No,' said Tom. 'Tears!'

'And her husband is not there now. He is gone.' Mme Annette said it as if he might have deserted his wife.

'Maybe he is away on a business trip. Has Madame Pichard made some friends in the village?'

Hesitation. 'I don't think so. She appears sad, m'sieur. May I prepare a soft-boiled egg for you, after I go to the bakery?'

Tom accepted that idea. He was hungry, and there was no keeping Mme Annette from the boulangerie.

Mme Annette turned on her way to the kitchen. 'Ah, M'sieur Clegg telephoned. I believe yesterday.'

'Thank you. Any message?'

'No. Salutations, that is all.'

So Mme Preechard was weeping. Another dramatic show of some kind, Tom supposed, and perhaps only for her own entertainment. Tom stood up and walked to the kitchen. When Mme Annette came in from her quarters with her handbag and took the shopping bag from a hook, Tom said, 'Madame Annette, please don't say to anyone that I am home or was home. Because I think that I shall go away again today . . . Yes, alas, so don't buy any extras for me! I shall tell you more later.'

Tom rang the Fontainebleau travel agency at 9 o'clock, and secured a first-class return ticket to London with open end, leaving that day at just after 1 p.m. from Roissy. Tom packed a suitcase with the usual, plus a couple of drip-dry shirts.

To Mme Annette he said, 'Tell anyone who might telephone that I am still in Maroc with Madame Héloïse, would you? And I shall be back before you know it! Maybe tomorrow, maybe the next day . . . No, no, I shall telephone you, tomorrow certainly, madame.'

Tom had told Mme Annette he was going to London, but not where he would be staying. He left no instructions in case Héloïse rang, simply hoping that she wouldn't, the Moroccan telephone system being discouraging.

Then Tom rang Ed Banbury from his bedroom upstairs. Though Mme Annette still knew no English, and as Tom often thought seemed impervious to the language, he preferred some conversations quite out of her hearing. Tom told Ed his arrival time, and said that probably a little after 3 p.m. he could be at Ed's house, if that was convenient.

Ed said he would make it convenient. No problem.

Tom checked Ed's Covent Garden address, to make sure he had it right. 'We have to consider Cynthia, find out what she's doing, if anything,' Tom said. 'We need quiet spies. We really need a mole. Think about it. Looking forward, Ed! Want anything from Frogland?'

'Um-m, well, bottle of Pernod from the duty-free?'

'No sooner said than done. A bientôt.'

Tom was carrying his light suitcase down the stairs when the telephone rang. He hoped it was Héloïse.

It was Agnès Grais. 'Tome – since you're alone, I thought it would be nice if you came for dinner at our place this evening. Only the kids are here, and they eat earlier, you know?'

'Thank you, dear Agnès,' he replied in French. 'Sorry to say, I have to take off again . . . Yes, today from Roissy. I was just about to ring for a taxi, in fact. What a shame.'

'A taxi to where? I am off to Fontainebleau now for shopping. Would that help you?'

That was just what Tom wanted, so he invited himself, with no trouble, to a ride as far as Fontainebleau. Agnès arrived five or ten minutes later. Tom had had time to say goodbye to Mme Annette when Agnès Grais' station wagon came through the gates he had opened. Then they were off.

'Where're you going now?' Agnès glanced at him with a smile, as if she thought he was the gadabout of all time.

'London. A little business – by the way –'

'Yes, Tome?'

'I'd be grateful if you didn't mention to anyone that I was home overnight. Or that I'm going to London for a day or so. It's not *very* important – to anyone – but I feel I should be with Héloïse, even though she's got her good friend Noëlle with her. You've met Noëlle Hassler?'

'Yes. Twice, I think.'

'I'll be going back to – Casablanca in a few days, very likely.' Tom assumed a more relaxed manner. 'Did you know that the curious Madame Pritchard is weepy lately? I heard this from my faithful spy Madame Annette.'

'Tears? Why?'

'No idea!' Tom wasn't going to say that M. Pritchard did not appear to be home just now. Mme Janice Pritchard must be keeping to herself pretty much, if Agnès hadn't noticed the absence of Janice's husband. 'Strange to go into the boulangerie wiping tears away, isn't it?'

'Very! And sad.'

Agnès Grais dropped Tom at the place he had, on the spur of the moment, suggested: in front of L'Aigle Noir. The porter who came down the steps and across the terrace might or might not have known Tom by sight, as Tom patronized only the hotel restaurant and bar, but he applied himself to getting a taxi that was willing to go to Roissy, for which Tom tipped him.

In what seemed like a short time, Tom was in another taxi that was driving on the left side of the road, heading for London. At his feet was the plastic bag containing Ed's Pernod and a carton of Gauloises. From the window, Tom saw red-brick factories and warehouses, huge company signs, promising nothing of the easy fraternity that Tom associated with visiting his pals in London. He had found more than £200 in cash in his UK-England envelope (a small drawer in his captain's chest was devoted to left-over foreign currencies), and also some traveller's cheques in pounds.

'And please watch it at Seven Dials,' Tom said to the driver in a polite but anxious tone, 'if you go that way.' Ed Banbury had warned him that taxi drivers could take a wrong turn which could be disastrous. Ed's block of flats, an old one renovated, he had said, was in Bedfordbury Street. The street was almost quaint, Tom saw when the taxi came to it. Tom paid the driver off.

Ed was in, as promised, and just as he buzzed Tom in, after verifying his voice on the speaker, a clap of thunder came that made Tom quake. Then, as Tom opened the second door, he heard the heavens open and the rain come down.

'There's no lift,' said Ed, leaning over the banister, then starting down. 'Second floor.'

'Hi, Ed,' Tom said in almost a whisper. He disliked speaking loudly when two flats on each floor might be able to hear. Ed took the plastic bag. The wooden banister was beautifully polished, the walls looked freshly painted white, and the carpeting was dark blue.

Ed's flat presented the same new and clean appearance as the hall. Ed made tea, because he usually did at this hour, he said, and also because it was raining cats and dogs.

'You spoke with Jeff?' asked Tom.

'Oh, yes. He wants to see you. Maybe tonight. I told him I'd ring once you arrived and we'd talked.'

They had tea in the room that was to be Tom's bedroom, a sort of library off the living-room, with a sofa that seemed made from a twin bed by dint of a cover and some cushions. Tom filled Ed in quickly as to David Pritchard's activities in Tangier, and the satisfying episode that had ended with Pritchard unconscious on the stone floor of La Haffa, a popular mint-tea-drinking and kif-smoking place on the Tangier coast.

'I haven't seen him since,' Tom went on. 'My wife's still there with a Paris friend called Noëlle Hassler. I suppose they'll go on to Casablanca. I don't want Pritchard harming my wife and I don't think he'll try. He's after me. I don't know *what's* on the bastard's mind.' Tom sipped his delicious Earl Grey. 'Pritchard may be a nut, okay. But what interests me is what he might be learning from Cynthia Gradnor. Any news there? Anything about the go-between, for instance – the friend of Cynthia's whom Pritchard spoke with at the big free-for-all?'

'Yes. We got his name. George Benton. Jeff got it, somehow, and it wasn't easy, had to do with photos taken at the party in question. Jeff had to ask questions, and he wasn't even at that party.'

Tom was interested. 'You're sure of the name? Lives in London?'

'Pretty much sure of the name.' Ed recrossed his lean legs, and frowned slightly. 'We saw three promising Bentons in the book. There are so many Bentons, and with the G. initial – we could hardly ring them up and ask if they knew Cynthia – '

Tom had to agree. 'What I'm worried about is how far will Cynthia go. In fact, is she even in touch with Pritchard now? Cynthia detests me.' Tom fairly shuddered as he said the words. 'She'd love to hit me hard. But if she decided to expose the forgeries, give the date when Bernard Tufts started forging' – here Tom's voice dropped to almost a whisper – 'she'll also be betraying her great love Bernard. I'm gambling that she won't go that far. It's strictly a gamble.' Tom sat back in this armchair, but still did not relax. 'It's more a hope and a prayer. I haven't seen Cynthia for a few years and her attitude towards Bernard may have changed – slightly. Maybe she'll be more interested in avenging herself on me.' Tom paused, and watched Ed think.

104

'Why do you say avenge herself on you, when you know it hits all of us, Tom? Jeff and I – we were doing articles with photos of Derwatt and his paintings – old ones,' he added with a smile, 'when we knew Derwatt was dead.'

Tom looked at his old friend steadily. 'It's because Cynthia knows I had the idea of Bernard's forging in the first place. Your articles came a little later. Bernard told Cynthia, and that's when Bernard and Cynthia began their split.'

'True. Yes, I remember.'

Ed and Jeff and Bernard, but especially Bernard, had been friendly with Derwatt the painter. And when Derwatt, in a depressed period, had gone off to Greece and deliberately drowned himself off some island there, the friends back in London had been understandably shocked, bewildered: in fact, Derwatt had merely 'disappeared' in Greece, because his corpse had never been found. Derwatt had been around forty, Tom thought, beginning to be recognized as a painter of the first category, with presumably his best work ahead of him. Tom had come up with the idea of Bernard Tufts, the painter, trying some Derwatt forgeries.

'Why're you smiling?' Ed asked.

'I was thinking of my confession. I feel sure a priest would say – could you write all that *out*?'

Ed put his head back and laughed. 'No – he'd say you've made it all up!'

'No!' Tom went on, laughing. 'The priest would say – '

The telephone had rung in another room.

'Excuse me, Tom, I'm expecting that,' Ed said, and went off.

While Ed spoke, Tom looked around the 'library' where he was to sleep. Lots of hardcover books, as well as paperbacks, he saw, in the two floor-to-ceiling walls of shelves. Tom Sharpe, Muriel Spark, almost side by side. Ed had acquired some good furniture since Tom had seen him last. Where was Ed's family from? Hove?

And what was Héloïse doing at this moment? Nearly 4 p.m.? The sooner she left Tangier and went to Casablanca, the happier he would be.

'It's all right,' Ed said, returning, tugging a red sweater down over his shirt. 'I cancelled something unimportant, and I'm free the rest of the afternoon.'

'Let's go to the Buckmaster.' Tom stood up. 'Isn't it open till five-thirty? Six?'

'Six, I believe. I'll just put the milk away, let's forget about the rest. If you want to hang up stuff, Tom, there's room in the cupboard here on the left.'

'I hung my spare trousers over a chair here – for now. Let's go.'

Ed reached the door and turned. He had put on a raincoat. 'You mentioned two things you wanted to say. Concerning Cynthia?'

'Oh – yes.' Tom buttoned his Burberry. 'The second – detail. Cynthia of course knows that the corpse I cremated was Bernard's, not Derwatt's. I don't have to tell you *that*. So in a way it's a further insult to Bernard that I've – further soiled his name, as it were, by telling the police that he was somebody else.'

Ed gave this a few seconds' thought, with his hand on the doorknob. Then he nervously released it and looked at Tom. 'But you know, Tom, in all this time, she hasn't said anything to us. To Jeff or me. All she does is ignore us, which is fine with us.'

'She never had an opportunity such as David Pritchard presents now,' Tom countered. 'A meddling, sadistic nut. Cynthia can simply use him, don't you see? And that's what she's doing.'

A taxi to Old Bond Street, to the discreetly lighted, brass and darkwood framed window of the Buckmaster Gallery. The fine old door still had its polished brass handle, Tom noted. A couple of palms in pots in the front window flanked an old painting and concealed much of the room beyond.

The man called Nick Hall, who had been described to Tom as about 30, was talking to an older man. Nick had straight black hair, was rather sturdy in build and inclined to keep his arms folded, it seemed.

Tom saw what he considered mediocre modern paintings on the wall, not a total exhibit of the same person, but a selection of three or four painters. Tom and Ed stood to one side until Nick had concluded his conversation with the older gentleman. Nick gave the man a card, and the older man departed. There was no one else in the gallery now, it seemed.

'Mr Banbury, good afternoon,' said Nick, coming forward, smiling, showing short, even teeth of the kind Tom disliked. Nick seemed straightforward, at least. And he plainly knew Ed, which indicated that they kept in good touch.

'Afternoon, Nick. May I introduce a friend – Tom Ripley. Nick Hall.'

'Very pleased to meet you, sir,' said Nick, smiling again. He did not extend a hand, but bowed a little.

'Mr Ripley's here only for a couple of days, and wanted to look in, meet you, and perhaps see an interesting painting or two.'

Ed's manner was light, and Tom kept his the same. Nick had apparently not heard Tom's name before. Fine. A far cry (and a good deal safer) from last time, when a gay chap named Leonard, as Tom recalled, had had Nick's position and been in on the fact that Tom was impersonating Derwatt and holding a press conference in the back room of this very gallery.

Tom and Ed strolled into the next room (there were only two showrooms) and looked at the Corot-like landscapes hanging on the walls. There were, in the second showroom, a few canvases leaning against the wall in a back corner. More would be in the back room, Tom knew, beyond the slightly smudged white door, where the press conference – two in fact – with Tom as Derwatt had taken place.

Out of Nick's hearing, Nick being then in the front room, Tom asked Ed to ask Nick if there had been any enquiries about Derwatts lately. 'And then, I'd like to take a look at the visitors' book – people who've signed.' It would be just like David Pritchard to sign, Tom thought. 'Anyway, the Buckmaster Gallery people – meaning you and Jeff, the owners – know that I like Derwatts, n'est-ce pas?'

Ed did ask.

'We have six Derwatts just now, sir,' said Nick, and straightened up in his snug grey suit, as if at the prospect of a sale. 'Of course I recall your name now, sir. They're this way.'

Nick showed the Derwatts by placing them on a chair seat and letting them lean against the back. The canvases were all Bernard Tufts, two Tom remembered, four he did not. 'Cat in Afternoon' pleased Tom most, a warm reddish-brown and nearly abstract composition in which a marmalade-and-white cat was not at once findable, a sleeping cat. Then 'Station Nowhere', a lovely canvas of blue, brown, tan spots with a chalky but dirty-looking building in the background, the railway station, presumably. Then – people again – 'Sisters in an Argument', which was a typical Derwatt, though to Tom a Bernard Tufts because of the date: a portrait of two females facing each other, mouths open. Derwatt's multi-lined outlines conveyed a sense of activity, noise of voices, and the dashes of red – a favourite device of Derwatt and copied by Bernard Tufts – suggested anger, maybe the scratching of fingernails and the blood therefrom.

'And what are you asking for this?'

'"The Sisters" – close to three hundred thousand, I believe, sir. I could check it. Then – if a sale is near, I am to notify one or two other people. That's a popular one.' Nick smiled again.

Tom wouldn't have wanted it in his house, but he had asked the price out of curiosity. 'And the "Cat"?'

'A little more. That's popular. We'll get it.'

Tom exchanged glances with Ed.

'You're remembering prices these days, Nick!' said Ed in a genial manner. 'Very good.'

'*Yes*, sir, thank you, sir.'

'Have you many enquiries for Derwatts?' Tom asked.

'Mm-m – not too many because they cost so much. He's the feather in our cap, I suppose.'

'Or the major jewel in our carcanet,' Ed added. 'The Tate people, Sotheby's, do come in to see what's turned up, Tom, what may have been given back to us for resale here. The auction people – we don't need them.'

The Buckmaster had its own auction method by notifying possible purchasers, Tom supposed. He was pleased that Ed Banbury talked freely before Nick Hall, as if Tom and Ed were old friends, client and art dealer. Art dealer: it sounded odd, but Ed and Jeff did do the choosing of what paintings they took in to sell, and what young artists, and also older artists, to represent. Their decisions were often based on the market, on fads, Tom knew, but Ed and Jeff had chosen well enough to pay the high Old Bond Street rent and also to make a profit.

'I presume,' Tom said to Nick, 'there are no more new Derwatts being found in attics and such?'

'Attics! – Not b – not likely, sir! Sketches – not even sketches for the last year or so.'

Tom nodded thoughtfully. 'I like the "Cat". Whether I can afford it or not – I'll think about it.'

'You have – ' Nick seemed to try to recollect.

'Two,' Tom said. '"Man in Chair" – my favourite – and "The Red Chairs".'

'Yes, sir. I'm sure that's on record.' Nick gave no sign of remembering or reminding himself that 'Man in Chair' was a forgery and the other wasn't.

'We should be moving on, I think,' Tom said to Ed, as if they had a date. Then to Nick Hall, 'Have you a visitors' book?'

'Oh, yes, sir. On the desk here.' Nick walked towards the desk in the front room, and opened a large book to the current pages. 'And here's a pen.'

Tom bent and looked, took up the pen. Scrawled signatures, Shawcross or something like it, Forster, Hunter, some with addresses, most without. A glance at the preceding page told Tom that Pritchard had not signed during the last year, at any rate. Tom signed, but gave no address; merely Thomas P. Ripley and the date.

Soon they were out on the pavement, where it was drizzling.

'Really, I'm glad to see that that Steuerman fellow is apparently not represented,' Tom said, grinning.

'Right. Don't you remember – you let out a scream of complaint from France.'

'And why not?' Now both of them were watching for a taxi. Ed or Jeff – Tom didn't want to point the finger at either individually – had a few years ago discovered a painter called Steuerman, who they thought could turn out passable Derwatts. *Passable*? Tom tensed even now under his raincoat. Steuerman could have blown everything, if the Buckmaster Gallery had been stupid enough to try marketing his productions. Tom had based his anti-Steuerman stance on colour slides the gallery had sent to him, as Tom recalled. No matter, he'd seen the slides somewhere, and they were impossible.

Ed was in the street, waving an arm, and it was going to be tough at this hour and in this weather to get a taxi.

'What's the arrangement with Jeff tonight?' Tom shouted.

'He's to come to my place around seven. Look!'

A taxi had loomed, with a blessed yellow light glowing at the front of its roof. They got in.

'I loved seeing the Derwatts just now,' Tom said, basking in recollected pleasure. 'I should say – the Tufts.' He made the last word soft as cotton. 'And I've thought of a solution to the Cynthia problem – hitch – what shall I call it?'

'What's the solution?'

'I'll simply ring her up and ask her. I'll ask if she's in touch with Mrs Murchison, for instance. And with David Pritchard. I'll pretend to be the French police. From your house, if I may?'

'Oh-h – certainly!' said Ed, suddenly understanding.

'You've got Cynthia's number? That's no problem?'

'No, it's in the book. Not Bayswater any more but – Chelsea, I think.'

11

At Ed's flat, Tom took a shower, accepted a gin and tonic, and composed his thoughts. Ed had written Cynthia Gradnor's number for him on a slip of paper.

Tom practised his French commissaire accent on Ed. 'Ees nearly se*ven*. Eef Jeff arrive – you let heem in, go on as usual, yes?'

Ed nodded, almost bowed. 'Yes. Oui!'

'I am reenging from ze bureau of police in – I'd better make it Paris instead of Melun – now – ' Tom was on his feet, walking around Ed's big workroom, where the telephone sat on a busy, paper-littered desk. 'Background noises. Leetle clack on type-writer, please. Zees is a *police* station. A la Simenon. We all know each ozzer.'

Ed obliged and seated himself, stuck a piece of paper into his machine. Clackety-clack.

'More thoughtful,' Tom said. 'Doesn't have to be fast.' He dialled, and braced himself to verify that he was speaking to Cynthia Gradnor, to say that David Pritchard had been in touch a few times, and could they ask a few questions in regard to M'sieur Reepley?

The telephone rang and rang.

'She ees not een,' Tom said. 'Damn. Et merde!' He looked at his watch. Ten past 7. Tom put the telephone down. 'Maybe she's out to dinner. Maybe she's out of town.'

'There's always tomorrow,' Ed said. 'Or later tonight.'

The doorbell rang.

'That's Jeff,' said Ed, and went to the front hall.

Jeff came in, with umbrella but still dampish. He was taller, bigger than Ed, and balder on top than when Tom had last seen him. 'Hello, Tom! An unexpected and welcome pleasure, as usual!'

110

The two shook hands warmly, almost embraced.

'Out of the wet raincoat and into a dry – something or other,' said Ed. 'Scotch?'

'You guessed it. Thank you, Ed.'

They all sat in Ed's living-room, which had a sofa plus a convenient coffee table. Tom explained to Jeff why he was here: things had hotted up since their last telephone conversation. 'My wife's still in Tangier, with a woman friend, at a hotel called the Rembrandt. So I came over to try and find out what Cynthia's doing – or maybe trying to do – in regard to Murchison. She might be in touch – '

'Yes, Ed's told me about that,' Jeff said.

' – in touch with *Mrs* Murchison in America, who of course would be interested in how her husband disappeared. I've got to sound that out, I think.' Tom turned his gin and tonic on a coaster. 'If it comes to looking for Murchison's corpse in my neck of the woods – they just might find it, the cops. Or a skeleton, anyway.'

'Just a few kilometres from where you live, you once said, didn't you?' Jeff spoke with a trace of fear or awe. 'In a river?'

Tom shrugged. 'Yes. Or a canal. I've conveniently forgotten exactly *where*, but I'd recognize the bridge Bernard and I dumped it from – that night. Of course' – Tom straightened up and his expression became more cheerful – 'nobody knows why or how Thomas Murchison disappeared. Could've been kidnapped at Orly, where I took him – you see.' Tom's smile widened. He had said 'took him', Murchison, as if he believed it. 'He was carrying "The Clock" and that disappeared at Orly. A genuine Tufts.' Now Tom laughed. 'Or Murchison could have decided *himself* to disappear. Anyway, somebody pinched "The Clock" and we never saw or heard of it again, remember?'

'Yes.' Jeff's high forehead wrinkled in thought. He was holding his glass between his knees. 'How long are these people, the Pritchards, staying in your neighbourhood there?'

'It could be a six-month rental, I suppose. Should've asked, but I didn't.' He would disembarrass himself of Pritchard in less than six months, Tom was thinking. Somehow. Tom felt his wrath mounting, and proceeded to tell Ed and Jeff about the house the Pritchards had rented, by way of letting off steam. Tom described the pseudo-antique furniture, and the pond in the lawn on which the afternoon sun shimmered, making designs on the living-room ceiling. 'Trouble is, I'd like to see them both drowned in it,' Tom

111

concluded, and the other two laughed.

'How's your drink, Tom?' asked Ed.

'No more, thanks, I'm fine.' Tom glanced at his watch: a little past 8. 'I want to try Cynthia again before we take off.'

Ed and Jeff cooperated. Background noise of typewriter provided by Ed again, as Tom limbered up by talking with Jeff. 'No laughter. Zees ees a police bureau een Paris. I 'ave 'eard from Preechard,' Tom said earnestly, on his feet again, 'and I must question Madame Gradnor, because she may know somezing about M'sieur Murcheeson or hees wife. Yes?'

'Oui,' said Jeff, with equal seriousness, as if he were swearing something.

Tom had pen and paper ready to jot anything down, plus the paper on which Cynthia's number was. He dialled.

On the fifth ring, a female voice answered.

''Ello, good evening, madame. C'est Madame Gradnor?'

'Yes.'

'Commissaire Edouard Bilsault here, een Paris. We are in communication with M'sieur Preechard concerning to a Thomas Murcheeson – whose name you know, I think.'

'Yes. I do.'

So far, so good. Tom was pitching his voice higher than normal, and making it more tense. Cynthia after all might recollect his usual pitch and recognize him. 'M'sieur Preechard ees now een l'Afrique du Nord as you may know, madame. We would like to know Madame Murcheeson's address americaine – een America, *eef* you have it.'

'For what purpose?' asked Cynthia Gradnor, sounding her old brusque self, which included the stiff upper lip, if circumstances demanded.

'Because we may 'ave some information – very soon – een regard to 'er 'usband. M'sieur Preechard has telephoned once from Tanger. But we cannot reach 'eem *now*.' Tom made his voice rise with urgency.

'Hm-m,' in a dubious tone. 'Mr Pritchard has his own way of dealing with – the matter you are talking about, I think. Not my affair. I suggest you wait until his return.'

'But we cannot – *should* not wait, madame. We 'ave a question to ask Madame Murcheeson. M'sieur Preechard was not een when we telephoned and telephone in Tanger ees *very-ry bad*.' Tom gave a grumpy throat-clearing that hurt him, and signalled for background noises. Cynthia had not seemed surprised that Pritchard was in Tanger, as the French called it.

Ed slammed a book on to a clear spot on his desk, continued pecking at the typewriter, and Jeff at a distance and facing a wall cupped his hands and created an end of a siren wail, exactly like the Parisian wails, Tom thought.

'Madame – ' Tom continued, in earnest tone.

'One moment.'

She was getting it. Tom took up his pen, without a glance at his friends.

Cynthia returned and read out an address in the East Seventies in Manhattan.

'Merci, madame,' said Tom politely, but as if it were no more than the police's due. 'And zee telephone?' Tom took this down too. 'Merci infiniment, madame. Et bonne soirée.'

'*Whee – ee – glug-glug.*' This from Jeff, as Tom politely bade his adieus, convincing cross-channel noises, Tom had to admit, but maybe unheard by Cynthia.

'Success,' Tom said calmly. 'But to think that she had Mrs Murchison's address.' Tom looked at his friends, who were for the moment silent and looking at him. He pocketed the data on Mrs Murchison, and again looked at his wristwatch. 'One more call, may I, Ed?'

'Go ahead, Tom,' said Ed. 'Want to be alone?'

'Not necessarily. This time France.'

The two drifted into Ed's kitchen, however.

Tom dialled Belle Ombre, where it would be half-past 9.

''Allo, Madame Annette!' said Tom. The sound of Mme Annette's voice conjured up the front hall, and the equally familiar kitchen counter by the coffee machine, where there was also a telephone.

'Oh, M'sieur Tome! I did not know where to find you! I have bad news. M – '

'Vraiment?' said Tom frowning.

'Madame Héloïse! She was kidnapped!'

Tom gasped. 'That can't be *true*! Who told you?'

'A man with an American accent! He telephoned – about four o'clock this afternoon. I did not know what to do. He said that, then he hung up. I spoke with Madame Geneviève. She said, "What can the police *here* do?" She said, "Tell it in Tangier, tell it to M'sieur Tome," but I did not know how to find you.'

Tom shut his eyes tight, as Mme Annette continued. Tom was thinking: Pritchard had told the lie, had discovered that Tom Ripley was no longer in Tangier, or not with his wife, anyway, and had decided to make more trouble. Tom took a breath and tried to get a coherent statement through to Mme Annette.

'Madame Annette, I think it is a trick. Please don't worry. Madame Héloïse and I changed our hotel, I think I told you that. Madame is now at the Rembrandt Hotel. But don't you worry about that. *I* shall telephone my wife there this evening and − I shall wager she is still there!' Tom gave a laugh, a real laugh. 'American accent!' Tom said with contempt. 'That would not be a North African, madame, or a police officer of Tangier, giving you correct information, now would it?'

Mme Annette had to concede that this was so.

'Now how is the weather? Here it is raining.'

'Will you telephone me, when you find out where Madame Héloïse is, M'sieur Tome?'

'Tonight? Y-yes.' He added calmly, 'I *hope* to speak with her tonight. Then I'll telephone you.'

'At any hour, m'sieur! Here I have locked every door carefully and the big gates.'

'Well done, Madame Annette!'

When he had hung up, Tom said, 'Whew!' He shoved his hands into his pockets and drifted towards his friends, who were now in the library or book room with their drinks. 'I have news,' Tom said, taking pleasure in being able to share the news now, bad as it was, instead of keeping silent, as he usually had to do with bad news. 'My housekeeper says my wife has been kidnapped. In Tangier.'

Jeff frowned. 'Kidnapped? Are you joking?'

'A man with an American accent rang my house and informed Madame Annette − then hung up. I feel sure it's false. It's typical Pritchard − making all the trouble he can.'

'What should you do?' Ed asked. 'Ring her hotel, see if she's there?'

'Exactly.' But meanwhile Tom lit a Gitane, savouring a few seconds of detesting David Pritchard, hating every ounce of his body, even his round-rimmed glasses and his vulgar wristwatch. 'Yes, I'll ring the Rembrandt in Tangier. My wife usually comes back to her room around six or seven to change for the evening. The hotel can at least tell me if she's been in.'

'Of course. Go ahead, Tom,' said Ed.

114

Tom went back to the telephone near Ed's typewriter, and fished his memo book from an inside pocket of his jacket. He had written down the Rembrandt number with the Tangier code. Hadn't somebody said that 3 a.m. was the best time to ring Tangier? Tom still tried now, dialling carefully.

Silence. Then a buzzing, three short buzzes that gave promise of activity. Then silence.

Tom tried the operator, asked the woman please to put the call through, and gave Ed's number. The operator told him to hang up. She rang back after a minute and said she was trying the Tangier number. The London operator gave saucy, irritated replies to someone whose voice Tom could barely hear, but she also had no luck.

'Sometimes at this time of the evening, sir – I suggest you try again, much later tonight.'

Tom thanked her. 'No,' he said in answer to her question, 'I have to go out. I'll try again myself later.'

Then he went into the book room, where Ed and Jeff had almost finished making up his bed. 'No luck,' Tom said. 'I couldn't get through. I've heard that about the Tangier telephone. Let's go out and have a bite and forget it for now.'

'Hellish,' Jeff said, straightening up. 'I heard you say you'll try again later.'

'Yes. By the way, my thanks to you fellows for making my bed. That's going to look welcome tonight.'

A few minutes later, they were out in the drizzle, two umbrellas among them, making their way to Ed's recommended pub-restaurant. It was close by, full of warm brown rafters and wooden booths. They sat at a table, which Tom preferred because he could see more of the patrons from a table. He ordered roast beef and Yorkshire pudding, for old times' sake.

Tom asked Jeff Constant about his work, which was freelance. Jeff had to take on some jobs for money, which he didn't like as much as what he called 'artistic interiors with people or no people'. He meant good-looking house interiors, maybe with a cat or plants. The commercial work had to do with industrial design a lot of the time, Jeff said, close-ups of electric irons.

'Or buildings out of town,' Jeff went on, 'in a half-finished state. I have to photograph them, sometimes in weather like this.'

'Do you and Ed see each other very often?' Tom asked.

Both Ed and Jeff smiled and glanced at each other. Ed spoke first.

'I wouldn't say so, would you, Jeff? But if one needs the other – we're there.'

Tom was thinking of the early days, when Jeff had made the excellent photographs of Derwatt (genuine) paintings, and Ed Banbury had talked them up, had written articles on Derwatt, carefully dropped a word here and there that would start the publicity ball rolling, they had hoped, and the ball had started rolling. Derwatt had been living in Mexico was the story, still lived there, but was a recluse, refused interviews, and refused even to tell the name of the village where he lived, though it was believed to be near Veracruz, from which port he shipped his paintings to London. The former owners of the Buckmaster Gallery had been handling Derwatt without impressive success, because they hadn't tried to push him. Jeff and Ed had done that only after Derwatt had gone to Greece and drowned himself. They had all known Derwatt (all except Tom, curiously, though Tom often felt as if he *had* known him). Before his death, Derwatt had been a good and interesting painter, ever on the edge of poverty in London, an admired acquaintance of Jeff and Ed and Cynthia and Bernard. Derwatt was from some dreary northern industrial town, Tom forgot which. It was the talking up that had done it, Tom realized. Curious. But then Van Gogh had suffered from the lack of talking up. Who had talked Vincent up? No one, maybe only Theo.

Ed's narrow face frowned. 'I'll ask it just this once tonight, Tom. Are you really not at all worried about Héloïse?'

'No. I was thinking about something else just now. I know this Pritchard, Ed. Slightly, but enough.' Tom gave a laugh. 'I never met anybody quite like him, but I've read about such types. Sadistic. Independent income, so says his wife, but I suspect them both of lying in their teeth.'

'He's got a wife?' Jeff asked, surprised.

'Didn't I tell you? American. It looks like a sado-masochistic set-up to me. They love and hate each other, you know?' Tom continued to Jeff, 'Pritchard told me he was studying marketing at INSEAD – it's a business school near Fontainebleau – absolutely untrue. His wife has bruises on her arms – and neck. He's in my neighbourhood solely to make my life as rotten as possible. And now Cynthia has fired his imagination by bringing up Murchison.' Tom realized, as he cut into his roast beef, that he did not wish to tell Ed or Jeff that Pritchard (or wife) had attempted to imitate Dickie Greenleaf by telephone and had spoken with both Tom and

Héloïse. Tom did not like harking back to Dickie Greenleaf.

'And followed you even to Tangier,' Jeff said, pausing with knife and fork in his hands.

'Without wife,' Tom said.

'How does one get rid of a pest like that?' Jeff asked.

'That *is* the interesting question.' Then Tom laughed.

The other two looked a bit surprised by his laugh, then managed smiles, too.

Jeff said, 'I'd like to come back to Ed's, if you're going to try for Tangier. I'd like to know what's happening.'

'Come along, Jeff! How long does Héloïse intend to stay, Tom?' Ed asked. 'In Tangier? Or Morocco?'

'Maybe another ten days or so. I don't know. Her friend Noëlle has been there before. They want to go on to Casablanca.'

Espresso coffee. Then some shop talk between Jeff and Ed. It was evident to Tom that each could turn a bit of work the other's way from time to time. Jeff Constant was good at portrait photos, and Ed Banbury often interviewed people for Sunday supplements.

Tom insisted on paying for dinner. 'My pleasure,' he said.

The rain had stopped, and Tom proposed a turn around the block when they were near Ed's. Tom loved the little shops interspersed with entrances to flats, the polished brass slits in the doors for letters, even the cosy late-night deli, well-lit and with fresh fruit, tinned goods, shelves of bread and cereals and open at nearly midnight.

'Run by Arabs or Pakis,' Ed said. 'Anyway, a blessing, open on Sundays and holidays, too.'

They arrived back at Ed's doorway where Ed used his key to let them in.

Tom thought he had a slightly better chance now for a telephone connection with the Hotel Rembrandt, though perhaps not so good as at 3 a.m. Again he dialled carefully, hoping that someone competent and able to speak French would be manning the switchboard.

Jeff and Ed drifted in, Jeff with a cigarette, to hear the news.

Tom made a gesture. 'They're not answering yet.' He dialled the operator and put the matter into her hands. She was to ring back when she made contact with the Rembrandt. 'Damn!'

'You think there's any hope?' asked Ed. 'You could send a telegram, Tom.'

'The London operator's supposed to ring back. Don't wait up, you two.' Tom looked at his host. 'Do you mind, Ed, if I run and get it in here, if Tangier rings back tonight?'

'Of course not. I won't hear it in my bedroom. No phone there.' Ed patted Tom on the shoulder.

It was the first physical touch Tom could recall from Ed, apart from handshakes. 'I'm going to take a shower, which will surely make the call come through when I'm in the middle of it.'

'Go ahead! We'll give you a shout,' said Ed.

Tom got his pyjamas from the bottom of his suitcase, stripped, and fled into the bathroom, which was between his sleeping quarters and Ed's bedroom. He was drying himself when Ed gave the shout. Tom shouted a reply, composed himself, and put on pyjamas before exiting in mooseskin slippers. *Is it Héloïse or the desk?* Tom wanted to ask Ed, but he said nothing and picked up the telephone. ''Allo?'

'Bon soir, Hotel Rembrandt. Vous êtes – '

'M'sieur Ripley.' He continued in French. 'I should like to speak with Madame Ripley, room three seventeen?'

'Ah, oui. Vous êtes – '

'*Son mari,*' said Tom.

'Un instant.'

'*Son mari*' cut some ice, Tom felt. Tom looked at his attentive two friends. Then a sleepy voice said:

''Allo?'

'Héloïse! I was so worried!'

Ed and Jeff relaxed, smiling.

'Yes, you know – the dreadful *Preechard* – he telephoned Madame Annette to say you had been *kidnapped*!'

'Kidnapped! I did not even *see* 'eem today,' said Héloïse.

Tom laughed. 'I am going to telephone Madame Annette tonight, she'll be much relieved. Now look.' Tom then tried to ascertain Héloïse's plans with Noëlle. They had gone to a mosque today, to a market also. Yes, they intended to go to Casablanca tomorrow.

'To what hotel?'

Héloïse had to reflect, or look somewhere. 'Miramare.'

How original, Tom thought, still in good spirits. 'Even if you didn't see the creep, my dear, he may be prowling around, trying to find out where you – and I maybe – are staying. So I'm pleased that you go to Casablanca tomorrow. And then what?'

'Then?'

'Where do you go from there?'

'I don't know. I think Marrakesh.'

'Take a pencil,' Tom said firmly. He gave Ed's telephone number, and made sure she had it right.

'Why are you in London?'

Tom laughed. 'Why are you in Tangier? My dear, I may not be here every hour of the day, but you telephone and leave a message – I think Ed has an answering service – ' Ed nodded to Tom. 'Tell me your *next* hotel, if you go on from Casablanca . . . Good. Greetings to Noëlle . . . I love you. Goodbye, dear.'

'That's a relief!' said Jeff.

'Yes. For me. She said she hasn't even seen Pritchard around – which of course doesn't mean much.'

'Preek-hard,' said Jeff.

'Hard-preek,' Ed retorted, deadpan, strolling about.

'Enough!' Tom was grinning. 'Further phoning tonight – Madame Annette. I must. Meanwhile I've been thinking about Mrs Murchison.'

'Yes?' asked Ed, curious, resting an elbow on a bookcase. 'Do you suppose Cynthia's in touch with Mrs Murchison? Comparing notes?'

Horrible thought. Tom pondered. 'They may know each other's address, but how much can one tell the other? Also – it may be only since the advent of David Pritchard that they're in touch.'

Jeff, still on his feet, drifted restlessly. 'What were you going to say about Mrs Murchison?'

'That – ' Tom hesitated, not wanting to talk about his half-formed ideas; yet he was among friends. 'I'd love to ring her up in America and ask what's happening in regard to – finding out what happened to her husband. But I think she dislikes me almost as much as Cynthia does. Well, not quite, of course, but I was the last person anyone can reach who saw her husband. And why should I be ringing *her*?' Tom suddenly broke out, 'What the devil can Pritchard *do*? What does he know that's new? Damn all! Nothing!'

'Right,' said Ed.

'And if you telephoned Mrs Murchison – you're so good at mimicking, Tom – with the voice of that Inspector – Webster, wasn't it?' Jeff asked.

'Yes.' Tom disliked remembering the English Inspector Webster's name, even though Webster had not poked through to the truth. 'No, I'm not taking a chance, thanks.' Could Webster, who had come to Belle Ombre and gone even to Salzburg, still be on

119

the case, as the phrase went? Webster in touch with Cynthia and Mrs Murchison? Tom returned to the same conclusion: there was nothing new, so what was there to worry about?

'I'd best be shoving off,' Jeff said. 'Got work to do tomorrow. Will you let me know what you're doing tomorrow, Tom? Ed has my number. You too, I recall.'

Goodnights, and well-wishing.

'Ring Madame Annette,' Ed said. 'Pleasant task, at least.'

'At least!' said Tom. 'I'll say good night too, Ed, with my thanks for your hospitality. I'm asleep on my feet.'

Then Tom dialled Belle Ombre.

''El-lo-*o-o*?'' Mme Annette's voice was shrill with anxiety.

'Tome here!' said Tom. He informed her that all was well with Mme Héloïse, that the kidnapping story had been a false rumour. Tom did not utter the name of David Pritchard.

'But – do you know who told this evil story?' Mme Annette used the word *méchante*, with venom.

'No idea, madame. The world is full of people with evil intent. Their *pleasure* – curiously. All goes well at home?'

Mme Annette assured Tom that all was well. He said he would telephone her when he knew when he would return. About Mme Héloïse's return he was not sure, but she was still with her good friend Mme Noëlle, and amusing herself.

Tom fell into bed and slept like a log.

12

The next morning was as bright and clear as if yesterday's rain had never been, except that all appeared washed, or so Tom liked to think, when he looked out of the window onto the narrow street below. Sunlight twinkled on the window fronts, and the sky was a clear blue.

Ed had left a key on Tom's coffee table, and a note beneath saying Tom was to make himself at home, and Ed would not be back before 4 p.m. Ed had shown Tom the kitchen yesterday. Tom shaved, breakfasted and made his bed. He was downstairs by 9.30, walking towards Piccadilly, savouring the street scenes, the snatches of conversation, the variety of accents he heard from the people he passed.

In Simpson's Tom strolled about, inhaling the current floral aroma, which reminded him that he might pick up some lavender wax for Mme Annette while in London. Tom drifted towards the men's dressing-gowns, and bought one for Ed Banbury, a light-weight Black Watch wool, and for himself a bright red plaid one, Royal Stewart, Tom thought. Ed took a size smaller than Tom, Tom was sure. Tom carried them both in a big plastic bag, and walked out in the direction of Old Bond Street and the Buckmaster Gallery. It was nearly 11.

Nick Hall stood talking with a heavyish dark-haired man when Tom arrived, and nodded a greeting when he saw Tom.

Tom walked about, into the adjacent room with the sedate Corots or Corot-like canvases, back into the front room, where he over-heard Nick saying, ' – under fifteen thousand, I'm sure, sir. I could check, if you'd like.'

'No, no.'

'All prices subject to review by the Buckmaster Gallery owners, prices can go up or down, usually very slightly.' Nick paused.

121

'Depending on the market and not the person who wants to buy it.'

'Very good. Then check for me, please. I'll be assuming thirteen thousand. I – like it, rather. "Picnic".'

'Yes, sir. I have your number and I'll try to reach you tomorrow.'

Nice, Tom thought, that Nick hadn't said 'get back to you tomorrow'. Nick wore a handsome pair of black shoes today, different from yesterday's.

'Hello, Nick – if I may,' said Tom when they were alone. 'I met you yesterday.'

'Oh, I remember, sir.'

'Have you any drawings of Derwatt that I could see?'

Nick hesitated briefly. 'Y-yes, sir. They're in portfolios in the back room. Mostly not for sale. I think none is for sale – officially.'

Good, Tom thought. Sacred archives, sketches for paintings that had become classics, or would have become. 'But – is it possible?'

'Sure. Certainly, sir.' Nick threw a glance at the front door, and then went to it, maybe to check if it were locked, or to slide a bolt. He returned to Tom, and they went through the second room and into the smaller back room, with the still somewhat cluttered desk, the smudged walls, the canvases, frames and portfolios leaning against the once white walls. Had twenty journalists, Leonard the drinks-server, a couple of photographers and himself squeezed themselves in here? Yes, Tom recalled.

Nick squatted and lifted a portfolio. 'About half of these are sketches for paintings,' he said, holding the big grey portfolio in both hands.

There was an extra table near the door, and Nick laid the portfolio reverently on it and untied the three strings that closed it.

'More portfolios are in the drawers here, I know,' Nick said, nodding towards the white cabinet against the wall, which held at least six shallow drawers top to bottom; the top surface was hip-high. This fixture was new to Tom.

Each Derwatt drawing was in a transparent plastic envelope. Charcoal, pencil and *conte*. As Nick lifted one after the other, all in their plastic, Tom realized that he could not tell the Derwatts from the Bernard Tufts, not with total confidence, anyway. 'The Red Chairs' sketches (three), yes, because he knew that was a Derwatt creation. But when Nick came to the 'Man in Chair' preparatory sketches, a Bernard Tufts forgery, Tom's heart gave a leap, because he owned the painting and loved it and knew it well, and because the devoted Bernard Tufts had done his preparatory sketches with the same loving care as would Derwatt. And in these sketches, made to impress no one, Bernard had been fortifying himself for his real effort, the composition in colour or canvas.

'Do you sell these?' Tom asked.

'No. Well – Mr Banbury and Mr Constant don't want to. As far as I know we've never sold any. Not many people – ' Nick hesitated. 'You see, the paper Derwatt used – it wasn't always of the best quality. It gets yellow, crumbles at the edges.'

'I think they're marvellous,' Tom said. 'Keep on taking care of them. Out of the light and all that.'

Nick gave his ready smile. 'And minimum handling.'

There were more. 'Sleeping Cat' which Tom liked, done by Bernard Tufts (Tom thought), on rather cheap good-sized sheets, with colour indications in pencil: black, brown, yellow, red, even green.

It occurred to Tom that Tufts so blended with Derwatt that it was artistically impossible to separate them, at least in some or most of these drawings. Bernard Tufts had become Derwatt, in more senses than one. Bernard had died in a state of confusion and shame because of his success, in fact, in becoming Derwatt, in Derwatt's old lifestyle, in his painting, and in his exploratory drawings. In Bernard's efforts, at least those here at the Buckmaster Gallery, there was no sign of faint-heartedness in Bernard's pencil or colour pencil sketches. Bernard appeared the master of the composition in question, and decision about proportion and colour.

'Are you interested, Mr Ripley?' asked Nick Hall, standing now, sliding a drawer shut. 'I can speak with Mr Banbury.'

Now Tom smiled. 'Not sure. It's tempting. And – ' The question confused Tom for an instant. 'What would the gallery ask for a preliminary drawing – for one of the paintings?'

Nick looked at the floor, thinking. 'I couldn't say, sir. I really couldn't. I don't think I've got the drawing prices anywhere here – if they exist.'

Tom swallowed. Many, most of those drawings came from Bernard Tufts's modest little studio somewhere in London, where he had worked and slept in the last years of his life. Oddly, the sketches were the best guarantee of authenticity of Derwatt's paintings and sketches, Tom thought, because the sketches betrayed no change in the use of colour, which Murchison had been so hung up on.

'Thank you, Nick. We'll see.' Tom moved towards the door, and said goodbye.

Tom walked through the Burlington Arcade, untempted for the moment by the silk ties, the good-looking scarves and belts in the shop windows. He was thinking, if Derwatt was 'exposed' as having been forged for the bulk of his work, what would it matter, since Bernard Tufts's efforts had been equally good, absolutely similar and logical, had shown the same development that the real Derwatt might have shown if he had died at fifty or fifty-five instead of thirty-eight, or however old he was when he had committed suicide? Tufts, it could be argued, had improved upon Derwatt's earlier work. If the sixty per cent (Tom estimated) of Derwatt works now extant were to be signed B. Tufts, why would they be less valuable?

The answer, of course, was because they had been marketed dishonestly, their market value, ever climbing and climbing still, based on the value of Derwatt's name, which in fact had had little value when he died, because Derwatt had not been much known. But Tom had been at this impasse before.

He was glad to be brought to his senses in Fortnum and Mason by asking where he could find household goods. 'Little items – furniture wax,' he added to an assistant in morning jacket.

There he was then, opening a tin of lavender wax, sniffing and imagining with eyes shut that he was back in Belle Ombre. 'May I have three?' Tom said to the salesgirl.

These he dropped in their plastic bag into the big bag with the dressing-gowns.

No sooner was this small task done than Tom's thoughts returned to Derwatt, Cynthia, David Pritchard and the problems at hand. Why not try to see Cynthia, talk with her face to face, rather than over the telephone? Of course, it would be difficult making an appointment with her, she might hang up on him if he telephoned her, might snub him if he hung around waiting outside the house where she lived. But what was there to lose? Cynthia might indeed have brought up the Murchison disappearance to Pritchard, just might have emphasized it in Tom's curriculum vitae, which Pritchard had evidently looked into in newspaper files. In London? Tom might find out if Cynthia was in touch with Pritchard still, telephoning or writing an occasional note. And he might find out her plan, if she had any besides giving him minor annoyance.

Tom lunched in a pub near Piccadilly, then took a taxi to Ed Banbury's flat. He put Ed's dressing-gown in the big plastic bag on

Ed's bed, unceremoniously, without a card . . . Simpson's bag looked handsome, Tom thought. He retu. . . library-bedroom, laid his dressing-gown on a straight chair a. . . went in search of the telephone books. They were near Ed's work table, and Tom looked up Gradnor, Cynthia L., and found her.

He looked at his watch – a quarter to 2 – then began to dial.

A recorded voice, Cynthia's, answered after the third ring, and Tom seized a pencil. The caller was asked to ring a certain number during business hours, Cynthia's voice said.

Tom rang the number, got a female voice, announcing something that sounded like Vernon McCullen Agency, and asked if he might speak to Miss Gradnor.

Miss Gradnor came on. 'Hello?'

'Hello, Cynthia. This is Tom Ripley,' Tom said, making his voice a bit deep and also serious. 'I'm in London for a couple of days – been here a day or so, matter of fact. I was hoping – '

'Why are you ringing *me*?' she asked, bristling already.

'Because I'd like to see you,' Tom said calmly. 'I have a thought, an idea – which I think would be of interest to you and to all of us.'

'All of us?'

'I think you know – ' Tom stood straighter. 'I'm *sure* you know. Cynthia, I'd like to see you for ten minutes. Anywhere – in a restaurant, tea room – '

'*Tea room*!' Her voice did not quite go shrill; that would have been out of control.

Cynthia was never out of control. Tom continued with a determined air. 'Yes, Cynthia. Anywhere. If you'd tell me – '

'What's brought this on?'

Tom smiled. 'A *thought* – which might solve a lot of problems – unpleasantnesses.'

'I do not care to see you, Mr Ripley.' She hung up.

Tom pondered that rejection for a few seconds, wandered around Ed's workroom, then lit a cigarette.

He dialled the number he had scribbled, got the agency again, verified the name and got an address for it. 'Your office is open until when?'

'Um – five-thirtyish.'

'Thank you,' Tom said.

That afternoon, from about five past 5, Tom lay in wait outside a doorway in the King's Road where the offices of Vernon McCullen were. It was a newish, grey building that housed a dozen companies,

.. om saw from the list of firms on a wall in the lobby. He kept on the lookout for a rather tall, slender woman with light brown straight hair, who would not be expecting him to be waiting for her. Or would she? Tom had a long wait. By twenty to 6, he was looking at his watch for perhaps the fifteenth time, tired of letting his eyes drift over the mainly exiting figures and faces, male and female, some looking tired, some laughing and exchanging chatter, as if glad one more day was past.

Tom lit a cigarette, his first since his vigil, because a cigarette often, in circumstances in which a cigarette was soon to be forbidden, such as the arrival of a bus one was waiting for, made things happen. Tom went into the foyer.

'Cynthia!'

There were four lifts, and Cynthia Gradnor had just emerged from the back right one. Tom dropped his cigarette, stepped on it, snatched it up and dropped it into one of the sand containers.

'Cynthia,' Tom said again, as she certainly hadn't heard him the first time.

She stopped short, and her straight hair swung a little at the sides. Her lips looked thinner, straighter than Tom recalled. 'I told you that I don't care to see you, Tom. Why do you *annoy* me like this?'

'I don't mean to annoy you. Just the opposite. But I would like just five minutes – ' Tom hesitated. 'Can't we sit down somewhere?' Tom had noticed that there were pubs nearby.

'No. No, thanks. What is it that's so vital?' Her grey eyes shot him a hostile look, then avoided his face.

'It's something about Bernard. I should think – well, that it would interest you.'

'What?' she said in almost a whisper. 'What about him? You've another unpleasant idea, I suppose.'

'No, the opposite,' Tom said, shaking his head. He had thought of David Pritchard: was anything, any idea, more unpleasant than Pritchard? Not to Tom, at the moment. He looked down again at Cynthia's flat black slippers, at her black stockings, Italian-style. Chic but also grim. 'I'm thinking of David Pritchard, who could do Bernard quite a bit of harm.'

'What do you mean? How?' Cynthia was jostled by a passer-by behind her.

Tom put his hand out to steady her, and Cynthia recoiled from him. 'It's hellish talking here,' Tom said. 'I mean, Pritchard means nobody any good, neither you, nor Bernard, nor – '

'Bernard is dead,' Cynthia said before Tom could utter the pronoun 'me'. 'The damage is done.' *Thanks to you*, she might have added.

'It isn't all done. I have to explain it – in two minutes. Can't we sit down somewhere? There's a place just around the corner!' Tom tried his best to be both polite and adamant.

With a sigh, Cynthia yielded, and they walked around the corner. It was not too big a pub, consequently not so noisy, and they even found a small round table. Tom didn't care when or if anyone came to wait on them, and he was sure Cynthia didn't.

'What is Pritchard up to?' Tom asked. 'Besides being a prowler – a Paul Pry – and I strongly suspect a sadist in regard to his wife?'

'Not, however, a murderer.'

'Oh? I'm glad to hear that. Are you writing to David Pritchard, talking with him on the telephone?'

Cynthia took a deep breath and blinked. 'I thought you had something to say about Bernard.'

Cynthia Gradnor was in pretty close touch with Pritchard, Tom thought, though perhaps she was wise enough not to put anything on paper. 'I have. Two things. I – but first, may I ask why you associate with such crud as Pritchard? He's sick in the head!' Tom gave a smile, sure of himself.

Cynthia said slowly, 'I don't care to talk about Pritchard – whom I've never seen or met, by the way.'

'Then how do you know his name?' Tom asked in a polite tone.

Again an inhalation; she glanced down at the table top, then looked back at Tom. Her face suddenly looked thinner and older. She was forty by now, Tom supposed.

'I don't care to answer that question,' Cynthia said. 'Can you get to the point? Something about Bernard, you said.'

'Yes. His work. I saw Pritchard and wife, you see, because they're my neighbours now – in France. Perhaps you know that. Pritchard mentioned Murchison – the man who strongly suspected forgeries.'

'And who mysteriously disappeared,' said Cynthia, attentive now.

'Yes. At Orly.'

She smiled a bit cynically. 'Just took a different plane? To where? Never got in touch again with his wife?' She paused. 'Come on, Tom. I know you did away with Murchison. You may have taken his luggage to Orly – '

Tom remained calm. 'Just ask my housekeeper, who saw us leave the house that day – saw Murchison and me. Heading for Orly.'

Cynthia probably had no instant rejoinder for what he had just said, Tom thought.

Tom stood up. 'What may I get you?'

'Dubonnet with a slice of lemon, please.'

Tom went to the bar, put in Cynthia's order and his for a gin and tonic, and after some three minutes was able to pay and carry the drinks away.

'Back to Orly,' Tom continued as he sat down. 'I remember I dropped Murchison at a kerb. I didn't park. We didn't stand having a stirrup cup.'

'I do not believe you.'

But Tom believed himself, now at any rate. He would go on believing, until any undeniable evidence was put in front of him. 'How do you know what his relationship with his wife was? How do I know?'

'I thought Mrs Murchison came to see you,' Cynthia said sweetly.

'She did. In Villeperce. We had tea at my house.'

'And did she say anything about a bad relationship between herself and her husband?'

'No, but why should she have? She came to see me because I was the last person who'd seen her husband – as far as anybody knows.'

'Yes,' said Cynthia smugly, as if she had information that Tom hadn't.

Well, if so, what was the information? He waited, and Cynthia didn't go on. Tom did. 'Mrs Murchison – I suppose – could bring up the forgery matter again. Any time. But when I saw her, she admitted that she didn't understand her husband's reasoning or his theory about the later Derwatts being forgeries.'

Now Cynthia pulled a packet of filter cigarettes from her handbag, and took one out delicately, as if she rationed them.

Tom extended his lighter. 'Do you hear anything from Mrs Murchison? In Long Island, I think it was?'

'No.' Cynthia shook her head slightly, calm still, and appearing uninterested.

Cynthia showed no sign of connecting him, Tom, with the telephone call from the French police asking Cynthia for Mrs Murchison's address. Or could Cynthia possibly be putting on a good act?

'I asked you that,' Tom continued, 'because – in case you're not aware – Pritchard is trying to make trouble in regard to

Murchison. Pritchard has it in for me especially. Very odd. He doesn't know beans about painting, certainly doesn't care about the arts – you should see the furniture in his house and the stuff on the *walls*!' Tom had to laugh. 'I was there for a drink. Not a friendly atmosphere.'

Cynthia reacted with a tiny, pleased smile, as Tom had expected. 'Why are you worried?'

Tom kept his pleasant expression. 'Not worried, annoyed. He took several photographs of my house, the exterior, one Sunday morning. Would you like that from a stranger, without a by your leave? Why does he want pictures of my house?'

Cynthia said nothing, and sipped her Dubonnet.

'Are you encouraging Pritchard in his anti-Ripley game?' Tom asked.

At that moment, the table behind Tom gave a clap of laughter like an explosion.

Cynthia hadn't flinched, as had Tom, but pushed a hand lazily against her hair, in which Tom now saw some grey. Tom tried to imagine her apartment – modern but with homey touches from her family, probably – an old bookcase, a quilt. Her clothes were good-looking and conservative. He dared not ask, was she happy. She'd sneer or throw her glass at him. Would she have a painting or a drawing by Bernard Tufts on a wall?

'Look, Tom, do you think I don't know that you killed Murchison and got rid of him – somehow? That – that it was Bernard who went over the cliff in Salzburg and whose body or ashes you passed off as *Derwatt's*?'

Tom was silent, silenced in the face of her intensity, at least for the moment.

'Bernard died for this rotten game,' she went on. '*Your* idea, the forgeries. You ruined his life – almost ruined mine. But what did you care as long as the paintings kept coming, signed Derwatt?'

Tom lit a cigarette. A prankster standing at the bar was banging his heel against the brass rail, laughing, adding to the noise. 'I never forced Bernard to paint – to keep painting,' Tom said softly, although they were out of anybody's hearing. 'That would've been beyond my powers, anybody's powers, you know that. I hardly knew Bernard when I suggested the forging. I asked Ed and Jeff if they knew anybody who might be able to do it.' Tom wasn't sure that was true, that he hadn't straight away suggested Bernard, because

Bernard's painting, what little Tom had seen of it, wasn't drastically different from or at odds with Derwatt's style. Tom went on, 'Bernard was more a friend of Ed's and Jeff's.'

'But you encouraged – all of it. *You* applauded!'

Now Tom was irked. Cynthia was only partly right. He was getting into enraged female territory, which scared Tom. Who could deal with it? 'Bernard could've quit any time, you know, quit painting Derwatts. He loved Derwatt as an artist. You mustn't forget the personal in all this – between Bernard and Derwatt. I – I honestly think what Bernard was doing was out of our hands finally – even pretty soon, when Bernard began assuming Derwatt's style.' Tom added with conviction, 'I'd like to know who could've stopped him.' Certainly Cynthia hadn't, he thought, and she'd known about Bernard's forging from the start, because she and Bernard had been very close, both living in London, and intending to marry.

Cynthia kept silent, and drew on her cigarette. Her cheeks looked hollow for an instant, like those of someone dead or ill.

Tom looked down at his drink. 'I know there's no love lost between you and me, Cynthia, so it doesn't matter to you how much Pritchard annoys me. But is he going to start talking about *Bernard*?' Again Tom had lowered his voice. 'Just to hit at me – it seems? It's absurd!'

Cynthia's gaze was fixed on him. 'Bernard? No. Whoever mentioned Bernard in all this? Who's going to bring him in now? Did Murchison even know his name? I don't think so. And what if he did? Murchison's dead. Did Pritchard mention Bernard?'

'Not to me,' Tom said. He watched her drink the last red drops in her glass, as if she were calling their meeting concluded. 'Would you have another?' he asked, glancing at her empty glass. 'I will if you will.'

'No, thank you.'

Tom tried to think, and fast. A pity that Cynthia knew – or was so convinced – that Bernard Tufts's name hadn't ever been mentioned in connection with the forgeries. Tom had uttered Bernard's name to Murchison (as Tom recalled) when trying to persuade Murchison to stop his forgery enquiry. But as Cynthia had said, Murchison was dead, because Tom had killed him a few seconds after that vain conversation. Tom could hardly appeal to Cynthia's desire – he assumed she had such a desire – to keep Bernard's name clean, if his name had never been mentioned in the newspapers. Still, he tried.

'You surely wouldn't want Bernard's name dragged in – in case loony Pritchard keeps on and learns it from someone.'

'From whom?' Cynthia asked. '*You?* Are you joking?'

'No!' Tom could see that she had taken his question as a threat. 'No,' he repeated, seriously. 'In fact, quite another – a happier turn of thought crossed my mind, if it came to attaching Bernard's name to the paintings.' Tom bit his underlip, and looked down at the humble glass ashtray, which made him recall his equally dismal conversation with Janice Pritchard in Fontainebleau, where the ashtray had held butts from strangers' cigarettes.

'And what's that?' Now Cynthia gathered her handbag, and sat up straight with an air of departure.

'That – Bernard was at this for so long – six, seven years? – that he developed and improved – and in a way became Derwatt.'

'Didn't you say this before? Or was it Jeff repeating to me what you'd said?' Cynthia was unimpressed.

Tom persisted. 'More important – what would the catastrophe be, if the last half or more of Derwatt productions were revealed as those of Bernard Tufts? Are they worse as paintings? I'm not talking about the value of good forgeries – in the news these days, and even a fad or a new industry. I'm talking about Bernard as a painter who developed *from* Derwatt – went on, I mean.'

Cynthia stirred restlessly, almost stood up. 'You never seem to realize – you and Ed and Jeff also – that Bernard was most unhappy with what he was doing. It broke *us* up. I – ' She shook her head.

The table behind Tom was on a roar again, wild laughter. How could he state to Cynthia, in the next half-minute, that Bernard had also loved and respected his work, even when doing 'forgeries'? What Cynthia objected to was the dishonesty in Bernard's trying to imitate Derwatt's style.

'Artists have their destinies,' Tom said. 'Bernard had his. I did my best to – to keep him alive. He was at my house, you know, I talked with him – before he went off to Salzburg. Bernard was confused at the end, thinking he'd betrayed Derwatt – somehow.' Tom moistened his lips, quickly drank the last of his glass. 'I said, "Very well, Bernard, quit the forgeries, but shake off the depression." I kept hoping he'd speak with you again, that you two would get back – ' Tom stopped.

Cynthia looked at him with thin lips parted. 'Tom, you are the most evil man I've ever met – if you consider that a favourable distinction. You probably do.'

'No.' Tom got up, because Cynthia was rising from her chair, throwing her handbag strap over one shoulder.

Tom followed her out, knowing she would be delighted to say goodbye as soon as possible. Tom judged from the address in the telephone book that she might be able to walk to her flat from here, if she was going there, and he was sure she did not want him to accompany her to the door. Tom had the feeling that she was living alone.

'Goodbye, Tom. Thank you for the drink,' Cynthia said when they were outside.

'A pleasure,' Tom replied.

Then suddenly he was alone, facing the King's Road, then turning again to watch Cynthia's tall figure in the beige sweater disappear among the others on the pavement. Why hadn't he asked more questions? What did she intend to get out of egging Pritchard on? Why hadn't he asked her outright if she telephoned the Pritchards? Because Cynthia wouldn't have answered, Tom thought. Or if Cynthia had ever met Mrs Murchison?

13

Tom got a taxi, after several minutes' effort, and asked the driver please to aim for Covent Garden, and gave Ed's address. Seven twenty-two by Tom's watch. His eyes jumped from shop sign to rooftop, to a pigeon, to a dachshund on a lead crossing the King's Road. The driver had to turn and head in the other direction. He was thinking, if he had asked Cynthia if she was in frequent touch with Pritchard, she might have replied with her catlike smile: 'Certainly not. What's the need?'

And this might have meant that a type like Pritchard would keep going under his own momentum, without even further ammo, though she'd given him some, because he had decided to hate Tom Ripley.

Tom was pleased to find both Jeff Constant and Ed Banbury in the flat when he arrived.

'How was your *day?*' asked Ed. 'What did you do? Besides buying me that handsome dressing-gown. I showed it to Jeff.'

They were in the room where Ed's typewriter and desk lived, plus a telephone.

'Oh, I – looked in at the Buckmaster this morning, talked with Nick, whom I like more and more.'

'Isn't he nice,' said Ed, rather mechanically in his English way.

'First, Ed, are there any telephone messages for me? I gave your number to Héloïse, you know.'

'No, I checked when I came in around half-past four,' Ed replied. 'If you want to try Héloïse now – '

Tom smiled. 'Casablanca? At this hour?' But Tom was a bit worried, thinking of Meknès or perhaps Marrakesh next, inland towns that evoked visions of sand, distant horizons, camels that walked with ease while men sank in the softness which in Tom's imagination took on the evil powers of quicksand. Tom blinked.

'I'll – maybe try her late again tonight, if that's all right with you, Ed.'

'My house is your house!' said Ed. 'Like a gin and tonic, Tom?'

'In a minute, thanks. I saw Cynthia today.' Tom saw Jeff's attention focus.

'Where? And how?' Jeff gave a laugh on the last question.

'Stood in wait outside her office building. Six o'clock,' Tom said. 'With some difficulty, I persuaded her to join me for a glass at a local pub.'

'*Really*!' said Ed, impressed.

Tom sat down in the one armchair to which Ed had gestured. Jeff looked comfortable on Ed's slightly sagging sofa. 'She hasn't changed. She's pretty grim. But – '

'Relax, Tom,' said Ed. 'Back in a flash.' He went off to the kitchen, and was indeed back in a flash with an iceless gin and tonic with a slice of lemon.

Meanwhile Jeff had asked, 'Is she married – do you think?' Jeff was serious, but he looked as if he realized that Cynthia would not have answered yes or no, if Tom had posed the question.

'I have the feeling no. Just a feeling,' Tom said, and accepted his glass. 'I thank you, Ed. Well, it seems to be *my* problem and not yours – either of you – and not the Buckmaster Gallery's or – Derwatt's.' Tom lifted his drink. 'Cheers.'

'Cheers,' they echoed.

'By problem, I mean, Cynthia having got a message through to Pree-chard – whom she says she's never met, by the way – to try to investigate the Murchison business. That's what I mean by *my* problem.' Tom grimaced. 'Pritchard is still in my neighbourhood. At least his wife is, at this moment.'

'What can he do – or she, exactly?' Jeff asked.

Tom said, 'Heckle me. Keep on ingratiating himself with Cynthia. Find Murchison's corpse. Ha! But – at least Miss Gradnor does *not* seem to want to spill the beans about the forgeries.' Tom sipped his drink.

'Does Pritchard know about Bernard?' Jeff asked.

'I'd say no,' Tom replied. 'Cynthia said, "Who said anything about Bernard in all this?" Meaning nobody has. She's got a defensive attitude about Bernard – thanks be to God, and lucky for all of us!' Tom leaned back in the comfortable chair. 'In fact – I tried again to do the impossible.' As he had with Murchison, Tom thought, tried and failed. 'I asked Cynthia, quite seriously, weren't

Bernard's paintings at the last as good as or better than what Derwatt might have produced? Also in Derwatt's same style? What's the horror if the name Derwatt were to be changed to Tufts?'

'Oof,' Jeff said, and rubbed his forehead.

'I can't see it,' said Ed, arms folded. He was standing at the end of the sofa where Jeff sat. 'As to the value of the paintings, I can't see it – as to their *quality* though – '

'Which ought to be the same thing but isn't,' said Jeff with a glance at Ed, and gave a mocking laugh.

'True,' Ed conceded. 'Did you talk with *Cynthia* about this?' he asked, looking a bit worried.

'N-not profoundly,' Tom said. 'More a rhetorical question or two. I was trying to take the steam out of her attack, if she had any, but in fact she hadn't. She told me that I'd ruined Bernard's life and almost ruined hers. True, I suppose.' Now Tom rubbed his forehead and stood up. 'Mind if I go wash my hands?'

Tom went to the bathroom between his library-bedroom and Ed's bedroom. He was thinking of Héloïse, wondering what she was doing now, wondering if Pritchard had followed her and Noëlle to Casablanca.

'What other threats, Tom – from Cynthia?' Ed asked in a soft voice, when Tom came back. 'Or hints of threats?'

Ed had almost grimaced as he spoke: he had never been able to handle Cynthia, Tom knew. Cynthia made people uncomfortable sometimes, because she had an air, always, of being undisturbed by and somehow above anything and everything anyone else might think or do. Towards Tom and his Buckmaster Gallery associates, of course, she had shown frank contempt. But the fact remained, Cynthia had not been able to persuade Bernard to stop his forging, and she had presumably tried.

'None, I think, that she stated,' Tom said finally. 'She enjoys knowing that Pritchard is annoying me. She's going to help him do that, if she can.'

'She talks with him?' asked Jeff.

'On the telephone? I dunno,' Tom said. 'Maybe. Since Cynthia's in the book, it's easy for Pritchard to telephone – if he wants to.' Tom was thinking, what else, what of import could Cynthia give Pritchard, if she wasn't going to betray the forgeries? 'Perhaps Cynthia wants to annoy us – all of us – just because she *could* spill the beans any time she wishes.'

135

'But you said she didn't give a hint of that,' said Jeff.

'No, but then Cynthia wouldn't,' Tom replied.

'No,' Ed echoed. 'Think of the publicity,' he added softly, as if musing, and his tone was earnest.

Was Ed thinking about unfavourable publicity for Cynthia, or for Bernard Tufts and the gallery, or all three? At any rate, horrid it would be, Tom thought, not least because it would be provable not by analysis of canvases but by absence of provenance records, and the already only half-explained disappearances of Derwatt, Murchison *and* Bernard Tufts would add weight.

Jeff's sizeable chin lifted, and he smiled his wide and easy-going smile that Tom hadn't seen for a long time. 'Unless we could prove that we knew nothing about the forgeries.' He said it with laughter, as if of course it was impossible.

'Yes, if we were not chummy with Bernard Tufts, and he never came to the Buckmaster Gallery,' said Ed. 'In fact, he never did come to the gallery.'

'We dump the blame entirely on Bernard,' said Jeff, more soberly now but still smiling.

'Won't hold water,' Tom said, pondering what he had heard. He drained his glass. 'My second thought is, Cynthia would tear our throats out with her fingernails, if we dumped the blame on Bernard. I shudder to contemplate it!' Tom laughed loudly.

'Ho-ow *true!*' said Ed Banbury, smiling at the black humour of it. 'But then – how could she prove we were lying? If Bernard had been sending his stuff from his London atelier – and not from Mexico – '

'Or would he take the trouble to get it sent from Mexico so we'd believe the postal labels?' asked Jeff, his face alight with the joy of fantasy.

'At the prices of those paintings,' Tom put in, 'Bernard might have taken the trouble to post them from China! Especially with the aid of a pal.'

'A *pal!*' Jeff said, raising a forefinger. 'We've got it! The pal's the culprit, we can't find the pal, neither can Cynthia! Ha-ha!'

They guffawed again. It was a relief.

'Nonsense,' Tom said, and stretched his legs out. Were his friends possibly tossing him 'a thought' to play with, by which playing all three of them and the gallery might free themselves of Cynthia's veiled threats and all past sins? If so, the pal idea was not viable. Tom was really thinking of Héloïse again, and of trying Mrs

Murchison while in London. What could he ask Mrs Murchison? Logically, plausibly? As Tom Ripley, or as the French police, as he'd successfully done with Cynthia? Would Cynthia already have rung Mrs Murchison to say that the French police had wanted her address? Tom doubted that. Though Mrs Murchison would be easier to fool than Cynthia, it was wise to be careful. Pride goeth before a fall. Tom wanted to know if busybody Preechard had spoken recently or ever with Mrs Murchison by telephone. Well, Tom wanted to know that mainly, but he could ring on the pretence of checking her address and telephone number, in regard to the quest for her husband. No, he'd have to pose a question of some kind: did she know where M'sieur Preechard was at this minute, because ze police had lost him in North Africa, and M'sieur Preechard was aiding them in regard to her husband.

'Tom?' Jeff took a step toward Tom, extending a bowl of pistachios.

'Thank you. May I have several? I love them,' Tom said.

'As many as you want, Tom,' said Ed. 'Here's the waste-paper basket for the shells.'

'I've just thought of something obvious,' Tom said, 're Cynthia.'

'And what's that?' asked Jeff.

'Cynthia can't have it both ways. She can't tease us or Pritchard by asking "Where's Murchison?" without admitting there was a reason to get rid of him, namely to shut him up about the forging. If Cynthia keeps on, she'll – expose the fact that Bernard was doing the forging, and I think she doesn't want to expose Bernard to *anything*. Not even to having been exploited.'

The others were silent for a few seconds.

'Cynthia knows Bernard was an odd one. We exploited him, his talents, I grant you.' Tom added musingly, 'Would she ever have married him?'

'Yes,' said Ed, nodding. 'I think so. She's the motherly type, underneath it all.'

'*Motherly*!' Sitting on the couch, Jeff laughed, and his feet left the floor. 'Cynthia!'

'All women are, don't you think?' said Ed, earnestly. 'I think they'd have married. That's one reason why Cynthia is so sore.'

Tom shook his head quickly to clear it, and munched another salty pistachio.

'Is anyone interested in food?' Jeff asked.

'Oh – yes,' Ed replied. 'I know a place – no, that's Islington.

There's another good place near here, different from last night, Tom.'

'I want to try Madame Murcheeson,' Tom said, getting up from his chair. 'New York, you know. Might be a good time, if she's in for lunch.'

'Go ahead,' said Ed. 'Want to use the phone in the living-room? Or here?'

Tom knew he looked as if he wanted to be alone, frowning and a bit nervous. 'Living-room, fine.'

Ed gestured, and Tom pulled his little notebook out.

'Make yourself at home,' Ed said, and set a chair near the telephone.

Tom stayed on his feet. He dialled the Manhattan number, and rehearsed himself silently for the French police officer's introduction of himself, Edouard Bilsault, Commissaire, Paris – and thank God he had noted the unlikely name under Mrs Murchison's address and telephone number, or he might not have remembered it. This time, he might make his accent not so pronounced, but rather like Maurice Chevalier's.

Unfortunately, Mrs Murchison was not at home but was due back at any minute, said a female voice, of a type Tom thought could belong to a servant or cleaning woman, though he was not sure of this, and so kept up his French accent with care.

'Weel you zay, please, zat I – Commissaire Bilsault – non-non, no need to write – weel ring again – tonight – or tomorrow . . . Zank you, madame.'

No need to say that the telephone call had been in regard to Thomas Murchison, because Mrs Murchison would guess that. Tom supposed he should try later tonight, as the lady was expected back so soon.

Tom was not sure what he should ask her, if he got her on the telephone: had she heard from David Pritchard, of course, with whom for the moment the French police had lost touch. Tom fully expected a 'No, I haven't' when he posed this question, but still he ought to pose something, or state something, because Mrs Murchison and Cynthia just might be in touch, at least now and then. He had no sooner entered Ed's study or workroom, when the desk telephone rang.

Ed answered. 'Oh – yes! Oui! Just a moment! Tom! It's Héloïse!'

'Oh!' said Tom, and took the instrument. 'Hello, my dear!'

138

''Allo, *Tome*!'

'Where are you?'

'We are in Casablanca. Ver-ry breezy – nice! And – what do you know? This Mister Preechard has turned up? We arrived at one in the afternoon – and he must have come very soon later. He must have found out our hotel, because – '

'Is he in the *same* hotel? The Miramare?' asked Tom, impotent and livid, squeezing the telephone.

'*Non*! But he – *looked* in here. He saw us, Noëlle and me. But he did not see you, we could see him looking around. Now Tome – '

'Yes, my sweet?'

'Zis was seex hours ago! Now – Noëlle and I looked around. We telephoned a hotel, two hotels, he is not in them. We think he has departed because you are not with us.'

Tom was still frowning. 'I'm not so sure. How can you be sure?'

There was a conclusive click, as if they had been cut off by some malicious hand. Tom took a deep breath, and refrained from uttering a four-letter word.

Then Héloïse's voice came back, speaking more calmly, through oceanic noises: ' . . . is now the evening and we don't see him anywhere. Of course it is disgusting that he follows us. *Le salaud*!'

Tom was thinking that Pritchard might have returned to Ville-perce by now, believing that he, Tom, had also returned. 'You should still be careful,' Tom said. 'This Pritchard is full of tricks. Don't trust even any stranger who may say, "Come with me – " somewhere. Even into a shop, for example. You understand?'

'Oui, mon cher. But now – we go around just in daytime, look and buy little things of leather, brass. Don't worry, Tome. Just the opposite! It is fun here. Hey! Noëlle wants to say a word.'

Tom was often startled by Héloïse's 'Hey!' but it sounded homely tonight, and made him smile. 'Hello, Noëlle. It seems you are having a good time in Casablanca?'

'Ah, Tome, wonderful! It has been three years since I was in Casablanca, I think, but I remember the port so well – a better port than Tangier, you know? Much bigger here . . . '

Sea-like noises swelled, drowned her voice. 'Noëlle?'

' . . . not to have seen this monster for several hours is a *pleasure*,' Noëlle continued in French, apparently unaware of the interruption.

'Preechard, you mean,' Tom said.

'Preechard, oui! C'est atroce! Cette histoire de kidnapping!'

'Oui, il est atroce!' Tom said, as if echoing the French words could confirm David Pritchard as insane, a figure to be hated by all mankind, and put behind bars. Alas, Pritchard wasn't behind bars. 'You know, Noëlle, I may go to Villeperce very soon, tomorrow, because Pritchard *may* be there – causing some kind of trouble. May I try to check with you tomorrow?'

'But of course. Say, midday? We can be here,' Noëlle replied.

'Don't worry if you don't hear from me, because daytime phoning is difficult.' Tom verified the Miramare number with Noëlle, who in her efficient way had it handy. 'You know Héloïse – she sometimes isn't worried *enough*, when situations are dangerous. I do not wish her to walk out in the street alone, Noëlle, even in daylight to buy a newspaper.'

'I understand, Tome,' said Noëlle in English, 'and here it is so easy to *hire* somebody to do anyzing!'

Horrid thought, but Tom said gratefully, 'Yes! Even if Preechard has gone back to France.' Tom added in coarse French, 'Wish to hell he'd drag his' – Tom had to leave it unsaid – 'out of our village.'

Noëlle laughed. 'Till tomorrow, Tome!'

Tom again pulled out his notebook with the Murchison number in it. He realized that he was seething with anger against Pritchard. He picked up the telephone and dialled.

Mrs Murchison answered, or so Tom thought.

Tom introduced himself once more: Commissaire Edouard Bilsault in Paris. Was this Madame Murcheeson? Yes. Tom was prepared to give precinct and arrondissement, made up on the spot, if need be. Tom was also curious to know – if he could gracefully learn it – if Cynthia had already tried to ring Mrs Murchison this evening.

Tom cleared his throat, and pitched his voice higher. 'Madame, this concerns your 'usband who ees missing. We are at the moment not able to find David *Preechard*. We are recently in touch with 'eem – but M'sieur Preechard went to Tanger – did you know zat?'

'Oh, yes,' Mrs Murchison said calmly, in her civilized voice that Tom now recalled. 'He said he might go, because Mr Ripley was going there – with his wife, I believe.'

'Oui. Exact, madame. You 'ave not 'eard from Meester Preechard since he was in Tanger?'

'No.'

'Or from Madame Cynthia Gradnor? I believe she ees also in touch weet you?'

'Yes, lately – she writes or telephones me. But not in regard to anybody in Tangier. I can't help you there.'

'I zee. Zank you, madame.'

'I don't – um-m – know what Mr Pritchard is doing in Tangier. Did you suggest that he go? Is it the idea of the French police, I mean?'

It was the idea of a loony, Tom thought, loony Pritchard to follow Ripley, not even to assassinate but to heckle. 'No, madame, eet is M'sieur Preechard who wanted to follow M'sieur Reepley to – Afrique du Nord, not our idée. But usually 'e ees in better touch with us.'

'But – what is the news about my husband? Are there any new facts?'

Tom sighed, and heard a couple of New York cars honk outside an open window near Mrs Murchison. 'None, madame, I am sorry to report. But we try. Ees a delicate situation, madame, because M'sieur Reepley ees a respected man where 'e leeves and we 'ave *nozzing* against M'sieur Reepley. Ees M'sieur Preechard who 'as his own idées – wheech of course we note, but – you understand, Madame Murcheeson?' Tom continued in a polite tone, but slowly drew the telephone away, so that his voice would fade. He made a sucking noise, a gurgle, and hung up, as if they'd been cut off.

Whew! It had not been as bad as Tom had feared, not dangerous at all, he thought. But Cynthia definitely in touch! He hoped it would be the last time he had to ring Mrs Murchison.

Tom then went back to the typewriter room, where Ed and Jeff showed signs of readiness to depart for dinner. He had decided not to ring Mme Annette tonight but tomorrow morning after her shopping hour, which he was sure hadn't changed. Mme Annette would know from her faithful sentinel – Geneviève, wasn't it? – whether M. Preechard had returned to Villeperce or not.

'Well,' Tom said, smiling. 'I spoke with Madame Murcheeson. And – '

'We thought it best not to hover, Tom.' Jeff looked interested.

'Preechard has been in touch enough to let Mrs Murchison know he went to Tangier. Imagine! I gather one telephone call did that. And she told me Cynthia rings or writes – sometimes. Bad enough, isn't it?'

'All in touch, you mean,' said Ed. 'Yes – rather.'

'Let's go out and get something to eat,' Tom said.

'Tom – Ed and I've been talking,' Jeff began. 'One or the other of us or both will come over to France and help you – versus this' – Jeff sought a word – 'obsessed nut Pritchard.'

'Or to Tangier,' Ed Banbury put in promptly. 'Wherever you have to go, Tom. Or wherever we're useful. We're all in this together, you know.'

Tom let it sink in. It was comforting, indeed. 'Thanks. I shall think – or zink – about what I or we must do. Let's go out, shall we?'

14

Tom didn't think too hard about his current problems while having dinner with Jeff and Ed. They had finally taken a taxi to a place Jeff knew of in the Little Venice area, quiet and small. It was indeed so quiet and unpatronized that evening that Tom kept his voice low, even when talking of innocent matters like cooking.

Ed said he had been giving some attention to his neglected cooking talents, if any, and next time he would venture to cook for both of them.

'Tomorrow evening? Tomorrow lunch?' asked Jeff, smiling incredulously.

'I've got a little book called *The Imaginative Cook*,' Ed went on. 'It encourages combining things and – '

'Left-overs?' Jeff lifted a piece of asparagus, with butter dripping from it, and put the tip into his mouth.

'Have your fun,' Ed said. 'But next time, I swear.'

'But you're not game for tomorrow,' said Jeff.

'How do I know Tom's here tomorrow night? Does Tom know?'

'No,' said Tom. He had espied, a couple of (empty) tables away, a very pretty young woman with fair straight hair, talking to a young man opposite her. She wore a black sleeveless dress, gold earrings, and had that happy self-assurance that Tom seldom saw outside of England and the kind of good looks that made his eyes keep drifting toward her. The young woman had made him think about a present for Héloïse. Gold earrings? Absurd! How many pairs had Héloïse already? A bracelet? Héloïse liked a surprise, even a small one, when he came back from a trip. And when would Héloïse be back home?

Ed glanced to see what fascinated Tom.

'Pretty, is she not?' said Tom.

'Is – she – not,' Ed agreed. 'Look, Tom – I could be free at the end of this week. Or even by Thursday – two days from now – to go

143

to France – or anywhere. I have an article to polish up and type. I'll hurry, if necessary. If you're in straits.'

Tom didn't reply at once.

'And no word-processor for Ed,' Jeff put in. 'Ed's the old-fashioned type.'

'*I* am a word-processor,' said Ed. 'How about your old cameras, for that matter? *Some* of them are old.'

'And they're excellent,' Jeff said quietly.

Tom saw that Ed stifled a retort to this. Tom was enjoying delicious lamb chops, and a good red wine. 'Ed, old pal, I am most grateful,' Tom said in a low voice, glancing to his left, where beyond one empty table, the next table now had three people.'Because you could get hurt. Mind you, I don't know exactly how, because I haven't seen Pritchard with a gun, for instance.' Tom lowered his head and said as if to himself, 'I may have to tackle the son of a bitch hand to hand. Really finish him, I dunno.'

His words hung in the air.

'I'm pretty strong,' Jeff said in a cheerful tone. 'You may need that, Tom.'

Jeff Constant was probably stronger than Ed, Tom thought, because he was taller and heavier. On the other hand, Ed looked as if he could be fast-moving, if necessary. 'We must all keep in condition, n'est-ce pas? Now who's for a nice gooey dessert?'

Jeff wanted to pay the bill. Tom invited them to a Calvados.

'Who knows when we'll meet again – like this?' Tom said.

The proprietress told them that the Calvados was on the house.

Tom awakened to the sound of rain pattering against the window panes, not hard but determined. He put on his new dressing-gown, price tag still dangling, washed in the bathroom, and went to Ed's kitchen. It seemed Ed was not yet up. Tom boiled some water, and made a filter coffee for himself, strong. Then a quick shower and a shave, and Tom was tying his tie when Ed surfaced.

'Lovely day! God morning!' Ed said, smiling. 'You see I'm sporting the new dressing-gown.'

'I see.' Tom's mind was on ringing Mme Annette, and the happy thought that it was an hour later in France, and that in about twenty minutes she might be back from shopping. 'I made coffee, if you'd like some. What'll I do with my bed?'

'Make it for the time being. Then we'll see.' Ed went on to the kitchen.

Tom was glad that Ed knew him well enough to know that he would either want to make the bed or take the sheets off, and to say make the bed was a welcome to stay another night, if need be. Ed put some croissants into the oven for warming, and there was also orange juice. Tom drank the juice, but was too tense to eat anything.

'I'm supposed to ring Héloïse at noon, or try to,' Tom said. 'Forgot if I told you.'

'You're most welcome, as ever, to my telephone.'

Tom was thinking that he might not be here at noon. 'Thank you. We'll see.' Then Tom jumped at the sound of Ed's telephone ringing.

After a few words from Ed, Tom knew it was a business call, something about a caption.

'Okay, sure, easy,' Ed said. 'I've got the carbon here . . . I'll ring you back before eleven. No problem.'

Tom looked at his watch, and saw that the minute hand had hardly moved since the last time he had glanced at it. He was thinking that he might borrow an umbrella from Ed and spend some of this morning walking about, and perhaps look in at the Buckmaster Gallery to choose a drawing for possible purchase. A drawing by Bernard Tufts.

Ed was back, silent, and he headed for the coffee pot.

'I'll try my house now,' Tom said, and got up from the kitchen chair.

In the living-room, Tom dialled the Belle Ombre number, and let it ring eight times, then twice more before he gave it up.

'She's out shopping. Maybe gossiping,' Tom added to Ed with a smile. But Mme Annette was growing a bit deaf, too, he had noticed.

'Try later, Tom. I'm getting dressed.' Ed went off.

Tom did in a very few minutes, and Mme Annette answered on the fifth ring.

'Ah, M'sieur *Tome*! Where are you?'

'London still, madame. And I spoke with Madame Héloïse yesterday. She is well. In Casablanca.'

'Casablanca! And when is she coming home?'

Tom laughed. 'How can I say? I am telephoning to ask how things are at Belle Ombre.' Tom knew Mme Annette would report a prowler, if any, or M. Pritchard and by name, if he had possibly had time to return and snoop.

'All goes well, M'sieur Tome. Henri was not here, but all the same.'

145

'And do you know by chance if M'sieur Preechard is at home in Villeperce?'

'Not yet, m'sieur, he has been away, but he returns today. I have just learned that from Geneviève this morning in the bakery, and she learned it from the wife of M'sieur Hubert the electrician, who did some work for Madame Preechard only this morning.'

'Really,' Tom said, with respect for Mme Annette's information service. 'Returns today.'

'Oh, yes, that is sure,' said Mme Annette calmly, as if she were talking about the sun rising or setting.

'I shall telephone again before – before – well, before I go anywhere else, Madame Annette. Now, you keep well yourself!' He signed off, then gave a great sigh.

Tom thought he should go back home today, so booking his reservation for the return to Paris was his next job. He went to his bed and began removing the sheets, when he bethought himself of the possibility that he might return before Ed had a next guest, so he remade the bed as it was.

'I thought you'd finished that,' said Ed, entering the room.

Tom explained. 'Old Preekhard's coming back to Villeperce today. So I'll meet him there next. And if need be, I'll lure him to London, where' – Tom threw a smile at Ed, because he was talking fantasy now – 'the streets are numerous and dark at night, and Jack the Ripper did all right, didn't he? What he'd – ' Tom paused.

'What he'd what?'

'What Pritchard would get out of ruining me, I don't know. Sadistic satisfaction, I suppose. Or out of exposing the Murchison story. He might not be able to prove anything, you know, Ed? But it would look bad for me. Then if he managed to kill me, he could see Héloïse an unhappy widow, going back to Paris to live, perhaps, as I can't see her living in our house alone – or even marrying another man and living there.'

'Tom, stop your dreaming!'

Tom stretched his arms, trying to relax. 'I don't understand cracked people.' But he had understood Bernard Tufts fairly well, he realized. And with Bernard he had lost, in the sense that he had not been able to stop Bernard from killing himself. 'Now I'll see about a plane, if I may, Ed.'

Tom rang up the Air France reservation, and found he could get on a flight leaving Heathrow at 13.40 that afternoon. Tom so informed Ed.

'I shall take my knapsack and drift off,' Tom said.

Ed was about to sit down at his typewriter, and had some work laid out on his desk. 'I'll be hoping to see you soon, Tom. I loved seeing you here. My thoughts will be with you.'

'Are there any Derwatt drawings for sale? I gathered that in principle they're not for sale.'

Ed Banbury smiled. 'We are hanging on – but for you – '

'How many are there? And at what price – about?'

'Fifty or so? Prices maybe from two thousand up to – fifteen, perhaps. Some Bernard Tufts's, of course. If they're *good* drawings, the price goes higher. Doesn't always depend on size.'

'I'd pay the normal price, of course. Be happy to.'

Ed almost laughed. 'If you're fond of a drawing, Tom, you deserve it as a gift! Who gets the profit after all, finally? All three of us!'

'I may have time to look into the gallery today. Haven't you anything here?' Tom asked, as if Ed must have.

'One in my bedroom, if you want to have a look.'

They went to the room at the end of the short hall. Ed lifted a framed drawing which had been leaning, face inward, against his chest of drawers. The *conte* and charcoal drawing showed vertical and slanting lines that might have depicted an easel, and behind it a suggestion of a figure just a bit taller than the easel. Was it a Tufts or a Derwatt?

'Nice.' Tom narrowed his eyes, opened them, advanced. 'What's it called?'

'"Easel in Studio",' Ed replied. 'I love the warm orangey-red. Just these two lines to indicate the size of the room. Typical.' He added, 'I don't hang it all the time – just six months out of the year perhaps – so it's fresh to me.'

The drawing was nearly thirty inches high, maybe twenty broad, in an appropriately grey and neutral frame.

'Bernard's?' Tom asked.

'It's a Derwatt. I bought it years ago – for absurdly little. I think about forty pounds. Forgot where I found it! He did it in London. Look at the hand.' Ed extended his right hand in the same position towards the painting.

In the drawing, the right hand with an indication of a slender brush in the fingers was extended. The painter was approaching the easel, left foot delineated by a stroke of dark grey for the shoe sole.

'Man going to work,' said Ed. 'It gives me courage, this picture.'

'I understand.' Tom turned in the doorway. 'I'm off to see the drawings – then a taxi to Heathrow. My thanks, Ed, for your kindnesses here.'

Tom collected his raincoat and small suitcase. Under his key on the night table he had left two twenty-pound notes for telephone calls, which Ed might find today or tomorrow.

'Shall I make it definite when I arrive?' Ed asked. 'Such as tomorrow? You've only to say the word, Tom.'

'Let me see how things look. Maybe I'll ring you tonight. And don't worry if I don't ring. I should be home by seven or eight this evening – if all goes well.'

They shook hands firmly at the door.

Tom walked to what looked like a promising taxi-flagging corner, and when he got one asked the driver to go to Old Bond Street.

This time, Nick was alone when Tom arrived, and got up from a desk where he had been looking at a Sotheby's catalogue.

'Good morning, Nick,' said Tom pleasantly. 'I am back – for another look at the Derwatt drawings. Is that possible?'

Nick drew himself up, smiled, as if he considered this request something special. 'Yes, sir – this way, as you know.'

Tom liked the first Nick pulled out, a sketch of a pigeon on a window sill, which had a few of Derwatt's extra outlines that suggested a shifting of the alert bird. The paper, yellowish but originally off-white and of fair quality, was nevertheless deteriorating at the edges, but Tom liked that. The drawing was in charcoal and *conte*, under transparent plastic now.

'And the price of this?'

'Um – Maybe ten thousand, sir. I would have to verify that.'

Tom was looking at another in the portfolio, a busy restaurant interior, which did not appeal to him, then a pair of trees and a bench in what looked like a London park. No, the pigeon. 'If I make a down payment – and you speak with Mr Banbury?'

Tom signed a cheque for two thousand pounds, and handed it to Nick at the desk. 'A pity it's not signed by Derwatt. Just not signed,' Tom said, interested in what Nick might reply.

'Well – y-yes, sir,' Nick answered pleasantly, almost rocking back on his heels. 'That was Derwatt, I've heard. Makes a sketch on the spur of the moment, doesn't think of signing it, forgets to do it later, and then he's – no longer with us.'

Tom nodded. 'True. Bye-bye, Nick. Mr Banbury has my address.'

'Oh, yes, sir, no problem.'

Then Heathrow, which looked to Tom more crowded every time he saw it. The cleaning women with brooms and bins on wheels apparently could not keep up with the dropped paper napkins and discarded flight-ticket envelopes. Tom had time to buy a box of six kinds of English soap for Héloïse, and a bottle of Pernod for Belle Ombre.

And when would he next see Héloïse?

Tom bought a gossip sheet, a newspaper he would not get on the aeroplane. In his first-class seat, Tom took a nap after a lobster lunch with white wine, and awakened only when the stewardess asked for seatbelts to be fastened. The neat pale green and darker green-and-brown patchwork of French fields had spread itself below. The plane tilted. Tom felt much fortified, ready for anything – almost. It had occurred to him in London that morning to make a trip to the newspaper archives, wherever that was, to look up David Pritchard, as Janice Pritchard had said Pritchard had done in the United States re Tom Ripley. But what would be on record about David Pritchard, if that was his real name? Misdemeanours of a spoilt adolescence? Tickets for speeding? A drug offence at eighteen? Hardly worthy of being on record, even in America, and of no interest in England or France. Still, curious to think that Pritchard *might* be on the books for torturing a dog to death at the age of fifteen, some horrid little nugget like that just might have turned up in London, if the computers ground exceeding small and copied it. Tom braced himself as the plane landed, smoothly, and began to brake. His own record – well, a list of interesting suspicions might sum it up. No convictions, however.

After passport control, Tom went to the next available telephone booth, and rang home.

Mme Annette answered on the eighth ring. 'Ah, M'sieur *Tome*! Où êtes-vous?'

'Roissy airport. I can be home in two hours with luck. Is all well?'

Tom ascertained that all was well and as usual.

Then a taxi homewards. He was too eager to get home to worry about the driver being interested in his address. The day was warm and sunny, and Tom opened the taxi windows a slit on both sides, hoping the driver would not complain of a *courant d'air*, which the French were apt to do at the mildest of breezes. Tom mused about London, the young man Nick, the readiness of Jeff and Ed to help, in case of need. And what was Janice Pritchard doing? How much

149

did she assist her husband, cover for him, and how much did she tease him about just such matters? Stand him up and let him down when he needed her? Janice was the loose cannon, Tom thought, an absurd term for someone as frail as she.

Mme Annette's ears were good enough for her to hear the taxi's wheels on the gravel, because she had opened the front door and was on the stone porch before the taxi came to a halt. Tom paid the driver, tipped him, and carried his case to the door.

'Non, non, I shall carry it!' Tom said. 'This tiny weight?'

Mme Annette's old habits never died, habits such as still wanting to carry the heaviest of cases, because a housekeeper should.

'Did Madame Héloïse telephone?'

'Non, m'sieur.'

That was good news, Tom thought. He entered the front hall and inhaled its smell of old rose petal, or something similar, but without the lavender-wax smell just now, which reminded him that he did have the wax in his suitcase.

'A tea, M'sieur Tome? Or a café? A drink with ice?' She was hanging up his raincoat.

Tom hesitated, walked into the living-room and glanced out of the french windows on to the garden lawn. 'Well, yes, a café. And no doubt a drink too.' It was just past 7. 'I think I'll take a quick shower first.'

'Oui, m'sieur. Ah! Madame Berthelin has telephoned. Last evening. I told her that you and madame were away.'

'Thank you,' said Tom. The Berthelins, Jacqueline and Vincent, were neighbours who lived a few kilometres away in another town. 'Thank you, I'll telephone her,' said Tom, walking towards the stairs. 'No other phone calls?'

'N-non, je croix que non.'

'I'll be down in ten minutes. Oh, first – ' Tom set his suitcase flat on the floor, opened it and extracted the tins of wax in their plastic bag. 'A present for the house, madame.'

'Ah, cirage de lavande! Toujours le bienvenu! Merci!'

Tom was down again in ten minutes, in a change of clothing and in sneakers. He elected to drink a small Calvados with his café, just for a change. Mme Annette hovered, ascertaining if what she had prepared for dinner would be satisfactory, though it always was. Her description went in one of Tom's ears and out the other, because he was thinking of ringing Janice Pritchard, the loose cannon.

'That sounds most tempting,' Tom said politely. 'I only wish

Madame Héloïse were here to join me.'

'And when is Madame Héloïse returning?'

'Not sure,' Tom replied. 'But she is enjoying herself – with a good friend, you know.'

Then he was alone. Janice Pritchard. Tom got up from the yellow sofa and walked with deliberate slowness into the kitchen. He said to Mme Annette, 'And Monsieur Preechard? I think he is back today?' Tom tried to sound as casual as he might in enquiring about any other neighbour, who was not yet a friend. In fact, he went to the fridge to get a wedge of cheese, or whatever might be visible at a glance, to munch on, as if he had come in for that purpose.

Mme Annette helped him, with a small plate and a knife. 'He was not back this morning,' she replied. 'Perhaps by now.'

'But his wife's still here?'

'Oh, yes. She is sometimes in the grocery.'

Tom returned to the living-room, small plate in hand, and set it down by his drink. On the hall table was the note-pad, which Mme Annette never touched, and soon Tom had found the number of the Pritchard house, not yet in the official telephone book.

Before Tom reached for the telephone, he saw Mme Annette approaching.

'M'sieur Tome, before I forget, I learned this morning that les Preechards have bought their house in Villeperce.'

'Really?' said Tom. 'Interesting.' But he said it as if it did not interest him. Mme Annette turned away. Tom stared at the telephone.

If Pritchard himself answered, Tom thought, he'd hang up without a word. If Janice answered, he'd take a chance. He might ask how David's jaw was, assuming Pritchard had told Janice about their set-to in Tangier. Would Janice know that Pritchard had told Mme Annette, in French with an American accent, that Héloïse had been kidnapped? Tom would not bring that up, he decided. Where did politeness end and insanity begin, or vice versa? Tom stood straight, reminding himself that courtesy and politeness were seldom a mistake, and dialled.

Janice Pritchard answered with a singing American 'Hel-lo-o-o?'

'Hello – Janice. Tom Ripley,' Tom said with a smile on his face.

'Oh, Mr Ripley! I thought you were in North Africa!'

'Was but I returned. Saw your husband there, as you may know.' Beat him unconscious, Tom thought, and smiled politely again, as if Janice could see him over the telephone.

'Ye-es. So I understand – ' Janice paused. Her tone was dulcet, soft anyway. 'Yes, there was a fight – '

'Oh, not much of one,' said Tom modestly. He had the feeling David Pritchard was not at home yet. 'I hope David is feeling all right?'

'Of course he's all *right*. I *know* he *asks* for these things,' Janice said earnestly. 'If you give it out, dish it out, you've got to take it, too, isn't that so? Why did he *go* to Tangier?'

A chill went through Tom. Those words were more profound than perhaps Janice knew. 'You're expecting David back soon?'

'Yes, tonight. I'm going to pick him up at Fontainebleau, after he calls me,' Janice replied in her steady, earnest way. 'He told me he'd be a little late, because he's buying some sports goods today in Paris.'

'Oh. Golf?' Tom asked.

'No-o. Fishing, I think. Not sure. You know the way David talks, all around the subject.'

Tom didn't know. 'And how are you faring all by yourself? Not lonely or bored?'

'Oh, no, never am. I listen to my French grammar records, try to improve.' Here a little laugh. 'The people are nice around here.'

Really. Tom thought at once of the Grais, two houses away, but did not want to ask if she'd made acquaintance with them.

'Well – David. Next week it could be tennis rackets,' Janice said.

'As long as he's happy,' Tom replied with a chuckle. 'Perhaps it will take his mind off *my* household.' He spoke in a tolerant and amused tone, as if of a child with a temporary obsession.

'Oh, I doubt it. He's bought the house here. He finds you *fascinating*.'

Tom again recalled Janice, smiling and plainly in good humour, driving her husband away from Belle Ombre, after Pritchard had been prowling about with his camera, snapping. 'You seem to disapprove of some of his doings,' Tom went on. 'Has it ever occurred to you to discourage him? Even leave him?' Tom ventured.

Nervous laugh. 'Women don't abandon their husbands, do they? Then he'd come after *me*!' Her last word was shrill, said through laughter.

Tom was not laughing, not even smiling. 'I understand,' he said, not knowing what else to say. 'You're a loyal wife! Well, my best to you both, Janice. Maybe we'll see you soon.'

'Oh, maybe, yes. Thank you for calling, Mr Ripley.'

'Bye-bye.' He hung up.

What a madhouse! *See* them soon! He'd said 'we' just now, as if Héloïse were back home. Why not? It might lure Pritchard to further adventure, derring-do. Tom realized that he had a desire to murder Pritchard. It was similar to his desire to hit at the Mafia, but that had been impersonal: he hated the Mafia *per se*, considered them brutal and well-organized blackmailers. Whichever Mafia member he killed, and he had killed two, didn't matter, it was two fewer. But Pritchard was a personal matter, Pritchard had stuck his neck out and was asking for it. Could Janice help? Don't count on Janice, Tom reminded himself; she'd let him down at the last minute, and save her husband so she could enjoy more mental and physical discomfort, presumably, at his hands. Why hadn't he finished Pritchard in La Haffa, with the aid of his new knife right there in his pocket?

He might have to get rid of both Pritchards to have any peace, Tom thought, lighting a cigarette. Unless they both decided to quit the neighbourhood.

The Calvados and the café. Tom finished the last drops, and returned the cup and saucer to the kitchen. Mme Annette would not be ready to serve for a good five minutes or so, he saw at a glance, so Tom informed her that he wanted to make one more telephone call.

He then rang the Grais, whose number he knew by heart.

Agnès answered, and from the background clatter Tom thought he had interrupted in the middle of dinner.

'Yes, back from London today,' Tom said. 'I'm interrupting you, I think.'

'No! Silvie and I are just tidying up. Is Héloïse with you?' Agnès asked.

'She's in North Africa still. I just wanted to announce my return. Can't tell when Héloïse will decide to come home. And did you know that your neighbours the Pritchards have bought that house?'

'*Oui!*' Agnès said at once, and informed Tom that she had learned this from Marie in the bar-tabac. 'And the *noise*, Tome,' she continued, with a certain amusement in her voice. 'I believe madame is alone now, but she plays loud rock music till all hours! Ha-ha! Does she dance by herself, I wonder?'

Or watch kinky video cassettes? Tom blinked. 'No idea,' replied Tom, smiling. 'You can hear it where you are?'

'If the wind is right! Not every night, to be sure, but Antoine was furious last Sunday night. But not furious enough to go to their house and tell them to shut up. And he could not find their telephone number.' Agnès laughed again.

They signed off, pleasantly and cordially like good neighbours. Then Tom sat down to a solitary dinner with a magazine propped up in front of him. As he ate his excellent braised beef, he chewed mentally on the two Pritchard nuisances. Back even this minute was David, perhaps, with fishing gear? Fishing for Murchison? Why hadn't that occurred to Tom at once? Murchison's corpse?

Tom's eyes left the page he had been reading, and he sat back, touched his lips with his napkin. Fishing gear? It would take a grappling iron, a strong rope, and more than a rowing boat. It would take more than standing on a river or canal bank with a delicate pole and line, as some locals did, catching if they were lucky small white-coloured fish, presumably edible. Since Pritchard's money was in good supply, according to Janice, was he going to buy a fancy motorboat? Even hire a helper?

But then, he might be quite on the wrong track, Tom thought. Maybe David Pritchard really liked fishing.

The last thing Tom did that evening was address an envelope to his National Westminster Bank branch, because he needed to shift money from deposit to current to cover the £2000 cheque. The sight of the envelope by his typewriter would remind him tomorrow morning.

15

After his first coffee the next morning, Tom walked out on the terrace and into the garden. It had rained during the night, and the dahlias looked good; they could use a deadheading, and it would be nice to cut a few for the living-room. Mme Annette seldom did that, knowing Tom liked to choose the colours for the day himself.

David Pritchard is back now, Tom reminded himself, back last night presumably, getting down to his fishing today, perhaps. Was he?

Tom did some bill-paying, spent an hour in the garden pottering, and then had lunch. Mme Annette said nothing about news of the Pritchards in the bakery this morning. He took a look at the two cars in the garage, and the one that stood outside, at the moment the station wagon. All three started properly. Tom washed the windows of them all.

Then he took the red Mercedes, which he seldom drove and which he considered Héloïse's car, and headed in a westerly direction.

The roads through the flat landscape were fairly familiar, but they were not the roads he took to go to Moret, for instance, or Fontainebleau, the shopping places. Tom could not even have said exactly what road he had taken that night with Bernard to dispose of Murchison's body. Tom had been in quest only of a canal, any fairly distant stream into which he could dump the tied-up corpse with fair ease. Tom had put a few large stones in the canvas sheet that shrouded Murchison, he remembered, to make the body sink and stay sunk. Well, it had, as far as Tom had ever learned. At a glance, Tom saw that there was a folded roadmap in the glove compartment, perhaps of the vicinity, but for the moment he preferred to trust his instinct. The main rivers in the area, the Loing, the Yonne

155

and the Seine, had canals and tributaries, numerous and some nameless, and Tom knew that into one of these he had dropped Murchison, and from over the parapet of a bridge which he might recognize if he came to it.

Hopeless quest, perhaps. If anyone elected to try to find Derwatt in Mexico, in some small village, it would be the task of a lifetime and then some, Tom thought, as Derwatt had never lived in Mexico, only in London, and had gone to Greece to kill himself.

Tom glanced at the petrol gauge: more than half-full. He made a U-turn at the next safe spot, and headed north-east. Only every three minutes or so did he see another car. Green fields of high, thickly planted corn spread left and right, corn planted for cattle consumption. Black crows circled and cawed.

As Tom recalled, he and Bernard had driven seven or eight kilometres from Villeperce that night, and westward. Should he go home and make a circle on a map, with its centre west of Villeperce? Tom now chose a road that he thought would lead him past the Pritchard house, then the Grais' house.

Must ring the Berthelins, Tom thought out of the blue. Jacqueline and Vincent.

Did the Pritchards know Héloïse's red Mercedes? Tom thought not. As he approached their two-storey white house, he slowed and tried to see as much as he could and still keep his eyes on the road. A white pick-up in the driveway in front of the porch steps caught Tom's eye. A delivery of sports goods? It had a grey lumpish cargo which projected over the floor at the back. Tom heard what he thought was a man's voice, maybe two men's voices, though Tom wasn't sure, and then he was past the Pritchard establishment.

Could that have been a small boat in the pick-up? The grey tarpaulin that covered it reminded Tom of the darker grey tarpaulin or canvas that had covered Thomas Murchison. Well! Perhaps David Pritchard had acquired a pick-up, and a boat, and maybe even an assistant? A rowing boat? How could one man get a row-boat into canal water (the height of the water varied with the action of the locks), plus the motor, plus descending by rope himself? The canal banks were sheer. Had Pritchard been discussing payment with his delivery man, or someone he intended to employ?

If David Pritchard was back, Tom could not pump Janice, his unreliable ally, versus her husband, as David would either pick up the phone or possibly overhear, and snatch the telephone from Janice's thin hand.

The Grais' house showed no sign of life at the moment. Tom turned left into an empty road, then right a few metres on, which put him on the road where Belle Ombre stood.

Voisy, Tom thought suddenly. The name entered his mind for no reason, and it was like a light being turned on unexpectedly. That was the village near which the stream or canal ran, where he had dropped Murchison's body. Voisy. Westward, Tom thought. Anyway, he could look it up on the map.

Tom did just that when he got home, having found a detailed map of the Fontainebleau region. A little westward, not far from Sens. Voisy on the Loing river itself. Tom felt relieved. Murchison's corpse would have moved northward towards the Seine, Tom thought, if it had moved at all, and that he doubted. He tried to take into consideration heavy rains, reversals of current. Would there have been reversals? Not in an inland river, he thought. And lucky it was a river, as canals were from time to time drained empty for repairs.

He rang the Berthelins' number and Jacqueline answered. Yes, he and Héloïse had been away for a few days in Tangier, Tom said, and Héloïse was still there.

'And how are your son and daughter-in-law doing?' Tom asked. Their son Jean-Pierre had finished his studies at the Beaux-Arts, which had been interrupted a couple of years ago by the girl to whom he was now married, and against whom Vincent Berthelin, Jean-Pierre's father, had railed, Tom recalled. '*The girl is not worth it!*' Vincent had shouted.

'Jean-Pierre is fine and they are expecting a baby in December!' Jacqueline's voice was full of joy.

'Ah, congratulations!' Tom said. 'Now that house of yours had better be warm for the baby!'

Jacqueline laughed, and yielded on this sore point. She and Vincent had for years had no hot water, she admitted, but they were going to install a *second* WC even, off their guest-room, plus a washbasin.

'Good!' Tom said, smiling, remembering when the Berthelins, for some reason determined to rough it in their country house, had boiled water on the kitchen stove in a kettle to wash with, and had had an outside toilet.

They promised to see each other soon, a promise not always kept, as some people seemed always busy, Tom thought, but still he felt better after hanging up. Good neighbourly relations were important.

Tom relaxed with the *Herald Tribune* on the sofa. Mme Annette, he thought, was in her part of the house, and Tom fancied he could hear her television set. He knew she watched certain soap operas, because in the old days she had used to mention them to Héloïse and him until she realized that the Ripleys didn't watch soap operas.

At half past 4, when the sun was still far above the horizon, Tom took the brown Renault and drove off in the direction of Voisy. Such a difference, he thought, between the sunlit farm landscape today and that night with Bernard, a moonless night as he remembered, when he had been uncertain where he was going. Until now, he told himself, that watery grave of Murchison had been a most successful hiding place, and perhaps it still was.

Tom came to the town marker 'VOISY' before he saw the town, which in fact was out of sight around a curve to the left and behind trees. Tom saw the bridge to his right, horizontal and with a ramp at either end, and some thirty metres long, maybe more. Over that bridge with its waist-high parapet he and Bernard had heaved Murchison.

Tom drove on at a slower but steady speed. At the bridge, he turned right and drove across it, not knowing or caring where the road beyond might lead. As he remembered, he and Bernard had parked and dragged the tarpaulin bundle on to the bridge. Or had they dared to drive the car some way on to the bridge?

In the next convenient spot, Tom stopped and consulted his map, saw a crossroads and went on, knowing that a signpost would point the way to Nemours or Sens and thus orient him. Tom was thinking of the river he had just glanced at: dirtyish blue-green, its surface a couple of metres (today anyway) below the upper level of its soft and grassy banks. No one could walk to the edge of that bank without slipping in, or falling in because of losing their balance.

And why in the name of – anything – would David Pritchard think of coming to *Voisy*, when there were twenty or thirty more kilometres of river and canal much closer to Villeperce?

Tom got home and, after removing shirt and blue jeans, took a nap in his bedroom. He felt safer, more relaxed. It was a delicious nap of three-quarters of an hour, after which Tom felt he had got rid of the strain of Tangier, the anxiety of London and talking with Cynthia, and the Pritchards' possible acquisition of a boat. Tom wandered into the room in what he thought of as the 'back right' corner of Belle Ombre, which was his studio or workroom.

The fine old oak flooring still looked good, though not so shiny and polished as the other floors of the house. Tom kept a few lengths of old canvas or sailcloth on the floor, which in his view were decorative, kept paint drips, if any, from staining the floor, and also served as rags when he wanted to give a brush a wipe or a cleaning.

'The Pigeon'. Where should he hang that yellowish sketch? In the living-room, surely, to share it with his friends.

Tom looked for a few seconds at a painting he had done, which now leaned against a wall. Mme Annette stood with cup and saucer in hand, his morning coffee: Tom had made sketches for that, so as not to tire Mme Annette. She wore a purple dress and white apron there. Then one of Héloïse, gazing out of the curved window in the corner of Tom's studio, her right hand resting on the window frame, left hand on her hip. Again preliminary sketches, Tom recalled. Héloïse did not like to pose for more than ten minutes at a time.

Should he try a landscape from his window? It had been three years since he had, Tom thought. The dark, dense woods beyond his own property line, where in fact Murchison's body had known its first resting place – not a nice memory. Tom steered his thoughts back to composition. Yes, he would try it, first sketches tomorrow morning, the handsome dahlias in foreground left and right, pink and red roses beyond. One could make something soppy and pretty out of that idyllic view, but such was not Tom's intention. He might try working with palette knife only.

Tom went downstairs, seized a white cotton jacket from the front closet, mainly so he could carry his wallet in an inside pocket, and went towards the kitchen, where Mme Annette was already astir. 'At work? It's hardly five, madame.'

'The mushrooms, m'sieur. I like to prepare them beforehand.' Mme Annette glanced at him with pale blue eyes and smiled. She was at the sink.

'I'm going out for half an hour. Can I buy something you need?'

'Oui, m'sieur – *Le Parisien Libéré*? S'il vous plaît?'

'With pleasure, madame!' Tom was off.

He picked up the newspaper first in the bar-tabac, lest he forget to buy it. It was early for men getting off from work for the day, but the usual buzz had started, a call for 'Un petit rouge, Georges!' and Marie was getting into her rhythm for the evening. She gave Tom a wave, being at that moment far to the left behind the bar. Tom found himself glancing around, quickly to be sure, for David Pritchard, and not finding him. Pritchard would have stood out: taller than most, round-rimmed eyeglasses in evidence, staring, not mixing.

Tom got into the red Mercedes again, drove off in the direction of Fontainebleau, then took the next left-hand turning for no reason. His direction now was south-west, more or less. What was Héloïse doing now? Strolling back to the Hotel Miramare, Casablanca, with Noëlle, both carrying plastic bags and newly acquired baskets full of afternoon purchases? Both talking about a shower and a nap before the dinner hour? Should he try Héloïse at 3 a.m. tonight?

At a Villeperce sign, Tom headed for home, remarking the eight-kilometre distance to his village. He slowed up, stopped to let a farmgirl steer her geese across the road with a long stick; beautiful, Tom thought, three white geese headed where they ought to go, but going at their own pace, unruffled.

Around the next gentle curve, Tom had to slow because of a pick-up which was going slowly, and he noticed at once that a grey shape projected from the back of it. And a canal or a stream lay to the right of the road, some sixty or eighty metres away. Pritchard and company, or David Pritchard alone? Tom was close enough to see, through the back window, that the driver was engaged in conversation with someone in the seat beside him. Tom imagined that they were both looking at and talking about the water, the stream on their right. Tom slowed still more. He was sure that the pick-up was the same one that he had seen in the Pritchard back or front yard, whichever they called it.

Tom thought of taking any road off, left or right, then decided to go right on, past them.

As Tom accelerated, a car approached from the opposite direction, a big grey Peugeot which had an air of caring for nobody. Tom slowed, let the Peugeot pass, then stepped on the accelerator.

The two men in the pick-up were still in conversation, and the driver was not Pritchard but a stranger to Tom, with wavy light brown hair. Pritchard sat beside him, talking and pointing towards the stream as Tom passed. Tom was reasonably sure that they had not heeded him.

Tom went on towards Villeperce, watching in his mirror till the last moment, however, to see if the pick-up ventured across a field, for example, to get a closer look at the stream. It did not while Tom was watching.

16

Tom felt restless after dinner that evening, unwilling to try television as a diversion, or to ring the Cleggs or Agnès Grais. He debated ringing Jeff Constant or Ed Banbury. One or the other might be in. What would he say? Come over soon as possible? Tom thought he might ask one of them to join him – for physical assistance in case of need, Tom admitted to himself – and he would not mind admitting it to Ed and Jeff. It *could* be like a little vacation for either of them, Tom thought, especially if nothing happened. If Pritchard fished or grappled for five or six days unsuccessfully, surely he'd give up? Or was he such an obsessive nut, he would go on for weeks, months?

The thought was frightening, yet that was possible, Tom realized. Who could predict what a mentally disturbed person would do? Well, psychologists could predict, Tom realized, but prediction would be based on past case histories, similarities, likelihoods, nothing that even doctors could call definite.

Héloïse. She'd been away from Belle Ombre for six days. Nice to think there were two of them there, Héloïse and Noëlle, even nicer to know that Pritchard was not there.

Tom looked at the telephone, thinking of Ed before Jeff, and thinking it was fortunate for him that London time was an hour earlier, in case he felt inspired to ring one of them later.

Nine-twelve now. Mme Annette had finished in the kitchen, and was probably deep in television. Tom thought he might make a sketch or two for his view-from-the-window oil.

The telephone rang as he was approaching the stairs.

Tom picked it up in the hall. 'Hello?'

'Hel-lo, Mr Ripley,' said a smiling, confident American voice. 'Dickie again. Remember? I've been keeping tabs on you – I know where you've been.'

161

It sounded like Pritchard, screwing his voice up a bit higher than normal, to make himself sound 'young'. He imagined Pritchard's face with a forced grin, mouth twisted as he attempted something like a New York drawl, or absence of consonants. Tom kept silent.

'Getting scared, Tom? Voices from the past? From the dead?'

Did Tom hear or imagine a remonstrative word from Janice in the background? A titter of laughter?

The speaker cleared his throat. 'Day of reckoning's very soon, Tom. All actions have their price.'

And what did that mean? Nothing, Tom thought.

'Still there? Maybe you're struck dumb with fear, Tom.'

'Not at all. This is being recorded, Pritchard.'

'Oh-ho – Dickie. Starting to take me seriously, eh, Tom?'

Tom kept silent.

'I'm – I'm not Pritchard,' the high voice went on, 'but I *know* Pritchard. He's doing some work for me.'

They'd soon know each other in the afterworld, perhaps, Tom thought, and decided not to say another word.

Pritchard went on. '*Good* work. We're accomplishing things.' A pause. 'Still there? We're . . . '

Tom cut it off by hanging up, gently. His heart was beating faster than usual, which he detested, but there had been times in his life when it had beat faster than this, he reminded himself. He got some adrenalin out of his system by running up the stairs two at a time.

In his studio, he turned on the fluorescent lights, and reached for a pencil and a pad of cheap paper. At a table convenient for standing at, Tom drew first the scene out his window as he knew it: vertical trees, the nearly horizontal line where his garden edge met the higher grass and bushes of land that did not belong to him. Retracing the lines, trying for an interesting composition, took his mind from Pritchard, but only to some extent.

Tom tossed his Venus pencil down and thought – the *nerve* of the bastard to ring him up a second time as Dickie Greenleaf! The third time, if he counted the telephone call Héloïse had had. He and Janice were indeed working as a team on this, it seemed.

Tom loved his hearth and home, and he was determined that the Pritchards should not become fixtures on his landscape.

On another piece of paper, Tom drew a primitive Pritchard portrait, harsh of line, with dark, round-rimmed glasses, dark eyebrows, mouth open and nearly round with speech. The brows scarcely frowned: Pritchard was pleased with his activities. Tom used coloured pencils, red for the lips, some purple under the eyes, green too. A rather forceful caricature. But Tom tore the sheet off, folded it and slowly tore it into bits and dropped it in his waste-paper basket. He would not want anybody finding that, he realized, in case he eliminated Mr Pritchard.

Then Tom went into his bedroom, where he had plugged in the telephone that was, most of the time, in Héloïse's bedroom. He was thinking of ringing Jeff. Barely 10 p.m. in London now.

Then he asked himself, was he collapsing under asshole Pritchard's heckling? Was he scared, whining for assistance? After all, he'd got the better of Pritchard in a fistfight, in which Pritchard might have put up a lot more resistance, but hadn't.

Tom started as the telephone rang. Pritchard resuming, he supposed. Tom was still on his feet. 'Hello?'

'Hello, Tom, Jeff here. I – '

'Oh, Jeff!'

'Yes, I checked with Ed, you hadn't telephoned him, so I thought I'd ask how things are.'

'Um, well – hottening – a little. I think. Pritchard's back in town – here. And I think he's bought a boat. Not sure. Maybe a small boat with outboard motor. I'm only guessing, because it was under wraps in a pick-up. I saw it when I was driving past his house.'

'Really? For – to do what?'

Tom had supposed that Jeff could guess. 'I suppose he could try dredging – grappling in the canals!' Tom laughed. 'With grappling irons, I mean. I'm not sure. And he's got a long way to go before he finds anything, I can guarantee that.'

'Now I get you,' Jeff said in a whisper. 'That man's obsessed, is he not?'

'Is he not,' Tom repeated pleasantly. 'I haven't seen him at it, mind you. But it's only wise to think ahead. I'll report again.'

'We're here, Tom, if you need us.'

'That means a lot to me. Thank you, Jeff, and tell Ed thanks. Meanwhile I'll hope a barge hits Pritchard's canoe and sinks it. Ha-ha!'

They hung up after wishing each other well.

It was comforting to have reinforcements in view, Tom thought. Jeff Constant, for instance, was stronger and more alert than Bernard Tufts had been, certainly. He'd had to explain to Bernard each manoeuvre and its purpose when they were getting Murchison out of his grave behind Tom's garden with the minimum of noise and car lights, then exactly what Bernard should say to a police investigator in case there were any, and there had been one.

In the present circumstances, Tom said to himself, the objective for him should be to keep Murchison's decaying and canvas-wrapped corpse under water, provided any of the corpse still existed.

Just what did happen to a corpse under water for four, five years, even three? The tarpaulin or canvas would rot, perhaps more than half of it would disappear; the stones would likely have fallen out, therefore, enabling the corpse to drift more easily, even rise a little, provided any flesh was left. But wasn't rising only due to bloating? Tom thought of the word maceration, the flaking off in layers of the outer skin. Then what? The nibbling of fish? Or wouldn't the current have removed pieces of flesh until nothing but bones were left? The bloated period must be long past. Where was he going to find information on such as Murchison?

After breakfast the next day, Tom informed Mme Annette that he was going to Fontainebleau or perhaps Nemours for garden clippers, and did she need anything?

She did not, she replied with thanks, though with the air, which Tom knew by now, of possibly thinking of something before his departure.

Having heard nothing from Mme Annette, Tom took off before 10, and thought to try Nemours first for the clippers. Tom found himself taking unknown lanes again, because he had ample time: he had only to glance at the next cluster of signs on a post for directions. At a petrol station, he stopped and filled the tank. He was driving the brown Renault.

He took a road northward, thinking to go a couple of kilometres then head left towards Nemours. Farmlands, a tractor moving slowly across yellow stubble, such were the sights from Tom's open window, and the vehicles he passed were as likely to be four-wheel farm cars with big rear tyres as passenger cars. Now another canal, with an arched black bridge visible, and bucolic clumps of trees near either end of the bridge. Tom's route would take him over the bridge, he saw. He drove slowly, because he was not holding up anyone behind him.

Tom had just rolled on to the black iron bridge when a glance to his right revealed two men in a rowing boat, one seated, holding what looked like a very wide rake. The man standing had his right arm lifted high, a rope in his right hand. Tom's gaze returned to the road for an instant, then back to the men, who were paying no attention to him.

The man seated, in light-coloured shirt, and with black hair, was David Pritchard, no less, and the man standing in beige trousers and shirt was a stranger to Tom, tall and with fair hair. They were handling a meter-or-more-wide metal bar with at least six small hooks on it, which in a larger version Tom would think of as grapnels or grapnel irons.

Well, well. So engrossed were they, they hadn't looked up at his car, which by now just might be familiar to David Pritchard. On the other hand, recognizing the car, Tom realized, would only have fed David Pritchard's ego: Tom Ripley was worried enough to cruise around to see what Pritchard was up to, and what had Pritchard to lose?

That boat had had an outboard motor, Tom had noticed. And maybe they had two such rake-like devices with grappling hooks?

The fact that they would have to cringe against the canal side when a barge passed, and absent themselves somehow if two barges wanted to pass each other, was not of much comfort to Tom at the moment. Pritchard and his companion looked as if they meant business and as if they would stick with their task. Perhaps Pritchard was paying the helper well too? Was he sleeping at the Pritchard house? And who was he, a local or from Paris? What had Pritchard told him they were looking for? Agnès Grais just might know something about the fair-haired stranger.

What chance had Pritchard of finding Murchison? Pritchard was about twelve kilometres from his quarry right now.

A crow came zooming down from Tom's right with an ugly and insolent 'Caw! Caw! *Caw!*' like a laugh. Who was the bird laughing at, him or Pritchard, Tom wondered. Pritchard, of course! Tom's hands gripped the wheel harder and he smiled. Pritchard was going to get what he deserved, the meddling bastard.

17

Tom had had no word from Héloïse in days, and he could only assume they were still in Casablanca, and that a couple of postcards had been written and launched in the Villeperce direction: they would probably arrive a few days after Héloïse was back home. That had happened before.

Tom felt restless, rang the Cleggs and managed a most relaxed and cheerful conversation with both of them, spoke about Tangier and Héloïse's further travels. But he wriggled out of a drinks date with them. They were English, he a retired lawyer, very reliable and proper, knowing nothing of Tom's connection with the Buckmaster Gallery people, of course, and probably the name Murchison had gone out of their heads, if it had ever much entered.

His inspiration having changed, Tom made sketches for a room interior as his next painting, a room giving on a hall. He wanted a composition of purples and near-blacks, relieved by one pale object, which he envisioned as a vase, perhaps empty, or maybe with a single red flower which he could add later, if he so chose.

Mme Annette thought he was a little 'mélancholique, because Madame Héloïse has not written'.

'Very true,' said Tom, smiling. 'But you know – the atrocious postal service there – '

One evening he went around 9.30 to the bar-tabac, for a change of atmosphere. At this time, it was a slightly different crowd from the 5.30 after-work crowd. Now there were a few card-playing men, who Tom had once supposed were mostly bachelors, but he knew now that this wasn't so. Many married men simply liked to spend their evenings in the local tavern, instead of watching TV, for instance – which in fact they could do also at Marie and Georges'.

'Ah-h, people who don't know the facts should shut up!' Marie was screaming at someone, or maybe the whole room, as she drew a *bière pression*. She gave Tom a quick, red-lipped grin and a nod.

Tom found a place at the bar. He always preferred to stand when he was here.

'M'sieur Reepley,' said Georges, his plump hands planted on the rim of the aluminium sink on the other side of the bar.

'M-m – un demi pression,' said Tom, and Georges went off to get it.

'He is a slob, he *is*!' said a man on Tom's right, and the same man was jostled by his companion, who retorted something both belligerent and comical, and laughed.

Tom edged further to his left, as the two were tipsy. He heard snatches of conversation: about North Africans, about a building project somewhere, about a construction entrepreneur who was going to need masons, at least six.

' . . . Preechard, non?' A short laugh. 'Fishing!'

Tom tried to listen, without turning his head. The words had come from a table behind and to his left, and he saw at a glance that the three men seated were in work clothes, all about forty. One was shuffling the deck.

'Fishing in – '

'Why doesn't he fish from the bank?' asked another. '*Une péniche arrive*' – a crunching sound and gesture with hands – 'he's going to get sunk in that silly boat!'

'Hey, do you know what he's doing?' said a new voice, and a younger man strolled over with his glass. 'He's not fishing, he's dragging the bottom! Two gadgets with hooks!'

'Ah, oui, I saw them,' said a card-player, uninterested and ready to return to the game.

Cards were being dealt.

'He won't catch any gardons with those.'

'No, only old rubber boots, sardine cans, bicycles! Ha-ha!'

'Bicycles!' said the younger man, still on his feet. 'M'sieur, you do not jest! He has already caught a bicycle! I saw it!' He guffawed. 'Rusted – bent!'

'What's he after?'

'*Antiques*! With Americans, you never know their tastes, eh?' This from an older man.

Laughter, and someone coughed.

'It is true he has an assistant,' a man at the table piped up, just as the slot-machine game with the motorcyclist gave somebody a jackpot, and a whoop from that direction (near the door) drowned out the words uttered in the following seconds.

' . . . another American. I heard them talking.'

'For fish, it is absurd.'

'Americans – if they have the money for such nonsense . . . '

Tom sipped his beer, slowly lit a Gitane.

'He is really trying. I saw him near *Moret*!'

Tom continued to listen, his back to the table, even as he exchanged a friendly word with Marie. But nothing more came from the men in regard to Pritchard. The card-players were back in their own closed world. Tom knew the two words the men had used, *gardons*, a type of roach, and *chevesnes*, an edible fish also, and of the carp family. No, Pritchard wasn't fishing for those silvery creatures, and also not for old bicycles.

'Et Madame Héloïse? Encore en vacances?' asked Marie, dark hair and eyes looking a bit wild as usual, but she was wiping, automatically, the wooden bar top with a damp cloth.

'Ah, well, yes,' Tom said, reaching for his money to pay. 'The charms of Morocco, you know.'

'*Maroc*! Ah, how beautiful! I have seen photos!'

Marie had said the same words several days ago, as Tom recollected, but Marie was a busy woman, having to be hospitable to a hundred or so customers morning, noon and night. Tom bought a packet of Marlboros before he quit the premises, as if the cigarettes would bring Héloïse sooner back to him.

At home, Tom chose the tubes of colour he thought he would want for tomorrow's work, and set up the canvas on the easel. He thought of his composition, dark, intense, with a focus on a still darker area in the background which would remain undefined, like a small room without a light. He had made several sketches. Tomorrow he would begin with pencil strokes on the white canvas. But not tonight. He was a bit tired, and afraid of failing, of smudging, of its simply not being good enough.

The telephone by 11 p.m. had not rung. It was 10 p.m. in London, and his friends there might be thinking that no news from Tom was good news. And Cynthia? Very likely reading a book this evening, secure and almost smug in her conviction that Tom was guilty of murdering Murchison – she must know of Dickie Greenleaf's questionable means of departing this life, too – and sure that fate would at last dominate, put its stamp on Tom's existence, whatever that meant. Annihilate him, perhaps.

As for books, Tom was glad to have Richard Ellmann's biography of Oscar Wilde as bedtime reading that night. He was enjoying every paragraph. Something about Oscar's life, reading it, was like a purge, man's fate encapsulated; a man of goodwill, of talent, whose gifts to human pleasure remained considerable, had been attacked and brought low by the vindictiveness of *hoi polloi*, who had taken sadistic pleasure in watching Oscar brought low. His story reminded Tom of that of Christ, a man of generous goodwill, with a vision of expanding consciousness, of increasing the joy of life. Both had been misunderstood by contemporaries, both had suffered from a jealousy deeply buried in the breasts of those who wished them dead, and who mocked them while they were alive. No wonder, Tom thought, that people of all types and ages kept reading about Oscar, not even realizing perhaps, why they were so fascinated.

As these thoughts went through Tom's head, he turned the page and read about Rennell Rodd's first book of poetry, a copy of which he, as a friend, had given Oscar. Rodd had written in his own hand an inscription in Italian – oddly, it was stated – which translated as:

> At thy martyrdom the greedy and cruel
> Crowd to which thou speakest will assemble;
> All will come to see thee on thy cross,
> And not one will have pity on thee.

Now that was prophetic, strange, Tom thought. Had he possibly read those lines before somewhere? But Tom didn't think he had.

Tom, as he read, imagined Oscar's thrill on learning that he had won the Newdigate Prize for poetry – after having suffered rustication not so long before. Then, despite Tom's ease in bed against his pillows, and anticipation of the next pages, he thought of Pritchard and his damned boat with the motor. He thought of Pritchard's assistant.

'God damn,' Tom murmured, and got out of bed. He was curious about the neighbourhood, the waterways in the vicinity, and though he had looked at his area on a map more than once, he felt compelled to do so again.

Tom opened his big *Times* atlas – the *Concise Atlas of the World.* As to rivers and canals, the district around Fontainebleau and Moret, south to Montereau and beyond, looked like a *Gray's Anatomy* drawing of part of a circulatory system: veins and arteries, thick and thin, intersecting, separating, rivers and canals. Each, however, would probably be big enough for Pritchard's rowboat-with-motor. Very well, Pritchard would have a task.

How he'd love to speak with Janice Pritchard! What did she think of all this? 'Any luck, dear? Any fish for dinner? Another old bicycle? Or boot?' And what did Pritchard tell her he was grappling for? Very likely the truth, Tom thought, Murchison. Why not? Did Pritchard keep a map, a record? Probably.

Tom still had the first map he'd looked at, of course, with the circle drawn. His pencilled circle went as far as Voisy and a little beyond. In the *Times Concise Atlas*, the canals and rivers were clearer, and appeared certainly more numerous. Would Pritchard have taken a 'wide radius', with the intention of closing in, or the immediate vicinity, and expanding? Tom thought the latter. A man with a corpse on his hands might not have had the time to go twenty kilometres' distance, Tom thought, but might have had to settle for ten or less. Tom reckoned Voisy was eight kilometres from Villeperce.

On a quick estimate, Tom judged that there were about fifty-four kilometres of canal and river within a circle with a radius of ten kilometres. What a task! Was Pritchard possibly going to hire another outboard-motor with another pair of helpers?

How soon would a person get tired of such a task? Tom reminded himself that Pritchard was not normal.

How much would he have scoured now in seven days, or was it nine? Cruising once up a canal, in the middle logically, at two kilometres an hour, three hours morning, same in afternoon, would cover twelve kilometres a day, but not with difficulties, such as another boat every half-hour, plus perhaps loading the boat on to the pick-up to take it to another canal. On a river, a back and forth trip might be necessary to cover the width.

Then in toto, some fifty kilometres to scour, at a rough estimate, made it look as if another three weeks or less might discover Murchison, if he was still there to be discovered, throwing in a bit of luck, too.

That time-span was vague, however, Tom told himself, after having felt a mild inner shudder. And suppose Murchison had even drifted north, out of the area Tom was thinking about?

And also, what if Murchison's tarpaulin-with-corpse had drifted into a canal in months past, been discovered when the canal had been drained for repair work? Tom had seen many a dry canal, water

170

held back by locks somewhere. Murchison's remains might have been given to the police, of course, who might not have been able to identify them. Tom had seen no such report in the newspapers – of an unidentified bag of bones – but he had not been looking for any, and would it necessarily have been mentioned in the newspapers? Well, *yes*, Tom thought, just what the French public or any other public loved to read about: a bag of unidentified bones dredged up by – a Sunday fisherman? Male, probably victim of violence or murder, not a suicide. But somehow Tom just couldn't believe that the police or anybody else had ever found Murchison.

One afternoon, when Tom had made good progress on his oil of 'the back room', as he thought of it, he felt inspired to ring Janice Pritchard. He might hang up if David Pritchard answered; if it was Janice, then he would pursue it and see what he could learn.

Tom laid a brush with ochre gently down beside his palette, and went downstairs to the hall telephone.

Mme Clusot, the woman for what Tom called 'the more serious' cleaning, was now busy in the downstairs loo, which had a basin and a door that gave on to the steps to the cellar. As far as Tom knew, she did not understand English. She was now only some four metres away. Tom looked at the number he had jotted down for the Pritchards, and was reaching for the telephone, when it rang. Great if it's Janice, Tom thought as he picked it up.

No. It was from overseas, two operators murmuring, one emerging the victor and enquiring, 'Vous êtes M'sieur Tom Reepley?'

'Oui, madame.' Had Héloïse been hurt?

'Un instant, s'il vous plaît.'

''Ello, Tome!' Héloïse sounded fine.

'Hello, my sweet. How are you? Why didn't you – '

'We are very well . . . Marrakesh! Yes . . . I *did* write a postcard – in an envelope, but you know – '

'All right. Thank you. The main thing is – you're well? Not sick?'

'No, Tome, chéri. Noëlle knows most wonderful medicines! She can buy them, if we need them.'

Well, that was something, of course. Tom had heard stories of strange African diseases. He gulped. 'And you're coming back when?'

'Oh-h – '

Tom heard another week, at least, in that 'Oh-h'.

'We want to see – ' Loud noises of static, or a near cut-off, then

Héloïse came back, calmly, '*Meknès*. We fly there – something is happening. I say goodbye, Tome.'

'*What's* happening?'

'. . . *okay*. Bye-bye, Tome.'

End.

What in God's name was happening? Another person wanting the telephone? It sounded as if Héloïse had rung from her hotel lobby (other people in background), which Tom thought a logical thing to do. Semi-infuriating, yet at least he knew that at this moment Héloïse was all right, and if flying to Meknès, that was north, in the direction of Tangier, whence surely she'd catch the aeroplane for home. Pity there'd been no time to speak with Noëlle. Nor did he even know the name of their hotel now.

Cheered, in the main, by Héloïse's call, Tom picked up the telephone again, checked his watch – ten past 3 – and dialled the Pritchard number. It rang five, six, seven times. Then Janice's high-pitched, American voice said, 'Hel-lo-o-o?'

'Hello, Janice! Tom here. How are you?'

'Oh-h! How nice to hear from you! We're fine. And yourself?'

Uncannily friendly and cheerful, Tom thought. 'Well, thank you. Enjoying the nice weather? I am.'

'Isn't it lovely? I was just out doing some weeding round my roses. I barely heard the phone.'

'And I hear David's fishing,' Tom said, forcing himself to grin.

'Ha-ha! Fishing!'

'Isn't that so? I think I saw him once – when I was driving along some canal near here. Fishing for carp?'

'Oh, no, Mr Ripley, he's fishing for a *corpse*.' She laughed gaily, apparently amused by the similarity of the words. 'It's ridiculous! What'll he ever find? Nothing!' Another laugh. 'But it gets him out of the house. Exercise.'

'A corpse – whose?'

'Someone called Murchison. David says you knew him – even killed him, David thinks. Can you imagine?'

'No!' Tom said with a laugh. He put on an amused air. 'Killed him when?' Tom waited. 'Janice?'

'Sorry, I thought for a minute they might be coming back, but it was another car. Years ago, I think. Oh, it's so absurd, Mr Ripley!'

'That it is,' said Tom. 'But as you say, it provides exercise – sport – '

'Sport!' Her shrillness, plus a laugh, told Tom that she was loving every minute of her husband's sport. 'Dragging a hook – '

'And the man with your husband – an old friend?'

'No! An American music student David picked up in Paris! Lucky for us he's a nice young man, not a thief – ' Janice gave a giggle. 'Because he's sleeping in the house, is why I say that. Name's Teddy.'

'Teddy,' Tom echoed, hoping for the last name, which did not come. 'How long do you think this is going to go on?'

'Oh, till he finds something. David's determined, I'll say that for him. Between buying gasoline, dressing cut fingers, cooking for these men – my life's been pretty busy. Can't you come around for a coffee or a drink some time?'

Tom was flabbergasted. 'I – thank you. Just now – '

'Your wife's away now, I heard.'

'Yes, and for several weeks more, I think.'

'Where is she?'

'I think she's heading for Greece next. A little holiday with a friend, you know. And I'm trying to catch up on garden work.' He smiled, as Mme Clusot backed out of the downstairs loo with bucket and mop. Tom was not going to add that Janice Pritchard could visit him for coffee or a drink, because Janice might be naïve or malicious enough to report that to David, and it would then appear that Tom was curious about David's activities, therefore worried. David surely knew also that his wife was unpredictable: that would be part of their sadistic fun. 'Well, Janice, my best wishes to your husband – neighbourly good wishes – ' Tom paused, and Janice waited. He knew David had told her about his beating up David in Tangier, but in their world, right and wrong, politeness and impoliteness seemed not to count or even be remembered. It was in fact odder than a game, because in a game there were rules of some kind.

'Goodbye, Mr Ripley, and thank you for calling,' said Janice, friendly as ever.

Tom stared out on to his garden, and pondered the strangeness of the Pritchards. What had he learned? That David might go on *ad infinitum*. No, that *couldn't* be. Another month from now, and David would have scraped the bottom of an area seventy-five kilometres in diameter! Maniacal! And unless Teddy were absurdly well paid, Teddy would get tired of it too. Of course, Pritchard could hire someone else, as long as he had the money.

Just where were Pritchard and Teddy now? The energy necessary, Tom thought, to lift that boat several times daily off the pick-up and back on to it again! Could the pair of them be scraping the Loing bottom near Voisy this minute? Tom had a desire to go there – maybe in the white station wagon for a change – to satisfy his curiosity now, at half-past 3. Then he realized that he was too afraid to do that, to cruise for a second time around the scene of the disposal. Suppose someone had noticed and remembered his face, the day he had driven to Voisy and crossed the bridge? Suppose he ran smack into David and Teddy dragging their hooks just there?

That would disturb Tom's sleep, even if they missed their goal there. Tom decided definitely not to go.

Tom stared at his finished painting, reasonably satisfied, more than that. He had added a vertical stripe of bluish-red to the left side of the composition, a curtain of the house interior. The blues and purples and blacks intensified from the borders to the soft-edged rectangle of the black, back-room doorway, which was not quite in the centre. The picture was higher than it was wide.

Another Tuesday came, and Tom thought of M. Lepetit, the music teacher, who usually came on Tuesdays. But Tom and Héloïse had temporarily stopped their lessons: they had not known how long they would be in North Africa, and Tom had not rung up M. Lepetit since his return, though he had practised. The Grais invited Tom for a meal one weekend, but Tom declined, with thanks. Tom did ring Agnès Grais on a weekday, and invited himself at about 3 one afternoon.

The change of scene was welcome to Tom's eyes. They sat in the Grais' functional and orderly kitchen at a marble-topped table big enough for six, and drank express café with a nip of Calvados on the side. Yes, Tom said, he had heard two or three times from Héloïse by telephone – and at least once they had been cut off. Tom laughed. And a postcard written ages ago, three days after his own departure, had arrived yesterday. All was well, as far as Tom knew.

'And your neighbour is still fishing,' Tom said with a smile. 'So I hear.'

'Fishing.' Agnès Grais' brown eyebrows drew together for a moment. 'He's looking for something, won't say what. He's dragging with little hooks, you know? His companion also. Not that I've seen them, but I heard people talking in the butcher's.'

People always talked in the bakery and at the butcher's, and since baker and butcher joined in, service was slow, but the longer one lingered, the more one could learn.

Tom said finally, 'I'm sure one could drag up fascinating items from these canals – or rivers. You'd be surprised at the items I've found in the *décharge publique* here – before the authorities closed it, damn them. It was as good as an art exhibit! Antique furniture! Some might have needed a small repair, to be sure, but – the metal pitchers by my fireplace – they hold water, late nineteenth-century. They're from the *décharge publique.*' Tom laughed. The *décharge publique* was a field to one side of a road going out of Villeperce, and here people used to be allowed to throw broken chairs, old refrigerators, old anything, such as books, of which Tom had rescued several. Now that field was closed with metal fence and lock. Modern progress.

'People say he's not collecting anything,' said Agnès, as if she were not much interested. 'He throws back metal junk, someone said. Not very nice of him. He ought to toss it up on the bank where the garbage people could collect it, at least. That would be doing the community a service.' She smiled. 'Another little Calvados, Tome?'

'No thanks, Agnès. I should be going home.'

'Now *why* should you be going home? Work? To an empty house? Oh, I know you can amuse yourself, Tome, with painting and your harpsichord – '

'Our harpsichord,' Tom interrupted. 'Héloïse's and mine.'

'Correct.' Agnès tossed her hair back and looked at him. 'But you seem a little tense. You're making yourself get back home. All right. I hope Héloïse rings you.'

Tom was on his feet, smiling. 'Who knows?'

'And you know you're always welcome here for a meal or just to drop in.'

'I prefer to telephone first, as you know.' Tom's tone was equally pleasant. Today was a weekday, Antoine would not arrive until Friday evening or Saturday noon. And the children were due any minute now from school, Tom realized. 'Bye-bye, Agnès. Many thanks for the nice expresses with.'

She walked with him to the kitchen door. 'You look a little sad. Don't forget your old friends are here.' She patted his arm before he walked off to his car.

Tom gave a final wave from his car window, and pulled on to the road just before the yellow school bus, coming from an opposite direction, paused to drop off Edouard and Sylvie Grais.

He found himself thinking of Mme Annette, of her due holiday. It was early September. Mme Annette did not like to take her holiday in August, the traditional French holiday month, because there was too much traffic and congestion if she travelled anywhere, she said, and in August the other housekeepers of the village had more than usual free time, as their employers were often away, so she and her cronies had time for visiting. Should he suggest to Mme Annette now, however, that she might begin her holiday, if she wished?

Should he, for safety's sake? There was a limit to what he wanted Mme Annette to see or hear in the village.

Tom became aware that he was worried. The realization made him feel weaker. He would have to do something about that feeling, and the sooner the better.

Tom decided to ring Jeff or Ed, they each seemed now of equal value to Tom. It was a friend's presence that he needed, a helping hand or arm if necessary. After all, Pritchard had one in Teddy.

And what was Teddy going to say if Pritchard hit his quarry? Just what had Pritchard told Teddy he was looking for, anyway?

Tom suddenly doubled over with laughter, nearly staggered in the living-room, where he had been slowly walking about. That Teddy, the music student – was he? – maybe finding a corpse!

At that moment, Mme Annette walked in. 'Ah, M'sieur Tome – I am so glad to see you in good humour!'

Tom was sure that his face was pink with mirth. 'I just recalled a good joke . . . no, no, madame, hélas, it does not translate well into French!'

18

A few minutes after those words, Tom checked the number of Ed Banbury in London and dialled it. He heard Ed's recorded voice requesting the caller to give name and telephone number, and Tom was about to speak when, to his relief, Ed came on.

'Hello, *Tom*! Yes, just got in. What's the latest?'

Tom took a breath. 'The latest is the same. David Preekard is still fishing in the neighbourhood, dragging his hooks from a rowboat.' Tom spoke with deliberate calm.

'No kidding! And how long is it now? Ten – well, more than a week, certainly.'

Ed had plainly not been counting the days, nor had Tom, but Tom knew it was more like two weeks that Pritchard had been at work. 'About ten days,' Tom said. 'To be honest, Ed, if he keeps this up – and he shows every sign of doing so – he just might come up with you know what.'

'Yes. It's incredible – I think you need support.'

Tom could hear that Ed understood. 'Yes. Well, I might. Pritchard's got a helper. I told Jeff that, I believe. A man called Teddy. They work together on this indefatigable rowboat-with-motor, dragging their two rakes – rather, rows of hooks. They've been at it so long – '

'I'll come over, Tom, to do whatever I can. Sounds like the sooner the better.'

Tom hesitated. 'I confess I'd feel better.'

'I'll do my best. Got a job to finish by Friday noon, but I'll try to finish it by tomorrow afternoon. Have you talked to Jeff?'

'No, I was thinking of it – but maybe not if you're able to come over. Friday afternoon? Evening?'

'Let me see how this work goes and perhaps I can make it earlier, such as Friday, midday. I'll ring you again, Tom – with the flight time.'

177

Tom felt better after that, and at once went in quest of Mme Annette to inform her that they would likely have a weekend guest, a gentleman from London. Mme Annette's room door was closed. Silence. Was she napping? She didn't often.

He looked out of a kitchen window and saw her stooped by a patch of wild violets to the right. The violets were pale purple and impervious to draught, cold or predatory insects, or so they seemed to Tom. He went out. 'Madame Annette?'

She stood up. 'M'sieur Tome – I am admiring the violets from very near. Are they not *mignons*!'

Tom agreed. They peppered the soil near the laurel and box hedge there. Tom imparted his good news: someone to cook for, to prepare the guest-room for.

'A good friend! That will cheer you, m'sieur. Has he been to Belle Ombre before?'

They were walking back towards the side or service entrance which led to the kitchen.

'Not sure. I don't think so. Curious.' It did seem odd, considering he'd known Ed such a long time. Perhaps unconsciously Ed had stayed away from contact with Tom and household, because of the Derwatt forgeries. And the Bernard Tufts fiasco of a visit, of course.

'And what do you think he might take pleasure in eating?' asked Mme Annette, once she was back in her domain, the kitchen.

Tom laughed, trying to think. 'He'll probably want something French. In this weather – ' It was warm, but not hot.

'Lobster – cold? Ratatouille? Of course! Cold. Escalopes de veau avec sauce madère?' Her pale blue eyes brightened.

'Ye-es.' The way Mme Annette pronounced all this did summon the appetite. 'Good ideas. It seems to be Friday that he arrives.'

'And his wife?'

'Not married. M'sieur Ed will be by himself.'

Then Tom drove to the *bureau de poste* to buy stamps and also to see if anything had come from Héloïse by the second post, which was not delivered to the house. There was an envelope addressed in Héloïse's hand, which made his heart jump. The postmark was Marrakesh, date quite illegible due to faint ink on the stamp. Inside was a postcard on which she had written:

Cher Tom,

All is well, an actif town here. So beautiful! Purple sands at evening view. We are not sick, eat couscous every noon almost. Meknès comes next. We go par avion. Noëlle sends love, I much love.

H.

Nice to receive, Tom supposed, but he had known days ago that they were going from Marrakesh to Meknès.

Tom then worked in the garden with inspiration, driving the spade in to sharpen edges that Henri had missed. Henri had a whimsical idea of what his chores should be. He was to some extent practical, even wise about plants, then he would get sidetracked and do a neat job on something of no great importance. But then he was not expensive or dishonest, and Tom told himself he couldn't complain.

After his labours, Tom had a shower and read the Oscar Wilde biography. As Mme Annette had predicted, he was cheered by the prospect of a visit. He even looked in *Télé 7-Jours* to see what might be on TV tonight.

He found nothing that excited his interest, but thought he might try one programme at 10, unless he had something more interesting to do. Tom did switch on at 10 p.m., but in five minutes switched off, and walked with a torch to Marie's and Georges' bar-tabac for an express.

The card-players were at it again, the game-machines clacked and slammed. But Tom picked up nothing about David Pritchard, the curious fisherman. Tom supposed that Pritchard might well be too tired in the evening to come out to the bar-tabac for a late beer, or whatever he drank. Tom, however, still kept an eye out for him when the front door opened. Tom had paid and was about to leave, when a glance towards the door – which had just opened again – told him that Pritchard's companion Teddy had entered.

Teddy seemed to be alone, and looked freshly washed in his beige shirt and chino trousers, but he looked also a bit sullen, or perhaps simply tired.

'Encore un express, Georges, s'il vous plaît,' said Tom.

'Et bien sûr, M'sieur Reepley,' answered Georges without even looking at Tom, and turned his round figure towards the steam machine.

The man called Teddy seemed not to have noticed Tom, if indeed Tom had ever been pointed out to Teddy, and took a place standing near the door end of the bar. Marie brought him a beer, and greeted him as if she had seen him before, Tom thought, though he couldn't hear what she had said.

Tom decided to chance it and glance at Teddy more often than a stranger would, to see if Teddy showed any recognition. Teddy did not.

Teddy frowned and stared down at his beer. An exchange with a man on his left was a brief one, without a smile.

Was Teddy contemplating pulling out of Pritchard's employ? Was he missing a girlfriend in Paris? Was he fed up with the atmosphere in the Pritchard house, because of David's and Janice's odd relationship? Could Teddy hear Pritchard hitting his wife in the bedroom, because he hadn't found his quarry that day? More likely Teddy wanted a breath of fresh air. Teddy was the strong type, judging from his hands. Not the brainy type. A music student? Tom knew that some American colleges had curricula that read like trade-school curricula, anyway. To be a 'music student' need not mean that the student knew or cared anything about music; it was the diploma that mattered. Teddy was over six feet, and the sooner he quit the scene, the happier Tom would be.

Tom paid for his second coffee and headed towards the door. Just as he passed the motorcycle game, the rider hit a barrier, his crash simulated by a flashing star that finally stayed fixed. Game over. 'INSERT COINS INSERT COINS INSERT COINS'. Low moans from the onlookers had given way to laughter.

The man called Teddy had not glanced at him. Tom came to the conclusion that Pritchard had not told Teddy what they were looking for, Murchison's corpse. Maybe Pritchard had said they were looking for jewellery from a sunken yacht? A suitcase with valuables in it? But as Tom saw it, Pritchard had not said that it had anything to do with a neighbour who lived in the same town.

When Tom looked back from the doorway, Teddy was still hunched over his beer, and not in conversation with anybody.

Since it was warm, and Mme Annette seemed inspired by the prospect of lobster on the menu, Tom offered to drive in to Fontainebleau to aid with the shopping and to look in at its best fish shop. With not too much difficulty – Mme Annette always had to be asked twice for such outings – Tom persuaded her to accompany him.

In spite of the list, assembling shopping bags and baskets and some clothes of Tom's to go to the cleaner's, they had left the house

180

by 9.30. Another glorious day of sunlight, and Mme Annette had heard on her radio that fine weather was predicted for Saturday and Sunday. Mme Annette asked what M. Edouard did for a living?

'He's a journalist,' Tom replied. 'I never really tested him out on his French. He's bound to know *some*.' Tom laughed, imagining what was coming.

When their bags and baskets were full, the lobsters tied up in a great white plastic bag that the fishmonger assured Tom was double, Tom fed the parking meter again and invited Mme Annette (twice) to come into a nearby pastry shop–tearoom for 'a treat', *un petit extra*. She yielded, smiling with pleasure.

A great globe or scoop of chocolate icecream with two ladyfingers perched like rabbit's ears upon it, a generous daub of whipped cream between the ears, was Mme Annette's choice. She glanced discreetly around her at the matrons chatting away about nothing at nearby tables. Nothing? Well, one could never be sure, Tom supposed, despite the broad smiles as they plunged into their sweets. Tom had an express. Mme Annette loved her treat and said so, which pleased Tom.

Suppose nothing happened this weekend, Tom thought as they walked back to the car. How long could Ed Banbury stay? Till Tuesday? Would Tom then feel he had to call upon Jeff Constant? The question was, Tom supposed, how long would Pritchard keep at it?

'You will be happier when Madame Héloïse returns, M'sieur Tome,' said Mme Annette, as they were driving back toward Villeperce. 'What is madame's news?'

'News! I wish I had some! The post – well, the post seems to be worse than the telephone. I would think in less than a week, Madame Héloïse will be back home.'

As Tom turned into the main street of Villeperce, he saw Pritchard's white pick-up cross the street from his right. Tom did not quite have to slow down, but he did. The stern of the boat with motor removed projected over the pick-up's floor. Did they take the boat out of the water during the lunch period? Tom supposed so, or it would not be safe, merely tied to the bank, from either thieves or the bumping of a barge. The dark canvas or tarpaulin was now on the floor by the boat. They were going out again after lunch, Tom supposed.

'M'sieur Preechard,' Mme Annette remarked.

'Yes,' Tom said. 'The American.'

'He is trying to find something in the canals,' Mme Annette continued. 'Everyone talks about it. But he doesn't say what he wants to find. He spends so much time and money – '

'There are stories – ' Now Tom could smile as he spoke. 'You know, madame, stories about sunken treasure, gold coins, jewellery boxes – '

'He brings up skeletons of cats and dogs, you know, M'sieur Tome. He leaves them on the bank – just throws them up there or his friend does! It is annoying for the people living nearby, the people walking . . . '

Tom didn't want to hear about it, but he listened nonetheless. Now he turned right, into the still open front gates of Belle Ombre.

'He can't be happy here. He's not a happy man,' Tom said with a glance at Mme Annette. 'I can't imagine that he'll be living in this neighbourhood very long.' Tom's voice was soft, but his pulse ran a bit faster. He detested Pritchard, and there was nothing new about that, he reminded himself. It was just that in the presence of Mme Annette, he could not curse Pritchard aloud or even under his breath.

In the kitchen, they put away the extra butter, the beautiful broccoli, lettuce, three kinds of cheeses, an especially good coffee, a good section of beef for roasting, and of course the two living lobsters, which later Mme Annette could handle, as Tom did not wish to. To Mme Annette, they might be worthy of hardly more concern than haricots verts dumped into boiling water, Tom knew, but Tom imagined that he heard them screaming, wailing at least, as they were boiled to death. Equally depressing was something Tom had read about microwave cooking (of lobsters – baked, presumably), which said that one had fifteen seconds after switching on to run out of the kitchen before having to hear and possibly watch the beating of claws against the glass windows of the oven, before the lobsters died. There were people, Tom supposed, who could go about peeling potatoes while the lobsters got roasted to death – in how many seconds? Tom tried not to believe that Mme Annette was such a type. At any rate, they did not yet possess a microwave oven. Neither Mme Annette nor Héloïse had showed any interest in acquiring one, and if either did, Tom had some counter-ammunition: he had read that microwave-baked potatoes came out more like boiled than baked, a point which Héloïse, Mme Annette and Tom would take seriously. And in regard to cooking, Mme Annette was never in a hurry.

'M'sieur Tome!'

Tom heard Mme Annette's cry, from the back terrace steps, when he was in the greenhouse, with its door open just in case of a shout. *'Yes?'*

'Téléphone!'

Tom trotted, hoping it was Ed, thinking it might be Héloïse. Two leaps and he was up the terrace steps.

It was Ed Banbury. 'Tomorrow around midday looks fine, Tom. To be precise – got a pencil?'

'Yes, indeed.' Tom wrote down 11.25 arrival at Roissy, flight 212. 'I'll be there, Ed.'

'That would be nice – if it isn't a lot of trouble.'

'No-o. A nice drive – it'll do me good. Anything from – well, Cynthia? Anybody?'

'Not a thing. And at your end?'

'He's still fishing. You'll see – oh, one more thing, Ed. What's the price of "The Pigeon" drawing?'

'Ten thousand for you. Not fifteen.' Ed chuckled.

They signed off cheerfully.

Tom began to think of a frame for the pigeon drawing: light brown wood, either slender or quite broad, but warm in tone, like the pale yellowish paper of the drawing. He went into the kitchen to tell Mme Annette the good news: their guest would be in time for lunch tomorrow. Something not too heavy for lunch, in view of the warm temperature.

Then he went out and wound up his chores in the greenhouse, including giving it a sweep. He also dusted the inside of the slanting windows with a soft floor broom that he fetched from the house. Tom wanted his house to be looking its best for an old friend like Ed.

That evening, Tom watched a video cassette of *Some Like It Hot*. Just what he needed, light-minded relaxation, even the insanity of the forced smiles of the male chorus.

Before going to bed, Tom went to his workroom and made some sketches at the table, at which he could comfortably stand. He drew in heavy black lines his recollection of Ed Banbury's face. He might ask Ed if he would be willing to pose for five or ten minutes for preliminary sketches. It would be interesting to do a portrait of Ed's blondish and very English face, the receding hairline, the thin, straight, light brown hair, the polite but quizzical eyes, the slender lips, ready to smile or shut straight on short notice.

183

19

Tom was up unusually early, as was his wont when he had engagements ahead. By 6.30, he had shaved and put on Levis and shirt, and was downstairs walking deliberately quietly through the living-room towards the kitchen to boil some water. Mme Annette usually got up only at quarter-past or half-past 7. Tom carried his drip pot and cup and saucer on a tray into the living-room. The coffee was not yet through, so he went to the front door, thinking to open it for the fresh morning air, to glance at the garage and decide whether to take the red Mercedes or the Renault to Roissy.

A long grey bundle at Tom's feet made him jump back a little. It lay across the doorstep and Tom knew, with horror, and instantly, what it was.

Tom could see that Pritchard had wrapped it in what could be called a 'new' grey canvas sheet, which looked to Tom like the same sheet Pritchard had been using to cover his boat, now tied with rope. Pritchard had also stabbed this canvas with a knife or scissors in several places – why? For fingerholds? Pritchard had had to transport the thing here, and maybe alone. Tom bent and pulled a flap of the new canvas back, out of curiosity, and at once saw the old canvas, threadbare and failing, and some grey-whiteness of bone.

Belle Ombre's big iron gates were still closed and padlocked from the inside. Pritchard must have driven into the lane beside Tom's lawn, stopped his car and dragged or carried the bundle across the grass and about ten metres of gravel to arrive at his front door. The gravel would have made a noise, of course, but both Mme Annette and Tom had been sleeping at the back part of the house.

Tom fancied he could smell something unpleasant, but perhaps it was only a stink of moisture, staleness – or imagination.

The station wagon was a good idea for the moment, and thank

184

God Mme Annette was not yet awake. Tom went back into the hall, grabbed his keyring from the hall table, dashed out and opened the back of the car. Then he took a firm grip with both hands under two cords on the bundle, and heaved, expecting a much heavier weight.

The damned thing weighed no more than fifteen kilos, Tom thought, maybe less than forty pounds. And some of that was water. The bundle dripped a little, even as Tom staggered with it towards the white station wagon. Tom felt that he had been paralysed with surprise for several seconds on the doorstep. Mustn't let that happen again! Tom could not tell head from feet, he realized, as he heaved the burden on to the floor of the car. He got into the driver's seat and gave one cord a tug, so that he could close the back.

No blood. Absurd thought, Tom realized at once. The stones he had put in with Bernard Tufts's help must be long gone also. The bones had stayed sunken because no flesh was left, Tom supposed.

Tom locked the back of the car, then the side door. This car was outside the two-car garage. What next? Go back to his coffee, say 'Bon jour' to Mme Annette. And meanwhile think. Or scheme.

He returned to the front door, where some drops of water were visible on doorstep and mat, to his annoyance, but the sunlight would soon take care of that, and by 9.30, Tom thought, when Mme Annette usually went out shopping. In fact, most of the time she departed and returned by the kitchen door. Inside the house, Tom made for the hall loo, and washed his hands at the basin. He noticed some sandy wetness on his right thigh and brushed it off into the basin as best he could.

When had Pritchard found his bonanza? Probably late yesterday afternoon, though of course it could have been yesterday morning. He'd have kept his trove hidden in his boat, Tom supposed. Had he told Janice? Probably, why not? Janice seemed to make no judgements of any kind concerning right or wrong, pro or con on anything, and certainly not her husband, or she would not be with him now. Tom corrected himself: Janice was just as cracked as David.

Tom entered the living-room with cheerful air, on seeing Mme Annette adding toast, butter and marmalade to his breakfast on the coffee table. 'How nice! Thank you,' said Tom. 'Bon jour, madame!'

'Bon jour, M'sieur Tome. You are up early.'

'As always when I have a guest coming, isn't it so?' Tom bit into his toast.

Tom was thinking that he should put a cover over the bundle, newspapers, anything, so that it didn't look like what it was to anyone glancing through a window of the car.

Had Pritchard dismissed Teddy by now, Tom wondered. Or had Teddy dismissed himself, scared of becoming an accomplice in something he had nothing to do with?

What did Pritchard expect him to do with the bag of bones? Was he going to arrive at any moment with the police and say, 'Look! Here's the missing Murchison!'?

Tom stood up at this thought, with coffee cup in hand, frowning. The corpse could jolly well go straight back into a canal, Tom thought, and Pritchard could go to hell. Of course Teddy could witness that he and Pritchard had found something, *some* corpse, but what was the proof that it was Murchison's?

Tom glanced at his wristwatch. Seven minutes to 8. He thought he should leave the house at ten minutes before 10 at the latest to fetch Ed Banbury. Tom moistened his lips, then lit a cigarette. He was walking slowly about the living-room, prepared to stop walking if Mme Annette should reappear. Tom recalled that he had decided to leave Murchison's two rings on his hands. Teeth, dental records? Had Pritchard gone so far in America as to get photostats of police documents, maybe via Mrs Murchison? Tom realized that he was torturing himself, because he couldn't, with Mme Annette in the kitchen, which had a window, go outside now and take a good look at what was in his station wagon. The car stood parallel to the kitchen window, part of the canvas bundle perhaps just visible to Mme Annette, if she peered, but why should she? The postman was also due at 9.30.

He'd simply drive the station wagon into the garage and take a look, and right away. Meanwhile Tom finished his cigarette calmly, got his Swiss knife from the hall table and pocketed it, and took a handful of old newspapers, folded, from the basket near the fireplace.

Tom backed the red Mercedes out in readiness for Ed Banbury, and drove the white station wagon into the place where the Mercedes had been. Sometimes Tom used a small vacuum cleaner with the electric power point in the garage, so at the moment Mme Annette could think what she wished as to his activities. The garage doors were at right-angles to the kitchen window. Nevertheless, Tom closed the garage door on the side where the station wagon was, and left the other open, where the brown Renault stood. He switched on the wire-guarded light on the right wall.

Again he got on to the flat floor of the station wagon and forced himself to make sure which was head and which the feet of the wrapped object. This was not easy, and just as Tom was realizing that the corpse was rather short, if it was Murchison, he realized also that it had no head. The head had fallen off, separated. Tom made himself slap the feet, the shoulders.

No head.

That was comforting, as it meant no teeth, no characteristic nose-bone or whatever. Tom got out and opened the windows of the car by the driver's and passenger's seats. It was a funny, musty smell that emanated from the canvas-wrapped bundle, not like death but like something very wet. Tom realized that he would have to look at the hands in order to see about the rings. *No head.* Where was the head, then? Rolling down with the current somewhere, Tom supposed, rolling back again, maybe? No, not in a river.

Tom got out of the car quickly, tried to sit on a tool case, which was too low, and ended by leaning against a front fender with his head bent low. He was near fainting. Could he risk waiting till Ed got here, to supply moral support? Tom faced the fact that he couldn't investigate the corpse further. He would say . . .

Tom straightened up and forced himself to think. He would say, in case Pritchard turned up with the police, that of course he had had to put the revolting bag of bones – Tom *had* seen some bones and had certainly felt them – out of his housekeeper's vision for decency's sake, and he had been so nauseated that he had not yet contacted the police himself.

It would be highly disagreeable, however, if the police arrived (summoned by Pritchard) when he was away from the house fetching Ed Banbury from Roissy airport. Mme Annette would have to deal with them, the police would certainly look for the corpse Pritchard told them about, and it would not take them too long to find it, less than half an hour, Tom estimated. Tom bent and wet his face at an outside standpipe on the lane side of the house.

Now he felt better, though he realized that he was waiting for Ed's presence to bolster his courage.

Suppose it was somebody else's corpse, not Murchison's? Funny, the things that ran through one's mind. Then Tom reminded himself that the tan tarpaulin was all too familiar as the one he and Bernard had used that night.

Suppose Pritchard kept on fishing for the head, in the vicinity of where he had found the corpse? What were the people of Voisy saying? Had any of them noticed anything? Tom gave it a fifty-fifty chance that someone had. There was often a man or woman taking a walk along a river-bank, over the bridge there, where the view would have been better. Unfortunately the object retrieved looked as though it might be a human body. Obviously the two (three?) ropes that he and Bernard had used had lasted, or the tarpaulin wouldn't have been there.

Tom thought of working in the garden for half an hour to ease his nerves, and then didn't feel like it. Mme Annette was ready to depart for morning shopping. There was only half an hour or so before he had to take off for Ed.

Tom went up and took a quick shower, though he had had one that morning, and put on different clothing.

Now the house was silent when he went downstairs. If the telephone rang now, Tom decided that he would not answer it, even though it might be Héloïse. He hated being away from the house for nearly two hours. His watch said five to 10. Tom strolled to the bar cart, chose the tiniest glass (stemmed) and poured a minuscule Rémy Martin, savoured it on his tongue and sniffed the glass. Then he washed and dried the glass in the kitchen and brought it back to the bar cart. Wallet, keys, all set.

Tom went out and locked the front door. Mme Annette had thoughtfully opened the iron gates for him. Tom left them wide open still when he departed northward. He drove at a medium or normal speed. Loads of time, in fact, though one never knew what the *périphérique* would present.

Exit at Pont La Chapelle, northward towards the huge and dismal airport, which Tom still didn't like. Heathrow was so huge, its sprawling entirety was hard to imagine, until of course one had to walk a kilometre or so with luggage. But Roissy in its arrogant inconvenience was easily conceived: a circular main building, and a gaggle of roads off, all marked of course, but it was too late to turn around if you hadn't found the first marking.

Tom parked, being fifteen minutes early at least, in an open-air lot.

Then there was Ed, looking warm with open-necked white shirt and a knapsack of some kind slung over one shoulder. He had an attaché case in one hand.

'*Ed*!' Ed hadn't seen him. Tom waved.

'Hello, Tom!'

They shook hands warmly.

'My car's not far away,' Tom said. Ed had a smallish suitcase, a raincoat over one shoulder. 'Let's get this navette! And how's everything in London?'

Everything was all right, said Ed, his coming over had not been difficult, no one was annoyed. He could stay till Monday with no problems, longer if necessary. 'And your end? Any news?'

Straphanging in the little yellow bus, Tom wrinkled his nose, winced. 'Well – a little something. Tell you later, not just here.'

Once in Tom's car, Ed asked how Héloïse was faring in Morocco. Had Ed been to his house in Villeperce before, Tom asked, and Ed said he hadn't.

'Funny!' Tom said. 'Almost unbelievable!'

'But it's worked out pretty well,' Ed replied, with a friendly smile at Tom. 'A business relationship, is it not?'

Ed laughed, as if at the absurdity of his statement, because in a sense their relationship was as deep as that of friendship, yet different. A betrayal by either of them of the other could lead to disgrace, a fine, maybe imprisonment. 'Yes,' Tom agreed. 'Speaking of that, what's Jeff doing this weekend?'

'Um – I dunno exactly.' Ed looked as if he were enjoying the summer breeze through his window. 'I rang him last night, told him I was coming over to see you. I also said you might need him. Saw no harm in it, Tom.'

'No,' Tom agreed. 'No harm.'

'Are we going to need him, do you think?'

Tom frowned at the congestion on the *périphérique*. The weekend departures were of course already beginning, and the drive south would also present more cars. Tom turned and turned again in his mind the question of whether to tell Ed about the corpse before or after lunch. 'I really don't know as yet.'

'What beautiful fields here!' Ed said as they rolled away from Fontainebleau eastward. 'Broader than in England – it seems.'

Tom said nothing, but he was pleased. Some guests made no comment, as if they were blind or day-dreaming out of the window. Ed was equally appreciative of Belle Ombre, much admired the impressive gates, which Tom reminded him with a laugh were not

189

bullet-proof, and praised the balance in the design of the house from the front.

'Yes, and now – ' Tom had parked the Mercedes not far from the front door, its back to the house. ' – I have to tell you something most unpleasant which I didn't know till this morning before eight, Ed – I swear.'

'I believe you,' said Ed, frowning. He had his luggage in his hand. 'What is it?'

'In the garage there – ' Tom lowered his voice and took a step nearer Ed. 'Pritchard deposited the corpse on my doorstep this morning. Murchison's corpse.'

Ed frowned harder. 'The – you don't *mean* it!'

'It's a bag of bones,' Tom said in almost a whisper. 'My house-keeper doesn't know about it, and let's keep it that way. It's in the back of the station wagon there. Doesn't even weigh much. But something's got to be done.'

'Obviously.' Ed spoke softly too. 'Take it to some woods and leave it, do you mean?'

'I dunno. Have to think. I thought – better to tell you now.'

'Here on the doorstep?'

'Right there.' Tom indicated with a nod. 'He did it in the dark, of course. I didn't hear a thing, where I sleep. Madame Annette didn't mention hearing anything. I found it around seven this morning. He came by the side here – maybe with his helper Teddy, but even alone he could've dragged it without too much trouble. From the lane. Hard to see the lane now, but you can drive a car into it, stop, and walk into my land.' As Tom glanced in that direction, he fancied he could see a faint depression in the grass, a path such as a person walking would have made, since the bones weren't heavy enough to have had to be dragged.

'Teddy,' Ed said musingly, and half-turned towards the house door.

'Yes. I learned that from Pritchard's wife, I think I told you. I'm wondering if Teddy is still employed or does Pritchard consider the job done? Well – let's go in, have a drink and try to enjoy a nice lunch.'

Tom used his key on the ring he still held in one hand. Mme Annette, busy in the kitchen, had perhaps seen them but also seen that they wanted to talk for a minute.

'How nice! Really, Tom,' said Ed. 'Beautiful living-room.'

'Want to leave your mac down here?'

Mme Annette came in and Tom introduced them. She of course wanted to carry Ed's case upstairs. Ed remonstrated, smiling.

'This is a ritual,' Tom murmured. 'Come on, I'll show you your room.'

Tom did. Mme Annette had cut a single peach-coloured rose for the dressing table, very effective in its narrow vase. Ed thought the room splendid. Tom showed him the bath adjacent, and asked him to make himself comfortable and come down soon for a pre-lunch drink.

It was then just past 1 p.m.

'Have there been any telephone calls, madame?' Tom asked.

'No, m'sieur, and I have been home since a quarter past ten.'

'Good,' said Tom calmly, thinking that it was very good. Surely Pritchard had told his spouse of his trove? His success? What had her reaction been, Tom wondered, besides silly laughter?

Tom went to his CD collection, hesitated between a Scriabin string composition – beautiful but dreamy – and Brahms's Opus 39, and chose the latter, a series of sixteen brilliant waltzes played on the piano. That was what he and Ed needed, and he hoped Ed would like it too. He set the volume not too loud.

He made himself a gin and tonic, and by the time he had twisted the lemon peel and dropped it in, Ed was down.

Ed wanted the same.

Tom made the drink, then went to the kitchen to ask Mme Annette to hold lunch for another five minutes or so, please.

Tom and Ed lifted their glasses, and exchanged a look in silence, but for Brahms. Tom felt the drink at once, but he also felt the Brahms making his blood run faster. One rapid and thrilling musical idea followed another, as if the great composer were deliberately showing off. And with that talent, why not?

Ed strolled towards the french windows on the terrace side. 'What a pretty harpsichord! And the view here, Tom! All yours?'

'No, just to where the row of bushes is. Behind's woods. Anybody's sort of.'

'And – I like your music.'

Tom smiled. 'Good.'

Ed strolled back to the centre of the room. He had put on a fresh blue shirt. 'How far away does this Pritchard live?' he asked quietly.

'About two kilometres that way.' Tom gestured over his left shoulder. 'By the way, my housekeeper doesn't understand English – or so I fancy,' he added with a smile, 'or I prefer to think.'

191

'I remember – from somewhere. Convenient.'

'Yes. Sometimes.'

They lunched on cold ham, cottage cheese with parsley, Mme Annette's homemade potato salad, black olives and a nice bottle of Graves, chilled. Then a sorbet. Their mood was outwardly cheerful, but Tom was thinking of their next job, and he knew Ed was too. Neither wanted coffee.

'I'm going to change into Levis,' Tom said. 'Are you okay? We have to – may have to kneel in the back of the car.'

Ed was already in blue jeans.

Tom nipped upstairs and changed. When he came down, he again got his Swiss knife from the hall table, and gave Ed a nod. They went out through the front door. Tom deliberately did not glance at the kitchen window, lest he attract Mme Annette's eye.

They went past the brown Renault, where the garage door was open. There was no wall between the cars in the garage.

'It's not too bad,' Tom said as cheerily as he could. 'The head's missing. What I'm after now – '

'Missing?'

'It probably rolled off, don't you think? After three, four years? Cartilege dissolving – '

'Rolled off where?'

'This thing's been under water, Ed. The Loing river. I don't suppose the current reverses, as in a canal, but – there is a current. I just want to check on the rings. He had two, I remember, and I – I left them on. Okay, are you game?'

Tom could see that Ed tried to look game as he nodded. Tom opened the side door, and they had a view of most of the dark grey canvas-wrapped form, on which Tom saw two coils of rope, one apparently at waist-, one at about knee-level. What Tom thought were the shoulders were towards the front of the car. 'Shoulders this way, I think,' Tom said, gesturing. 'Excuse me.' Tom got in first, crept to the other side of the corpse to give Ed room, and pulled out his Swiss knife. 'I'm going to look at the hands.' Tom began sawing away at the rope, not a quick job.

Ed put a hand under the end of the sack, the feet end, and tried to lift it. 'Quite light!'

'I told you.'

With his knees on the car floor, Tom attacked the rope from below, sawing upward with his knife's little saw blade now. It was Pritchard's rope, and new. He got it cut. Tom loosened the rope and braced himself, because he was at the abdominal part of the remains now. There was still only a stale, dampish smell, not the kind to make one ill unles one thought about it. Now Tom could see that some bits of flesh still clung, pale and flabby, to the spinal column. The abdomen was of course rather a hollow. *The hands*, Tom reminded himself.

Ed was watching closely, and had murmured something, maybe his favourite exclamation.

'Hands,' Tom said. 'Well – you can see why it's light.'

'Never saw anything *like* it!'

'I hope you never will.' Tom loosened Pritchard's cloth, then the worn-out beige tarpaulin which seemed ready to fall apart everywhere, like a mummy's disintegrating tapes.

The hand and wrist bones almost separated from the two bones of the forearm, Tom thought, but at any rate, they didn't. It was the right hand (Murchison lay on his back by accident), and Tom saw at once the heavy gold ring with purple stone, which he vaguely recalled, and remembered thinking was probably a class ring. Tom took it carefully from the little finger. It came off easily, but he did not want to tear off the delicate bones of that finger. Tom pushed his thumb into the ring to clean it, then pushed it into a front pocket of his Levis.

'You said two rings?'

'As I recall.' Tom had to back up, as the left arm was not bent but straight down at the side. Tom loosened more tarpaulin, then twisted and lowered the window behind him. 'You all right, Ed?'

'Sure.' But Ed looked white in the face.

'This'll be quick.' Tom got to the hand, and there was no ring on it. He looked under the bones, to see if it had fallen off, even into Pritchard's oilcloth. 'Wedding ring, I think,' Tom said to Ed. 'Not here. Maybe it fell off.'

'Certainly logical it *could've* fallen off,' replied Ed, and cleared his throat.

Tom could see that Ed was struggling, that he would have preferred not to watch. Once more, Tom groped under the femur, the pelvic bones. He felt crumbs, soft and not so soft, but nothing like a ring. He sat back. Should he take both wrappings off? Yes. 'I've got to look for that – here. You know, Ed, if Madame Annette gives us a shout, about a telephone call or some such, you step out and tell her we're in the garage, and I'll be there in a minute. I'm not sure if she knows we're here or not. If she asks – which she won't –

what we're *doing*, I'll say we're polishing something.'

Then Tom went at his task with a will, cut the other rope in the same manner (it had a hard knot), wishing he had his pruning saw from the greenhouse. He lifted ankle and shin bones, looked and felt, down to the end. Useless. Tom noticed that the little toe was missing from the left foot. And so had a phalange or two of the fingers been missing. But that class ring proved it was Murchison, Tom thought.

'Can't find it,' Tom said. 'Now – ' Tom hesitated about stones. Should he gather some, as he had with Bernard Tufts, to sink the bones? What was he going to do with the thing, anyway? 'I think tie it up again. Could look almost like skis, you know?'

'Won't this Pritchard bastard get the police, Tom? Tell the police to come here?'

Tom gave a gasp. 'Yes, you'd think! But we're dealing with loonies, Ed! Just try and predict them!'

'But what if the police come?'

'Well – ' Tom felt his adrenalin rising. 'I'll tell them these bones are in the car because I wanted them out of sight of my guest, and that I intended to deliver them to the police as soon as I'd recovered from the shock of finding them. And also – who notified the police? *There's* the culprit!'

'You think Pritchard knows about that ring? Identification?'

'I doubt it. Doubt if he looked for a ring.' Tom began tying up the lower part of the carcass again.

'I'll help you with the top,' Ed said, reaching for the rope that Tom had laid to one side.

Tom was grateful. 'Got to make two loops around instead of three, thanks to that knot, I think.' Pritchard had given three circles round with his new rope.

'But – what're we going to do with it finally?' Ed asked.

Throw it back in some canal, Tom thought to himself in which case, they'd have to – or he'd have to – untie the ropes again to get some stones into Pritchard's canvas. Or throw the damned thing into Pritchard's little pond. Tom laughed suddenly. 'I was thinking we could throw it back at Pritchard. He's got a pond on his lawn.'

Ed gave a short laugh, unbelieving. They were both tugging at the final knots to secure their ropes.

'I've got more rope in my cellar, thank goodness,' Tom said. 'Excellent, Ed. Now we know what we've got here, right? A headless corpse, pretty hard to identify, I'd say, fingerprints long ago washed off with the skin, head missing.'

Here Ed forced a laugh that sounded sick.

'Let's get out,' Tom said at once. Ed got down to the garage floor and Tom slid out after him. Tom looked at the stretch of the road in front of Belle Ombre, as much of it as he could see. He couldn't believe that Pritchard wasn't curious enough to be snooping now, and Tom was half expecting Pritchard at any moment. But he didn't want to tell Ed this.

'I thank you, Ed. I couldn't have done it without you!' Tom gave Ed's arm a pat.

'Are you kidding?' Ed tried to grin.

'No. I bogged down on it this morning, as I said.' Tom wanted to look for extra rope now and put it handy in the garage, but he noticed that Ed's pallor did not leave his face. 'Want to take a turn in the back garden? Out in the sun?'

Tom put out the inside light in the garage. They strolled around by the kitchen side of the house – Mme Annette had likely finished there, and was in her own room by now – and on to the back lawn. The sunshine fell warm and bright on their faces. Tom chatted about his dahlias. He'd cut a couple now, he said, because he had his knife with him. But there was the greenhouse, quite near, so Tom went in and got his clippers, his second pair, which lived there.

'You don't lock this at night?' Ed asked.

'Usually not. I know I should,' Tom replied. 'Most people would around here.' Tom found himself glancing at the side road, the unpaved lane, for a car or for Pritchard. After all, Pritchard had made his delivery by that road. Tom cut three blue dahlias and they went into the living-room, via a french window.

'Nice little brandy?' Tom suggested.

'Frankly, I feel like lying down for a couple of minutes.'

'Nothing easier.' Tom poured a very small Rémy Martin, and handed it to Ed. 'I insist. Moral support. Won't do you any harm.'

Ed smiled, and tossed it down. 'Um-m. Thank you.'

Tom went up with Ed, took a hand towel from the guest bathroom, and wet it with cold water. He told Ed to lie down with the folded towel on his forehead, and if he wanted to sleep for a while, fine.

Then Tom went down and got an appropriate vase for the dahlias from the kitchen, and set them on the coffee table. Héloïse's pricy jade Dunhill lighter lay on the coffee table. How wise she had been to leave it behind! Tom wondered when she would next pick it up.

Tom opened the door of the tiny room he called the downstairs loo, then the smaller door, and put on the light. Down the stairs to the wine department, to the unused picture frames that leaned against the wall, to the old bookcase which now served as reserve for extra mineral water, milk, soft-drink bottles, potatoes and onions. A rope. Tom looked in corners, lifted plastic grain sacks, and finally found what he wanted. He shook the rope out, and coiled it again. He had nearly five metres here, and might need it, if he made three ties and put rocks into the canvas. Tom went up and out of the house via the front door, closing all doors behind him.

Was that Pritchard's car – a white one – creeping slowly towards Belle Ombre from the left? Tom walked on to the garage, and dropped the rope in the far left corner, near the Renault's left wheel.

It was Pritchard. He had stopped his car to the right of the gates from Tom's view, and stood outside them lifting a camera to his eyes.

Tom advanced. 'What's so fascinating about my house, Pritchard?'

'Oh, plenty! Have the police been here yet?'

'No. Why?' Tom paused with hands on hips.

'Don't ask silly questions, Mr Ripley.' Pritchard turned and walked towards his car, looked back once with a faint and stupid smile.

Tom stood as he was until Pritchard's car had moved on. The photograph had perhaps included him, Tom thought, and so what? Tom spat on the gravel in the direction of Pritchard, turned and walked back to his front door.

Had Pritchard possibly kept the head of Murchison, Tom wondered. Like a guarantee of victory?

20

Mme Annette was in the living-room when Tom entered the house.

'Ah, M'sieur Tome, I did not know where you were – earlier. The police telephoned perhaps one hour ago. The Nemours commissariat. I thought you had gone for a walk with the gentleman.'

'Telephoned about what?'

'They asked if there had been any disturbance during the night. I said no, not – '

'What kind of disturbance?' Tom asked, frowning.

'Noise – of some kind. A car. They even asked me, and I said, "Non, m'sieur, absolument pas de bruit."'

'I can say the same. Good, madame. They didn't say what kind of noise?'

'*Yes*, they said a big package had been delivered, someone reported – someone with an American accent – a package of interest to the police.'

Tom laughed. 'A package! Must be a joke.' Tom looked for his cigarettes, took one finally from the box on the coffee table and used Héloïse's lighter. 'The police are going to telephone again?'

Mme Annette paused in her wiping of the shining dining-room table. 'I am not sure, m'sieur.'

'They didn't say who the American was?'

'Non, m'sieur.'

'Maybe I should telephone them,' Tom said as if to himself, and he thought he certainly should, to ward off a possible visit from the police. He also realized that he would be sticking his neck out, endangering himself, or in a plain word lying, if he said he didn't know anything about a package, as long as that sack of bones was on his land.

Tom consulted the telephone book for the commissariat's number in Nemours. He dialled and gave his name, and said where he lived. 'There was a telephone call from the commissariat today, my housekeeper told me. From *your* commissariat?' Tom was passed to someone else, and had to wait.

To the next person, Tom repeated what he had said.

'Ah, oui, M'sieur Reepley. Oui.' The male voice continued in French. 'A man with American accent told us that you had received a package that would be of interest to the police. Therefore we telephoned your home. This would have been about fifteen hours this afternoon.'

'I have not received a package,' Tom said. 'A couple of letters today, yes, but not a package.'

'A big package, the American said.'

'Not any package, m'sieur, I assure you. I can't imagine why anyone – did the man leave his name?' Tom kept a light and unworried tone.

'Non, m'sieur, we asked but he did not give his name. We know your house. You have a handsome gate there – '

'Yes, thank you. The postman can ring, if he has a package, of course. Otherwise there is a letterbox outside.'

'Yes – that is normal.'

'I thank you for telling me,' Tom said. 'But as it happens, I have walked quite around my house a few minutes ago, and there is no package anywhere, small or big.'

They hung up amicably.

Tom was glad that the officer had not connected the American-accented caller with Pritchard, the American who lived now in Villeperce. That might come later, if there was any later, and Tom hoped there wouldn't be. And the officer he had just spoken to would probably not be the same who had visited Belle Ombre in connection with Murchison's disappearance years ago. But of course that visit would be on police records. Hadn't that officer been based in Melun, a bigger town than Nemours?

Mme Annette was hovering discreetly.

Tom explained. There had been no package, he and M. Banbury had walked around the house, no one had come through the gates, not even the postman this morning (again nothing from Héloïse), and Tom had declined to have the police from Nemours come to look round for a strange package.

'Very good, M'sieur Tome. That is a relief. A package – ' She shook her head, indicating that she had no patience with pranksters and liars.

Tom was glad that Mme Annette did not suspect Pritchard as the culprit either. That was the kind of thing she would come out with, if she did suspect. Tom looked at his watch: 4.15. He was delighted that Ed was having a good nap after today's stress. Maybe a cup of tea? And should he ask the Grais over for a pre-dinner drink? Why not?

He went into the kitchen and said, 'A pot of tea, madame? I'm sure our guest is going to wake up any minute. Tea for us two . . . No, no need of sandwiches or cake . . . Yes, Earl Grey would be perfect.'

Tom returned to the living-room, hands in the front pockets of his jeans; in the right-hand pocket was Murchison's rather thick ring. Best into a river with that, Tom thought, maybe dropped from the bridge in Moret some time soon. Or if he were in haste, straight into the rubbish bag in the kitchen. The plastic rubbish bag swung out when one opened the door under the sink, and the bags were put out at the edge of the road and collected Wednesday and Saturday mornings. Tomorrow morning, for instance.

Tom was climbing the stairs to rap on Ed's door, when Ed opened it, smiling cautiously.

'Hello, Tom! Had a great nap! Hope it didn't bother you. It's so lovely and quiet here!'

'Certainly didn't bother me. How about a spot of tea? Come down.'

They drank their tea, and watched two sprinklers that Tom had put on in his garden. Tom had decided not to mention the telephone call from the police. What good would it do? And it might well make Ed more edgy, unsure of himself.

'I was thinking,' Tom began, 'by way of relieving the atmosphere of this afternoon – I might ask a couple of neighbours to come for a pre-dinner drink. Agnès and Antoine Grais.'

'That'd be nice,' said Ed.

'I'll buzz them. They're friendly – live not far away. He's an architect.' Tom went to the telephone and dialled, expecting, nay hoping, for a flood of information on Pritchard at the sound of his voice. But no. 'I'm ringing to ask if you and Antoine – if he's there and I hope so – can come for a glass around seven? I've an old friend from England here for the weekend.'

'Oh, Tom, how nice! Yes, Antoine's here now. But why don't you both come to us? Change of scene for your friend. What is his name?'

'Edward Banbury. Ed,' Tom replied. 'Very well, Agnès, my dear. We'd be delighted. What time?'

'Oh-h – six-thirty, is that too early? The children want to watch something on télé after dinner.'

Tom said it was fine.

'We're going there,' he said to Ed, smiling. 'They live in a round house, like a turret. Climbing-rose-covered. Only two houses away from the accursed – Pritchards.' Tom whispered the last word, and glanced at the doorway in the kitchen direction; sure enough, Mme Annette was just coming through the doorway to ask if the messieurs would care for more tea. 'I think not, madame, thank you. Or do you, Ed?'

'No, thanks, really.'

'Oh, Madame Annette – we are gong out to the Grais' at half-past six. I suppose we shall return at half-past seven, quarter to eight? So dinner perhaps about eight-fifteen?'

'Very good, M'sieur Tome.'

'And a good white wine with the lobsters. A Montrachet, perhaps?'

Mme Annette was pleased to oblige.

'Should I put on a jacket and tie?' Ed asked.

'I wouldn't bother. Antoine's probably already in jeans, even shorts. He's come down from Paris today.'

Ed stood up, finished the last of his cup, and Tom saw him look out of the window towards the garage. He glanced at Tom, then away. Tom knew what was on his mind: what were they going to do with it? He was glad Ed didn't ask now, because Tom had no ready answer.

Tom went upstairs and so did Ed. Tom changed to black cotton trousers and a yellow shirt. He put the ring into the right-hand pocket of the black trousers. Somehow he felt safer having the ring with him. Then out to the garage, where Tom looked at the brown Renault, then turned his glance to the red Mercedes in the drive, as if debating which to take – in case Mme Annette were looking out of the kitchen window. He went into the closed half of the garage, and ascertained that the canvas-wrapped bundle still lay on the car's floor.

If the police did come during this absence, Tom intended to say that the bundle must have been deposited during the night without his knowledge. Was David Pritchard going to turn up and remark the difference in the ropes and so on? Tom doubted that. Tom did not want to say all this to Ed, however, lest it make Ed more tense. Tom would just have to hope that Ed was not present, or would catch on to his lie and go along with him, in case the police spoke to both of them together.

Ed was down and they took off, as it was time to go.

The Grais were hospitable and curious about their new guest, Ed Banbury of London, a journalist. The teenagers stared a little, amused by Ed's accent, perhaps. Antoine was in shorts, as Tom had predicted, and his tanned legs with bulging calf muscles looked utterly untirable, capable of a marathon walk around the border of France, for instance. Tonight he was using his legs merely to go back and forth from living-room to kitchen.

'You work for a newspaper, M'sieur Banbury?' asked Agnès, in English.

'I am freelance. Independent,' Ed replied.

'Amazing,' Tom said, 'all the years I've known Ed – I admit we have not been very close friends – he's never been to Belle Ombre! I'm glad to say he – '

'It is very beautiful,' said Ed.

'Ah, Tome, some news since yesterday,' said Agnès. 'The assistant, or whatever one may call him, of Preechard has departed. Yesterday afternoon.'

'Oh,' said Tom pretending little or no interest. 'The boat man.' He sipped his gin and tonic.

'Let's sit down,' said Agnès. 'Anyone want to sit? I do.'

They were standing, because Antoine had shown Ed and Tom round their house to some extent, at least to the upstairs 'observatory tower' as Antoine called it, where his workroom was, and on the opposite side, or curve, two bedrooms. Still up, there was another bedroom for their son, Edouard, and an attic room.

They all sat.

'Yes, this Teddy,' Agnès went on. 'I happened to see him driving past yesterday around four, by himself in the peek-up away from the Preechard house. So I thought, they are finishing early today. Does your friend know that they have been scraping the local waterways?'

Tom looked at Ed and said in English, 'We're talking about Teddy, the helper of Pritchard. I told you about the odd two, dredging the rivers – for treasure.' Tom laughed. 'There are two odd couples, one's Pritchard and wife, the other Pritchard and helper.' He continued in French to Agnès. 'What were they looking for?'

'Nobody knows!' Now Agnès and Antoine laughed, because they had both said the words almost at once.

'No, seriously, this morning at the bakery – '

'The bakery!' said Antoine, as if in contempt of a gossip centre for women only, then listened with attention.

'Well, Simone Clément told me in the bakery that she'd heard it from Marie and Georges. Teddy was in the bar-tabac for a couple of glasses yesterday, and he told Georges he was finished with Preechard and he was in bad humour and did not say why. It seems they had a quarrel. I am *not* sure. That's the way it sounded,' Agnès finished with a smile. 'Anyway, Teddy is not here today, his truck is not.'

'Curious people. These Americans. Sometimes,' Antoine added, as if he thought Tom might be offended by his '*curious*'. 'And what is the news from Héloïse, Tome?'

Agnès passed round her little sausage canapés and the bowl of green olives once more.

Tom filled Antoine in with what he knew, meanwhile thinking that it was a decided advantage that Teddy had departed, and in foul mood. Had Teddy finally realized what Pritchard's quarry had been, and thought it best to have nothing to do with it? Wouldn't quitting the scene be a normal reaction? And perhaps Teddy – even if well paid – had had enough of the oddball personalities of both Pritchard and wife. Normal people, Tom thought, were made uneasy by seriously abnormal people. Tom was still managing to speak of other things, as his inner thoughts roved.

Five minutes later, after Edouard had reappeared and asked permission to do something in the garden, Tom had another thought: Teddy just might report the bones to the Paris police, not necessarily today even, but tomorrow. Teddy could probably honestly say that he had been told by Pritchard that Pritchard was after a treasure trove, a sunken suitcase, anything but a corpse, and that he (Teddy) thought the police ought to know about the corpse. That would be an excellent way for Teddy to hit back, too, if Teddy were so inclined.

So far, the news was good. Tom felt his face relax. He accepted a canapé, but not a freshener of his drink. Ed Banbury seemed to be holding his own pretty well in French with Antoine, Tom saw. Agnès Grais looked particularly nice in her peasant-style white blouse, embroidered, with puffy short sleeves. Tom paid her a compliment on it.

'It really is time Héloïse gave you another telephone call, Tome,' Agnès said as he and Ed were leaving. 'I have a feeling she will telephone you tonight.'

'Have you?' said Tom, smiling. 'I wouldn't bet my life on it.'

The day had shaped up nicely, Tom thought. So far.

21

To add a small bit to his luck today, Tom thought, he had not had to witness or hear or imagine that he heard the squeals of two lobsters being boiled alive. And as he bit into another succulent morsel covered in warm lemon butter, he reminded himself that the police had not paid a visit while he and Ed were at the Grais'. Mme Annette would have said something at once, if they had.

'Delicious, Tom,' said Ed. 'Do you dine like this every night?'

Tom smiled. 'No, it's in your honour. I'm glad you like it.' He took a bit of rucola salad.

They had just finished their salad and cheese when the telephone rang. Was that the police or had Agnès Grais' prediction come true and it was Héloïse?

'Hello?'

''Ello, Tome!' It was Héloïse, and she was with Noëlle at Roissy, and could Tom fetch her later tonight from Fontainebleau?

Tom took a deep breath. 'Héloïse, darling, I am delighted you are home, but – just tonight, could you possibly stay chez Noëlle?' Tom knew Noëlle had an extra room. 'I have an English guest tonight – '

'Who?'

Reluctantly Tom said, 'Ed Banbury,' knowing that the name would signify vague danger to Héloïse, because it was connected with the Buckmaster Gallery. 'Tonight – we have a bit of work, whereas tomorrow – how *is* Noëlle? . . . Good. Give her my love, would you? And you are well also? You don't mind, darling, staying in Paris tonight? Ring me any time tomorrow morning.'

'All right, chéri. It is so good to be back!' Héloïse said in English. They hung up.

'Holy – holy cow!' Tom said as he walked back to the table.

'Héloïse,' Ed said.

'She wanted to come down tonight, but she's going to stay with her friend Noëlle Hassler. Thank goodness.' The corpse in the garage was only bones, perhaps unidentifiable, Tom thought, but still the bones of a dead man, and instinctively Tom didn't want Héloïse anywhere near them. Tom swallowed, then took a sip of his Montrachet. 'Ed – '

At that moment Mme Annette came in. It was indeed time to remove the dinner and salad plates and replace them with the dessert plates. When Mme Annette had brought on her light and home-made raspberry mousse, Tom began again. Ed was faintly smiling, eyes alert.

'I have in mind to do something about the problem tonight,' Tom said.

'Thought you might – Another river? This would sink.' Ed spoke positively but softly. 'Nothing to float there.'

Tom knew he meant without rocks. 'No. I've another idea. Dump 'em right back into old Preekhard's pond.'

Ed smiled, then laughed softly, and some pink came into his cheeks. 'Right back,' he repeated, as if listening to or reading a comical horror story, and he took a spoonful of his dessert.

'Possibly,' Tom replied quietly, and began eating. 'Do you know this is made with my own raspberries?'

Coffee in the living-room, and neither wanted a brandy. Tom strolled to the front door, stepped out and looked at the sky. It was nearly 11. The stars were not in full summer glory because of a lot of clouds, and what was the moon doing? If they did the job quickly, Tom thought, who cared about moonlight? He could not find the moon now.

He returned to the living-room. 'Are you game to come with me tonight? I don't expect to *see* Pritchard – '

'Yes, Tom.'

'Back in a second.' Tom ran up the stairs, put on his Levis again, and transferred the heavy ring from his black trousers into his Levis. Was he developing some kind of neurosis about clothes-changing? Imagining that it helped somehow, gave new strength? Then Tom went to his atelier, took a soft pencil and some sketch paper, and went downstairs, feeling suddenly in more cheerful mood.

Ed sat where he had been before, at one end of the yellow sofa, now with a cigarette in hand.

'Can you bear it if I make a quick sketch?'

'Of *me*?' But Ed acquiesced.

Tom drew, with indications of sofa and pillow as background. He drew the puzzled concentration in Ed's blond brows and eyelashes, as Ed gazed at him, the thinnish English lips, and the casual lines of the open shirt collar. Tom moved his chair half a metre to the right, and took another page. Same thing. Ed could move, drink his coffee, and did. Tom worked for perhaps twenty minutes, and then thanked Ed for his cooperation.

'Cooperation!' Ed laughed. 'I was day-dreaming.'

Mme Annette had returned with more coffee, and had now retired for the evening, Tom knew.

'My idea,' Tom began 'is to approach the Pritchard estate from the other side – not the Grais' side – get out of the car and on foot take the thing on to the Pritchard lawn to the pond there, and just toss it. Doesn't weigh anything, you know. Well – '

'Not even thirty pounds, I'd guess,' said Ed.

'Just about,' murmured Tom. 'Well – they might hear something, Pritchard and wife, if they're home. Living-room has a window on that side, a couple of windows, I think. We'll just walk away. Let him complain!' Tom added boldly. 'Let him ring the police and tell his story.'

Silence for a few seconds.

'Do you think he would?'

Tom shrugged. 'Who knows what a *nut* will do?' He spoke in a resigned tone.

Ed stood up. 'Shall we?'

Tom pulled back the pages of his sketch-pad, and laid it, with his pencil, on the coffee table. He got a jacket from the hall table, and his wallet from the drawer of the hall table, just in case of police check, he thought with amusement: he never drove without his wallet, with licence, of course. A police officer might check his licence tonight, but not look into the package in the back of the car, which at a glance resembled a rug tied up for transport.

Ed came down from upstairs also with a jacket, a dark one, and in sneakers. 'Right, Tom.'

Tom turned off a couple of lights, they went out through the front door, and Tom locked it after them. He opened the big gates, assisted by Ed, then the tall metal door of the garage. Mme Annette's light might have been on at the back of the house, but Tom wasn't sure and didn't care. There was nothing unusual about his taking a guest for a late-night drive, possibly to a Fontainebleau café. They got in, and each lowered a window a bit, though Tom noticed not a hint of musty smell now. Tom drove through Belle Ombre's gates and turned left.

He crossed Villeperce at its southern part and took a road north when he could, as ever not caring much which road, as long as the general direction was correct.

'You know all these roads,' Ed said. It was half a question.

'Ha! Ninety per cent, maybe. It's easy to overshoot the side roads at night, where there's no marker.' Tom made a right turn, drove for a kilometre, then found a signpost which said among other towns 'VILLEPERCE', to the right. Tom took it.

Then he was on a road he knew, which would take them to the Pritchard house, the empty house, then the Grais'.

'This is their road, I think,' said Tom. 'Now my idea – ' He drove more slowly, and let a car pass him. 'We'll walk with it – thirty metres or so anyway, so they don't hear the car.' The clock on his dashboard said almost half-past midnight. Tom's car crept along, with dimmed lights.

'Is that it?' Ed asked. 'The white house on the right?'

'That's it.' Tom saw lights downstairs and up, but only one up. 'I hope there's a party!' Tom said with a smile. 'But I doubt it. I'm going to park by those trees back there and hope for the best.' He backed, and then cut the lights. He was near a curve, which led into a lane to the right, the unpaved kind used mainly by farmers. A car could still pass Tom's, of course, though Tom had not gone more to the right, lest he roll into a ditch, even a shallow one. 'Let's try it.' Tom took the torch which he had put on the seat between them.

They opened the back, and Tom put his fingers under the nearer rope around Murchison's lower legs, and pulled. It was easy. Ed was about to grasp the next coils of rope, when Tom said, 'Wait.'

They kept still and listened.

'Thought I heard something but maybe I didn't,' Tom said.

They had the bundle out now. Tom closed the back, almost: he did not want to make a noise. With a gesture of his head, Tom indicated departure, and they went off, along the right side of the road, Tom in front now, torch in left hand, but not on except from time to time when he flashed it downward at the road, because it was rather dark, after all.

'Hold it,' Ed whispered. 'Had a bad grip.' He got his fingers in better position under the rope, and they went on.

Tom paused again and whispered, 'About ten metres on, you see – we can get on to the grass. I don't think there's a ditch, even.'

Now they could see clearly the sharp corners of the lighted living-room windows. Did Tom hear music or was he imagining it? There was a ditch of sorts to their right, but no fence. On the other hand, just four metres on was the driveway, and neither of the Pritchards was in sight. Tom again indicated silently that they were to walk on. They walked into the driveway, and turned to the right towards the pond, which was now a dark oval, though nearly round. Their steps were silent on the grass. Tom heard music from the house, classical and not loud tonight.

'Now the old heave-ho,' Tom said, and led the manoeuvre. 'One – ' A swing. ' – two – and three right in the middle.'

Plu-ung! Then an echoing groan or burble from the pond's waters.

And much spatter, a gurgling of air rising, as Tom and Ed walked slowly away. Tom took the lead, and at the road turned left, torch flashing once on the road, for the benefit of both of them.

When they were some twenty paces from the driveway, Tom slowed and stopped, and so did Ed. They looked back at the Pritchard house, beyond the darkness.

' . . . awa . . . boaa-aa . . . ?' The fragments of a question had come from a female throat.

'That's his wife, Janice,' Tom whispered to Ed. Tom glanced to his right, and could just see the ghostly form of the white station wagon, mainly hidden by dark foliage. Tom looked back at the Pritchard house, fascinated. They had apparently heard the splash.

'You – oh – *wah*!' This came in deeper tone, and sounded to Tom like Pritchard's voice.

A light on the side porch's ceiling came on, and Tom saw Pritchard's figure in light shirt, darker trousers, on the porch. Pritchard looked to right and left, shone the torch all round at the lawn, stared at the road, then descended the few steps on to the lawn. He went straight to the pond, peered, then looked towards the house.

' . . . *pond* . . . ' That word came clearly from Pritchard, followed by a rough sound, maybe a curse. ' . . . am-mm-me . . . from *garden*, Jan!'

Janice had appeared on the porch, clad in light-coloured slacks and top. ' . . . wah . . . ma-ee?' asked Janice.

'No-o – one with the *hook*!' A favourable breeze must have carried those words straight to Tom and Ed.

Tom touched Ed's arm and found it rigid with tension. 'I think he's going to grapple for it!' he whispered, and stifled a burst of nervous mirth.

'Shouldn't we take off, Tom?'

At that moment Janice, who had disappeared, trotted into view again around the front corner of the house, bearing a pole, hurrying. Bent, peering through the wild bushes that grew on the Pritchards' lawn edge, Tom could just see that it was not the broad grappling-hook rake, but a three-pronged claw, perhaps, of the kind gardeners used to rake leaves and weeds from hard-to-get-at places. Tom had something similar, not two metres long, and this one looked shorter.

Mumbling, asking for something, maybe the flashlight (now lying on the lawn), Pritchard took the pole and appeared to push it downward into the pond.

'And what if he *does* get it?' Tom murmured to Ed, and stepped sideways in the car's direction.

Ed followed.

Then Tom thrust out his left hand towards Ed, and they paused. Through the bushes, Tom saw Pritchard, his figure bent forward from the waist, reach for something Janice was handing him, then Pritchard's white shirt vanished.

They heard a cry from Pritchard, then a heavy splash.

'*David*!' Janice's figure trotted halfway round the pond. '*Da* – vid!'

'Chrissake, he's fallen *in*!' said Tom.

'Ma – waa – aaa . . . ' That was Pritchard, surfacing, then 'P'too!' A spitting sound. A splash, as of an arm that threshed the water's surface.

'Where's that *hook*?' Janice cried shrilly. 'Hand . . . '

Pritchard had lost his grip on it, Tom thought.

'Janice! . . . Gimme . . . *mud* below! Y'*hand*!'

'Better a *broom* . . . or a *rope* . . . ' Janice dashed off towards the lighted porch, then swerved maniacally and returned to the pond. 'That *pole* . . . can't *see* it!'

' . . . y' *hand* . . . these . . . ' David Pritchard's words were lost, and there was another splashing sound.

Janice's pale figure wafted round the rim of the pond like a will-o'-the-wisp. 'Davy, where *are* you? Ah!' She had sighted something, and bent.

The pond's surface seethed audibly to Tom and Ed.

' . . . my *hand*, David! Grab the *edge*!'

Seconds of silence, then a shriek from Janice followed by another great splash.

'My God, they're *both* in!' said Tom, hysterically amused, having meant to whisper, but he had spoken almost normally.

'How deep is that pond?'

'Dunno. Five or six feet? I'm guessing.'

Janice cried out something, and was stifled by water.

'Shouldn't we – ' Ed looked at Tom anxiously. 'Maybe – '

Tom could feel Ed's tautness. Tom shifted his weight from left to right foot and back, as if weighing or debating something, yes or no. It was Ed's presence that made things different. The people in the pond were Tom's enemies. On his own, Tom wouldn't have hesitated, he would have walked away.

The splashing sounds had stopped.

'*I* didn't push them into that pond,' Tom said rather sternly, just as a faint sound – like a single hand stirring the surface – came from the direction of the pond. 'Now let's get out while we can.'

There were only some fifteen more paces to go in the dark. Great luck, Tom thought, that no one had passed by in those five or six minutes that the events had taken. They got into the car, and Tom backed into the nearby lane, in order to pull out and turn left, which would enable him to depart by the roundabout way he had come. He put his lights on now at their brightest.

'What a break!' Tom said, smiling. He was reminded of his euphoria with the unresponsive Bernard Tufts, after they had dumped – yes – the same bones, Murchison's bones, into the Loing at Voisy. He had felt like singing. Now he felt simply relieved and merry, but realized that Ed Banbury didn't, couldn't. So Tom drove carefully and said no more.

'A break?'

'Oh – ' Tom was now driving in a darkness that seemed dense; he was not sure where the next crossroad or signpost would turn up. But he thought his course could take him again south of Villeperce proper, and past the main street at right-angles. Marie and Georges' bar-tabac would be closed, probably, but Tom didn't want to be seen even crossing the main street. 'A break – that nobody drove by during those minutes back there! Not that I'd have cared much. What've I got to do with the Pritchards *or* the bones in their pond – which I assume will be found tomorrow?' Tom vaguely imagined two corpses floating an inch or so beneath the pond's surface. He gave a laugh and glanced at Ed.

Ed, smoking a cigarette, returned Tom's glance, then plunged his head down, held his forehead with one hand. 'Tom, I can't – '

'Do you feel sick?' asked Tom with concern, and let the car slow down. 'We can stop – '

'No, but we're leaving the scene and they're drowning back there.'

They have drowned, Tom thought. He thought of David Pritchard calling to his wife, 'Your *hand*!' as if to pull her deliberately in, as if in a final act of sadism, but Pritchard had had no footing then, and had wanted to live. Tom realized, with a sense of frustration, that Ed Banbury didn't understand it in the same way that he did. 'They're a pair of meddlers, Ed.' Tom again concentrated on the road, on the patch of now sandy-coloured surface that kept advancing under the car. 'Please don't forget tonight had to do with *Murchison*. That is – '

Ed put out his cigarette in the ashtray. He still rubbed his forehead.

I didn't enjoy watching that either, Tom wanted to say, but could he say it and be believed, when he had just been laughing? Tom took a breath. 'Those two would have loved to get at the forgeries – get at the Buckmaster Gallery, get at *all* of us via Mrs Murchison – probably,' Tom went on. 'Pritchard was after me, but the forgery would have opened up. They asked for what they got, Ed. They were absolute outsider meddlers.' Tom spoke with force.

They were nearly home; the bucolic few lights of Villeperce twinkled on their left. They were on the road that would take them to Belle Ombre. And now Tom saw the great tree opposite Belle Ombre's gates that leaned towards his home, protectively, Tom always felt. The big gates were still open. The faintest light from the living-room showed in a window left of the front door. Tom drove into the empty space on one side of his garage.

'I'll use the torch,' Tom said, and took it. With a rough cloth he found in a corner of the garage, Tom flicked out some grains of sand from the floor of the station wagon, grey crumbs of soil. Soil? It occurred to Tom that the crumbs might be, must be, the remnants of Murchison, indescribable (by him) remains of human flesh. There were very few, and Tom pushed them off the cement floor of his garage with his foot. Tiny they were, vanishing into the gravel, invisible, at least to the eye.

Tom held the torch as they walked to the front door. Ed Banbury had had a busy day, Tom realized, with a genuine taste of his own life – Tom's – and what he had to do, what had to be done now and then, to protect the lot of them. But Tom was by no means in the mood for making a speech to Ed, even a short statement. Had he not just done that in the car?

'After you, Ed,' said Tom at the house door, letting Ed precede him.

Tom put on another light in the living-room. Mme Annette had hours before drawn the curtains. Ed had gone into the downstairs loo, and Tom hoped he was not going to be sick. Tom washed at the kitchen sink. What to offer Ed? Tea? A stiff scotch? Didn't Ed prefer gin? Or a hot chocolate and bed? Ed rejoined Tom in the living-room.

Ed was trying to look as usual, and even pleasant, though his face held an element of puzzlement or worry, Tom thought.

'Something, Ed?' asked Tom. 'I'm going to have a pink gin, no ice. Say what you'd like. Tea?'

'The same. Same as you,' said Ed.

'Sit down.' Tom went to the bar cart and shook the Angostura bottle. He brought the identical drinks over.

After they lifted their glasses together, and sipped, Tom said, 'Thank you very much, Ed, for being with me tonight. It was a great help, your presence.'

Ed Banbury tried to smile, and could not. 'And if I may ask – what's going to happen now? What comes next?'

Tom hesitated. 'For us? Why should anything come?'

Ed sipped again, and swallowed with what seemed difficulty. 'At that house – '

'The Pritchard house!' Tom said in a low voice, with a smile. He was still on his feet. The question amused him. 'Well – I can see it tomorrow, for instance. The postman – probably – arrives around nine, let's say. He just might notice the garden hook, the wooden end of it, sticking out of the water and go closer to look. Or maybe not. He would see the house door open, unless the wind blew it shut, might notice the lights on – the light on the porch roof.' Or the postman might walk up from the driveway direction toward the main steps to the porch. And the hook utensil, being less than two metres long, might not project at all from the pond's surface, since the bottom was muddy. It could be more than a day before the Pritchards were discovered, Tom thought.

'And then?'

'Very likely in less than two days they'll be discovered. And so what? Murchison can't be traced, identified, I'll bet anything! Not even by his wife.' Tom thought quickly of Murchison's class ring. Well, he'd hide the ring somewhere in the house tonight, in case the most unlikely happened, police visiting tomorrow. The Pritchards' lights would remain on, Tom realized, but their lifestyle was so odd, he doubted if any neighbour was going to knock on their door because of lights burning all night. 'Ed, this is the simplest thing I've ever done – I think,' Tom said. 'Do you realize that we didn't lift a finger?'

Ed looked at Tom. He was sitting on one of the yellow straight chairs, leaning forward with forearms on his knees. 'Yes. All right, you could say that.'

'Very definitely,' Tom said firmly, and took another comforting sip of his pink gin. 'We know nothing about the pond. We were nowhere near the Pritchard house,' Tom said, speaking softly and going closer to Ed. 'Who knows that – bundle was ever here? Who's going to question *us*? Nobody. You and I took a drive to Fontainebleau, decided – maybe after all not to look in at a bar, and we drove back home. We were gone – less than forty-five minutes. And that's about right.'

Ed nodded, glanced up at Tom again and said, 'True, Tom.'

Tom lit a cigarette, and sat down on another of the straight chairs. 'I know it's unnerving. I've had to do much worse. Much, much – much worse,' said Tom, and gave a laugh. 'Now what time would you like coffee brought to your room tomorrow morning? Or tea? You should sleep as late as you wish, Ed.'

'Tea, I think. That's elegant – tea before – something else downstairs.' Ed tried to smile. 'Say – nine o'clock, quarter to nine?'

'Right. Madame Annette adores pleasing guests, you know? I'll leave a note for her. But I'll probably be up before nine. Madame Annette's up just after seven, as a rule,' Tom said in cheerful tone. 'Then she's apt to walk to the bakery for fresh croissants.'

The bakery, Tom thought, that information centre. What news would Mme Annette come back with at 8 a.m.?

22

Tom awoke just after 8. Birds sang beyond his partly open window, and it looked like another sunny day. Tom went – compulsively, like a neurotic, he felt – to his sock drawer, the bottom drawer of his captain's chest, and felt in a certain black woollen sock for the lump that was Murchison's class ring. It was there. Tom slid the brass-cornered drawer shut again. He had hidden the ring there last night, otherwise he would not have been able to sleep, knowing that the ring was – simply – in a trouser pocket. Hang the trousers absently over a chair, for instance, and there was the ring on the carpet for all to see.

In the same Levis as last night, a fresh shirt, and after his shower and shave, Tom went quietly downstairs. Ed's door was closed, and Tom hoped Ed was still asleep.

'Bon jour, madame!' Tom said with more than usual cheer, he realized.

Mme Annette reciprocated with a smile, and commented on the fine weather, yet another day of it. 'And now your café, m'sieur.' She went off to the kitchen.

Horrible news, if any, would have been already announced by Mme Annette, Tom thought. Though she may not have been to the bakery as yet, a friend could have telephoned. Patience, Tom told himself. The news would be all the more surprising when it came, and he had to look surprised, no doubt about that.

After his first coffee, Tom went out and cut two fresh dahlias, and three interesting roses, and got vases for them in the kitchen, with some help from Mme Annette.

Then he took a broom and went out to the garage. He began by giving the garage floor a hasty sweep, and found it so free of leaves and dust that his sweepings could go on to the gravel outside and disappear. Tom opened the back of the station wagon, and swept

214

the car floor of the greyish particles, so few he did not count them, and sent them finally into the gravel as well.

Perhaps Moret this morning would be a good idea, Tom thought. A little outing for Ed, and he could dispose of the ring in the river there. And perhaps, Tom indeed hoped, Héloïse would have rung by then, telling the arrival time of her train. They might combine all this, the Moret detour, Fontainebleau and the drive home in the station wagon, surely big enough to hold what Héloïse would have acquired in the way of extra suitcases.

The post that came just after 9.30 brought a card from Héloïse dated ten days back from Marrakesh. Typical. How welcome it would have been in the desert of last week with no word! The photograph on it was of a market scene with women in striped shawls.

Dear Tom,

　　　　Again camels but more fun! We have met two men from *Lille*! Amusants and nice for dinner. They take both vacations from wifes. Bises from Noëlle. XXX Je t'embrasse!

H.

Vacation from wifes, but not from women, it seemed. Nice for dinner sounded as if Héloïse and Noëlle might have eaten them.

'Morning, Tom.' Ed came down the stairs smiling, rosy-cheeked as he sometimes was for no reason, Tom had noticed, and Tom had to believe that it was an English peculiarity.

'Morning, Ed,' Tom replied. 'Another fine day! We're in luck.' Tom gestured towards the table in the dining alcove, which was set for two at one corner, with enough space for comfort. 'Does the sun bother you? I can close the curtain.'

'I like it,' said Ed.

Mme Annette arrived with orange juice, warm croissants and fresh coffee.

'Might you like a boiled egg, Ed?' Tom asked. 'Or coddled? Poached? I like to think we can do anything in this house.'

Ed smiled. 'No egg, thanks. I know why you're in a good mood – Héloïse is in Paris and she's probably coming home today.'

Tom's smile broadened. 'I hope. I trust. Unless something very tempting is on in Paris. Can't think what. Not even a good cabaret show – which she likes, and Noëlle too. I think Héloïse will telephone – any minute. Oh! Had a postcard this morning from

Héloïse. Took ten days to get here from Marrakesh. Can you imagine?' Tom laughed. 'Try the marmalade. Madame Annette makes it.'

'Thank you. The postman – would he come here before he got to that house?' Ed's voice was just audible.

'I don't know, really. I'd think he'd come here first. From the centre outward. Not sure.' Tom saw the worry in Ed's face. 'I thought this morning – once we hear from Héloïse – we might take a drive towards Moret-sur-Loing. Lovely town.' Tom paused, and was about to mention that he'd like to drop the ring in the river there when he thought better of it: the fewer angst-making items Ed Banbury had on his mind, the better.

Tom and Ed took a stroll on the grass beyond the french windows. Blackbirds pecked, barely showing wariness of them, and a robin looked them in the eye. One black crow flew over with its ugly cry that made Tom wince, as if at cacophonous music.

'Caw – caw – *caw*!' Tom mimicked. 'Sometimes only two caws, even worse. I wait for the third as if it were the second shoe that ought to drop. This reminds me – '

The telephone rang, they heard it faintly from the house.

'Probably Héloïse. Excuse me,' Tom said, and trotted off. In the house, he said, 'That's all right, Madame Annette, I'll get it.'

'Hello, *Tom*. Jeff here. I thought I'd ring and ask how things are.'

'Nice of you, Jeff! Things are – oh – ' Tom saw Ed coming quietly through the french windows into the living-room ' – rather quiet, so far.' He winked elaborately at Ed, and kept a sober face. 'Nothing exciting to report. Would you like a word with Ed?'

'Yes, if he's handy. But before you sign off – don't forget I'm willing to pop over *any* time. I trust you'll let me know – and don't hesitate.'

'Thank you, Jeff. I appreciate that. Now here's Ed.' Tom put the telephone on the hall table. 'We've been in the whole time – nothing's happened,' Tom whispered to Ed as they passed each other. 'Better that way,' he added as Ed picked up the telephone.

Tom drifted towards the yellow sofa, went past it and stood by the tall windows, practically out of hearing. He heard Ed say that all was quiet on the Ripley front, and that the house and the weather were beautiful.

Tom spoke to Mme Annette about lunch. It looked as if Mme Héloïse would not be here for lunch, so it would be M. Banbury and himself. He told Mme Annette that he was now going to ring Mme

Héloïse at Mme Hassler's apartment in Paris to ask what Mme Héloïse's plans were.

At that moment, the telephone rang.

'That must be Madame Héloïse!' said Tom to Mme Annette, and went off to answer it. 'Hello?'

''Ello, Tome!' It was Agnès Grais' familiar voice. 'Have you heard the *news*?'

'No. What news?' asked Tom, and he noticed that Ed was paying attention.

'Les Preechards. They were found dead this morning in their pond!'

'Dead?'

'Drowned. So it appears. It was — well, really quite an upsetting Saturday morning here for us! You know the Leferre boy, Robert?'

'I'm afraid I don't.'

'He goes to the same school as Edouard. Anyway, Robert came along this morning selling tombola tickets — with a friend of his, another boy whose name I don't know, doesn't matter, so of course we bought ten tickets to please the boys, and they went off. This was a good hour ago. The next house is empty, as you know, and they evidently went on to the Preechard house, which — alors, they came running back to *our* house, *scared to death*! They said the house was open — the doors. No one answered the bell, a light was on, and they went — out of curiosity, I'm sure — to take a look at the pond at the side of the house there, you know?'

'Yes, I've seen it,' Tom said.

'There they could see — because the water is pretty clear, it seems — two bodies — not quite floating! Oh, it's so *horrible*, Tom!'

'Mon Dieu, oui! Do they think it was suicide? The police – '

'Oh, yes, the police, of course, they're still at the house and one was even here to talk to us. We just said – ' Agnès gave a great sigh. 'Alors, what *could* we say, Tome? That those two kept strange hours, played loud music. They were newcomers here in the neighbour-hood, they had never been to our house, nor we to theirs. Worst is — oh, nom de Dieu, Tome — it is like black magic! Horrid!'

'What is?' asked Tom, knowing.

'Below them — in the water — the police found bones, yes – '

'Bones?' Tom echoed in French.

'The remains of — *human* bones. Wrapped up, a neighbour told us, because people went there out of curiosity, you know?'

'Villeperce people?'

'*Yes*. Till the police roped it off. *We* didn't go, I am not *that* curious!' Agnès Grais gave a laugh, as if to relieve her tension. 'Who knows what to say? Were they insane? Did they commit suicide? Did Preechard fish these bones up? We don't know any answers yet. Who knows how their minds worked?'

'True.' Whose bones could they be, Tom thought of asking, but Agnès wouldn't know, and why should he appear curious? Like Agnès, Tom was shocked, merely. 'Agnès, I thank you for telling me. It's really – incredible.'

'A fine introduction to Villeperce for your English friend!' said Agnès with another relieving laugh.

'Isn't it true!' said Tom, smiling. An unpleasant idea had come to him in the last seconds.

'Tome – we are here, Antoine till Monday morning, trying to forget the horror not so far away from us. It is good to talk to friends. And what do you hear from Héloïse?'

'She's in Paris! I had a telephone call from her yesterday evening. I expect her home today. She stayed the night with her friend Noëlle who has an apartment in Paris, you know?'

'I know. Give Héloïse our love, will you?'

'Indeed, yes!'

'If I learn anything more, I'll telephone you again today. After all, I am closer, unfortunately.'

'Ha! I realize. Thank you infinitely, dear Agnès, and my best to Antoine – and the kids.' Tom hung up. 'Whew!'

Ed stood some distance away, near the sofa. 'That's where we had drinks last night – Agnès – '

'Yes,' said Tom. He explained how two boys selling tombola tickets had looked into the pond and seen the two figures.

Even knowing the facts, Ed grimaced.

Tom narrated the events as if, indeed, they were news to him. 'Terrible for kids to have to come on that! I suppose the boys are about twelve. The water *is* clear in that pond, as I recall. Even though the bottom's mud. And those funny sides – '

'Sides?'

'Sides of the pond. Cement, I remember someone saying – probably not thick. But you can't see the cement at grass level, it doesn't come up that high, so perhaps it's easy to slip at the edge and fall in – especially carrying something. Oh, yes, Agnès mentioned the police finding a bag of human bones at the bottom.'

Ed looked at Tom, silent.

'I'm told the police are still there. I'll bet.' Tom took a deep breath. 'I think I'll go speak with Madame Annette.'

A glance told him that the big square kitchen was empty, and Tom had just turned to his right to go and rap on Mme Annette's door when she appeared in the short hall there.

'Oh, M'sieur Tome! Such a story! *Une catastrophe*! Chez les Preechards!' She was ready to narrate all. Mme Annette had a telephone in her room with her own number.

'Ah, yes, madame, I just heard the story from Madame Grais! Truly a shock! Two deaths – and so near us! I was coming to tell you.'

They both went into the kitchen.

'Madame Marie-Louise just told me. Madame Geneviève told her. All the *village* knows! Two persons *drowned*!'

'An accident – do they think?'

'People think they were quarrelling – that one slipped and fell in, perhaps. They were always quarrelling, did you know, M'sieur Tome?'

Tom hesitated. 'I – think I heard people say that.'

'But those bones in the pond!' Her voice fell to a whisper. 'Strange, M'sieur Tome – *very* strange. Strange *people*.' Mme Annette made it sound as if the Pritchards were from outer space, beyond normal comprehension.

'That is certain,' Tom said. '*Bizarre* – so everyone says. Madame – I must now go and telephone Madame Héloïse.'

Again the telephone rang, just as Tom was about to pick it up, and this time he cursed silently with frustration. The police? 'Hello?'

''Allo, Tome! C'est Noëlle! Bonnes nouvelles pour vous – Héloïse arrive . . . '

Héloïse should arrive in a quarter of an hour. She was driving down with a young friend of Noëlle's called Yves, who had a new car and wanted to run it in. Besides, the car had room for Héloïse's baggage, and was more convenient than a train.

'A quarter of an hour! Thank you, Noëlle. You are well? . . . And Héloïse?'

'We both have the health of the most rugged explorers!'

'I hope to see you soon, Noëlle.'

They hung up.

'Héloïse is being driven down – any minute,' Tom said with a smile to Ed. Then he went to impart the news to Mme Annette. Her expression brightened at once. Héloïse's presence was more

219

cheerful than thoughts of the Pritchards dead in their pond, Tom was sure.

'For the luncheon – cold meats, M'sieur Tome? I have bought very good chicken liver pâté this morning . . . '

Tom assured her that it all sounded excellent.

'And for this evening – tournedos – sufficient for three. I was expecting madame certainly this evening.'

'And baked potatoes. Can you do that? Really well done. No! *I* can do it all outside on the grill!' Certainly the most cheerful and tasty way of baking potatoes and grilling tournedos. 'And a good sauce béarnaise?'

'Bien sûr, m'sieur. Et . . . '

She would buy fresh string beans this afternoon, and something else, and perhaps a kind of cheese Mme Héloïse liked. Mme Annette was in seventh heaven.

Tom returned to the living-room where Ed was looking at that morning's *Herald Trib*. 'All is well,' Tom announced. 'Want to take a walk with me?' Tom felt like jogging, or leaping a fence.

'Great idea! Stretch our legs!' Ed was ready.

'And maybe run into Héloïse in that fast car? Or is Yves running the car in? Anyway, it's due.' Tom went to the kitchen again, where Mme Annette was calmly at work. 'Madame – M'sieur Ed and I are going out for a short promenade. Back in fifteen minutes.'

Then Tom rejoined Ed in the hall. Again he thought of the depressing possibility that had occurred to him that morning, and Tom paused, hand on the door-knob.

'What's the matter?'

'Nothing specific. Since I've – so taken you into my confidence – ' Tom pushed his fingers through his straight brown hair. 'Well, it occurred to me this morning that old Preekhard might have kept a diary – or even *she*, more likely. They might have written down that they found the bones,' Tom continued, lowering his voice, glancing into the broad doorway to the living-room, 'and dumped them on my doorstep – just yesterday.' Here Tom opened the door, needing sunlight and fresh air. 'And that they hid the head somewhere on their property.'

They both went out on to the gravelled forecourt.

'The police would find the diary,' Tom went on, 'and learn soon enough that one of Pritchard's pastimes was harassing me.' Tom disliked talking out his anxieties, usually so fleeting anyway. But certainly Ed was to be trusted, he reminded himself.

'But both of them were so cracked!' Ed frowned at Tom, and his whisper was hardly louder than their tread on the gravel. 'Whatever they wrote – might be fantasy or not necessarily true. And even so – their word against *yours*?'

'If they've written anywhere that they delivered any bones here, I'm simply going to deny it,' Tom said in a quiet and firm tone, as if that were the end of the matter. 'I don't think it'll happen.'

'Right, Tom.'

They walked on, as if to get rid of nervous energy, able to walk side by side because cars were few or none. What colour was Yves' car, Tom wondered, and did people have to run in any new car these days? He imagined the car yellow, *très sportif*.

'D'you think Jeff might like to come over, Ed? Just for fun?' Tom asked. 'He said he could make himself free now. By the way, I hope you'll stay on at least two more days, Ed. Can you?'

'I can.' Ed glanced at Tom. The English pink was back in his cheeks. 'You might ring Jeff up and ask. That's a nice idea.'

'There's a couch in my atelier. Quite comfortable.' Tom much wished to enjoy even two days of holiday at Belle Ombre with his old friends; at the same time, he was wondering if his telephone was ringing at this moment, ten past 12, because the police would like to speak with him about something. 'There! Look!' Tom jumped into the air and pointed. 'The yellow car! I'll bet!'

The car with its top down rolled toward them, and Héloïse was waving from the passenger seat. She raised herself as much as her seatbelt permitted, and her blonde hair blew back.

'Tome!'

Tom and Ed were on the same side of the road as the car.

'Hi! Hello!' Tom waved both arms. Héloïse looked very suntanned.

The driver braked, but still went past Tom and Ed who trotted back towards it.

'Hello, darling!' Tom kissed Héloïse on the cheek.

'This is Yves!' said Héloïse, and the dark-haired young man smiled and said, 'Enchanté, M'sieur Ripley!' He was driving an Alfa-Romeo. 'Would you like to get in?' he asked in English.

'This is Ed.' Tom gestured. 'No, thank you, we'll follow,' he replied in French. 'See you at the house!'

The back seat of the car had been laden with small suitcases, one definitely new to Tom, and Tom had not seen room even for a small dog there. He and Ed went off trotting, then running, laughing, and they were no more than five metres behind the yellow Alfa by the time it turned right and went through the gates of Belle Ombre.

Mme Annette appeared. Much chatter and greetings and introductions. Somehow they all helped with the luggage, because there were innumerable small items in plastic bags in the boot. For once, Mme Annette was permitted to carry the lighter items upstairs. Héloïse hovered, pointing out certain plastic bags which contained 'pâtisserie et bonbons de Maroc', and which no one should squeeze.

'I shall not squeeze,' said Tom, 'just take them to the kitchen.' He did, and returned. 'May I offer you a glass of something, Yves? And you are also welcome to stay for lunch.'

Yves declined both with thanks, and said he had a date in Fontainebleau and was a bit late now. Goodbyes and thanks between Héloïse and Yves.

Then Mme Annette served two bloody Marys at Tom's request, for himself and Ed, and an orange juice for Héloïse, her choice. Tom did not want to take his eyes from her. She had not lost or gained weight, he thought, and the curve of her thighs under the pale blue trousers seemed things of beauty, works of art. Her voice, as she chattered on, half in French and half in English, about Maroc, Morocco, was music to him, more delicious than Scarlatti.

When Tom looked at Ed, who stood with his tomato-coloured drink in hand, he found Ed equally fixated, gazing at Héloïse as she looked out of the french windows. Héloïse asked about Henri, and when was the last time it had rained? She had two other plastic bags in the hall, and brought them in. One contained a brass bowl, plain and not decorated, Héloïse pointed out with pleasure. Another item for Mme Annette to polish, Tom thought.

'And this! Look, Tom! So pretty and it costed so little! A briefcase for your desk.' She produced a rectangle of soft brown leather, tooled, but not too elaborately, and just at its borders.

What desk, Tom wondered. He had a writing-table in his room, but –

Héloïse was opening it, showing Tom the four pockets within, two on each side, also made of leather.

Tom still preferred to stare at Héloïse, so close to him now that he imagined he could smell the sun on her skin. 'It is l-lovely, darling. If it's for me – '

'Of course it is for *you*!' Héloïse laughed and gave a quick glance at Ed, pushed her blonde hair back.

Again her skin was a bit darker than her hair. Tom had seen this a few times before. 'It's a wallet, darling – no? I think not a briefcase – which usually has a handle.'

'Oh, Tome, you are so serious!' She gave him a playful push in the forehead.

Ed laughed.

'What would you call this, Ed? A letter-holder?'

'The English language – ' Ed began and didn't finish. 'Anyway not a portfolio. I'd say a letter-holder.'

Tom agreed. 'It *is* beautiful, my dear, and I thank you.' He seized her right hand and gave it a quick kiss. 'I shall love it and keep it polished – or cared for.'

Tom's thoughts were more than half elsewhere. Where and when could he tell her about the Pritchard tragedy? Mme Annette would not mention it in the next two hours, because she was occupied with serving lunch. But the telephone might ring at any moment with more news from someone, the Grais, perhaps, even the Cleggs if the news had spread for kilometres. Tom decided at any rate to enjoy a pleasant lunch, and listen to accounts of Marrakesh and the two French gentlemen who were nice for dinner, André and Patrick. There was much laughter.

Héloïse said to Ed, 'We are so glad to have you here at our house! We hope you will enjoy your visit.'

'Thank you, Héloïse,' Ed replied. 'It's a beautiful house – *very* comfortable.' Ed glanced at Tom.

Tom was at that moment thoughtful, biting his underlip. Maybe Ed knew what he was thinking: that he had to inform Héloïse soon about the Pritchards. If Héloïse had asked about them during lunch, Tom was prepared to be evasive. He was happy that she didn't mention them.

23

No one wanted coffee after lunch. Ed said that he felt like taking a longer walk, 'all through the village'.

'Do you think you'll ring Jeff – really?' Ed asked.

Tom explained to Héloïse, who was having a cigarette at the table. He and Ed thought that their old friend Jeff Constant, a photographer, might like to come over to visit for a couple of days. 'We happen to know he's free now,' Tom said. 'He's a freelancer, like Ed.'

'*Mais oui*, Tome! Why not? Where will he sleep? Your atelier?'

'I'd thought of that. Unless I join you for a couple of days and he takes my room.' Tom smiled. 'As you wish, my sweet.' It had been done before, Tom recalled, several times: it was easier for him to sleep chez Héloïse, somehow, than for her to move necessities into his room. Each of their rooms had a double bed.

'But of course, Tome,' Héloïse said in French. She stood up, and then Tom and Ed did.

'Excuse me a sec,' Tom said, mainly to Ed, and went off to the kitchen.

Mme Annette was putting plates into the dishwasher, just as on any other day.

'Madame, an excellent lunch – thank you. And two matters.' Tom lowered his voice, and said, 'I shall tell Madame Héloïse now about the Preechard affair – so that she does not hear it from a stranger in – well, so it is not such a shock, perhaps.'

'Oui, M'sieur Tome. You are right.'

'And the second thing, I shall invite another English friend to come tomorrow. I'm not sure he can, but I shall inform you. In which case he'll have my room. I'm going to telephone London in a few minutes, then I'll let you know.'

'Very good, m'sieur. But about the meals – le menu?'

Tom smiled. 'If there are difficulties, we'll dine out somewhere tomorrow evening.' Tomorrow was Sunday, Tom realized, but the village butcher was open tomorrow morning.

He then hurried up the stairs, thinking that at any minute the telephone could ring – the Grais, for instance, who knew Héloïse was due home – and someone might start talking about the Pritchards. The upstairs telephone was now in Tom's room, not in Héloïse's as it usually was, but she would likely answer it if it rang in his room.

Héloïse was in her own room, unpacking. Tom noticed a couple of cotton blouses that he had not seen before.

'Do you like this, Tome?' Héloïse held a vertically striped skirt against her waist. The stripes were of purple, green and red.

'It *is* different,' Tom said.

'Yes! That's why I bought it. And this belt? Then I have something for Madame Annette too! Let me – '

'Darling,' Tom interrupted, 'I have to tell you – something – rather unpleasant.' Now he had her attention. 'You remember the Pritchards – '

'Oh, the *Pree*chards,' she repeated, as if she thought them the most boring or unattractive people on earth. 'Alors?'

'They – ' It was painful to get the words out, even though he knew Héloïse disliked the Pritchards. 'They had an accident – or committed suicide. I don't know which, but the police can probably tell.'

'They are *dead*?' Héloïse's lips stayed parted.

'Agnès Grais told me this morning. She telephoned. They were found in that pond on the lawn. Remember? The pond we saw when we went to look at that house – '

'Oh, yes, I remember.' She was standing with the brown belt in her hands.

'They may have slipped – one could have dragged the other in, I don't know. Then the bottom's mud – de la boue – not easy perhaps to get out of.' Tom winced as he spoke, as if he felt sympathy for the Pritchards, but it was the sheer horror of that muddy drowning that made him wince, the nothing underfoot but mush and softness, mud in the shoes. Tom hated the thought of drowning. He continued, and told Héloïse of the two boys selling tombola tickets, who had come running to the Grais' house afterward, scared, with the news of seeing two people in the pond.

'*Sacrebleu*!' Héloïse whispered, and sat down on the edge of her bed. 'And Agnès called the police?'

'No doubt. And then – I don't know how she heard, or I forgot, the police found *below* the Pritchards a bag of human bones.'

'*Quoi?*' Héloïse gasped with shock. 'Bones?'

'They were odd – strange. The Pritchards.' Now Tom sat down in a chair. 'All this was just a few hours ago, darling. We'll learn more later, I suppose. But I wanted to tell you before Agnès or someone else did.'

'I should telephone Agnès. They're so *close* there. I wonder – that bag of bones! What were they doing with it?'

Tom shook his head and stood up. 'And what else will they find in that house? Instruments of torture? Chains? Those two belong in Krafft-Ebing! Maybe the police will find *more* bones.'

'How terrible! People they have *killed*?'

'Who knows?' And in fact Tom didn't know, and thought it a possibility that David Pritchard might have among his treasures some human bones that he had dug up somewhere, or which were just possibly of someone he had done in; Pritchard was a good liar. 'Don't forget, David Pritchard liked to beat his wife. Maybe he has beaten other wives.'

'*Tome!*' Héloïse put her hands over her face.

Tom went and pulled her to him, put his arms around her waist. 'I shouldn't have said that. But it is possible, that's all.'

She held him tightly. 'I thought – this afternoon – could be for us. But not with this horrible story!'

'But there's tonight – and lots of time ahead! You want to ring Agnès, I know, dear. And then I'll telephone Jeff.' Tom stepped away. 'Didn't you meet Jeff once in London? A little taller and heavier than Ed? Also fair-haired?' Tom did not want to remind her just now that Jeff and Ed were among the original Buckmaster Gallery founders, as was Tom, because that would evoke Bernard Tufts, with whom Héloïse had never been comfortable, Bernard having been visibly cracked and peculiar.

'I remember the name. You should ring him first. Agnès will know more if I wait.'

'True!' Tom laughed. 'By the way – Madame Annette of course heard the news about the pond this morning, from her friend Marie-Louise, I think.' Tom had to smile. 'With Madame Annette's telephone network, she'll probably know more now than Agnès!'

Tom found that his personal address book was not in his room, therefore probably down on the hall table. He went downstairs, looked up Jeff Constant's number and dialled. On the seventh ring, he had luck.

'Tom here, Jeff. Now look – all is at the moment quiet, so why don't you come over for a short holiday with Ed and me – or a longer one, if you can. How about tomorrow?' Tom realized that he was speaking as cautiously as if his line might be tapped, but so far it had never been. 'Ed's out for a walk just now.'

'Tomorrow. Well, yes, tomorrow, I suppose I could. With pleasure, airlines permitting. You're sure there's room for me?'

'Absolutely, Jeff!'

'Thank you, Tom. I'll look into the plane schedules and ring you back – I hope in less than an hour. Is that all right?'

Of course it was all right. And Tom assured Jeff that he would be happy to pick him up at Roissy.

Tom informed Héloïse that the telephone was free, and that it looked as if Jeff Constant could come over tomorrow and stay for a couple of days.

'Very nice, Tome. So now I telephone Agnès.'

Tom drifted off, downstairs again. He wanted to check the charcoal grill, get it ready for tonight. He was thinking, as he folded up the waterproof cover and rolled the grill to a convenient place, what if Pritchard had informed Mrs Murchison about his find, saying he was sure the bones were those of her husband, because of the class ring on the little finger of the right hand?

Why hadn't the police rung him by now?

His problems were perhaps far from over. Pritchard, if he had informed Mrs Murchison – and maybe informed Cynthia Gradnor also, good God – might have added that he had dumped or intended to dump the bones on Tom Ripley's doorstep. He wouldn't have said dump, Tom thought, but deliver or deposit, certainly to Mrs Murchison.

On the other hand – and Tom had to smile at his wandering thoughts – in speaking to Mrs Murchison, Pritchard might not have said he intended to deliver the bones anywhere, because there would have been something disrespectful in doing so: the correct thing, Tom supposed, would be to have transported the bones to his house, Pritchard's, as Pritchard had done, and then called the police. In view of Tom's old undisturbed ropes, maybe Pritchard hadn't looked for rings.

Still another possibility, Pritchard having made small gashes in the old canvas, was that Pritchard *might* have removed the wedding ring himself, stored it in his house somewhere, and the police just might find it. If Mrs Murchison had been informed of the bones by Pritchard she might have mentioned the two rings that her husband had always worn, and might be able to identify the wedding ring – if the police found it.

His thoughts were becoming ever thinner, wispier, Tom felt – meaning that he could not believe in the reality of the last: suppose Pritchard had hidden the ring in a place only he knew of (this was assuming that the wedding ring had not fallen off in the Loing), that place might be so unlikely that no one would ever find it unless the house were burnt quite down, and the ashes sifted through. Did Teddy possibly –

'Tom?'

Tom started, and turned. 'Ed! Hi!'

Ed had come round the house and was behind Tom. 'Didn't mean to scare you!' Ed had his sweater tied around his neck by its arms.

Tom had to laugh. He had jumped as if shot. 'I was day-dreaming. I reached Jeff and it sounds as if he can come tomorrow. Isn't that great?'

'Is it? It sounds nice for me. And what's the latest news?' he asked in a lower tone. 'Anything?'

Tom carried the charcoal bag to a corner of the terrace. 'I think the ladies are comparing notes now.' He could just hear the voices of Héloïse and Mme Annette in lively discourse near the front hall. They were talking simultaneously, but Tom knew that each was understanding the other perfectly, albeit after some repetition. 'Let's go and see.'

They walked into the living-room via a french window.

'Tome, they have searched – hello, M'sieur Ed.'

'Ed, please,' said Ed Banbury.

' – searched the house, the police,' Héloïse continued, while Mme Annette appeared to listen, though Héloïse spoke in English. 'The police were there till after three this afternoon, Agnès told me. They even came again to talk with the Grais.'

'That was to be expected,' Tom replied. 'Do they say it was an accident?'

'There was no suicide note!' Héloïse replied. 'The police – maybe they think it could have been an accident, Agnès said, when

228

they were throwing these – these – '

Tom glanced at Mme Annette. 'Bones,' he said softly.

' – bones – in. Ugh!' Héloïse waved her hands with nervous revulsion.

Mme Annette moved away, with an air of returning to her duties, as if she had not known what the word bones meant, and probably she hadn't.

'Didn't the police find out whose bones?' Tom asked.

'The police don't know – or they don't say,' Héloïse answered.

Tom frowned. 'Did Agnès and Antoine *see* the bag of bones?'

'Non – but the two children went over and they say they saw it – on the grass – before the police asked them to leave. I think there is a cordon around the house and a police car – which stays. Oh – Agnès said the bones were old. The officer of police told her that. Some years old – and had been in the water.'

Tom glanced at Ed, who was listening with admirable serious-ness and interest, Tom thought. 'Maybe they *fell* in – trying to pull the bones out?'

'Ah, oui! Agnès said the police thought something like that, because there was a – *utensil* – for the garden with a *crochet* in the water with them.'

Ed said, 'They're taking the bones to Paris – or somewhere, I suppose, for identification? Who owned that house before?'

'I dunno,' said Tom, 'but it's easily found out. I'm sure the police have looked *that* up by now.'

'The water was so clear!' Héloïse said. 'I remember the time I saw it. I thought, pretty fish could even live there.'

'But the bottom was mud, Héloïse. Something could sink and – What a subject,' Tom said, 'when life is usually so quiet here.'

They now stood near the sofa, but no one sat.

'And do you know, Tome, Noëlle knows already? She heard it on one o'clock radio news, not télé.' Héloïse pushed her hair back. 'Tome, I think tea would be nice. Maybe M'sieur Ed, too? Can you tell madame, Tome? Now I want to walk by myself – in the garden.'

Tom was pleased, because some moments alone would make Héloïse relax. 'You do that, my sweet! Of course I'll ask madame to make some tea.'

Héloïse went off, and she ran down the few steps to the grass. She wore white slacks and tennis shoes.

Tom went off to find Mme Annette, and had just told her that they would all like tea when the telephone rang.

'I think that's our friend in London,' Tom said to Mme Annette, and went back through the living-room to get it.

Ed was at the moment not in view.

It was Jeff, and he had his time of arrival: 11.25 tomorrow morning, BA flight 826. 'Open end,' Jeff said, 'in case.'

'Thank you, Jeff. We all look forward! Lovely weather but bring a sweater.'

'Can I bring you anything, Tom?'

'Just yourself.' Tom laughed. 'Oh! A pound of cheddar *if* convenient. It always tastes better from London.'

Tea. This the three of them enjoyed in the living-room. Héloïse sat back with her cup in a corner of the sofa, and hardly talked. Tom didn't mind. Tom was thinking of the 6 o'clock news on television, some twenty minutes from now, when he saw Henri's huge figure near a corner of the greenhouse.

'Well, well, Henri,' said Tom, setting his cup down. 'I'll go see what he wants – if anything. Excuse me, please.'

'You have a rendez-vous with him, Tome?'

'No, dear, I have not.' Tom explained to Ed. 'He's my informal gardener, the friendly giant.'

Tom went out. As he had suspected, Henri was not about to begin work at this hour on a Saturday evening, but wanted to talk about *les événements* at the *maison Preechard*. Even a double suicide, as Henri called it, did not stir his great form into liveliness, or even cause tension, that Tom could see.

'Yes, indeed, I heard about it,' said Tom. 'Madame Grais telephoned me this morning. Truly shocking news!'

Henri's thick-soled boots shifted left to right and back again. His great hands twiddled with a clover stem on the end of which bobbed a round lavender blossom. 'And the bones below,' Henri said in an ominous low tone, as if the bones somehow sealed a judgement on the Pritchards. 'Bones, m'sieur!' Twiddle, twiddle. 'What strange people – just *here*! Before our noses!'

Tom had never seen Henri disturbed before. 'Do you think – ' Tom looked off at the lawn, then back at Henri – 'they both really decided to commit suicide?'

'Who knows?' asked Henri, with a lift of bushy brows. 'Maybe it was a strange game? They both tried something – but what?'

Very vague, Tom thought to himself, but probably Henri's ideas were a reflection of those of the whole village. 'It will be interesting to know what the police say.'

'Bien sûr!'

'And whose bones *are* they? Does anybody know?'

'Non, m'sieur. Bones of a certain age! As if – alors – you know – everyone knows – Preechard had been dragging the canals and rivers around here! For what? For his pleasure? Some people say these bones are what Preechard got out of a canal and he and his wife – they were *fighting* over them.' Henri looked at Tom as if he had disclosed an unsavoury secret in regard to this pair.

'Fighting over them,' Tom echoed, in true country style.

'Strange, m'sieur.' Henri shook his head.

'Oui, ah oui,' said Tom in a reconciled tone and with a sigh, as if each day presented something puzzling, which one simply had to live with. 'Maybe this evening's télé will bring us some news – if they bother with a small village like Villeperce, eh? Well, Henri, I must return to my wife now, as we have a guest from London and we're expecting another tomorrow. You surely don't want to start any work at this hour, do you?'

Henri didn't, but he accepted a glass of wine in the greenhouse. Tom kept a bottle there – changed often enough, so that it wouldn't become stale – for Henri, plus a couple of glasses. The two glasses were not very clean, but they lifted them anyway and drank.

Henri said in a low tone, 'It is good that these two will be removed from the village – those bones too. Those people were *bizarre*.'

Tom nodded solemnly in agreement.

'Salutations à votre femme, m'sieur,' said Henri, and drifted off across the lawn, heading for the lane at the side.

Tom returned to the living-room to drink his tea.

Ed and Héloïse were talking about Brighton, of all things.

Tom turned the set on. It was almost time. 'Be interesting to know if Villeperce merits a minute on international news,' Tom said, mainly to Héloïse. 'Or even national.'

'Ah, yes!' Héloïse sat up.

Tom had rolled the set more to the centre of the room. The first item was about a conference in Geneva, then came a boat race somewhere. Their interest wavered, and Ed and Héloïse chatted again, in English.

'There it is. Look,' said Tom, rather calmly.

'The house!' said Héloïse.

They all looked. The two-storey white house of the Pritchards provided the background for the commentator's voice. Plainly the photographer had not been able to get closer than the road, and maybe just for the one shot, Tom thought. The announcer's voice said, '. . . a bizarre accident discovered this morning in the village of Villeperce near Moret, the bodies of two adults, David and Janice Preechard, Americans, both in their mid-thirties, in a pond of water two metres deep on their own lawn. The deceased pair were clothed and wearing shoes, and their deaths are believed to be an acccident . . . M'sieur and Madame Preechard had recently bought their house . . . '

No mention of the bones, Tom thought as the announcer came to an end of the Pritchard story. He looked at Ed, and imagined from Ed's slightly raised brows that Ed was thinking the same thing.

Then Héloïse said, 'They didn't say anything about – about those bones here.' She looked anxiously at Tom. Whenever Héloïse had to mention the bones, she seemed pained.

Tom collected his thoughts. 'I'd think – they'd be taken somewhere – to find out how old they are, for instance. That's probably why the police didn't allow the bones to be mentioned.'

'Interesting,' Ed said, 'the way they cordoned the place off, don't you think? Not even a shot of the pond, just a distant shot of the house. The police are taking precautions.'

Still investigating, Tom supposed Ed meant.

The telephone rang, and Tom got up to get it. He had guessed correctly, it was Agnès Grais, who had just seen the evening news.

'Antoine says, "Good riddance,"' Agnès told Tom. 'He thinks those people were insane, and they happened to dredge up some bones, so they became – overly enthusiastic – and fell in them-selves.' Agnès sounded on the brink of a laugh.

'Would you like to speak with Héloïse?'

She would.

Héloïse went to the telephone, and Tom returned to Ed, but remained standing.

'An accident,' Tom murmured, with thoughtful air. 'And so it was, in fact!'

'True,' Ed replied.

Neither of them was listening, or trying to, to Héloïse's lively conversation with Agnès Grais.

Tom was thinking, maybe for the second time, that it was lucky Murchison had not been wearing a belt, but braces. A belt might have lasted, a leather belt, might have been another trinket removed by David Pritchard, and more easily found in a house than a wedding ring. *Had* Murchison worn a belt? Tom had, in truth, forgotten. He picked up a last little chocolate biscuit from the plate on the coffee table. Ed declined one.

'I'm going up to relax for a few minutes, and I'll see about our charcoal at a quarter to eight,' Tom said. 'Out on the terrace.' He smiled. 'We're going to have a nice evening.'

24

Tom had just descended the stairs, having put on a fresh shirt and a sweater over it, when the telephone rang. He answered from the hall telephone.

A male voice identified himself as Commissaire de Police Divisionnaire, or something which sounded like that, Etienne Lomard in Nemours, and could he come now to speak with M. Ripley for a moment?

'It will be brief, I believe, m'sieur,' the officer said, 'but it is of sufficient importance.'

'But of course,' Tom replied. 'Now? . . . Very good, m'sieur.'

Tom gathered that the police officer knew where his house was. Héloïse had told him, after her telephone conversation with Agnès Grais, that the police were still at the Pritchard house, and that a couple of police cars were parked on the road there. Tom had an impulse to go up and warn Ed, but decided against it: Ed knew what Tom's story would be, and there was no need for Ed to be present when the officer was here. Instead, Tom went to the kitchen, where Mme Annette was washing salad, and told her that a police officer would call, in perhaps five minutes.

'Officier de police,' she repeated with only mild surprise, because it was not her domain. 'Very good, m'sieur.'

'I'll let him in. He won't be here long.'

Then Tom took a favourite old apron from a hook behind the kitchen door, put it round his neck and tied the waist. 'OUT TO LUNCH' was written in black letters on a red pocket in front.

When Tom went into the living-room, Ed was coming down the stairs. 'A police officer is coming in a minute,' Tom said. 'Probably because somebody said we – Héloïse and I – knew the Pritchards.' Tom gave a shrug. 'And because we speak English. Not many such around here.'

Tom heard the door knocker. There was both knocker and bell, but Tom made no judgement about people who used one or the other.

'Shall I vanish?' asked Ed.

'Make yourself a drink. Do as you like. You're my house-guest,' said Tom.

Ed did make his way to the bar cart in a far corner.

Tom opened the door, and greeted the police officers, two, whom he thought he had not seen before. They said their names, touched caps and Tom invited them to come in.

They both elected to take the straight chairs rather than the sofa.

Ed came into view, and Tom, still on his feet, introduced him as Edward Banbury, of London, an old friend who was a guest for the weekend. Then Ed took his drink out to the terrace.

The police officers, of about the same age, might have had the same rank. At any rate, they both spoke, and the matter was, a Mrs Thomas Murchison had telephoned the Pritchard house from New York, and had expected to speak with David Pritchard or his wife, and the police had answered. Mrs Murchison – was M. Ripley acquainted with her?

'I believe,' Tom said earnestly, 'she was here in this house for one hour – some years ago – after the disappearance of her husband.'

'Exactement! Just what she told us, M'sieur Reepley! Alors – ' The officer went on in French with gravity and assurance. 'Madame Murcheeson informed us that she had heard yesterday, Friday, from – '

'Thursday,' corrected the other officer.

'Possibly – the first telephone call, yes. David Preechard informed her that he had found the – the bones, yes, of her husband. And that he, Preechard, was going to speak with you about them. *Show* you these bones.'

Tom frowned. 'Show me? I don't understand.'

'Deliver them,' said the other officer to this colleague.

'Ah, yes, *deliver* them.'

Tom took a breath. 'Mr Pritchard said nothing to me about this, I assure you. Madame Murchison said he telephoned *me*? That is not true.'

'He was *going* to deliver them, n'est-ce pas, Philippe?' asked the other officer.

'Yes, but Friday, said Madame Murcheeson. Yesterday morning,' replied his colleague.

They both sat now with their caps on their laps.

Tom shook his head. 'Nothing was delivered here.'

'You knew M'sieur Preechard, m'sieur?'

'He introduced himself to me in the bar-tabac here. I went once to his house to take a glass. Weeks ago. They had invited me and my wife. I went alone. They were never in this house.'

The taller, blonder officer cleared his throat, and said to the other officer, 'The photographs?'

'Ah, oui. We found in the Preechard house two photographs of your house, M'sieur Reepley – from outside.'

'Really? Of my house?'

'Yes, plainly. These photographs were propped up on the mantel in the Preechard house.'

Tom looked at the two snapshots in the officer's hand. 'Very odd. My house is not for sale.' Tom smiled. 'However – yes! I remember once seeing Pritchard in the road outside. A few weeks ago. My housekeeper called it to my attention – someone taking pictures of my house with a small – quite ordinary camera.'

'And you recognized him as M'sieur Preechard?'

'Oh, yes. I didn't like his taking pictures, but I chose to ignore it. My wife saw him too – also a friend of my wife's who was visiting us that day.' Tom frowned, recollecting. 'I remember seeing Madame Pritchard in a car – she picked up her husband a few minutes later, and they drove away together. Strange.'

At this point Mme Annette came into the room, and Tom gave his attention to her. She wished to know if the gentlemen would like something? Tom knew she wanted to lay the table soon.

'A glass of wine, messieurs?' asked Tom. 'Un pastis?'

Both declined politely, being on duty or *de jour*.

'Nor for me just yet, madame,' said Tom. 'Ah – Madame Annette – was there a telephone call for me Thursday – or Friday' – Tom asked with a glance at the officers, and one nodded – 'from a M'sieur Preechard? About delivering something to the house?' Tom asked this with real interest, as he had suddenly thought that Pritchard might have spoken with Mme Annette about a delivery, and she might have forgotten (though it was unlikely) to inform Tom.

'Non, M'sieur Tome.' She shook her head.

Tom said to the officers, 'Naturally, my housekeeper learned of the Pritchard tragedy this morning.'

Murmurs from the officers. Of course, news like that would spread quickly!

'You may ask Madame Annette about anything being delivered here,' said Tom.

One officer did, and Mme Annette replied in the negative, shaking her head once more.

'No packages, m'sieur,' said Mme Annette positively.

'This' – Tom chose his words – 'this also concerns M'sieur Murcheeson, Madame Annette. Remember – the gentleman who disappeared at Orly airport? The American who was here overnight a few years ago?'

'Ah, oui. A tall man,' said Mme Annette rather vaguely.

'Yes. We talked about pictures. My two Derwatts – ' Tom gestured towards his walls for the benefit of the French officers. 'M'sieur Murchison had also a Derwatt, which was alas stolen at Orly. I drove him to Orly the next day – around noon as I recall. You remember, madame?'

Tom had spoken casually, without emphasis, and Mme Annette rewarded him, luckily, by replying in the same tone.

'Oui, M'sieur Tome. I remember helping with his valises – to the car.'

That was good enough, Tom thought, though he had heard her say that she remembered M. Murchison walking out of the house and getting into the car.

Now Héloïse came down the stairs. Tom stood up and so did the officers.

'My wife,' Tom said, 'Madame Héloïse – '

The two officers again said their names.

'We speak about the Preechard house,' Tom said to Héloïse. 'Something to drink, dear?'

'No, thank you. I wait.' Héloïse looked as if she wanted to drift off, perhaps to the garden.

Mme Annette returned to the kitchen.

'Madame Reepley, did you perhaps see any package – this long – delivered – left anywhere on your property here?' The officer gestured with arms spread to indicate length.

Héloïse looked puzzled. 'From a florist?'

The officers had to smile.

'Non, madame. Canvas – tied with rope. Late Thursday – or Friday?'

Tom left it to Héloïse to state that she had arrived from Paris only today at midday. She had spent Friday night in Paris, and Thursday she had been in Tangier, she said.

That settled that.

The officers consulted, then one said, 'May we speak to your friend from London?'

Ed Banbury was standing by the roses. Tom gave him a shout. Ed came trotting.

'Police want to ask you about a package brought here,' Tom said on the terrace steps. 'I haven't seen any, neither has Héloïse.' Tom spoke easily, not knowing if a police officer were behind him on the terrace or not.

The officers were still in the living-room when Ed Banbury went in.

Ed was asked if he had seen any greyish package, more than a metre long, in the driveway, under the hedges – anywhere, even outside the gates. 'Non,' Ed replied. 'Non.'

'When did you arrive here, m'sieur?'

'Yesterday – Friday – midday. I had lunch here.' Ed's serious blond brows gave his face a most honest expression. 'M. Ripley met me at Roissy airport.'

'Thank you, sir. Your profession?'

'Journalist,' Ed replied. Ed then had to print his name and London address on a notepad one of the officers produced.

'Please convey my kind regards to Madame Murchison, if you speak with her again,' Tom said. 'I remember her pleasantly – if a bit vaguely,' he added, smiling.

'We shall speak again with her,' said an officer, the one with brown straight hair. 'She is – well – she thinks the bones we found – or Preechard found – may be those of her husband.'

'Her husband,' Tom repeated incredulously. 'But – where did Pritchard find them?'

'We don't know exactly, but perhaps not far from here. Ten, fifteen kilometres.'

The Voisy inhabitants had not yet spoken up, Tom thought, assuming they had seen anything. And Pritchard hadn't mentioned Voisy – or had he? 'Surely you can identify the skeleton,' Tom said.

'Le squelette est incomplet, m'sieur. Il n'y a pas de tête,' said the blond officer, with serious face.

'C'est horrible!' Héloïse murmured.

'We shall determine first its time in water – '

'Clothing?' asked Tom.

'Ha! All rotted away, m'sieur. Not even a button in the original shroud! The fish – the flow of the water – '

'Le fil de l'eau,' repeated the other officer, gesturing. 'The current. This wears away – the clothing, the flesh – '

'Jean!' The other officer waved a hand quickly, as if to say, Enough! A lady is present!

There was a silence of a few seconds, then Jean went on.

'Do you recall, M'sieur Reepley, if you saw M'sieur Murchison go into the departure door at Orly that day so long ago?'

Tom did remember. 'I did not park my car that day – I paused at the kerb, helped M'sieur Murchison out with his luggage – and the wrapped picture – and I drove on. It was the pavement in front of the departure door. He could have carried his few things easily. So I did not – as it happened – watch him go through the door.'

The officers consulted, murmured, and looked at their notes.

Tom supposed that they were verifying that he had said to the police years ago that he left Murchison with his luggage on the pavement at the departure gate at Orly. Tom wasn't going to emphasize that his statement to that effect had surely been on record all this time. Nor was he going to mention that it seemed odd to him that anyone would have brought Murchison back to the area here to murder, or that Murchison would have committed suicide in the vicinity. Tom suddenly stood up, and went over to his wife.

'You are all right, sweet?' he asked in English. 'I think the gentlemen are soon finished here. Won't you sit down?'

'I am fine,' Héloïse replied somewhat coldly, as if to say that Tom's odd and unknown activities had brought the police here in the first place, and that their presence was not pleasant to endure. She was leaning with folded arms against a credenza cabinet, a good distance from the police.

Tom returned to the police officers, and sat down, so as not to appear to be urging their departure. 'Would you please say to Madame Murchison – if you speak with her – that I am willing to talk with her again? She knows all that I can say, but – ' He paused.

The blond officer called Philippe said, 'Yes, m'sieur, we shall tell her. She has your telephone number?'

'She once had it,' Tom said pleasantly. 'It hasn't changed.'

The other officer held up a finger to his colleague, demanding audience, and said, 'And a woman called Cynthia, m'sieur – in England? Madame Murcheeson mentioned her.'

'Cynthia – yes,' Tom replied, as if with slow recollection. 'I know her slightly. Why?'

'I believe you saw her recently in London?'

'Yes, true. We had a drink in a pub anglais.' Tom smiled. 'How did you know that?'

'Madame Murcheeson told us, as she is in touch with Madame Cynthia – '

'Gradno-or,' the blondish officer supplied, after looking at their notepad.

Tom began to feel uneasy. He tried to think ahead. What questions were coming next?

'Did you see her in London – speak with her for any particular reason?'

'Yes,' said Tom. He turned in his chair so that he could see Ed, who was leaning on the back of a straight chair. 'Remember Cynthia, Ed?'

'Ye-es, vaguely,' Ed replied in English. 'Haven't seen her in years.'

'My reason,' Tom continued to the police, 'was to ask her what M'sieur Pritchard wanted from me. You see, I found M'sieur Pritchard – a little overly friendly, wanting to be invited to my house, for instance – which I knew for a fact my wife did not want!' Here Tom laughed. 'The one time I visited les Pritchards for a glass, M'sieur Pritchard mentioned Cynthia – '

'Gradno-or,' the officer repeated.

'Yes. M'sieur Pritchard when I had a glass at his house suggested that this Cynthia was unfriendly to me – had something against me. I asked Pritchard what it was, and he did not tell me. This was not pleasant, but was typical Pritchard! So when I was in London, I managed to find Madame Gradno-or's number, and I asked her: What is the matter with Pritchard?' Tom recalled swiftly that Cynthia Gradnor intended (in Tom's opinion) to protect Bernard Tufts from acquiring the label of forger. Cynthia had her self-imposed limits, and these were going to work in Tom's favour.

'What else? What did you learn?' The brown-haired officer looked interested.

'Not much, unfortunately. Cynthia told me that she had never met Pritchard – had never even seen him. He had telephoned her out of the blue.' Tom thought suddenly of the go-between, George something, at the big party in London for journalists, at which Pritchard had been, and also Cynthia. The go-between, after listening to Pritchard talk about Ripley, had told Pritchard that there was a woman in the house who detested Ripley. Thus had Pritchard learned her name (and Cynthia Pritchard's, it would seem) but they had not crossed the room to meet face to face. Tom was not going to furnish the police with that information.

'Strange,' mused the fair-haired officer.

'Pritchard *was* strange!' Tom stood up, as if sitting for so long had made him stiff. 'I believe, since it is nearly eight, I shall make a gin-tonic for myself. And for you, gentlemen? Un petit rouge? A scotch? Whatever you might like.'

Tom spoke in a tone that took for granted the gentlemen would accept something, and so they did: both chose *un petit rouge*.

'I shall tell madame,' said Héloïse, and went off to the kitchen.

The two officers complimented Tom on his Derwatts, the one over the fireplace especially, the creation of Bernard Tufts. And Tom's Soutine.

'I am glad you like them,' Tom said. 'I am very happy to possess them.'

Ed had freshened his drink at the bar, Héloïse had joined them, and with a glass in everyone's hand the atmosphere was lighter.

Tom said in a quiet tone to the brown-haired officer, 'Two things, m'sieur. I shall also be happy to speak with Madame Cynthia – if she wants to speak with me. And number two, why do you think – ' Tom glanced around, but no one was listening now.

The blond officer, Philippe, with cap under arm, seemed enchanted by Héloïse, and happy to talk of nothing, probably, instead of bones and rotted flesh. Ed had also joined Héloïse.

Tom continued, 'What do you think M'sieur Pritchard intended to do with the bones in his garden pond?'

The officer Jean appeared to ponder.

'If he got them from a river – why throw them back into water, and then – maybe deliberately kill themselves?'

The police officer shrugged. 'It may have been an accident – one slipped and fell, then the next, m'sieur. With that garden implement they were trying to pull something out – it seems. Their télé was still on – their café – a drink' – a shrug – 'unfinished in the living-room. Maybe they were hiding the bones temporarily. We may learn something tomorrow or the next day and then maybe not.'

The officers were standing with their stemmed glasses in hand.

Tom had another thought: Teddy. He decided to mention Teddy, and moved closer to Héloïse's group. 'M'sieur,' he said to

Philippe. 'M'sieur Pritchard had a friend – or in any case a man with him when he was fishing in the canals. Everyone says that.' Tom used the word *pêcher*, to fish, rather than 'to search'. 'I heard, somewhere, that his name was Teddy. Have you spoken with him?'

'Ah – Teddy, Théodore,' said Jean, as both officers exchanged a glance. 'Oui, merci, M'sieur Reepley. We heard about him from your friends the Grais – very nice people, they are. Then we found his name and Paris telephone number by the telephone in the Preechard house. This afternoon someone has spoken with him in Paris. He said that when Preechard found the bones in a river, his work for Preechard was finished. And he – ' The officer hesitated.

'That he then departed,' Philippe said. 'Pardon, Jean.'

'Departed, yes,' said Jean with a glance at Tom. 'He was surprised, it seems, that the bones – the skeleton – seemed to be the objective of Preechard.' Here Jean looked hard at Tom. 'And when this Teddy saw them – he returned to Paris. Teddy is a student. He wanted to earn some money – that's all.'

Philippe started to say something, but was silenced by a gesture from Jean.

Tom ventured, 'I think I heard something like that in the bar-tabac here. That this Teddy was surprised – and decided to bid adieu to Pritchard.' Now it was Tom's turn to give a slight shrug.

The officers made no comment. They did not wish to stay for dinner, which Tom invited them to do, although Tom had been sure they would not accept. Nor did they wish their glasses refilled.

'Bon soir, madame, et merci,' they both said cordially to Héloïse, with bows.

They asked how long Ed would be staying.

'At least three more days, I hope,' said Tom, smiling.

'Not sure,' said Ed pleasantly.

'We are here,' Tom said firmly to both officers, 'my wife and I, in case we can be of any help.'

'Thank you, M'sieur Reepley.'

The officers wished them an agreeable evening, and went out to their car, which they had left in the forecourt.

Tom, returning from the front door, said, 'Quite pleasant fellows! Didn't you think so, Ed?'

'Yes – yes, indeed.'

'Héloïse, my sweet, I want *you* to light the fire. Now. We're running a bit late – but we're going to have an excellent meal.'

'Me? What fire?'

'The charcoal, dear. On the terrace. Here are the matches. Just come out and strike one!'

Héloïse took the matchbox and stepped on to the terrace, graceful in her long striped skirt. She wore a green cotton blouse, with its sleeves partly rolled up. 'But you always do this,' she said, striking a match.

'Tonight is special. You are the – the – '

'Goddess,' Ed supplied.

'Goddess of the house,' Tom said.

The charcoal took fire. Short and even yellow and blue flames danced over the coals. Mme Annette had wrapped at least a half-dozen potatoes in foil. Tom put his apron back on and got to work.

Then the telephone rang.

Tom groaned. 'Héloïse, you get it, please. It's either les Grais or Noëlle, I'll bet you.'

It was les Grais, Tom could tell as he went into the living-room. Héloïse was of course filling them in on what the police had said and asked. Tom spoke with Mme Annette in the kitchen: her sauce béarnaise was under control, also the asparagus which was the first course.

The meal was indeed delicious and memorable. So said Ed. The telephone did not ring; nobody mentioned the telephone. Tom said to Mme Annette that tomorrow morning after breakfast she might make up his room for their English guest, M. Constant, who was to arrive at 11.30 at Roissy airport.

Mme Annette's face reflected her pleasure at the prospect. It was as if guests, friends, made the house come alive for her, as flowers or music did for other people.

Tom did venture to ask Héloïse, as they drank coffee in the living-room, if Agnès or Antoine Grais had had any news.

'Non-n – just that the lights are still on in that house. One of the children took a walk with the dog to there. The police are still looking – for something.' Héloïse sounded bored with it.

Ed glanced at Tom and smiled slightly. Tom wondered if Ed had thought that – well, Tom could not put his thoughts into words, even for himself, much less in Héloïse's presence! Considering the Pritchards' peculiarities, no extreme was too far, when it came to imagining what the police might be looking for, and what they might be finding.

25

The next morning, after his first coffee, Tom asked Mme Annette please to buy what newspapers she could (it was Sunday) when she went into the village.

'I could go immediately, M'sieur Tome, unless – '

He knew she meant Mme Héloïse's breakfast of tea and grapefruit. Tom offered to prepare it, in case Mme Héloïse awakened, which he said he doubted. And as to M'sieur Banbury, Tom simply didn't know, as the two of them had sat up late last evening.

Mme Annette was off, as much to hear the local gossip in the bakery, Tom knew, as to buy the newspapers. And which would be the more reliable? The bakery would be lively, exaggerated, but one could always pare away a bit and get down to the truth, which might well be several hours ahead of the press.

By the time Tom had deadheaded some roses and dahlias, and chosen a frizzy orange dahlia plus two yellows, Mme Annette was back. He heard the click of the door latch.

Tom looked at the papers in the kitchen. Mme Annette was extracting croissants and a flute of bread from her net.

'The police – they search for the *head*, M'sieur Tome,' Mme Annette whispered, though no one but Tom could have heard her.

Tom frowned. 'In the *house*?'

'Everywhere!' Again it was a whisper.

Tom read: the headlines said something about 'extraordinary household in vicinity of Moret-sur-Loing', and went on to state that David and Janice Pritchard, Americans in their thirties, had either slipped to their deaths or committed a bizarre suicide in a pond on their own property. They had been in the water about ten hours, said officials, when discovered by two boys under twelve years of age, who had reported the corpses to a neighbour. From below in the muddy subsoil of the pond, the police had dredged up a sack of human bones, a partial skeleton with its head and one foot missing. The skeleton was of a male of mature age, and up to now had not been identified. Neither of the Pritchards had employ, and David Pritchard derived his income from his family in the United States. A following paragraph stated that the incomplete skeleton had been in water for an undetermined number of years. Neighbours reported that Pritchard had been exploring the bottoms of canals and rivers in the region, apparently for this sort of cache, as his exploring efforts had come to a halt last Thursday with the discovery of the partial skeleton.

The second newspaper said essentially the same, more briefly, and gave an entire sentence to the suggestion that the Pritchards had been an unusually quiet couple during the mere three months they had lived in the house, keeping to themselves, apparently finding their sole amusement in playing records loudly late at night in their isolated two-storey house, finally taking up the hobby of dragging canal and river bottoms. The police had managed to get in touch with the respective families of David and Janice Pritchard. The house lights had been on, door open, and there were un-finished drinks in the living-room, when the two corpses had been discovered.

Nothing new, Tom thought, but still a bit shocking to him, whenever he read it.

'What are the police now looking for – really, madame?' Tom asked, hoping to learn something, as well as please Mme Annette, who loved to impart knowledge. 'Surely not the head,' Tom whispered earnestly. '*Clues*, maybe – whether it was suicide or accident.'

Mme Annette, at the sink, her hands wet, leaned towards Tom. 'M'sieur – I heard this morning they have found a *whip*. Someone else – Madame Hubert, you know, the wife of the electrician, she said a *chain* was found. Perhaps not a big chain, but a chain.'

Ed came downstairs, and Tom greeted him and handed him the two newspapers in the living-room.

'Tea or coffee?' asked Tom.

'Coffee with some warm milk. May I?'

'You may. Sit down at the table, more comfortable.'

Ed wanted a croissant with marmalade.

Just suppose they *did* find the head, Tom was thinking, as he went to convey Ed's order, in the Pritchard house? Or the wedding ring hidden in an incredible place, for instance hammered into an interstice between two floorboards? A wedding ring with initials?

And the head somewhere else – and maybe this had been the last straw for Teddy?

'Can I come with you to Roissy?' Ed asked when Tom returned. 'I'd enjoy that.'

'Of course! And I'd like your company. We'll take the station wagon.'

Ed read on in the newspapers. 'Nothing new here, is there, Tom?'

'Not to me.'

'You know, Tom – well – ' Ed broke off, smiling.

'Come on! Something cheerful!'

'That it is – and now I've ruined it, the surprise. I *think* Jeff's going to bring your pigeon sketch in his suitcase. I mentioned it to him before I left.'

'Won't that be nice!' Tom said, and took a glance at his living-room walls. 'What an inspiration that will be!'

Mme Annette arrived with a tray.

Hardly an hour later, when Tom and Héloïse too had checked on the appearance of Tom's room, now assigned to Jeff, and had set a red rose in a flute-like glass vase on the dressing table, Tom and Ed departed for Roissy. They would be back for lunch, Tom said to Mme Annette, just after 1, with luck.

Tom had taken Murchison's ring from the black woollen sock in his sock drawer, and it was in his left-hand trouser pocket now. 'Let's go by Moret. The bridge is so pretty, and it's hardly at all out of the way.'

'Okay,' said Ed. 'Lovely.'

The day was lovely too. It had rained early that morning, around 6 from the look of things, which was just what had been needed to freshen the garden and the lawn, and of course save Tom from watering today.

The towers of the bridge at Moret, a single stocky tower on either side of the river, came into view – pinkish tan, venerable and protective.

'Let's try to get near the water – somehow,' Tom said. 'It's two-way on the bridge, but it's narrow through the towers, so sometimes we have to wait and take turns.'

Each tower had an arched passageway, wide enough for only one car. Tom had to pause only a few seconds for a couple of oncoming cars, then they crossed the Loing, where Tom so much wanted to throw the ring, but it was impossible to stop. Once through the second tower, he took a street to his left, and despite a yellow li̶ drew up at the kerb.

'Let's walk to the bridge and take a quick look at least,' Tom said.

They did reach the bridge road, Tom with hands in pockets, left hand gripping the ring. He pulled his hand out of his pocket and held the ring in his fist.

'Sixteenth-century architecture, a lot of this,' Tom said. 'And Napoleon spent a night here on his return from Elba. The house where he did has a plaque, I believe.' Tom pressed his palms together and transferred the ring to his right hand.

Ed said nothing, and seemed to be trying to absorb everything. Tom stood nearer the rail along the bridge, as two cars passed behind him. A few metres below, the Loing looked comfortably deep to Tom.

'M'sieur – '

Tom turned in surprise, and saw a police officer in dark blue trousers, short-sleeved pale blue shirt, sunglasses.

'Oui,' said Tom.

'You have the white station wagon in – '

'Oui,' Tom said.

'It is forbidden to park there – where you are.'

'Ah, oui! Excusez-moi! We shall be moving off at once! Thank you, officer.'

The officer saluted and moved off, white-holstered gun on hip.

'Did he know you?' asked Ed.

'Not sure. Maybe. Nice of him not to slap me with a fine.' Tom smiled. 'I don't *think* he will. Let's go.' Tom swung his arm back and hurled the ring, aiming for the middle of the river, which was not in full flood at the moment. It plunked near enough in the middle to satisfy Tom. He smiled slightly at Ed, and they walked back in the direction of the station wagon.

For all Ed knew, he might have thrown a stone, Tom supposed, and that was just as well.

ALSO AVAILABLE BY PATRICIA HIGHSMITH
CAROL

With a new introduction from Val McDermid

'Some books change lives. This is one of them ... This is a book that is hard to set aside; it demands to be read late into the night with eyes burning and heart racing'
VAL McDERMID

Therese is just an ordinary sales assistant working in a New York department store when a beautiful, alluring woman in her thirties walks up to her counter. Standing there, Therese is wholly unprepared for the first shock of love. Therese is an awkward nineteen-year-old with a job she hates and a boyfriend she doesn't love; Carol is a sophisticated, bored suburban housewife in the throes of a divorce and a custody battle for her only daughter. As Therese becomes irresistibly drawn into Carol's world, she soon realizes how much they both stand to lose...

First published pseudonymously in 1952 as *The Price of Salt*, *Carol* is a hauntingly atmospheric love story set against the backdrop of fifties New York.

＊

'A document of persecuted love ... perfect'
INDEPENDENT

'Very recognizably Highsmith, full of tremor and of threat and of her peculiar genius for anxiety'
SUNDAY TIMES

'Magnificent ... Gently exploratory, genuinely moving'
MAIL ON SUNDAY

'An original, honest novel, a remarkable imaginative achievement by any standard ... as compelling as any of Highsmith's thrillers'
FINANCIAL TIMES

＊

ISBN 978 1 4088 0897 9   PAPERBACK   £7.99

BLOOMSBURY

THE TREMOR OF FORGERY

Howard Ingham finds it strange that no one has written to him since he arrived in Tunisia – neither the film director that he is supposed to be meeting in Tunis, nor his lover in New York who is, he hopes, missing him. While he waits around at a beach resort, unable to get going on the film script he is there to write, he starts work on a new novel, about a man living an amoral double life. Howard also befriends a fellow American who has a taste for Scotch and a suspicious interest in the Soviet Union, and a Dane who appears to distrust Arabs intensely. When bad news finally arrives from home, Howard thinks he may as well stay and continue writing, despite the tremors in the air of violence, tensions and ambiguous morals.

✻

'Highsmith's finest novel'
GRAHAM GREENE

'One of her best books ... She creates a lot of dread and
a lot of apprehension very casually'
JONATHAN LETHEM, CHICAGO TRIBUNE

'Highsmith lived in her imagination, and, ultimately, it's in her uniquely
disturbing stories that you'll find her'
LA WEEKLY

✻

ISBN 978 0 7475 7501 6   PAPERBACK   £6.99

BLOOMSBURY

ELEVEN

Unsuspecting victims are devoured by their own obsessions in this perfectly chilling collection. A man becomes devoted to his pet snails, with fatal results. A young nanny turns arsonist in a bid to become heroine of the hour. A boy finally stands up to his mother, with knife in hand. Highsmith weaves a world claustrophobic in its intensity, disturbing in its mundanity, as she probes the dark corners of the human psyche. *Eleven* is a collection of masterpieces of Highsmith's particular art, full of compulsion, foreboding and cruel pleasures.

∗

'Fabulous, in all senses of that word'
PAUL THEROUX

'The mood of nagging apprehension is consistent, skilfully underplayed so that just the right amount of chill is induced with an economy of means'
NEW YORK TIMES

'What is striking about these stories is their integrity: they are all of a piece ... a brilliant collection'
SUNDAY TIMES

∗

ISBN 978 0 7475 7500 9   PAPERBACK   £7.99

BLOOMSBURY